REAPER

REAPER

C. Terry Cline, Jr.

DONALD I. FINE, INC.
New York

Library of Congress Cataloging-in-Publication Data

Cline, C. Terry.
Reaper / by C. Terry Cline, Jr.
p.   cm.
ISBN: 1-55611-149-5
I. Title.
PS3553.L53R4   1989
813'.54—dc20   89-45334
                                    CIP

Manufactured in the United States of America

10   9   8   7   6   5   4   3   2   1

This novel is a work of fiction. Names, characters, places and
incidents are either the product of the author's imagination or
are used fictitiously. Any resemblance to actual events, locales,
organizations or persons, living or dead, is entirely coincidental
and beyond the intent of either the author or publisher.

Designed by Irving Perkins Associates

To
JOHN D. HEALD
and
NANCY LEWIS

REAPER

CHAPTER ONE

IN A CROWDED MALL, he was just one body among many, a laboring man in a sea of humanity. GRAND OPENING, a sign said. DOOR PRIZES! CASH WINNERS! WELCOME!

Jaydee folded his horoscope and tucked it in a shirt pocket. He wiped perspiring hands down his faded blue denim trousers, tugged his garments to create folds which hid the pistol in his belt. Sweat gathered in his eyebrows and crawled down his flesh.

He'd left his twenty-year-old station wagon in a mosaic of parked cars baking under the relentless South Florida sun. Even inside, a petroleum smell from freshly pressed paving perfumed the air.

This shopping center was the newest commercial blister to pock the West Palm Beach suburbs. He had come here because here the herd congregated. For one among these patrons today, he was destiny.

A sense of power condensed and at this moment—he was a god. He selected a bench outside a bank and lit a cigarette, using an ashtray as a pretext for sitting. He shifted to relieve the prod of his weapon, blew a trickle of smoke lazily, his slate-gray eyes almost sleepy as he lounged. He saw everything, stared at nothing. To the casual passerby, he was a man patiently awaiting someone. Which, indeed, he was.

1

A pregnant woman pushed a stroller, her toddler sleeping among sacks of wares. A boy counted his allowance and skipped away from his parents to spend it. An elderly man slumped in a wheelchair, palsied hands fluttering. His companion, a woman decades his junior, shouted in his ear, "Sit here and watch the people!"

Abandoned, the old man shook and stared.

The image made Jaydee think of his grandfather. Resolve intensified.

He was impelled by forces he didn't truly understand. He was having difficulty sleeping nights, a vague uneasiness kept him depressed. Sometimes he could shake it off, other times it overwhelmed him. Finally, driven by the same compulsion that makes a beast gorge, or procreate, his body demanded relief.

He imagined himself a specter, invisible and omniscient, dispensing mercy, or death, at will. A river of humanity flowed around the old man in his wheelchair, around planters and benches—they sensed no peril.

In the civilized pod of a modern mall, the world without was forgotten. In here, background music provided subliminal assurance, an artificial sanctum with a carnival atmosphere. Artisans crafted baubles in wide center aisles. There was a puppet show for children. A camera club had mounted a photo display.

As if filled with ennui, Jaydee peered through double-wide doors of the bank, observing first-of-the-month transactions. The herd ebbed from J. C. Penney's to Sears, past fast food outlets and lethargic guards. Every store boasted special discounts for the elders, free fun for the juniors. No gamble: *satisfaction guaranteed . . .*

Different shopping malls catered to varying segments of society. This was a Wal-Mart and Woolworth crowd; no Cartier or Neiman-Marcus here. These merchants advertised "Retirees Welcome!" That meant women, really. *Old women.*

Jaydee hated old women as much as he loathed astrology. Elderly women looked to their children and their horoscopes, convinced that one or the other would shelter them.

The desire to mingle was a strong geriatric impulse. Widows in particular sought continuity to their existence, a chance to be part of the whole, even if among strangers. And here, they were safe. Beneath these skylights the sun never set, rains never fell. The air was always cool and constant. Who among them would suspect a predator had penetrated the fold?

He watched, as all predators do, for a hint of infirmity; the hesitant step, a lax awareness, a straggler away from the flock. They had forgotten, or never knew, the hot breath of a hunter. To these flaccid specks of humanity, pestilence was a thing of the past, famine banished. Lightning struck; barns burned; outside crime stalked the unwary. But in here, they were coddled and nurtured. They expected discounts, they insisted. They had *earned* them!

Their men died after years of toil, supporting creatures more thick of thigh and hale of heart than themselves. Always, it seemed, their men died just before the family savings were threatened by rising medical costs.

Jaydee took a deep breath, a study in languor.

Down a far corridor, a queue awaited the start of an early movie. Silver-haired ladies sold tickets to a raffle—WORTHY CAUSE, a sign pledged.

Inside the bank, a woman in her seventies cashed a check. She sheltered her money from prying eyes and counted it twice.

Something about her . . .

She was thin, frail, but posture correct. Her full pink cheeks were dabbed with a tint of rouge, accenting summer-sky eyes that flitted from face to face as if seeking recognition.

She emerged from the bank and paused to get her bearings. She looked this way, then that, and stepped into the stream of shoppers, letting them sweep her toward a pet shop window where kittens cavorted on artificial trees.

Jaydee moved nearer.

"I have too many cats as it is," she sparked conversation with a younger mother. "Someone else must give these pussies a home—not I."

"We live in an apartment," the mother remarked.

"Mother," her daughter pleaded, "I'd look after a kitty of my own, I promise I would."

"No pets," the mother said. "It's in the lease."

Jaydee stubbed out his cigarette, listening.

"My husband and I never had children, but, oh, how we loved them. We taught school for fifty years, my Eugene and I. After he died, I needed my pussies. They're all the company I have."

Widowed. Teacher. Alone.

She meandered from one display to another. She sat beside an indoor fountain watching spurts of water change patterns, talking to anyone who paused long enough to listen. She bought an ice cream cone, taking tiny licks to make it last.

Jaydee trailed her through a store she would have called "the five and dime." She sniffed samples of perfume, fingered the weave of a shawl. It cost nothing to look, touching was free.

He knew old women. They moved on a dreary treadmill timed to some inner clock. They could waste a day dawdling, then suddenly demand speed and action. Oh, yes, he knew them. Wheedling, whining, commanding—they lived in the past.

On her vanity, he would find loose face powder, Pond's cleansing cream, Jergens hand lotion. In her dresser drawers, lace-up corsets with garter straps, step-in panties, sachets of dried herbs. There would be a saucer filled with large hairpins, old hats in boxes on shelves of her closet, awaiting a revival of popularity.

In her icebox (she would call it that), homemade mayonnaise. Bibbed aprons would hang behind the kitchen door. The cupboards would contain cans of evaporated milk, a box of Argo starch, a tin of baking powders. In the laundry would be Octagon soap flakes, because she didn't fully trust detergents. The medicine cabinet would be stocked with epsom salts, rubbing alcohol, iodine and castor oil.

He closed his eyes, opened them again—watching.

She had taken a seat outside a bookstore, looking at customers come and go. Behind her, Jaydee waited.

No hurry.

He knew old women.

And this one was his . . .

Inez Cumbie watched people browsing in a bookstore. Libraries were everywhere and the price of books so high, yet there remained those who could afford them, obviously.

She loved books, had always treasured words. During a half century of teaching she was known for her ability to define almost any term in an unabridged dictionary. Then, she would trace the etymology, giving a word weight and substance, relating the way the Greek and Latin intended it to be. She could parallel the development of civilization with changes in the language. War brought societies together, melded tongues, altered speech. Armies of occupation left a linguistic stamp on foreign lands. Immigration and commerce transported idioms abroad, and America had become the richest recipient of all.

Well. Her memory was not as it had been. She suffered the lapses of incomplete connections between axons and synapses. She despaired that all her hard-earned knowledge was evaporating as she aged.

Exercise of the mind was as critical as calisthenics to the body. A part of her pension always went to Dell publishing for a crossword puzzle book filled with jumbles, anagrams and IQ teasers.

So she would not finish the book too quickly, she allotted herself one puzzle per day. She admired those wordsmiths who outsmarted her—except when one cheated, inventing a variation to make his puzzle complete.

Before Eugene died, they had worked the puzzles together. Nearly always she bested him and, oh, how he enjoyed her victory!

"Too smart for me, Inez," he'd say. "Always were. Too smart for me."

It was a loving lie. Eugene was an analyst, the mathematician in the family. But his grasp of abstracts seemed confined to logarithms and algebraic deductions. Synonyms and antonyms eluded him.

Theirs had been such a good marriage. She had no regrets about a day of it. They were both third-generation Floridians, products of the Great Depression, childless but with great regard for children. They began teaching in the same rural Palm Beach County school the year they married.

Five decades ago, where she now sat there had been sand dunes and marshlands. She and Eugene had come here to watch sea eagles soar in utterly blue skies. She wasn't sure where the old oak tree had been—Eugene would have known—in the housewares section of Sears, she thought. Under that tree they always spread a picnic lunch and, once, as newlyweds, they'd made love in the twilight. Of course, the nearest neighbor was miles away in those days and winter was the best time for picnics, because the insects ruled summer. She could still remember the rustle of palmetto fronds in a breeze, the whispering oak overhead, a tinkle of trace chains as their mule stamped his hooves restlessly; the feel of Eugene's hands, the kiss on her neck, the sigh of satisfaction.

So long ago, but yesterday.

Good memories are deposits for withdrawal in less happy times. She and Eugene had made many fine deposits.

Teaching had been a life of penury back then. There were no unions. The satisfaction was not in the money. But somehow they always had nearly enough. With that first mule, Eugene had tilled a garden. They never felt deprived. It didn't occur to them to change professions. Together, they had taught nearly nine thousand students, watched them go off to wed, to war—

"Forty-two were reprobates," Eugene once commented, "but the others weren't so bad."

If contentment was success, they were Rockefellers. Eugene taught math and she taught English and they both taught moral values, developing character.

Enough of this. She would buy her crossword puzzle book, catch a bus out to the West Palm Beach city limits, walk home in the sunset. Daylight Saving Time made for a late nightfall. There was no reason for haste. The buses ran every twenty minutes.

So she watched the passersby, smiling when her eyes met theirs. By their raiment she guessed their occupations, education and social status. By their demeanor she calculated the degree of their success, imagining burdens they secretly bore.

Enough . . .

She purchased a crossword book, strolled back through the crowded mall toward the bus lines.

One would think, among so many people, she would meet a former student, at least one person she knew.

There were familiar faces.

But nobody noticed her.

The sun was a golden globe on a russet horizon when Inez stepped off the bus at the last stop. Long shadows fell across the road. The hiss of air brakes released and the bus turned to leave.

That's when she had seen him—the setting sun bathed the old station wagon in tones of ocher.

Followed her. She realized that now.

Now was too late—her legs were bound to a sturdy wooden chair, one arm tied to the arm of the furniture, her body strapped against the back.

Killing her cats.

Inez heard a tumble of drawers thrown aside, the crash of breaking glass. Then, a shriek—*killing her cats.*

How could this be happening? This nightmare—how could this be! He appeared at the kitchen door, asking mildly, "Are you writing?"

"I'm trying to."

"Be about it," he said.

The smell of blood was nauseating. Inez stared at the notebook paper on the table, a pen quivered in her free hand.

"Dear Violet Day—"

She listened to the bump of things he threw, the spit of a trapped feline. A thud. Another.

He hated cats, he'd said. But he said it after he'd gained entry.

She thought back to their meeting—the bus gone, Inez walking in the dusk.

"Hello there!" he'd called through his opened car window.

She'd had difficulty seeing his face in the dark of the interior. "Do I know you?"

"You ought to," he'd said, pleasantly.

He wore a cowboy hat, work shirt and jeans. On the side of his station wagon, in faded places where once there'd been a painted sign, she read OR O—a farm or ranch, perhaps. South Florida had become the cattle capital of the nation. Corporations controlled most of the farming these days. But she couldn't remember an OR O ranch hereabouts.

"How are your cats?" he'd asked.

He obviously knew her. The son or grandson of a former student, maybe. Inez remembered smiling, trying to recall a similar high brow, the unruly sandy hair and such straight, even teeth.

"Taught my folks and me, too," he'd said without accent. Tourists were the invading influence here—even native-born Floridians had lost their drawls.

"Are you Wilma's boy?"

"Lived about five miles away most of my life," he'd said. By then the door was open. *Expecting her to get in.*

"Still got your cats?"

"Oh, yes!"

"Come on, let me give you a lift. It's good to see you again," he'd said.

One of her students, certainly. Wilma's boy, perhaps. "Whatever happened to Wilma?"

"Mama's fine."

The car smelled of exhaust fumes, the floorboard was littered with soft drink cans, wrappers from hamburgers. Ants crawled the windshield, she remembered. She'd scrutinized his profile in fading light. *Wilma had gray eyes,* the same short neck.

"I heard your husband died," he said.

"Several years ago. I miss him."

"I'll bet you do. Tell me where to turn."

"End of the fence coming up. I can walk from here."

"No problem. I'll take you to the door."

"I need the exercise," she'd said.

"No problem." He turned into the long, unpaved drive toward the house a quarter mile away.

"You're retired now?" he'd commented.

"Nearly nine years ago. You can stop here. The ruts aren't worth driving over."

But he kept driving, the vehicle lurching on squeaking springs, the undercarriage scraping, the sun bleeding away beyond the last rise.

"House is dark," he'd said. "Nobody home."

"Well, thank you for the ride, son."

"No problem."

He let her out, his forehead and eyes masked by shadow, teeth white in a boyish smile.

"Tell me your name," she'd said.

"Jaydee."

Wilma had married, perhaps twice or more. Inez didn't ask rude questions. She patted the car door, having closed it. "Thanks again for the ride."

"Aren't you going to ask me in?"

"In? Well, no, actually, I—I'm not prepared for guests."

He was getting out by then. Eyes squinting—shoulders broad, muscular. His shirt hung outside his trousers. Boots rough—a laboring man.

"Long way from anywhere out here," he mused. "But I remember when it was further. City folks are moving this way, though. New shopping mall and all."

Then she recalled—that's where she'd seen him.

He had her by the arm, as if to steady her, but his grip was too strong—she tried to ease away.

"Kitty-kitty," he said in a monotone. "How many do you have?"

"I-I-I don't know for certain. They come and go. Thanks again for—"

"No problem," he said. He pushed her through the door into the hallway, into the kitchen.

"Cats stink," he said. "I hate cats."

Everything was so methodical. So deliberate. Like a bad dream. He tied her to a chair. He found paper and pen and sat down, leaning toward her with an elbow on the table.

"When were you born?" he asked.

"What are you going to do here?" she'd demanded.

"I am your destiny."

"I don't think so."

"Ah, but I am. Here we are. Tell me the day and month of your birth."

"July 25th."

"Leo." He removed a folded newspaper page from his pocket. "Do you know your horoscope for today?"

Horoscope . . .

She watched him spread the page, find a column and trace it. "Leo—'this is a good day for bargains,' " he read. Looking up, he asked, "Did you buy something at a good price?"

"Is it money you want?"

Still reading, he intoned, " 'A stranger may bring good news.' "

"What is this?" she questioned. "Are you playing a game with me?"

He folded the newspaper, stuck it in his top pocket. "Cats stink, don't they?"

"You don't have to endure it. You could leave. My money is in my purse."

He swiped at his face, making a dry spitting sound. "Fur all over the place—the stench—Jesus."

"Young man, what is the meaning of this?"

"I'm going to clean up a bit. Get rid of these cats. While I do that, I want you to write a letter."

"A letter?"

"A letter to Violet Day. You know who she is."

"The astrologer?"

He turned full circle, looking at the cats, mewing, waiting for their evening meal. He grabbed a mop and swung at one—the cat was thrown across the room.

"Violet said today was a good day for bargains and you got no bargain," he said, stalking another cat. "Violet said a stranger might bring good news. I am a stranger."

He faced her then, the boyish smile now insanely menacing. "The news is not good."

"Why are you doing this?" she cried. "I don't deserve this. I've always been good to people. I gave my life to help people. You're making a mistake!"

"Oh?" He sat again. She could smell his breath. "Have we made a mistake?" he asked. He took her one free arm, turned it so her palm was up on the table. He fingered her flesh, peering at the creases.

"This is your life line," he murmured. "Fate, heart, marriage—you see, it tells about your one marriage. One tiny line, right here—see it?"

"Please," she sobbed. "What are you going to do?"

He learned her name from identification in her purse. "Inez," he said, "I'm going to make a deal with you. I'm going to give you a chance to make peace with your god. You believe in God, don't you?"

"God will not let you hurt me."

"You say you've been a good girl, Inez," he said, smiling. "But all girls say that. I wonder what your husband would have said? When he became ill, did you take him to a hospital, Inez?"

"God will not allow this," she prayed.

"Oh, yes, God." He put his hand on the table, showing his own palm. "See that little mark—that hourglass mark? That's the mark of Cain, Inez. My grandmother told me about it. Cain and his children and all their children for all time bear that mark—I am not good news."

He chatted conversationally, trapping cats, killing them.

"As long as you write, you live, Inez. But when you've said all you have to say—I must kill you."

So calmly. Stuffing a cat into a sack, beating it with a piece of firewood. Dumping the dead animal and going for another—room to room—

"What do you want me to say?" she wept.

"Anything you wish. It is your last letter. Tell Violet about yourself. She'll be interested in that. Tell her when you were born and where. Give her as much information as you can, Inez. Tell her she lied to you—the stranger did not bring good news. You got no bargain today."

Her hand cramped. She'd urinated in fear. Her fingers were too stiff to hold the pen. She'd written of Eugene and crossword puzzles, anagrams and IQ teasers. She'd reminisced about her life as a teacher.

As he read it over, he chuckled. "You don't mention me."

"I didn't think you'd want me to."

"You could tell her I've killed your cats. I'm about to kill you. Tell her that. You forgot to mention she lied to you, Inez. That's important—tell her that."

Inez worked her fingers. Her mouth was so dry she couldn't get enough saliva to moisten her tongue. She wrote. Hours passed. The windows were black with the night beyond. Her cats lay broken and bloodied about the room.

Violet—

The bastard. Evil bastard!

I am about to die, he tells me.

She prayed that Eugene's spirit was here, waiting. She begged forgiveness for sins of omission and a few of commission. She thanked God for the good years, the good deposits.

He took a gun from his belt, stood over her, that smile, that terrible smile—

"A good letter, Inez," he said. "Surely Violet will see she was wrong . . ."

He pulled the trigger.

CHAPTER
TWO

IF THERE HAD NOT BEEN three witnesses, Ken Blackburn might have lied to the court. If the alley had been dark, he could have alibied, claiming a potential assault. But there were mercury lights which made day of night and one of the witnesses was another cop.

The youth was shirtless, barefoot, wearing cutoff shorts that concealed nothing. Ken couldn't say that he'd feared a hidden weapon.

"Ain't nothing you can do to me," the young man sneered. "You take me in and they're going to let me out. I got no gun, so you can't shoot me."

Cold-blooded, the onlookers said.

Ken's revolver was empty. Ballistics proved it.

"Any regrets?" a Dallas reporter questioned, after the trial.

Not at the time. *No.*

"Why did you do it, Mr. Blackburn?"

What could he say that a reporter would understand? They hadn't seen the mutilated bodies, had not walked in the mind of such an animal. They did not know what it took Ken seventeen years of law enforcement to learn—such criminals welcomed the revulsion of the world. They had no fear of incarceration because their lives of isolation had always been jails to the mind. They couldn't be hurt, therefore they couldn't be punished. Couldn't be helped, either.

The rap of the gavel would ring in Ken's mind forever. The judgment no policeman ever expected against him had been delivered. Seventeen years of his career vanished; thousands of hours of experience became worthless.

He was a good man who had done bad. It was public record.

He'd left Dallas within an hour of the verdict. He couldn't remember the route he took, through bayous of Louisiana, across the delta of Mississippi and along Florida's Gulf Coast. Day and night he drove, filled with despair, sick with the results—and *now* he felt regret.

It was a shock to realize he wasn't the man he thought he was. Ken Blackburn was a cop. *Son of a cop.* He'd never been anything else and never wanted to be. He'd worked his way through Florida State University as a deputy sheriff in Leon County. With a master's degree in criminology, he'd made an unsuccessful bid to be elected sheriff and, failing that, had gone to Dallas.

His specialty became homicide. After two years at the FBI Academy, hundreds of hours in the lab, intensive studies in forensic sciences, his focus narrowed. *Lust murder,* the FBI called it.

When he first entered law enforcement, Ken had thought the world divided into good and bad. Bad men did evil things, but good men were intrinsically good. *Evil* was a term for theologians, not police officers. Good was—well, Godly. It's what he believed himself to be—good.

Vietnam, maturity and experience taught him that good men weren't always so, and bad men were not inevitably evil. There were gradations, shades of gray.

Then he encountered *evil.*

When he was in college, a deputy in Tallahassee, Florida, he encountered his first serial killer. Rape, molestation that involved cruelty; what kind of felon bit his victims fiercely, enjoying their torment?

That was the kind of man he'd killed in Dallas. After investigating eleven bodies and unspeakable brutality, he knew the sneering youth for what he was. Sane by legal standards, committing insane acts against women. No healthy man could imagine gratification in such torture and degradation as that man had perpetrated. Would the killer do it again? After years in prison, after years of psychiatric help—yes, he would do it again!

So then, when he stood there with gun drawn at the sneering youth,

Ken thought of that first serial killer back in Tallahassee—he'd gotten away, was out there yet so far as Ken knew, looking for new victims.

Execution, the prosecutor announced. *Deliberate murder,* the newspapers agreed. *Guilty,* the jury decreed, but *not guilty.* They'd let him go, but his career was over.

Driving mindlessly across the bayous and deltas, released from the consequences of trial—now, indeed, he had regrets.

After two days and into the second night of wandering, he stopped south of Tampa, at a crossroads called Arcadia. It was an all-night diner owned by Cubans. Sitting in a front booth by a large picture window, Ken could survey the street outside, the parking lot, the end of a dark alley—and with his backside against a wall, he watched migrant workers sitting along a counter to his right. Dressed in dirty coveralls, the men traded rumors of crops to pick, orchards up north, produce in the Glades. Past the counter, through a low open window, the cook toiled over a grill, his head bound in a bandana to trap the sweat on his forehead. The place smelled of refried beans and charred meat.

Outside, a police car cruised by slowly. At the end of the alley, a blind man ate sandwiches discarded as stale. When he put down his food, mice ventured into the light to nibble at crumbs. The sun was sinking and lights winked along the main street of Arcadia.

The police car returned. The patrolman was watching two young girls who studiously ignored him. Then, when he was out of sight, they stuck out their thumbs in a frantic effort to catch a ride.

"*Cafe, senor?*" the waitress asked Ken.

"*Si, gracias. Negro.*"

Ken sipped the beverage, watching the blind man and his mice, the girls hitchhiking unsuccessfully. When his vision shifted to shorter range, his own image met his gaze, a ghostly apparition with sad blue eyes under thick bushy eyebrows. His brown wavy hair was tipped with gray. Who was that vision who resembled himself?

Two tours in Vietnam. He'd volunteered for both.

Okay, he was a veteran.

But this mirrored face was older than the Ken Blackburn he knew—sad, so sad!

He'd never suffered an identity crisis before now.

Who was he? What did he do?

More importantly, what next?

*   *   *

Passing on the street again, the Arcadia Police car slowed. Definitely appraising the girls. Because of the cop's overt notice, they gathered their belongings, a bundle wrapped in a sheet and a cardboard suitcase, walking toward the diner. Outside Ken's window, they halted to confer, their faces painted by red neon signs.

One wore tight denim jeans, a western style man's shirt with imitation pearl snaps instead of buttons. She glanced at her Timex wristwatch, then at Ken. Their eyes met, lingered, and she lifted her chin slightly, returning to her companion.

The other girl was younger, fifteen at most. Her fingernails had been bitten to the quick. *Runaways, possibly.*

Ken drank the last of his coffee, but held his cup aloft, studying them. When they saw the patrol car returning, they ran toward the diner door and entered. They came straight to his booth and sat without invitation.

"You driving the Ford with Texas plates?" one asked.

Ken felt the eyes of other patrons. He saw the cop looking his way.

"Hey, listen," the older girl said, "I'm Diane. This is Sissie. That cop is going to take us in if we don't get out of here. How about a ride?"

A Mexican-American had turned on his stool at the counter, staring at them. Rolling a toothpick between his teeth, he ogled the girls.

"Nobody is after us, we aren't in any trouble," Diane insisted.

Ken indicated the cop with a sidewise jerk of his head.

"Him? He doesn't care. He doesn't want us loitering on the street, that's all."

"What about your parents?" Ken questioned.

She widened her eyes, two hazel orbs set in sunburned flesh and a galaxy of freckles. "Believe me," she said, emphatically, "our parents are *not* looking for us."

The patrolman was across the street, watching. His intention was to intimidate them.

Diane leaned nearer, voice lowered. "We pay our way, man. One way or another, we pay our way—right, Sissie?"

"You know what we mean?" Sissie asked.

"I think so."

The waitress watched all this, dourly. Ken saw the blind man feeling among the mice for his jacket.

Diane stole a glance at the police officer, pretending to use the window to check her own reflection. She brushed back her auburn hair.

"Okay?" she asked. "Deal, okay? You buy us something to eat, right now, give us a ride to the next town and we'll show you something you never saw before."

Ken smiled wryly. "Maybe I'll show you something. You don't know me. How do you know I can be trusted? This is a dangerous game you girls are playing. But, all right. If the cop doesn't come after you, I'll give you a ride. I want no trouble, girls."

"Believe me," she insisted, "we are not in trouble!"

"Yet," Ken said. He raised a hand to summon the waitress. They ordered cheeseburgers, cold drinks, and ate so hungrily, Ken ordered more. The customers rotated out, new ones wandered in. The blind man had disappeared into the alley. The cop passed twice more as he patrolled the town.

"What do we call you?" Diane asked Ken.

"Ken."

She sucked spittle between her teeth. "You live in Texas," she surmised from the auto tag. "What kind of work?"

"Between jobs at the moment."

Sissie was dozing, her head on Diane's shoulder. Solicitiously, Diane nudged her. "Need to pee before we go, Sissie?"

"Not really."

"Go anyway. Come on, let's wash up."

They gathered their bundles, retreating to the rear of the diner with feigned nonchalance. Ken paid for the food, went out to wait in his car. Through the windows across the front of the diner, he could see every booth, the counter, and the restroom doors. Diane appeared, looked this way and that, then she and Sissie slipped out the back exit.

Okay.

He'd fed them, would have given them a ride, but he had no craving for distraction. If they wanted to shake him off, it was easy to do because he didn't care.

The Arcadia police car arrived from nowhere, parked next to Ken. The officer took note of Ken's Ford, the Texas plate.

Ken backed his vehicle out, turned it toward the street. There, he paused. He'd been on the road since the trial. He was bone weary, but didn't want to sleep. With the cop watching him, Ken halted for a traffic light, still watching the cop's car in the rearview mirror.

The doors flew open and the girls piled in, shrieking.

"Kee-right!" Diane shrilled. "I thought he had you. We saw him across the street, waiting. Made sure he saw us sneaking out the back way."

Sissie looked through the back window. "He's going into the alley right now.

"Well?" Diane shoved Ken's shoulder. "Come on, come on! Let's go."

"Where?"

"Anywhere but here," she twisted to look back at the diner. "Anywhere you say, baby . . ."

They'd been riding about an hour, the headlights pushing back the night. Highway 70 was a monotonous straight line. *Okeechobee eight miles.* Australian pines rose like sentinels, then fell away behind. A new moon hung over the southern hemisphere, the stars brilliant in a darkened sky.

Beside Ken, Diane gazed across the swampland. In the rear seat, Sissie slumbered.

Of the two, Diane was more angular, with muscled thighs and a lean body. She'd been raised on a farm in Montana, she'd said. Milked cows, spread manure, tossed hay—but it was a lie. Those fingernails were manicured, her palms soft and pliant.

Sissie, on the other hand, was an hourglass of femininity. The nymphet destined to be a temptress.

Of the two, Diane was more appealing. She gave an impression of rustic, rural roots, but then some hint of refinement slipped through. That intrigued Ken.

For one thing, Diane was more mature than he'd first thought. Twenty-one, maybe twenty-two, she was also more sophisticated.

"What kind of work do you do?" she'd asked.

"This and that."

"Okay. Do you enjoy *what* you do?"

"I don't do many things I don't enjoy. I try to take things as they're dealt to me. What's been dealt to you?"

"*Bois de vache,*" she said. Then, "Know what that means? Buffalo dung."

She didn't speak French, she said. It was a phrase she'd "heard somewhere." Education by accident.

It seemed to be the way she did everything—by accident, to hear her tell it.

They rambled, she said. Tumbleweeds ripped from the soil, thrown hither and yon by the sweep of capricious winds, impelled by biological urges, nothing cerebral.

Lighting Diane's cigarette, the flare of Ken's match reflected in her eyes, the pupils appeared elliptical. Like a cat. The illusion had an eerie appeal.

"Oh, God," Sissie whimpered.

"What is it?" Diane asked.

"Oh, God, Diane. I lost the ring."

Diane whirled in the seat, on her knees, leaning over to help Sissie paw things about.

"I told you not to wear it," Diane snapped.

"I didn't! I had it in my pocket when we went into the restroom."

"Did you put it down?"

"No! I don't think so."

"You don't think so! Damn, Sissie. Ten thousand dollars worth of diamond and you lost it?"

"Ten thousand?" Ken said.

"Ten-goddamned-thousand!" Diane was seated again, glaring ahead. "We were going to hock it tomorrow. We tried to already, but they thought we stole it."

"Did you?"

She looked away, came back angry. "Sissie, I told you to let me carry it."

Sissie was crying.

"Are you positive you had it back at the diner?" Ken asked.

"She keeps taking the damned thing out, looking at it," Diane said. "Wanted to wear it, for god'ssake. Talk about stupid."

"Diane, I'm sorry!"

"Who told you it was worth ten thousand dollars?" Ken asked.

"The jeweler. Where we tried to sell it."

"Ten thousand?" Ken queried, skeptically.

"Well, maybe not ten thousand. He said that's what somebody paid for it. He might've offered five thousand."

"Or less."

"Three thousand, for sure. Trouble was, dressed like we are, he thought we stole it."

"I ask again, did you?"

Sissie's mother's ring, she said. Ken was driving more slowly.

"Hey, you know what?" Diane brightened. "I'll bet you could sell it. How about it, Ken? We'd split with you, fifty-fifty—what do you say?"

"I don't know," Ken hedged.

"Come on—what the hell—let's go back. If we find it, we'll split the money tomorrow after it's sold."

"Fifty-fifty?" Sissie protested.

"Hell yes, Sissie! He's going to have to go all the way back to Arcadia—he bought our supper, didn't he? We can't sell it at all. Fifty-fifty is fair. What say?"

"Fifty-fifty is a lot of money, Diane."

"Chances are you won't get it back," Ken predicted.

"Okay," Diane said, "let us out, okay? We'll hitch a ride back. I'm not leaving a five-thousand-dollar ring without trying."

Sissie was crying again.

Few houses, no cars. Mosquitoes would eat them alive. "All right," Ken relented. He swung in a wide arc, turning around. "We can try. But in that place, if somebody finds a ring, he won't turn it in."

Diane lit a cigarette, cracked her window to vent smoke. Driving faster now, Ken retraced their route.

"I hope it's there," Sissie said. "If we don't get a lot of money for it— we'll have to go home, Diane."

"We're not going home," Diane said, huskily. "We'll get it back, Sissie. Stop the bawling, will you?"

The warm wind roared in Ken's ears, the whine of tires a traveler's lullaby.

He had two petty thieves and one was a minor.

But what else did he have to do? Going home to West Palm Beach, back to his mother's house, thirty-nine years old and unemployed . . .

Depressed, Ken drove the arrow-straight highway toward Arcadia, Diane smoking beside him.

He had nothing better to do . . .

It was after midnight when Ken pulled into the diner parking lot. The cook and waitress were gone. A man in a rolled apron sat at the counter, reading a newspaper.

"Sissie, you check the booth where we were sitting," Diane instructed. "Then check the rest room. I'll talk to that guy and see if somebody found the ring."

Sissie started to get out with her bundle, and Diane said, "Why are you taking that?"

"I don't know."

"Leave it here," Diane commanded. "Ken will watch it."

"Don't leave without locking the car, okay?" Sissie asked Ken.

"I'll be right here."

With the motor idling, he watched Sissie search the seat and under the table where they'd been. Ken glanced into the rear seat—more jewelry in the bundle?

Diane was speaking to the man at the counter. Then, she and Sissie stood aside, talking to one another. Insects darted at the neon signs, the smell of them acrid where they fell to be smashed underfoot on a sidewalk.

Diane came out, leaned in the car window. "He has the ring, but he says he wants five hundred dollars reward."

"Five hundred dollars! Let me go talk to him."

She held the door as Ken tried to open it. "Hey, you don't want to do that. If he calls the cops they'll find out Sissie is fourteen. They'll want to know where we got the ring. It's better to forget it than to take a chance like that."

"I haven't got five hundred dollars."

"What do you have?"

"A hundred, maybe."

"Okay. Let me go tell him, a hundred or nothing."

Ken turned off the motor. He watched an animated exchange between the counterman and Diane. Sissie was in the rest room.

Diane came out again. "He says he'll take the hundred but he wants us to come back tomorrow and give him another four hundred when we sell the ring."

"Why did you tell him you were selling it?"

"Because I thought he wasn't going to take the hundred!"

"Did he show you the ring?"

"Yeah, yeah, he's got it."

Ken took a hundred dollar bill from his wallet. As he gave it to Diane, she said, "The bastard."

Inside, again, she stood with her back to Ken, conversing with the man. He wiped his counter, moved shakers of salt and pepper here and there. Then, he led the way to the back.

The neon sign hummed, the insects whirled. Behind Ken, a truck passed, gained speed to make a distant traffic light.

A couple of men entered the diner and sat at the counter.

Ken blotted his face with a sleeve, waiting. He turned to look in the rear seat again. The cardboard suitcase and bundle were there.

After another minute, one of the customers leaned across the counter, as if peering toward the rear where Diane and the counterman went.

There. The employee appeared, rolling down his apron. He took their orders, went into the kitchen.

Ken waited another few minutes. Then, angrily, he got out, went in.

"Where're the two girls?" he demanded.

"Gone."

"Did they get the ring?"

"What ring? She asked me to change a C-note and I did. She went out the back way."

Ken shoved through the rest room door—the window was open.

He ran out back into an alley.

The blind man was fumbling in a trash can. At the far end of the alley, a street light poured yellow hues over the rear of commercial buildings.

"Anybody go by here?" he asked the blind man.

"Two girls." He sniffed a package. "Running."

Conned.

Furious, Ken returned to his vehicle. He tore open the bundle and the suitcase—rags. Nothing but rags.

Conned—damn them—

He jammed the car into reverse, drove around the block, then around the next block, looking.

So slick—damn them—and he fell for it. It was the surest proof he was no longer a policeman.

His face prickled with heat, his jaw ached from clamping his teeth. He slammed the steering wheel with the flat of one hand. Driving at a crawl now, he peered into dark recesses, alert for movement.

But they were gone.

And he was nearly broke . . .

He counted his money. Nineteen dollars and change.

He drove in ever-widening circles. Defeated, he returned to the diner. He bought a newspaper and his eye fell on Violet Day's column:

Sagittarius:
Be patient and you will
get what you desire.
Luck is merely sleeping.

Impulsively, he drove back to Sarasota, then south toward Fort Myers. His head pounded with poorly contained anger. He was trembling for want of rest, his face a stubble of beard.

He was consumed by the thievery to which he'd been victim. He examined every car he overtook, watching for the girls.

God help them if he caught up.

He filled his tank in Fort Myers, using a credit card he knew he couldn't pay next month. Frustration engendered stupid thoughts—he considered robbing the attendant. God, was he that far gone? Robbery? God!

He took Highway 80, which crossed Florida into West Palm Beach. Nauseated with his status, enraged that he'd been duped, he'd never felt so whipped.

At Belle Glade, he pulled into a convenience store, bought chocolate milk and cookies.

Going home to his mother's house. He'd have to tell her—his career was ruined, law enforcement was a thing of the past. He'd killed a man.

Temporary insanity, they'd called it. The result of stress, his lawyer had said.

But it was execution. Three witnesses saw it. His own partner was one of them.

Ken sat in his car, the first hint of dawn diluting the black of night. *Killed a man.*

He'd told the doctors he didn't remember.

But he did.

The jolt of the weapon, the sharp crack of gunfire, the thud of slugs . . .

His revolver was under the seat. Loaded, ready.

It would be easy to end it.

But he thought of his mother, at home unsuspecting; his father, divorced and living in Miami. He thought of teachers who'd taught him, men who'd served beside him.

Suicide was the ultimate selfish act. He'd seen too many of them, with the survivors left to endure alone.

Suicide would make his dishonor complete.

He remembered Violet Day's horoscopic prophecy in the morning newspaper:

> *Patience . . .*
> *Luck is merely sleeping . . .*

CHAPTER THREE

LORRAINE DAY placed her mug of hot coffee on a glass tabletop and leaned back in a cushioned lawn chair to watch the sun rise. Her favorite hour . . .

The Atlantic Ocean spread away from Palm Beach in a molten crescent, pungent with seaweed, unruffled by waves. Around Lorraine, in predawn darkness, buried lawn sprinklers hurled misty spray in a constant whisper. The smell of oleander and frangipani was a reminder that she was home. Right where she'd been born, thirty-nine years ago.

"This is where you belong," her mother, Violet, had declared. "You will be the fourth Violet Day. Your daughter will be the fifth."

So, like it or not, this was the row she'd hoe, the plush rut she'd walk, from now until death.

"A goodly portion of the population would love these environs," Violet reasoned. "Besides, if it were not meant to be, you wouldn't be here. Do not find fault with the stars, my dear. We live by them."

There was no denying that. Violet Day's column appeared in one thousand six hundred newspapers, translated into thirty languages. Her books on horoscopy were best sellers. Thousands of letters came each week, asking for a ten-dollar "astrograph" tailored to the specific inquiry. The result: this thirteen-acre compound with sculpted lawns and five hundred feet of Atlantic beach front. The family and servants shared a twenty-two-room mansion designed by Addison Mizner. Completed in 1924, the residence had been commissioned by Lorraine's grandmother, Violet's mother, also known as "Violet Day."

The sprinklers quit, responding to a preset clock in the pump house. Droplets glistened on the grass, hung like crystal tears from the tips of palm fronds. Lorraine sipped coffee, watching stars disappear, a rim of cobalt sea under a platinum sunrise. She heard a distant clatter of pans. Annie preparing breakfast. The cook and gardener were laughing in the kitchen. *Cancer and Leo.* They'd become lovers when Lorraine was a child. Spying on their tryst in the greenhouse was an education in those days.

Lorraine's thoughts drifted, the next Violet Day, divorced with a teenage daughter, but financially secure—why was she depressed?

The decree became final yesterday. After eighteen years of marriage Tommy wanted a divorce, swearing he loved her even as they parted.

Their daughter, Becky, tried to intercede with all the wisdom of a sixteen-year-old. "Mom, think about this, now. Dad's a good man, isn't he?"

Yes. Tommy Linden was a good man.

"He's always looked after us. He's never been unfaithful, has he?"

No reason to think so.

How could she defend herself? Why *should* she? He'd asked for the divorce!

"Think about why you married in the first place," Becky attempted.

Just out of school, filled with youthful optimism, invincible adolescents with the world awaiting. Why *did* they marry? Violet had urged against it. "You are a Scorpio, Lorraine. Tommy is a Virgo. The signs don't mesh."

Tommy Linden, son of an accountant. His mother was a quiet woman who wore no lipstick and sang with Tommy's sisters in a church choir. No, they didn't mesh. Lorraine's whole family was peculiar even in a town where peculiarities were prized as individualism. She addressed her mother as "Violet." Even to granddaughter, Becky, Violet was "Violet."

"Relationships are fluid in terms of millennia," Violet rationalized. "I am your mother and I suppose you could call me mother, but that's this lifetime only. In previous existences, we have been father-son, sister-brother, husband-wife. With my overview of past relationships, it feels a bit odd to be addressed as 'mother' by an entity who was once my lover in Persepolis."

A sliver of sun cast a bloody dagger across the sea. The firmament was becoming a Chagall blue. A vee of pelicans swooped low over mirrored waters, flying belly to belly with their own reflections as they navigated south toward Lake Worth.

"Mom?" Becky's voice. "Bring you anything, Mom?"

"No, darling. I'm fine. Want to sit with me?"

Becky came, sat on the arm of Lorraine's chair. She had her father's high forehead, but everything else seemed to come from Violet; huge, azure-blue eyes, a fine, straight nose over sensual lips, a tiny dimple in each cheek.

They contemplated one another a moment, then Becky curled into Lorraine's lap like a small child. Lorraine stroked soft blonde hair, kissed Becky's forehead.

"I'm invited to a pool party," Becky said. "The MacArthurs or the Mellons or somebody. They live up Ocean Boulevard in the pink monstrosity with turrets."

Lorraine laughed softly.

"They want to introduce me to the right people, Violet said."

"I would say they do know the right people, Becky."

"Everybody seems so plastic, Mom. They drop names like I should know who they are. They drone on and on about Switzerland and Austria—"

"You've been to Switzerland and Austria."

"On vacation. That's where *they* go to school! They act as if we're impoverished because I'm going to school here. And they talk like they have rigor mortis. Have you ever noticed? Their jaws don't move."

"Becky, you have a prejudice against wealth."

"They're so false, Mom. They make a big deal out of nothing."

"Such as?"

"Getting dressed," Becky said. "They dress for tennis, to take a drive. Different clothes for everything. They even dress different ways for eating: breakfast, lunch, tea, cocktails, dinner—you wouldn't dare show up for supper wearing shorts and a T-shirt. That's a cardinal sin. 'Thou shalt not seem ordinary.' "

"They're trying to regiment their lives, Becky. Wealth has its burdens, believe it or not. That's why your father and I always sent you to public schools. To see how other people live. Besides, you don't have to go to this pool party."

"Violet said I ought to."

"That's not a command."

Becky pulled away, sat up, gazing out at the ocean, her brow furrowed. "I called Daddy," she said.

"You say that as if it were a confession. You know I don't mind."

"I called him last night and again a while ago."

"Five in the morning. I'm sure he was overjoyed."

"Said he was. Said he wasn't sleeping. He said he was thinking about me when the telephone rang."

After a long pause, Lorraine asked, "How is Tommy?"

"He said okay."

"Does he like Tucson?"

"Said he does. But not as much as Virginia. Too dry."

Another pause. Becky sighed, a rib-racking exhalation. "He says he has a ranch-style house and he's preparing a room for me when I visit. *If* I visit."

"Of course you'll visit."

"It won't be good, Mom. We'll be like two strangers in a public rest room. He'll talk funny and I'll act funny. He'll ask about everybody but you, hoping I'll talk about you. He'll raise his eyebrows—you know how Daddy lifts his eyebrows and makes his eyes bright when he's pretending to be interested in something. He makes little ohs with his mouth with every tiny detail, as if I were an idiot saying something surprisingly intelligent."

Becky sighed again. "He grins with tight lips when he disapproves of something, but pretends he doesn't. I can hardly wait to tell him I'm engaged or pregnant."

Lorraine took Becky's hand, squeezed it.

"So I understand why you didn't work it out," Becky said. "But I wish you had, Mom."

"I wish it could have been, Becky."

"I wish we still lived in Virginia, where boys talk like boys, about cars and girls, and girls talk about boys—instead of stupid things like schools in Switzerland."

The breakfast bell tolled and Lorraine watched Becky walk back toward the house. The sun shone on terra-cotta tile roofing and reflected in the swimming pool. An unseen bird greeted the dawn with shrill *cheer-up*s . . .

Yes, Lorraine wished that she and Tommy had been happy. But they weren't. For years she thought it was only her, before Tommy shocked her with a request for divorce.

She'd never find a better man. Good father. Loving, industrious, diligent—*and dull*.

How could she explain that to Becky?

"We cannot live together because your daddy finds me embarrassing and I find him tedious."

"Lorraine!" Violet called from the terrace.

She emptied cold coffee from her mug.

"Lorraine! Breakfast, m'love. This is going to be an exciting day— it's in the forecast."

The stars . . .

They lived by them.

In good weather, they took breakfast on the east terrace beneath a green- and white-striped canopy with scalloped buntings. Overlooking the golden yellow blossoms of glaucous Cassia trees and Spanish tile fountains, they dined on fresh fruits and juices.

"Try the chilled mango, dear," Violet suggested to Becky. "It's a culinary delight that's good for the system."

Violet peered over the rims of lavender-tinted sunglasses, her blue eyes probing. "How are you this morning, Lorraine?"

Before she got an answer, Violet shifted her inquiry to Becky. "Is your mother all right?"

By way of explanation, Becky said, "I called Dad this morning."

"*Folie à deux*," Violet said. "Thank heavens you are Pisces, child. That much good came of it. How is your father?"

"He said fine."

"Except for you, that union should never have been. I said so at the time, didn't I, Major?"

Major Drummond. It was his name, not a title. He'd been a part of the household since Lorraine was a toddler. He answered without raising his eyes from a book. "You said it, Violet."

"It was a case of two perfectly wonderful people who were perfectly incompatible," Violet stated. "The signs so decreed and I said as much. Did I not, Major?"

"So you did, Violet."

"Tommy Linden was Io to Lorraine's Jupiter, that's all. A satellite in the sway of celestial pull. He couldn't assert himself! But now, I predict, he will blossom magnificently."

"I hope so," Becky said.

"Oh, he will, I tell you! Lorraine's trajectory was immutable. Can you imagine a certified public accountant married to Violet Day? Good Lord—oil and water! Lorraine has always been a volatile, restless soul, hasn't she, Major?"

"Ran before she walked," he intoned. Major reclined on a chaise longue, turning a page as he read. *Cyrano de Bergerac* by Edmond Rostand.

Violet's tinted hair was an amber halo in the morning sun. Her fingernails were lacquered to match. Nobody could play the role better. With her claims of multiple lives, she tended to quote conversations from some ancient context so convincingly even Lorraine suffered occasional doubts.

Listening to her mother, Lorraine tried to imagine herself when she turned sixty-seven. Would she be athletic, as supple and captivating? Was it possible to learn the patter of this trade? From infancy she'd been steeped in it. While other children listened to tales of Jakob and Wilhelm Grimm, Lorraine had shivered under the covers at bedtime as Violet described robed priests who plucked the eyes from live black cocks, or slaughtered bleating lambs as they muttered incantations to summon the devil.

"You must never play games with incantations," Violet inevitably concluded. "Never tease the devil, Lorraine."

"Is he real?"

"Yes, child. The devil is real. He comes in evil form and claims to enjoy foul deeds."

"But, why?"

"Because," Violet had tutored, "he never learned to master good. His personality is quite different from God's."

And yet, reflecting on it then and now, Lorraine found the devil enthralling. God was—well—like Tommy Linden. *A bit dull.*

"Lorraine? Lorraine, are you listening?"

"I'm sorry, Violet. My mind wandered."

"I was saying," Violet enunciated, "what *you* always needed was a good man with a touch of the devil."

As if reading her thoughts.

Violet now spoke to Becky again, but her gaze remained on Lorraine. "Tommy is bereft of wickedness. If he'd had a touch of the imp, there might have been hope for the marriage. But Tommy Linden has not so much as a gram of the gremlin in him, and he never felt comfortable with those of us who do."

"Daddy is a good man."

"Indeed no doubt! But, Becky, to be really good, one must also be a little wicked. It's the seasoning of life."

A moment later, suddenly pensive, Violet said, "But evil—pure, unadulterated evil—does not require one to be good in the slightest. That's why evil is a weaker force than good. To be good, in the saintly sense, one must know evil and what nourishes it. Being good takes finesse, which pure evil does not possess."

Lorraine watched Violet's expression go absent as her thoughts ranged afar.

"Our foes are without mercy," Violet said softly. "They come from the halls of hell to torment us."

"Violet," Major sat up, "must we, for breakfast?"

Bees hummed in the hibiscus blossoms. Cumulus clouds gathered at sea. The ocean responded to some transatlantic surge and the morning sun rode gentle swells toward shore.

"I'm glad you've come home, Lorraine," Violet said, heavily. "I'm getting old."

"No, Violet," Major said sternly, "you are not."

Stunned, Lorraine saw tears in her mother's eyes.

"By whatever name," Violet said, "it is inevitable. Age is a sieve, youth seeps away. One morning, in the mirror, an old woman looked at me quizzically, asking, 'Where have the years gone?' "

Major knelt beside her, holding Violet's hand. "You've never been more beautiful or appealing," he murmured. "It defies nature that you become even more perfect with each year."

He glanced at Lorraine and she took the cue. "I'm going to the office," she announced. "Want to ride with me, Becky?"

As they walked the pebbled drive to the garage, Becky said, "She's talking about dying, isn't she, Mom?"

"That's part of it."

"She isn't *that* old," Becky said. "Besides, she's always saying that death is only a fresh start. You think she's afraid of dying, Mom?"

"I think Violet is feeling mortal because she's giving up the title of Violet Day. She sees herself in me at this same age—and she wonders where the years have gone."

Driving toward West Palm Beach with Becky beside her, Lorraine fought a tightening knot in her solar plexus. *This was it.*

For three months she'd been dreading October, and here it was—her first day at the office without Violet for support. While the retiring Violet Day went to Europe to fill a speaking tour, the younger would assume the day-to-day duties at home.

"Don't telephone asking for advice," Violet had warned. "I will not talk to you, Lorraine. It's like diving into frigid waters—sink or swim—it's up to you as of October first."

"Mom? Do you think Violet believes everything she says?"

"Like what?" Lorraine joined traffic on Poinciana, approaching the Middle Bridge.

"Like saying she's known Major for thousands of years. Violet said they met over a leg of antelope in a cave during the Ice Age."

"Only Violet could answer your question, Becky."

"She makes it real," Becky conceded, "—talking about how quiet it was, huge snowflakes drifting down over what is now the nation of France. Major acted like he believed her."

"They work well together," Lorraine noted, truthfully.

Maybe if *she* had a Major Drummond to share the lonely nights; if *she* had a confidant and constant companion, maybe then Lorraine could handle this damned job with confidence. *Job.* That's what it was. After all the glamour of travel and TV talk shows, when the glitter ended and the truth was distilled—this was a way to make a living, nothing else.

If she thought of it like that, she'd be all right. Nine-to-five, standard office procedure, selling a product like any other, except this was slightly more specialized than canned goods or hardware.

"I think she thinks she's dying, Mom."

"Violet? Nonsense. She's got a lot of years left and she'll enjoy every one of them."

"I think she thinks it, though."

They were stalled. The bridge lifted to let boating traffic pass. "Becky, don't worry about Violet. She tends to melodrama. You know that."

"You won't get that way, will you?"

"I hope not."

"Violet comes to my room at night," Becky said. "She comes in and tells me stories. Sometimes she holds my hand with all the lights off, telling me bedtime stories like I was four years old."

The bridge lowered, traffic inched forward.

"She told me about Saint Joseph of Copertino. He died in 1663, but Violet talks like she knew him. She said he went into divine ecstasy and flew. Do you think that's true?"

"Levitating? Or that she knew him?"

"Either one! Then she told me about Agrippa and asked if I'd read *Occult Philosophy*. I told her we'd just now gotten to civics."

Lorraine laughed. It eased the knot in her chest.

"Violet says she met Agrippa, who she knew as Heinrich Cornelis when they were students together in Cologne. I looked him up in the encyclopedia. He was born in 1486."

"Becky, take all this with good humor. If Violet wants to spin yarns, what does it hurt?"

"Nothing. I enjoy them, sometimes."

"So, okay then. Just listen. It pleases her."

"She thinks I'm not educated, Mom. She can't understand why I haven't studied all the heebeejeebee stuff. She said I won't be ready, when my time comes."

Lorraine entered the garage at the Stellar Building and parked in the space designated for Violet Day. The knot was returning, harder, more painful . . .

"I guess what's worrying me is you," Becky said. "I don't want you to embarrass me, like Violet embarrassed you when you were a kid."

"I won't do that to you. I promise."

As they reached the elevators, Becky wrinkled her nose. "Just when I think Violet is crazy, she says something that explains everything. Last night, I sort of insulted her. I asked how she could sell astrographs that are supposed to predict the future."

"What did she say to that?"

" 'We are not masters of our fate, but magnets.' The astrograph helps people recognize their best tendencies and avoid their worst, she said."

"Yes," Lorraine said, "she's convincing."

"She said, 'The stars impel, they do not propel.' That's pretty good, really. Keeps the customers coming and lets Violet off the hook at the same time. Smart, huh?"

They entered the elevator, rising rapidly.

"She said she'd prove it to me," Becky ruminated.

"Oh?"

"Said it sort of scary like. Like I really didn't want to know."

"You know your grandmother's sense of drama," Lorraine said. But she remembered the same offer to her, as a child. She hadn't the courage to call Violet's bluff, and it never came up again.

"I told her to go ahead, prove it," Becky said.

The elevator doors opened, and they stepped out into the receptionist's foyer.

"Did she?" Lorraine asked.

"I don't know yet. She said something about two birds with one stone and she'd let you do the job for her."

"I'm sorry to disappoint you."

"She said two things would happen today, according to the stars," Becky persisted. "She said a stranger will change our lives—and an old friend will come to help us."

"Then," Lorraine said, "we'll soon know, won't we?"

CHAPTER
FOUR

LORRAINE'S GRANDMOTHER had purchased the Stellar Building, downtown West Palm Beach, in 1930, after the stock market crash. While everybody else was going broke, Violet Day's wealth compounded. Desperate people requested astrological forecasts, hoping for signs of better times.

Back then, the preparation of such a prophecy was a "hands-on" process involving hours of research and mathematical computations. One horoscope might take a week to prepare.

Computers had changed all that.

Violet's office was tailor-made for her occupation. The ceiling was round, an inverted bowl with key celestial configurations calculated by computer. At the touch of a sensor, heavy drapes covered the windows, the lights extinguished and Violet's private planetarium became visible overhead, complete with shooting stars and the glittering tails of vanishing comets. It seemed to inspire Violet when she withdrew to ponder her annual predictions for the world to read.

The coffee table was an electronic reflection of the same skies—a computerized board with bright colored lights. On command, it could place the heavenly bodies as they had been at the time of Christ—or as they would be in the year 10,000. On Violet's desk were telephones linking her to the New York and Los Angeles offices, with direct connections to information banks from which her computers could draw. One wall was dominated by shelves behind glass. Locked and lighted for display, the shelves held rare and valuable arcane texts, a crystal ball reportedly owned by Doctor John Dee, the man who predicted the execution of Mary, Queen of Scots.

Magic.

"Man is enthralled by magic," Violet said, "because man wants to elevate himself to a level with God, to justify his existence and control his own destiny."

There was a framed quote in Violet's office. It was from G. K. Chesterton's *The Dagger With Wings:*

> *The soul goes round*
> *upon a wheel of stars*
> *and all things return . . .*

Becky viewed the sanctum with childish candor. The Boogey Room, she called it. To her, the computer banks were of great help with school work. But, usually, she subverted the expensive software to even more mundane uses. Major had rigged a channel offering a variety of electronic games and puzzles.

"No school today, Becky?" Violet's secretary, Cynthia Peebles questioned in passing.

"Teacher's conference or some such," Becky said.

"That's nice." Then to Lorraine, "The personal mail is on your desk, Miss Lorraine. Several pieces from subscribers require a reply from Violet Day."

Subscribers were the pinnacle of their clientele. Paying as much as a thousand dollars per month, they demanded, and got, astrological forecasts by the week, day and hour if so desired. They included the cycles when love, business and careers were lowest or most favorable. There were people who relied on Violet Day for investments, contract decisions, even the most propitious time to begin a project that might take years to complete.

An Arab oilman . . . a movie star . . .

Lorraine leafed through the wires first, letters second. *A banker . . . realtor . . .*

"Have the calculations been completed on these?" she asked.

Cynthia Peebles had been with Violet for twenty years. She knew the system. "The print-outs are ready for your signature, Miss Lorraine."

Lorraine reviewed the answers and okayed them. Through the connecting door to Violet's office, she saw Becky watching TV.

"The New York office called," Cynthia said. She scratched her head with the eraser of a pencil, used the same eraser to push up thick spectacles on the bridge of her nose. "They want Violet to do an extensive astrological work-up on all the candidates for president."

"Who commissioned it?"

"The John Birch Society."

"Tell them no."

Lips taut against her teeth, Cynthia peered down at her notes. "New York also wants to know if Violet decided to sell her condominium— they have an offer."

"Give that to Major."

"He said give it to you."

"Give it to Major."

"Yes, ma'am."

Then, on second thought, Lorraine instructed, "Tell New York no."

"Without giving it to Mr. Drummond?"

"Yes."

Cynthia shifted her weight to the other leg, very fat calves squeezed to tiny ankles. She wore nylon stockings, loafers, a skirt that revealed dimpled grins on her knees.

"Mrs. Wheeler wants to see you," Cynthia said. "She has several letters which don't fit the codes."

"All right. Let's get the worst behind us and have coffee before we begin dictation. Send in Mrs. Wheeler."

And that was it.

The organization ran itself, really. Lorraine would devote an hour to personalizing a reply to this correspondent or that—she would take Becky to lunch—she would tend to a few minor details like Mrs. Wheeler—*and that was it.*

Her desk was uncluttered and dust-free. A photo of Becky and her father peered at Lorraine from a sterling silver frame. A digital clock winked away the hours.

Anybody who would refuse this job was crazy.

If only it weren't so boring . . .

*   *   *

Lorraine was never comfortable with Donna Wheeler. The woman was, at age eighty-two, the only employee who had known all three Violet Days. Even Lorraine's mother was intimidated by Mrs. Wheeler.

"You haven't the insight of your grandmother, nor the charisma of your mother," Mrs. Wheeler once accused Lorraine. "To you, this is mumbo jumbo, a mishmash of numbers."

It was true, wasn't it?

Lorraine saw herself in the assessing eyes of Donna Wheeler and came up wanting. At five feet six, Lorraine was damned with a long waist and fiery red hair perpetually unruly. In contrast to Violet's riveting blue eyes, Lorraine's were chocolate brown. Violet's hands were butterflies, given to sudden darting flights while speaking. Lorraine had shed such mimicry, forcing herself to movement only by conscious command. She had become, Mrs. Wheeler stated, "Reticent."

She meant *dull*.

"We have several letters which don't fit the codes," Mrs. Wheeler said. She looked Lorraine over, from wispy hair to freckled forearms.

"For every inquiry there is a coded response," Mrs. Wheeler advised needlessly.

"For example," Mrs. Wheeler expounded, "if we get a letter pleading for money it is Code Nine; if the plea is for a dying spouse, it is Code Nine-dash-one. If it is a plea for surgery, it is Code Nine-dash-one-one."

"I think you've explained this to me before," Lorraine said.

"And," Mrs. Wheeler continued, "if it is a request for charity, it is Code Nine-dash-nine."

"Yes, I recall."

Mrs. Wheeler preferred to stand. A tall, thick-shouldered monolith with the backbone of a granite slab. "If it is an inquiry that shows promise of development, it is another code. Our letter is personalized, there are key inserts responding directly to the writer . . ."

She wore a dark blue jacket and skirt, a ruffled white blouse. A mole on her upper lip kept cadence with the words. "We encourage the writer to send for an updated and personalized horoscope—that's the business we're in."

"Yes," Lorraine said, a bit peeved. "I've noticed."

The sarcasm wasn't lost, but it was ignored. Mrs. Wheeler clutched a large Manila envelope—the object of this meeting.

"We have codes for the bereaved, the newly married, the bankrupt and the ill," Mrs. Wheeler said. "We have codes for just about anything one might imagine. And, as you may know—"

"I do know."

"—every answer we send encourages the respondent to the next level. If he sends for the general astrograph, we suggest he may want the more expensive personal horoscope. If he orders the personal horoscope, we suggest the specific, which covers love life, business and so forth."

"So now," Lorraine coaxed, "you have a letter that doesn't fit the codes."

"Within each of the specific categories," Mrs. Wheeler persisted, "we have subspecifics: love and sex, love and dating, love and siblings, love and spouse."

"Mrs. Wheeler—the letter?"

"Under the subspecific, we have double-subs. Love and spouse has sixteen addendums covering menopause, impotence, premature ejaculation—you get the picture, don't you?"

"Quite."

"*If,*" Mrs. Wheeler took a breath, "it is something from a luminary, such inquiry always goes to Violet herself."

"Is that what this is?"

"*If,*" she said, "it is a politician of note, a head of state, a member of royalty—Violet always answers such mail herself."

"And I shall see that it is done," Lorraine said.

"*However,*" Mrs. Wheeler's mole paused mid-beat, "this is not to say that the code system is fixed. I have had to update and revise it from time to time as society evolved into promiscuity, debauchery, and me-ism. The concern with AIDS is a recent example of necessary modifications in the code system. I rewrote the letter once used for leprosy and poliomyelitis when those horrid afflictions were usually terminal."

"We couldn't function without you, Mrs. Wheeler."

"But this," she held the thick envelope with both hands, "this is something else."

Lorraine saw Becky change channels on the TV in Violet's office. Beyond her own door she could see Cynthia typing, listening surreptitiously.

"This is the third one like this," Donna Wheeler said. "The first two I attributed to Code Coo-Coo."

Obscene. Death threats. Usually from someone the newspaper horoscope led astray. *Invariably anonymous.*

Mrs. Wheeler took a short step forward and placed the packet before Lorraine. "I think I should be giving this to Violet. It shouldn't be handled by any of us."

"Thank you, Mrs. Wheeler. Is there anything else?"

"No."

"How are things in data and analysis?"

"My staff is dedicated and diligent. Everything is as it should be, except for this letter."

"You said there were three."

"They're there. Two brief, the one longer, but substantially the same."

"Thank you, Mrs. Wheeler."

Still not moving, Mrs. Wheeler said, "I find it awkward to go through an intermediary to reach Violet. It was never necessary before."

"My mother and Major Drummond left for New York this morning, Mrs. Wheeler. As of today, these duties are mine. I know you will help me do what is right."

The woman's shoulders lifted slightly. "I live for my work, everyone knows that. This isn't merely a way to earn wages, Lorraine."

"You are what makes this place tick, Mrs. Wheeler. Everybody knows that, too."

After a moment, Mrs. Wheeler nodded curtly, turned and strode past Cynthia, who was working, eyes down. A moment later, Cynthia looked at Lorraine and shook one hand as if she'd dropped something hot.

Lorraine examined the smallest envelope first, a single page on canary-yellow stationery.

Dear Violet

I am about to die . . .

The letter was so incredible, Lorraine assumed it was a hoax.

Pinned to it was a copy of Violet Day's horoscope from the Orlando *Sentinel.* The letter writer's sign was circled in the column.

"*I was born 1-11-,*" the writer said. "*You was wrong about me to day. This man ant joken. Hes gone kill me.*"

The second letter was on twenty-pound bond typing paper. She'd met a man in a grocery store during a heavy rain, she said. He offered her a ride.

Her horoscope predicted, "Relief from past financial woes, a turning point in a troubled relationship."

"*My horoscope was wrong*," she concluded. "*A man is about to kill me, he says. I am going to die*" . . .

A shiver made the hair on Lorraine's arm stand straight out from her flesh.

The third letter convinced her these were not from the same person, were mailed from different places.

In the thick brown envelope were twenty-eight pages on ruled note-book paper. A former teacher, from West Palm Beach. The penmanship was shaky, each word carefully crafted, the choice of phrase sometimes poetic.

> *Husbands enviably have a special grace regarding all yester-days; eventually yesterdays emerge sweet and blissful, loving, utterly euphoric with all grief only nebulous—only lovely dreams.*

She spoke of evenings with her husband, working anagrams, poring over difficult crossword puzzles. She described picnics beneath a solitary oak on a rolling sandy dune where white-tail deer cavorted and ospreys rode thermal currents in the sky.

Lorraine could almost feel the woman beside her.

Her name was Inez Cumbie.

They'd lived a simple life, she and Eugene, but then Inez described the rich rewards of such "ascetic simplicity."

If the letters were a hoax, they were effective.

Lorraine could understand why Mrs. Wheeler had no code for them. How does a computer respond to correspondence that ends with the first letter? They certainly weren't prospects for astrological charts and heavenly advice.

If the letters were to be believed, they each died moments after the signatures were affixed.

Killing my cats. Her "poor pussies," Inez called them.

Lorraine turned pages, perspiration cold in the palms of her hands. Three postmarks, the first dated several months ago, the most recent, day before yesterday.

What to do with these?

She considered calling the police. But such a story would make the tabloids for sure. The *National Enquirer*, a few miles south of here in Lantana, would hound Violet for interviews. The *Star* would use the enclosed predictions to sensationalize astrology in general, Violet in particular.

And if this was a ruse, what could come from public scrutiny except to encourage more of the same?

"Mom, what about lunch?" Becky called from Violet's office.

Lorraine's fingers tingled as she held the letters, placing them back into their envelopes. She had a breathless sense that something was pressing her—tormented souls wailing in the ether. She closed her eyes, her early morning fear returning, a bad taste in her mouth.

Please God—let these be false.

"Mom?"

Lorraine swallowed repeatedly, struggling to subdue the surge of gastric acids, trying to push away imagined images of squealing felines, the horror Inez Cumbie must have felt—if the letter was true.

"Mom!" Becky screamed.

Lorraine jolted forward, pushed the letters away.

"Are you all right, Mom?"

"Yes, Becky."

"What were you doing?"

"I—I don't know."

Becky's blue eyes darted, searching, her distress so obvious that Lorraine forced a laugh to disarm her.

"What did it look like I was doing?" she joked, lamely.

"I thought you were having an attack or something."

"I'm sorry, Becky. Let's go home."

"You looked like—"

Lorraine put the letters in her satchel, paused, turning.

"You looked like Violet," Becky said. "Like Violet looks when she's pretending to conjure something."

Surprised, Lorraine thought a moment.

Surprised—because, for some reason—she felt complimented.

In the shadows of late afternoon Lorraine sat on her bedroom balcony with a telephone at her side. Down below, the gardener whistled softly as he trimmed a hedge.

Violet and Major had called from New York, the first leg of the speaking tour. They were going to a Broadway show tonight, leaving for England tomorrow.

Lorraine hadn't mentioned the letters. She was supposed to be shouldering the worries, relieving Violet of office details.

She had read Inez Cumbie's letter several times. It was too sincere to dismiss, too frightening to ignore.

Sitting in a wicker bottom rocker, gazing over the tops of sabal palms, she could see the ocean, blue green and ribbed with breakers.

Alone. Again. Becky was at her pool party.

She'd never had anyone she could confide in. *Except Ken Blackburn.* Other than Tommy Linden, Ken was the only constant male companion through her adolescent years.

He was the son of a woman who'd worked for Violet most of Lorraine's life. Educated, soft-spoken, Marian Blackburn was the wife of a tough Miami barrio cop. Their troubled marriage would not mend. During long separations, Marian would come back to Palm Beach and resume employment with Violet.

Even when Lorraine was married to Tommy, they'd never been able to talk meaningfully. Maybe they'd sensed their relationship was not permanent. Maybe because she didn't know how to say what she felt.

The truth was, all her life she'd tried to disguise a corrosive insecurity. Since she could not divorce her mother, Lorraine had developed a *who cares* posture. When Violet appeared at her school in flowing lavender dresses, with Major at her side, it was excruciatingly embarrassing.

"I do not understand Lorraine's low grade in history," Violet would protest. "It behooves you to listen to Lorraine's version of events rather than try to foist upon her the revisionist claptrap of several centuries of authors who were never there."

"Can you give me an example, Miss Day?"

"Absolutely! Take this business with Nero—"

"*God, it was awful.*

"Then there's the propaganda about Brutus—"

To mask her discomfort, Lorraine became a caricature of Violet—loud, wise-cracking, irreverent. Wearing garish clothes and outlandish hairdos, she wrapped herself in disdain, chin lifted, daring any and all to verbal jousts. Few accepted the challenge.

Tommy was her straight man, a willing butt to stinging one-liners.

Oh, yes, they were the life of every party. He clung like a whipped puppy. No insult could drive him away. Any attention was better than none at all, for Tommy.

She realized too late the harm she'd inflicted.

"I never minded the jokes about me in public, Lorraine. People laughed and that's what I most admired about you, the way people laughed. But at home, alone—you never quit. After a while I began to think you really meant those things."

Penile humor. Deliberately crude and cutting. "Why is Tommy's penis like a virus? They're both microscopic!"

"If a man loses sight, his hearing becomes better. A malfunction at one junction accentuates the other. Take Tommy—he goes to work with sex on his breath . . ."

Lorraine squirmed lower in the wicker rocker, a hand over her mouth, aching with regret. Eighteen years of marriage, eroding Tommy's confidence, which had been tentative at best. He didn't deserve that—she hated herself for it! Cruel, stupid . . .

The letters lay in her lap.

Trust—whom?

Her relationship with Ken Blackburn had been the opposite of what she'd known with Tommy.

She remembered Ken as a tall, strong boy. Like his mother, he had lustrous brown hair and melancholy blue eyes. His mouth was sensitive, slow to smile, as if a woeful thing had drained him of the will.

Ken *listened* to her. When those idiot slurs fell from her lips, he ignored them, trying to glean substance from inanities.

"I don't know why I say things like that," Lorraine once blurted.

"To avoid exposing what you really feel," Ken had noted.

It was pretty revealing from a fifteen-year-old high school junior. Ken understood her before Lorraine understood herself.

She could trust Ken. Even after all these years, she could. Keep a confidence? He already had.

In one of those spontaneous acts of childhood, Lorraine stole money from a teacher's desk. She didn't need it, didn't even want it. She didn't like the teacher.

The memory of that day was still bitter.

"When one cannot be trusted with pennies," the teacher expounded, "one cannot be trusted with dollars. A thief is a thief and the guilty student should step forward."

Hands clasped on their desks. Lorraine stared straight ahead. From a corner of her eye, she saw Ken watching her. *He knew.* She had no idea how he knew, but he knew!

"Very well," the teacher said, "we will search every pocket, purse and desk. A thief has no honor and deserves none. We will expose that person publicly."

The coins were in a distinctive, small felt bag with a drawstring pull. It was in Lorraine's purse.

Advancing, from one desk to the next, the search was thorough, the silence heavy. *No way out . . .*

"Stand up, Lorraine. Empty your desk."

Across the room, Ken said, "I stole the money."

"You, Kenneth?"

"It isn't here. I spent it."

He'd been expelled. Other students ostracized him. His mother, Marian, was horrified.

"They won't trust you in the main house," she'd cried. "Kenny, Violet and Mr. Drummond will never trust you again!"

The next day, Lorraine returned the purse, intact. Not a penny missing.

Thereafter, they were a trio, she, Tommy and Ken.

They hadn't discussed the incident. Lorraine never learned how Ken knew it was she.

The telephone rang. Cynthia calling back.

"I pulled the personnel file on Marian Blackburn," Cynthia reported. "She's on pension with us. You want her address?"

"I know it, Cynthia. What about her son, Kenneth?"

"I had to make several long distance calls, that's what took so long."

Cynthia delivered a litany of information regarding education, employment history, military service, with a curious blend of personal asides.

"He was engaged to marry a professor at Florida State University, but didn't. He's still single. He likes vanilla wafers and wears size thirteen-D shoes—"

Lorraine laughed. "Where do you get those things?"

"You know Mrs. Wheeler. When she finds out some little something, she adds it to the personnel file. I can give you Kenneth's grades from elementary up."

"Is he still in police work, Cynthia?"

"He was until last Friday. Dallas. But according to the Texas newspapers, he just got fired. 'Dismissed for conduct unbecoming an officer,' they said. Kenneth lost his job, his pension—he'll never get another one in police work, the reporter told me."

"What did he do?"

"He shot a man they were trying to arrest."

"Where is he now?"

"He's here. At his mother's. He arrived this morning."

Trust the heavenly bodies, Violet was fond of saying.

After she hung up, Lorraine took a breath, held it, steadying her nerves.

A stranger would change their lives.

An old friend would come to help them . . .

CHAPTER
FIVE

KEN WAITED for a call his mother said was coming. *Violet Day.*

"Did they say what she wanted?" he'd asked.

"Maybe they're going to offer you a job. Would you accept it?"

"Mama, they don't need me."

"I heard that Lorraine is taking over as the new Violet Day," his mother advised. "You and she were always chums."

"Long time ago, Mama."

"Those people turn to long associations, Kenny. You know how clannish they are."

Maternal concern softened her voice, "It would please me to have you here."

To live with her, she meant. Man around the house.

"Let's wait and see what they want, Mama. Probably nothing."

"If you need money—"

"No. I'm all right."

Coming home after a prolonged absence was an exercise in obituaries and legal documentation. Mama insisted on mentioning people Ken knew or should have known, people who had died or suffered a calamity. Marian Blackburn would halt any conversation with a snap of her fingers to mention marriages and divorces—including Lorraine Day's from Tommy Linden. "Have I mentioned that?" she'd ask, adding, "I think Lorraine knew the marriage wouldn't last. Why else would she have kept her maiden name?"

Come on, phone—ring!

And it did.

"Ken? This is Lorraine Day."

"Hi, Lori."

"Long time." Her voice was that same husky timbre from childhood. "How are you, Ken?"

"I'm getting along. How about you?"

She hesitated an instant and that told him. "Do you have a minute to talk, Ken?"

"Sure. End of the day."

"I could call later, if you prefer."

"No, Lori—what is it?"

Marian wrapped a dishtowel around her hand, listening.

"I have a problem that requires discretion, Ken. That is, *if* I have a problem."

"Tell me about it." He was a little surprised at the thump of his own heart.

She told him about three letters, *going to die* . . .

"Probably a hoax," she said, hopefully, "and if they are, okay. But the one that came today is from a woman named Inez Cumbie—the postmark is here in West Palm. Dated last Saturday."

He made a note of the name, listened while she read random passages—retired school teacher, widowed—

"What would you like me to do, Lori?"

"If it isn't too much trouble, could you verify any of this?"

"Suppose she's alive and well?"

"God, I hope so. Then I can assume the other letters are also fraudulent and forget the whole thing."

"All right, Lori. I'll check into it."

"Thank you, Ken."

Long pause. "Planning to stay in West Palm?"

So she knew about Dallas. "Been thinking about it."

"Drop by. We'll walk on the beach or something."

She gave him her private number. Talked about a daughter, Becky.

But really, they didn't have much to say and the call ended in a sputter of disappointment.

As it had always been . . .

After he hung up, his mother asked no questions. She knew cop talk when she heard it. Ken drove to the public library, caught them as the doors were closing. He pulled a city directory, searched the indexes.

CUMBIE, INEZ . . . *teacher, ret.*

Her address was a rural route. She had a telephone.

Ken dialed the number, rocking gently from heel to toe, standing in the foyer of the library, listening to the burr of repeated rings.

"We're closing, sir."

"Be through in a second."

A moment later, he hung up.

People like Violet Day provoked every haywire in the country . . .

Probably nothing. But, what else did he have to do?

Nothing. For the rest of his life, nothing.

He returned to his car, a breeze from the Atlantic side sweeping away the smell of rush hour traffic.

Nothing else to do—what the hell—he'd go see Inez Cumbie . . .

Ken allowed heavy traffic to dictate his progress, easing past a new shopping mall where palmetto and sandspurs had dominated a few years ago. Immersed in memories of Lorraine, he was in no hurry, responding to the flow of vehicles around him.

Every high school class had its intellectual comedian and Lorraine was typical of them all. Her sense of humor had been caustic, truisms etched in acid.

At first glance, she was not always pretty—an abundance of red hair, dark eyes that warned of ill will. She went through a phase in which she accentuated her features with brilliant ruby lipsticks and eye shadow that deepened the animosity of her glare. She wore frilled blouses with puffed sleeves, adding bulk to amplitude, suggesting that only forward momentum would keep her from toppling onto her face.

But when she smiled, she was transformed. As if a portal to a tender soul had opened, a grin revealed a timid and vulnerable Wizard of Oz beneath belligerent chicanery.

Always difficult to approach, she had few intimates. Yet, if anyone could get to know her, he would have found her extremely appealing.

Ken and his mother had lived in servants' quarters near the rear of the Violet Day compound, behind a huge greenhouse. His youth had never been secure—the son of a brusque father, a stern disciplinarian who ultimately drove them away for good. Then, to the fantasy land that was Palm Beach, surrounded by wealthy kids who looked upon their domestics as they viewed their pools and patios—objects to be used.

For years, he'd spied on Lorraine. When she swam alone, he hid behind the ornamentals, peeking over an elephant's ear. When she lounged on the terrace, he peeped through the balusters. He'd come to the conclusion Lorraine was as lonely as he. Her bravado was a shield not for combat but defense.

Ken pulled into a service station, checking his map of rural routes. *Not far now* . . .

Back in traffic, he recalled a gazebo near the beach that had been their rendezvous. They went there often—especially during stormy weather. Lori loved the lightning. Waves thundering on the shore, rain driven like grains of sand to sting their faces, the fronds of palms lashing wildly— at those moments she was most unguarded.

"I wish I were a seagull," she'd once confided, wistfully. "Imagine being so light and graceful, out there riding the wind."

Another time, she complained, "God made every creature perfect except man. You never see a cow and think, *What an udder!* Nobody looks at a crane and laughs at its skinny legs—that's the way they're supposed to be. But people—"

What is more rare than a beautiful woman who perceives herself otherwise? In a sea of suntans, Lori was an exotic creature, lightly freckled fair skin, a mass of curly red hair and dark mysterious eyes.

Two lonely children . . .

Ken slowed as a city bus reached the end of its route, circling for the return trip. The sun hung low in a hazy sky, the scrublands around him burning in hues of gold.

He consulted his map again, drove straight ahead, slowly. A barbed wire fence to his right stood as testimonial to early ranching efforts of decades past. It wouldn't be long before subdividers parcelled these acres into lots and paved streets. All of Florida seemed doomed to plastic plants and concrete estates.

A mailbox on a weathered post told him this was the place. He left the pavement, crawling over rutted bumps, moving toward a house still a quarter of a mile distant.

Suppose he stayed here in West Palm Beach? Was there any reason to believe he and Lori could go beyond those youthful years of friendly estrangement? More likely, they would feel uncomfortable, painfully polite, with less in common today than they'd had back then.

He pulled into the yard and stopped. With the motor off, a heavy silence enfolded him. The house needed paint. A barn to one side listed on rotting pillars. A corn crib, empty. An eroded, small water tank designed to catch and hold the rain. An algae-covered trough suggested a time when the family cow and other livestock might have slaked their thirst here.

He got out and stood a moment, straining for any sound of habitation. A joree warbled, a mocker replied. Gnats murmured in his ears.

There is, in man, a sixth sense which civilization tends to blunt. But some still have it—men in combat, police officers pounding a bad beat. A breeze put a whisper in the leaves of a nearby water oak, then died; gnats darted at his eyes.

He got his pistol from under the front seat and clipped the holster to his belt, unaware that he'd done it. It was a law officer's equivalent of checking his fly before leaving a urinal.

He stood away from the house, then walked around it. The windows on the west side were aflame with reflections of the setting sun. The other windows were black rectangles in weatherworn wood, clapboard siding twisted by sun and clime. Sandy loam crunched underfoot.

No dog barked. No animals remained in the coops and stalls. Nothing moved.

On the east side, he walked through a shadow so dark it felt liquid. He saw a bird's nest in the soffit, but no birds. Into the slanted rays of sunlight again, his footsteps and breathing the only audible things to be heard. Sweat gathered and he licked his lips—*salty*—and he felt perspiration trickle over his ribs.

"Hello, there!"

His voice was as foreign as the first glitter of an evening star. "Ho! Anybody home?"

He resisted an urge to look in a window. Officers had been shot as intruders before.

"Hello, inside! Hello?"

The steps groaned as he went onto a small back porch. He reached to knock and the pressure of his hand sent the door inward on weeping hinges.

The odor.

That's when he knew.

Nothing smells like a dead human. The olfactory memory of Vietnam was indelible. One whiff—and he knew what was in there.

His back to the wall, pistol drawn, he edged down a poorly lighted hall toward the first interior door. His foot struck something and instantly, a swarm of flies curled around his legs. He heard rodents scurry.

Cats. Dead cats in the hallway . . .

How could he not have heard the flies, even outside? The hum became a drone and then a roar as he looked through the door. The kitchen was laced with yellow rays from the dying sun. Broken bodies of cats lay here, there, eyes wide, fangs exposed in morbid grimace.

And in a chair, tied—head hung—a woman whose face had been blown away . . .

Homicide. Captain Wayne Dilling was a tall man, gaunt, eyes that said he'd seen more than he wished and the worst of mankind. He wore a police special .38 in a shoulder holster, a badge pinned to his belt. He dangled a cigarette between his lips, breathing around it, eyes squinted against rising smoke.

"Have a seat, Blackburn."

Ken's personnel file was on the captain's desk. Another report marked CUMBIE included photographs of the victim, the dead cats.

Herb Leibowitz leaned against a file cabinet, his beard so heavy that, even clean-shaven, his face looked sooty. He wore a sports jacket, unbuttoned, trousers that rode his girth so high his sheer stockings were exposed. He had been first man on the scene last night and his first words were, "You're a cop."

"Have been," Ken had admitted.

"Only a cop reports a homicide to homicide. Anybody else calls 911 and caterwauls."

Captain Dilling turned pages, reading. "You found the body?"

"Yes."

"But didn't know her."

"No."

"Out there on a tip, you said."

"Yes, Captain. A friend who knew me years ago. She received a letter from Mrs. Cumbie that worried her. She wanted to be sure everything was all right."

"But it wasn't," Dilling said. Ashes fell on his desk and he brushed them away with a little finger. "You wouldn't divulge the name of your friend—why not?"

"I told Leibowitz, she's something of a celebrity. She's worried about publicity. Captain, I'm not hard to get along with—"

"Neither am I. Normal police procedure. You were a cop long enough to know about procedure. Find a body, chase down the clues, suspects interrogated. You start with the closest one, right?"

"Yes."

"At the moment," Dilling said, "you're the closest one. We begin with you because you were there."

"My friend writes a newspaper column. Her business attracts a lot of mail. Other than the letter from Mrs. Cumbie, there's no connection whatsoever."

"They were friends, though."

"No connection whatsoever," Ken repeated.

"What did the letter say?" Dilling questioned.

"I haven't seen it."

"What did your friend say it said?"

"That Mrs. Cumbie was being threatened with death."

"Does that sound like evidence to you?"

"Yes, of course."

"And you're withholding information?"

"Captain, I'm going to her place. I'll get the letter."

"You're withholding information, Blackburn. It has already been noted by the investigating officer and I am about to make note of it again. That means your name is involved—a snag—a nagging question in an ongoing case."

"I promised to protect my source."

"You don't trust the West Palm Beach Police Department?"

"Can you assure me there will be no publicity sensationalizing my friend's name unnecessarily?"

"Blackburn, you're no rookie."

"No, I've seen what can happen when a case has a celebrity involved, no matter how remotely."

Dilling's eyes hardened an instant. "According to Dallas, you're a rogue cop. Disgraced. This temporary insanity thing—that's crap."

"The reason I didn't want to answer questions last night," Ken said. "There was a reporter taking my photograph. I don't need that."

"You're playing lone star cowboy here," Dilling said. "Maybe trying to crack a case single-handed. Trying to rectify the mess in Dallas?"

"That's not what I'm doing."

"You told Leibowitz last night there were extenuating circumstances. Want to explain that?"

"My friend said she also received similar letters from two other people."

Dilling lit another cigarette, gazed past Ken's head toward the outer offices. "Possible serial killer," he said. "That's a coincidence, isn't it? Your specialty."

He shifted to Herb Leibowitz. "What's the best guess on this Cumbie thing?"

"Robbery."

"It isn't robbery," Ken stated.

"She cashed a pension check at Barnett Bank in the new shopping mall," Leibowitz reported. "There was a bank envelope in her purse, check stub—no money, not even change. She'd bought one magazine, maybe paid bus fare."

"But you say it was not robbery," Dilling spoke to Ken.

"I don't think so."

"Mind sharing this education I'm reading about here, this file on you?"

"The assailant may have taken cash he found, possibly other items as well. But his primary motivation was sexual."

"Sex," Dilling said, flatly.

"The act was ritualistic," Ken explained. "The intruder went back at least once after the murder."

"How would you know that?"

"A couple of the cats had been moved. You could see the moist areas where they fell originally. I could see they were arched in an unnatural way for a limp body left undisturbed. The fur on the top was compacted. They'd been moved and turned over since rigor mortis set in."

Dilling and Leibowitz studied photographs.

"In the bedroom," Ken said, "the closets had been ransacked, dresser drawers emptied, things scattered as if to vandalize the place. But her underwear was on the bed, neatly smoothed, carefully spread.

"Was she raped?" Dilling asked.

"I doubt it. Not the way the body was bound. I didn't see signs of violation, which doesn't mean she wasn't—but it wasn't obvious. She was fully clothed."

"You lifted her skirt?"

"Yes."

"Says here," Herb said, softly, "you didn't touch anything."

"I touched the skirt."

"Anything else?"

"Back door maybe; down the hall. The phone to call here."

"And the skirt."

"Kinda man does this, Blackburn?"

"Sick. Twisted by an isolated childhood. Cruel or uncaring parents. Average or above IQ. Probably didn't finish high school, works a blue collar job. Difficulty in social situations, a loner. The FBI can give you the whole profile."

"Profiling was what you did, wasn't it? Dallas?"

"Yes."

"Did they give you the shaft out there, Blackburn? Politics and public pressure—"

"No."

"You shot the man in cold blood, emptied your revolver. He was unarmed, skimpily dressed, no way to conceal a weapon. Is that true?"

"Yes."

"Executed him. True?"

"I—that's what they said."

"What do you say?"

"I'm not sure."

He'd just spent the night in jail. Hadn't called his mother or Lori. The smell of death still clung to his clothes, filled his nostrils.

"I want those letters on my desk tomorrow latest," Dilling said.

"All right."

"You can go, Blackburn."

Herb Leibowitz gave Ken a ride to the city pound, helping clear the way to get Ken's car released. Then, with Ken behind the wheel, Leibowitz shut the door gently and leaned against it.

"Got anything to add about all this, Blackburn?"

"He's done it before. He'll do it again."

The detective rolled a dead cigar between his teeth. "This Dallas thing. Sorry you did it?"

When he didn't answer, Leibowitz said, "Any cop understands it. Can't admit that but they understand it. Okay. I'll be in touch."

Suddenly, Ken's arms felt weak, his legs trembling. He started the motor, but didn't dare move the vehicle, distrusting his own reflexes.

Somewhere out there a monster was only momentarily sated. Inez Cumbie, his most recent victim, had pacified him for now. But in a few days, or weeks, he would grow restless. Perhaps he would consult some piece of memorabilia he'd taken to fuel his fantasy. The adrenaline would flow as he relived the last assault.

He may not have penetrated the woman. But sex was the purpose—absolute control of the victim an essential part of the act.

And he enjoyed it.

That was what turned Ken's stomach, brought an ache to his abdomen. *He enjoyed it.*

He knew the man because of other men like him. The mother who bore him and the father who abandoned them were part of the reason for this man's existence—he'd developed in a cold womb. His infancy was controlled by uncaring authority figures who deprived him of security, tormented him with verbal abuse. His childhood concepts had been warped; he was flotsam, forever worthless—except during his fantasies.

In his deadly reveries, he was a god with the power of life and death. At this moment, he might be fondling Inez Cumbie's undergarments, reconstructing vivid images of his crime. To him, her fear was an expression of respect. She'd been at his mercy. He'd held her life with whimsical disdain, the horrified woman unable to alter the terrible flow of events. Only *he* could do that. And yes, he enjoyed it.

It was as if Dallas had followed Ken home, was determined to test him again.

Nauseated, Ken fought rising fear—for the murderer's next victim, another woman destined for future attack. And Lori—Violet Day—he feared for them.

The letters were part of the ritual. Designed to instill terror from afar, to kindle the same "respect" Inez Cumbie had shown facing her imminent mortality.

Sitting in his car, not yet moving, Ken clutched the steering wheel.

Admit it. His fear was for himself. The godawful cold sweats, anguish and frustration.

Oh, yes. Ken knew him.

But finding the man was something else . . .

CHAPTER
SIX

CATS RUBBED against Jaydee's legs under the kitchen table. He kicked them away. From his mother's bedroom down the hall came the sounds of a fight begun last night, gathering intensity, laced with vulgarities.

Jaydee looked in the refrigerator. *No milk.* He ate a bowl of corn flakes moistened with sugared water. He read Violet Day's column again— no mention of him; not a word about her mistakes. Soon enough, though . . .

There was a short item about Inez Cumbie, lost in the back pages of section two. *Murder. Name withheld.*

He imagined the moment of discovery, the scene as it looked to the visitor, transfixed with shock.

It pleased him to consider that.

A cat bounded into his lap and Jaydee knocked it to the floor. He heard his mother yelling at her most recent lover, the man's reply insults of a like kind.

Jaydee calculated the time it would have taken from the moment of mailing to delivery of Inez Cumbie's letter. Local mail; they should have received it yesterday. Even in a bag with hundreds of envelopes, it should've been noticed. Twenty-eight pages long. How often did they receive such a parcel?

Still, it took time to open everything, time to read and react.

Would Violet Day ever see it?

He blew on his coffee to cool it.

Surely by now Violet was not unaware. After three letters, after that magnificent thing Inez Cumbie composed? It had the ring of truth—a poignant reminiscence of a time Violet could relate to.

Yet, realistically, Jaydee knew the first two notes were so brief they might have been dismissed.

But not the one from Inez, certainly. It was too rich, too lucid. He'd gotten lucky with that one. Violet had to notice that one.

Mother's bedroom door flew open. Her lover came into the kitchen, shirt in hand, unshaven. "You know what your mother is?"

He knew.

Behind him, Mother wore a loosely bound faded pink chenille robe and slippers. "You drink my beer, eat my food," she accused.

With no reaction from Jaydee, the man flung wide the screened back door. The spring sang with a metallic hum.

Good riddance.

Estelle Reaper puffed her cheeks with a quick exhalation, clenched her fists and struck her own thighs. Cats curled around her ankles, mewing for attention.

She shifted the focus of her anger. "Have you fed these cats, Jaydee?"

He ate cereal, head down.

"Another thing," she said. "I want this place cleaned up, you hear me? I'm sick to my stomach with this mess. You walk through cat shit like it isn't there. What time is it? Are you going to work, or what?"

"Work."

"You'd better. They're shutting off the electricity next week. When are you supposed to be there?"

"Ten o'clock."

"It *is* ten o'clock! Jaydee, I got to wonder if there's any hope for you. Are you going to work looking like that? When's the last time you washed your hair? Get your chin out of the trough! You eat like a pig. A social misfit, is that what you want to be?"

"Mark of Cain," he said.

"You going through life blaming everything on a wrinkle in your hand? Blame it on a crease in your foot, why not?"

He laughed.

She bit her lower lip, looking toward the back door. More softly, she said, "Feed these cats before you leave. I want the litter boxes emptied. They're stinking up the place."

She opened the refrigerator, looked in. Cats pressed against her legs, tails erect, backs arched. Estelle moved to a cupboard, opened it, stared at the void. Cats were on the counters now, pleading. She talked baby talk to them.

There was nothing to feed them.

Estelle made a cup of instant coffee with hot tap water, then came to sit beside Jaydee. She took the morning newspaper and studied Violet Day's column. She read not only her own horoscope, but all twelve prophecies of the zodiac. She knew somebody for every sign.

"Lavern will be getting a long distance call today. Wonder who that could be?"

Every morning of his life, it'd been the same. Violet Day making promises.

"Your Aunt Reba has to be mindful of her health," Estelle continued reading. "Little late for that, I'd say. Diabetes, hardening arteries. I don't know how she's lived this long."

A cat leaped on the table and she brushed the animal back onto the floor with a sweep of a chubby forearm.

"Be careful driving today, Jaydee."

"I read it."

"Drive defensively, Violet says."

Another cat; another sweep of her arm.

"The new Violet Day begins writing the horoscope this month," Estelle reported.

She put her finger on her place and gazed away, dreamily. "The fourth Violet Day, imagine that. Four generations! Me, I got two daughters changed their names when they married and two sons, one I never see, the other sitting here late for work. You're never going to get anywhere, you know that, Jaydee? You aren't disciplined. You have to be disciplined to succeed. You got no respect for yourself. If you don't respect yourself, who does?"

As a child, he'd wait fearfully, to see if his plans for the day would be altered by something Violet Day said. A coveted camping trip was forfeited one year because Violet Day advised "Stay close to home." There were times when his mother remained in bed to avoid the chance of a mishap.

"Imagine living in one of those Spanish castles along the beach,"

Estelle contemplated. "If I ever win the sweepstakes or the lottery, first thing I'm going to do is buy a house in Palm Beach. The Atlantic side, not Lake Worth. I want to hear those waves. I'd get up early, go for walks—you find the best driftwood and shells early morning. I could make things with them, too. Driftwood and shells sell quick at the flea markets. A person could make good money doing that."

She peeled pages of the paper, going to the want ads.

"Listen to this. Swimming pool, cabana, guest cottage. Lolly could move into the cottage."

"I want the cottage."

"Okay, sure. Why not? You could live in the guest house and Lolly could take one wing, her and the babies. People talk about the cost of upkeep, but you could do that."

She threw back her head and screamed at the ceiling. "God! We need some money!"

Estelle believed you had to get God's attention. "You let a man in Pahokee win the lottery!" she yelled. "It's our turn!"

Jaydee stood to leave and Estelle returned to Violet's column. "Today's a good day for me to invest." She hollered at the ceiling again, "You hear that? A good day to invest! But first I need money!"

Then, to Jaydee, "Feed these cats before you go."

"I'm late."

"You can empty the litter boxes when you come home, but feed the cats."

"There's no cat food."

"Then go get some."

In the bathroom, he dipped a nylon bristle brush in warm water and raked his hair. He stirred things in his dresser until he found a shirt more or less clean.

He stepped around little piles of kitty manure, a desiccated, petrified obstacle course for bare feet during late-night runs to the toilet.

He departed by the front door with no pretense at stealth. His mother was engrossed in Violet's predictions, her yellowed blonde hair straggling, the cats insistent, but ignored.

Slaves to the stars begat slaves to the stars, he'd decided. His grandmother had been even more addicted than Estelle. To Grandmother, what Violet Day said was merely the first layer. The old woman would then extrapolate, reading omens "between the lines," adjusting her every move. Like a fundamentalist preacher manipulating his flock, Grandmother guided the lives of her family through Violet Day.

He considered going to Inez Cumbie's place, but decided against it. The body would be gone. Once they took the body, the excitement waned. Jaydee turned onto the Belle Glade road leading toward the storage depot where he'd pick up his route sheet and truck.

Today was Palm Beach day, first Tuesday of the month. Every two weeks he went there—lawns to fertilize, plants to spray, insecticides to deliver. Some accounts, such as towering condominiums, took an entire day, so those he tended on the first and third Wednesday of the month.

It was the nicer part of his job, Palm Beach days. Close to home, short hours.

He turned off the highway, driving toward a chain link fenced enclosure with huge white tanks laid on their sides like bloated weiners on a rotisserie. *Liquid fertilizers.*

He'd worked here since quitting school in the tenth grade. In the eleven years of his employment, he'd worked his way up to route man, finally to "regional manager." Which didn't mean anything except he was responsible for a region.

Still and yet, he got to travel some—as far north as Orlando, west to Fort Myers—spraying the citrus groves, staying in a motel, all expenses paid.

Jaydee parked his station wagon—he'd bought it from ORGRO Corporation, this wagon. It was old, but it ran good.

"You're late, Jaydee."

"Nothing but Palm Beach today, Mr. Gus."

Gus Chambers hurt a lot. World War II, he'd said. Twisted at the trunk, he lurched along on a bad leg and calcified spine. "How many times I explained about the route?"

Jaydee didn't like him.

"Dependability and service," the wizened old man said. "A thousand companies can sell hydrogen and potassium. Dependability and service, that's what holds a customer."

Jaydee pulled a pair of neatly pressed coveralls from a locker in a room that adjoined the small office. The company provided the uniform and a cap emblazoned ORGRO.

"You know what we're selling, don't you?" the manager rubbed salt in wounds of his own making. "Cow crap, that's what we're selling. It's glorified cow crap, Jaydee. We talk about it's liquid and we use fancy terms like 'intersystemic' but fertilizer is, and always has been, nothing but cow crap. It's what we used on the farm when I was a kid, and all we sell now is the same ingredients made in some laboratory. The customer senses that. So he looks for dependability and service. Understand?"

Jaydee took the clipboard with the route sheets attached.

"I don't think the dumb bastard hears me," Mr. Gus said to the air around him.

One of the deliveries Jaydee anticipated.

Maybe he'd see the new Violet Day . . .

"You know how to calculate the mix for this run, Jaydee?" Mr. Gus questioned, as if Jaydee had never mixed ingredients before.

"Indubitably."

That was a good one—*indubitably*. It was what Jaydee said when somebody tried to make him feel stupid.

But Mr. Gus wasn't reassured. He stood by, observing as Jaydee filled the tank truck, blending liquids to meet the demands of Palm Beach gardeners.

Jaydee knew words like indubitably. When he was in school his teachers used to say he had a good vocabulary.

But even they tried to make him look dumb. "Despite dyslexia," one teacher wrote on his report card, "Jaydee has a good command of the language."

For an idiot, it implied.

He had difficulty spelling. A mix-up between the eye and the brain, somebody explained.

When they let him take tests orally, he always scored better than if he had to write the answers.

"Watch your gauges, Jaydee."

Sonofabitch.

Vocabulary was imperative when Jaydee dealt with old women. Big words fell on their ears like soothing music. Maybe they figured that anybody that smart wouldn't hurt them.

So, he said things like *imperative* and *indubitably.*

Mr. Gus reached past Jaydee and tapped a gauge. "That ought to do it," he said. "Shut it off."

Jaydee slowed the flow, deliberately ignoring the command while seeming to comply.

It was one of the things he did best, resisting while appearing not to.

"Good enough," Mr. Gus said. "Okay, Jaydee, shut it off."

He let more trickle through.

"That's got it, Jaydee."

A little more . . .

"Damn it, Jaydee—that's enough!"

One last squirt, as if an involuntary jerk of the hand—five gallons in a quick squeeze of the fingers.

"All right," Mr. Gus directed, "you've got your route sheets, you know where you're going."

Jaydee capped the tanker, recoiled the hoses. Mr. Gus stood with his weight on the good leg, the bad one oddly postured at an angle. He turned pages, reciting the names and addresses to be serviced.

Jaydee lowered a nozzle, letting milky Malathion drain from a hose, an act designed to distract Mr. Gus.

"How many times I have to tell you?" Mr. Gus squawked. "We've been cited by EPA three times already—don't spill the insecticides!"

Finally, Jaydee was on his way. The truck rumbled from one gear ratio to the next, picking up speed, the liquid in the tank bucking a bit despite baffles designed to prevent surge. He was a good driver, though. He knew the rhythm required him to double-clutch, accelerate or brake, transporting his product. A cargo that shifted could be dangerous in sudden turns or stops.

Following the truck route, he passed a housing project where he'd lived until age thirteen. The low, rectangular brick buildings were inhabited mostly by Cubans and blacks now. He didn't care much for either.

It was there he'd learned about people—watching Saturday night crap shooting, listening to men brag about their conquests, reading graffiti on the walls. There was a camaraderie about the place back then. No drugs, although liquor was abundant.

His father had recently abandoned them, taking Jaydee's younger brother, to live with a lover in New Orleans. Moving to the public-subsidy housing was a necessity. "We aren't like these people," Mother boasted constantly. "They're uneducated lowlife."

But she adapted well enough. Various men, perpetually unemployed, took up residence long enough to get dictatorial. If Mother wasn't available, Jaydee was—

He'd tried to tell her what was happening, but she accused Jaydee of lying, shifting the subject from abuse to recrimination. "I work all day and clean house, too—straighten up your bed, Jaydee, goddamn it! Did you wash clothes like I told you? Hell no. What do you do after school?"

Jaydee made his first service call at a hotel, downtown Palm Beach. He sprayed boxwood hedges and fertilized potted palms in the courtyard.

His second contract was residential, farther north, more spraying and fertilizer dispensed.

He was saving the best for last.

The estate of Violet Day was like most palatial dwellings along the northern end of Palm Beach Island. Set back from the street, hidden by dense tropical foliage, only a glimpse of the red terra-cotta tile roof could be seen. The main drive was pebbled, branching away toward the rear of the house, past a four-car garage. Immediately beyond that, Jaydee had to turn, backing to a pump house.

He'd seen Violet Day several times. A small woman who wore lavender dresses, she liked to entertain on the east terrace overlooking the ocean. By three o'clock, the house cast a cooling shadow over the swimming pool, a canopy sheltered several patio tables creating an even darker haven for the pampered butts that sat there.

Jaydee turned off the motor and stepped out on the high running board. He could see over the cab of his truck, past a border of oleander—

A woman—red hair.

"What mix you got there?" the gardener inquired. "We need more nitrogen this time of year."

Jaydee presented the bill of lading and let him read it for himself.

To a man in his line of work, the pump house was a beauty. Two five-hundred-gallon stainless steel reservoirs, a bank of valves to direct the flow of nutrients, a clock to time the dispensation—the best of everything. Top of the line. Clean as a city hall rest room.

"Tell your boss the Crystal Ball is this month," the gardener advised.

Mr. Gus knew that.

The gardener blotted his face with a handkerchief, crammed it in a hip pocket. "Everything perfect." He surveyed the grounds. "That's the way they want it and so it is, until they tear up my yard with platforms and tent stakes."

Jaydee connected his hose to the intake spout of the stainless steel tanks. On a wall, a schematic displayed the area being favored. With a flip of the hand, the gardener could redirect nutrients, insect repellants or water to every square foot of the compound.

The delivery hose distended, thumping gently like a swollen vein. Trapped air inside the tanks whistled softly as liquid filled the void.

"Lock up when you finish," the gardener said.

"Indubitably," Jaydee replied.

He stood in the shadows, peering past bougainvillea at the terrace, the red-haired woman sitting there alone. A tickle ran up his spine.

The lone wolf. Hidden by shade and lush greenery, his eyes narrowed against refracting light, he watched the woman cross her legs, rotate her head slowly as if to ease taut muscles.

He glanced toward the gardener now occupied near the greenhouse. Jaydee walked along the blind side of his truck to the cab, got on the running board as if to enter.

There she was, gazing away at the ocean, oblivious to his presence. The rich were like the elderly, useless flecks of humanity, existing in a dream world. What would she be thinking, sitting there? What to wear? Whether to swim in that blue-green eye of the pool?

Again she twisted her neck, hunched her shoulders, drawing the muscles to relax them. She tossed her hair, took a sip from a tall iced drink.

A maid in uniform came onto the terrace, spoke to the woman and received a nod in reply. Alone again, the mistress peered across the yard toward the sea.

If she never worked she wouldn't be hungry. If she lifted a finger someone would rise to answer. *Spoiled.*

"Hey!" the gardener yelled.

Jaydee jumped down, flustered.

"You watching that pump?"

He waved.

The pump quit when the float said quit—he turned it off, unscrewed the delivery hose and recoiled it.

The machinery in the pump house hummed, preset to mix and deliver.

An automobile came down the drive, pebbles grinding underwheel. *Texas tags.* A man got out and stood there looking this way.

Waiting for him, she was.

Jaydee hung the delivery sheet on a nail in the pump house, closed the door and locked it.

On the running board again, he paused for a second to watch them— hugging one another—sitting down together.

Then, electrified, he saw the man pick up a brown Manila envelope.

Of course he couldn't be positive, not at this distance—but then, there were two other, smaller envelopes.

God—it was wonderful!

It *was* her.

The new Violet Day . . .

CHAPTER
SEVEN

SITTING ON the east terrace waiting for Ken, Lorraine worried that he would be startled by changes in her since they last met. She'd assessed herself—firm body, but definitely past the age of youthful bloom; maturity lined her eyes. Character had made her more interesting, perhaps.

She'd always hoped Ken would be attracted to her. But in high school, prepared for rejection, she'd rebuffed him, creating a hurdle to clear. It never happened.

Inez Cumbie—dead. That poor woman. Ken's voice on the telephone had been a monotone. *Murdered,* he'd said.

"Those letters are evidence," he'd stated. "The West Palm police want them."

"Oh, dear, Ken. Is there any way we can keep our name out of this?"

"I don't know. Is Violet aware of what's happening?"

"Not yet."

Violet was a great believer in predestination. Inez Cumbie's life had ended tragically, but at the exact moment it was predestined to end. That's what Violet would say. If, somehow, this affected them—that too was foreordained.

After talking to Ken this morning, Lorraine had telephoned their New York office.

"She's gone, Miss Day. Violet isn't due in London until next Monday, so they're probably taking a vacation before the speaking tour."

Violet had not bothered to tell anyone her schedule. There *was* no schedule until next Monday. It was vintage Violet. Why not? She was free. Lorraine was tending things.

"I could contact the airport and see if they filed a new flight plan, Miss Day."

"A flight plan wouldn't mean a thing to my mother," Lorraine had said. "Halfway to England, she might come home or go to Africa."

She'd heard a long distance sigh. "Isn't that delightful? Wouldn't it be nice to do that?"

A dual-wheel tank truck rumbled down the driveway, maneuvering to deliver liquid fertilizer to the lawn sprinkler system. The driver stepped out and stared this way. Then with a wave to the gardener, he began his chores.

Lorraine rotated her head, trying to ease creeping tension that threatened a headache. She anticipated seeing Ken, dreading it nevertheless. She wasn't the same woman he knew in high school—she *was* a woman, that was the difference.

"Miss Day," Annie reported. "Mr. Blackburn telephoned. He's on his way."

He too had changed, she must be prepared for it. Further investigation of the situation in Dallas had not been comforting.

Execution . . . temporary insanity plea . . .

Maybe this meeting was not wise. The studious boy she'd known was hardly capable of executing someone.

Violet liked to speak of "seeds." Ken came from good seed, she'd say. Whatever forces may have bent the tree, it began with good seed.

"Execution" had a chilling ring. "Temporary insanity" suggested instability.

Ken would know she knew about Dallas. He'd know they had run a check on him, routinely. Should she mention it, get it into the open? Did she *want* to?

And why was she feeling so—so—fluttery!

Seagulls swooped in spirals, following a fishing boat coming home from the sea.

One thing she vowed. No sophomoric wisecracks. Gibes had always been her armor—well, put the shield aside one time. Be natural. Hug him, allow a kiss on the cheek, a bit aloof, but not unattainable.

When he arrived, her first words defeated her plan. "How does it feel to have hair on your chest?" *Stupid!*

"I don't know," he said. "You tell me."

His frame thickened by manhood, he had stepped from his car and paused, as if taking in the scene. *Home again.* Was that his thought? Or did he harbor misgivings from some distant memory?

He came onto the terrace and held her at arm's length, his eyes darting here and there across her face. "You're more beautiful than ever, Lori. I hadn't realized how much I missed you until this moment."

Annie brought iced tea spiked with fresh mint. She offered sandwiches, but Ken declined. All the while, he stared at Lori with a faint smile.

"So what do you think?" she questioned.

"Time is good to you."

Impulsively, she said, "If you're planning to stay in Palm Beach awhile, why don't you come here? I'd love to have you as my guest."

"My mother likes having me around, Lori. But, thanks."

The thin scent of plant nutrients reached them from the pump house reservoir.

"No place smells so sweet," Ken said. "Look at those clouds, how blue the sky. I don't know what I was doing in Dallas."

He said it as if he'd returned wiser, rather than in defeat. Still, it didn't have the clarity of sincerity. Almost as if he realized it, Ken sobered, asking, "Are those the letters?"

He read the short ones first, handling the stationery by the very edges of the paper. Fingerprints? By now, half a dozen people had touched those pages.

Then he read the words of Inez Cumbie.

Twice he sighed, once with a barely audible moan, an involuntary expression of sadness.

Finally, he put the pages in order, replaced them in the Manila envelope. Absently, he watched the departure of the ORGRO truck. "I'll have to take these letters to the police, Lori."

"Keep us out of it."

"I'm not sure I can. Anyway, it isn't up to me."

"Pay somebody." Her tone was commanding. Lorraine softened it. "Do what you must. I'm worried about the tabloids. They'll make a circus of this. You know they will."

His eyes moved over the grounds, touching on the servants' quarters where he and his mother had lived, the greenhouse, the shoreline . . .

"Where do you go to eat, Lori?"

She named several restaurants. "Where would you like to go?"

"None of them. From now on, stop going where you normally would for anything. Change beauty parlors, drugstores. Alter your routine from day to day. Don't follow the same route or the same schedule. Tomorrow, I want to see your offices and evaluate the security system."

"There is no security system! The receptionist stops people at the door. Ken—" Lorraine affected a laugh. "Are you trying to frighten me? Listen, I'm concerned about these letters. This is a terrible thing. But I can't adopt a fortress mentality. Violet wouldn't allow it."

"You're the new Violet Day, aren't you?"

So that was it. Her life was in danger. And he cared.

But instead, "Ken, I'd like to put you on the payroll."

His expression set—the face of a professional cop, she thought.

"There are better men than me for what you need," he said.

"Ken, did I misunderstand? I'm sorry. Would you like to have dinner with me?"

But the moment was ruined. Ken hesitated so long, she withdrew. "Another time, maybe. Well."

Ken stood up. "You look terrific, Lori. I'd like to meet your daughter sometime. A blend of you and Tommy—she must be quite a girl."

"Yes. Ken, thank you."

He took the letters diffidently. "I'll deliver these to the police station. I'll ask them to protect you from publicity."

Damn it.

She considered calling him back. Then, angrily, she held her tongue. She had enough to worry about. She didn't have time to play psychologist to a bruised ego. If he needed a job, she'd offered one. For old times' sake, she'd offered. It was more than he should expect and generous to a fault. She didn't need a dishonored cop.

Besides, he was right. There *were* better men for her immediate purposes.

For a long, aching moment she felt immensely isolated and lonely. As he pulled out to drive away, she forced a smile, waved. Either he didn't see, or didn't care.

It had always been that way.

Ken sat in the glass-enclosed Florida room watching a torrential rain fall perfectly straight to the ground. It roared on the roof, beat down fronds of palms, flooded the lawn. His mother prepared breakfast.

"What did they want with you, Kenny?"

"Police business, Mama."

"It must be important. You haven't been home in eighteen months and now that you are you haven't been here two consecutive hours."

She placed cantaloupe before him, served Melba toast with guava jelly. Marian poured hot chocolate over a huge marshmallow. *Little boy breakfast.*

"Violet received three letters that seem threatening," he said.

"Nothing new in that. I remember years ago, a maniac said he'd plunge Mars to Earth if Violet didn't do whatever he wanted."

She sat across from him, searched his face as if seeking a familiar feature that had been disguised by time.

"More and more you look like your father," she said.

"How is Dad?"

"He seems healthy. I saw him at his mother's funeral. I wrote you about that."

"Yes. I sent flowers."

"Your father wondered why you weren't there, of course."

"I'm sorry."

"Never mind. I used his line to explain your absence—'police business.' It gave me some satisfaction."

She smiled with the thought of it, then frowned. "What did they want with you, Kenny?"

"To look at the letters, decide what to do with them. Keep it all quiet, if possible. Mama, what do you think of Lori?"

"I raised her."

"That doesn't tell me what you think."

"She's the next Violet Day."

"She isn't like Violet Day."

"She will be."

"I can't envision Lori as Violet," Ken said.

His mother dabbed spilled cocoa with a paper napkin and crumpled it. "I knew Violet when she was Lorraine's age. She wasn't like *her* mother, either. But when you want to do what she does, you must be what she has become."

Ken bit into crisp bread, guava bringing quick saliva. "I suppose you know as much about them as anyone. You've been so much a part of their personal lives."

"I was never a part of their personal lives, Kenny. Managing a part of their personal lives was my job. But we weren't friends. I was an employee. I bathed Lorraine as a baby, kissed her skinned knees, helped with arithmetic, saw her through a difficult menstruation. But even a child senses there's a difference when you're paid to care."

"I think Lori is fond of you," he said.

"I'm fond of her, but she doesn't love me. I don't love her. Lorraine is to me what a pupil is to her tutor."

Mildly surprised, Ken said, "Mama, you sound as if you resent having to be what you were to them."

"Oh, but I don't. Violet was always generous. When inflation ate away my pension, she doubled it without a word from me. There was always great mutual trust. She trusted me with her child and I trusted her with the balance of my life. But, yes, there was some resentment when I sat in Lorraine's room late at night listening to her troubles about whatever—while my own child tossed himself to sleep alone. I yearned to give you the same care. But there are only so many hours in a day. There's a Danish proverb: 'A rich child often sits in a poor woman's lap.' I would add, 'While the poor woman's child sits without.' "

"No complaints from me, Mama. Would you do it again?"

"Without doubt," she said. "You attended the best school right along with a wealthy woman who called you for help, because she knew you."

When he didn't respond to that, Marian Blackburn said, "She trusts you, Kenny. People like Violet Day can buy loyalty as long as there's money. But out of thousands of people they know worldwide, they don't trust a handful. For Violet Day, it's Major Drummond. Remember when the school accused you of stealing?"

"Well, I was just a kid."

"An honorable kid," Marian said, emphatically. "You can bet Lorraine thought of that when she called you."

"You knew?"

"Of course I knew. I know *you*. But I see the results of my loyalty sitting here before me, soon to be forty years old. Whatever happened to that girl you nearly married in Tallahassee?"

"Joanne Fleming—that's been ten years."

"Do you still correspond with her?"

"Christmas cards, mostly."

"Doctor, wasn't she?"

"Of criminology."

"I always liked her."

"You never met her, Mama."

"I know, but I liked what you wrote about her."

"Hey," Ken chided, "you're the one who advised, No marriage is better than a bad one."

"That's still true. But Lorraine is not substance for a good marriage."

"Mama, there's nothing romantic between—"

"Lorraine will be consumed by Violet Day, and into that vortex all around her will be consumed as well. It's the nature of their lives, their business."

"Don't worry about it."

"There are times when we imagine there are not so many differences between us," his mother said. "But they are so different as to be alien."

Ken laughed shortly. "Money. They have it and we don't."

"But it's more than that. You can tell me to the penny what you earn. If you ask Lorraine what she earns—or what Major Drummond earns—or Violet Day—"

"Do you know?"

"They don't earn anything," she said. "Replace the furniture, go to Europe, buy a car—an accountant pays the bills. They go out to dine, a credit card is presented. Money is an abstract."

"Should I be discouraged by this line of reasoning?"

"When you can have anything you want," she persisted, "you lose the joy of challenge. That's why wealthy men run for public office—money won't buy it. Although they try when popularity fails them."

"Lori isn't interested in romance," Ken said. "But for the sake of discussion, Violet Day is more than horoscopes. They have real estate, stock ventures, investments in—"

"Can you see yourself controlling that, Kenny? They have the best attorneys, the best realtors, the best accountants, the best investment counselors. Violet Day is not an individual, she's an industry. She doesn't manage anything—it manages her. It will Lorraine, too."

"Mama, hey—listen—this is a wasted conversation. Lori isn't interested in me. I did what she asked and that was it."

"Just remember, Kenny—ask yourself—do you want to be Lorraine's Major Drummond?"

He went for orange juice, trying to shake the mood. He laughed it away, kissed his mother as if condescendingly. But deep inside, he hurt a little.

As it had always been . . .

Ken shoved the push mower with hard, angry thrusts, chopping a carpet of St. Augustine grass. Sweat streamed down his bare chest and legs. The sun was unrelenting in rain-washed blue skies.

"You could work the shady places first," his mother suggested. But he pushed, pulled, pushed, the blades chattering.

"I pay a boy twenty-five dollars to mow the lawn," Marian said.

"Pay me. I need the money."

He'd been sacked, disgraced, robbed, jailed, snubbed—

"If you insist on doing this," Marian said, mildly, "there's a power mower in the shed."

"I saw it, Mama."

The front doorbell pulled her away. Ken's arms ached, his legs quivered—*push, pull, push*—

Detective Herb Leibowitz stepped into the backyard, shielding his eyes against the glare. "You always mow in the middle of the day?"

Ken completed his row. A twig clogged the blades. He joined the detective under an umbrella shading a round patio table.

Marian brought lemonade, busied herself with nearby plants, plucking away dead leaves.

"The other two letters were authentic," Leibowitz reported. "I thought you'd want to know. Same m.o., gunshot to the back of the head, victims bound in chairs. All three were elderly women who'd visited a shopping mall the day of death."

Ken sipped lemonade, watching his mother feign work.

"I called Joanne Fleming at F.S.U.," the detective said. "When I mentioned your name she said you were the best with this kind of crime."

Ken's mother stole a glance.

"I'd like you to take a look at what we have," Leibowitz said. "Fort Myers sent photos, but not much else. They had it down as simple robbery. No diagrams, very little hard evidence. Nothing serological."

"Are you putting me on the payroll?" Ken questioned.

Leibowitz looked away.

"I might be an assistant electrician by this time next week," Ken said. "Or working with a plumber. Who knows?"

"I could speak to a few security people in Palm Beach," the detective offered.

"Hire a man who executed a criminal?"

"Hey! There are folks who would take that as a high recommendation."

"Not interested."

"Okay. Listen. I lived in Mobile, Alabama, awhile. Started a guard dog service. Would you consider partners?"

"No."

"You spent a year in fingerprint science. I'll speak to the captain about that—get you some lab work, maybe."

"Leibowitz—"

"Herb—call me Herb."

"Herb. I don't want part-time work in a basement. If it isn't on-line, I don't want it."

"Blackburn, goddamn! If you'd retired, what would you do? Find a new way to go, man."

Ken sat forward, earnestly. "Every department has discretionary funds. You could pay me as a consultant. I know what you're up against with this killer. I know the sonofabitch better than he knows himself. The way he thinks, the dreams he has, the bastard's upbringing—what's happened so far is only a beginning, Herb. There'll be more to come— and the degree of cruelty will escalate, if he's true to type."

"I'll do what I can," Herb said softly.

"Forget it," Ken yielded, suddenly. "I know better."

The detective stood up. "If you have a minute somewhere along the way—we'd appreciate it."

Ken heard his mother making a final appeal as she ushered Herb through the house. "College degree . . . best grades at the FBI school . . . his father was a policeman, too . . ."

Wasted breath.

He was thinking like a schoolboy, fantasizing that some act of valor would absolve him.

His mother emerged and came to put a hand on his shoulder. "They're making a big mistake," she said.

He held her wrist to halt the caress. "Nobody wants a cop who went crazy for a minute."

"That could happen to anybody, Kenny. The pressures you're under. The things you've seen."

Repeating words he'd spoken to her.

He felt drained. *Beat.*

"Nothing is going to happen," he said, "unless I make it happen."

"Good for you. Be positive."

But that wasn't what he'd meant. He'd meant, the West Palm police would use him so long as he allowed it. Lori would, too.

He'd blown that prospect—so sure Lori would embrace him, put him on the payroll, no questions asked, a long-time friend who would set up alarms to warn of intruders. She needed him, whether she knew it or not.

But it wasn't going to happen unless he instigated it.

The irony . . .

For shooting a man just like this West Palm killer, he was in this mess. Now, the same kind of man, cast from the same defective mold, was his best hope for redemption.

As he thought, his abdomen twisted painfully. But pain or not, it was up to him to change things.

You and me, pal, Ken thought, bitterly. *You and me.*

CHAPTER EIGHT

"MISS LORRAINE," Cynthia advised, "there are things that need your attention this morning."

"All right, Cynthia. Ask Mr. Leibowitz to come on in." The detective sat in the outer office on the edge of a chair. He'd arrived unannounced.

"You don't have time for him," Cynthia said, rather firmly. "You'll be getting a phone call in a few minutes. One of our best clients. Here's a summary of his activity and past advice from Violet."

Cynthia placed a thick sheaf of papers on Lorraine's desk. *Actor. Age sixty-one. Aries.* Lorraine thumbed through twenty-two years of correspondence and past "consultations."

"Did you tell this man my mother isn't here?"

"No, of course not. He thinks he'll be speaking with Violet Day."

"What am I going to say to him?"

"You'll do fine."

Emmy. Academy Award nominations.

Herb Leibowitz leaned through the door, "May I come in, Miss Day?"

"Mr. Leibowitz—no—I'm sorry. Could you come back another time? I'm expecting a long distance call."

"Won't take long, ma'am. Police business."

Lorraine waved him to a chair, trying to concentrate on the actor's history: family, career, investments—apparently he'd turned to Violet Day with every major decision.

"It's about these letters you've been receiving," Leibowitz began.

"Miss Lorraine?" Cynthia's voice on the intercom. "New York realtor on line one—about the condo sale."

"Didn't we tell him no?"

"They've raised the offer. He insists on speaking to Violet."

Lorraine lifted the receiver with an apologetic smile at the detective. He stood up, walked around the room looking at the photographs of the Violet Days with celebrities past and present.

"They've upped their bid twenty percent," the realtor said.

Cynthia delivered a cup of coffee to the detective, held a tray while he added sugar and cream.

"Miss Day?" the caller persisted. "This is as good a proposal as we can expect."

"I'll consider it."

"May I sign the sales contract?"

"No. I'll consider it."

Leibowitz was tilting his head back, trying to read an autograph.

"The offer is seven hundred dollars a square foot," the realtor pressured.

"I understand. Let me think about it."

Cynthia on the intercom again, *the client on line three.*

Lorraine punched a blinking button.

"Violet?"

"I—uh—yes."

"Violet," the actor said, mellifluously, "I have two propositions. One is for money money money. The other is zilch, but the story is compelling, the role so commanding—"

"Do you need the money?"

"I haven't reached a station where a million dollars isn't attractive."

"All right. That's a lot of money."

"But," he faltered, "this other script—a true story about a truant boy living in a migratory labor camp in the Everglades right before World War II—skipping school, the boy is drawn to another free spirit, an elderly man who gathers orchids, pine cones, and rattlesnakes, flora and fauna, which he sells to botanists, zoos and such. That's the role I'd play. Finally, the authorities drag the old man into court to have him committed for contributing to the delinquency of a minor. The boy faces reform school. I say again, the money is paltry, but the role—"

"Obviously it appeals to you."

"It does. It really does."

Leibowitz was sitting now, on the edge of another chair.

Lorraine scanned the actor's astrological chart. "You stand at the threshold of some rather significant events over the next year or two. Your signs look favorable. But your caution is a holdover from less prosperous times. You can afford to be bold. Let me ask you a question."

"Yes?"

"If you were on your deathbed, which would be more important to you: the million-dollar film offer, assuming it is a masterful film, or the role of the old man in the swamp, assuming it, too, is a masterful film?"

In the long pause following, Lorraine closed her eyes, waiting.

"You're right. You're always right," he said. "When should I sign a contract?"

She searched his graph. "In the morning hours. Tuesday would be good. But if you could wait until the first Tuesday of next month, your influence will be ascending."

"Outstanding! Thanks, Violet. You sound wonderful. Younger than ever."

"Lucky genes, Florida sunshine and vitamins," Lorraine replied.

When she hung up, Cynthia leaned across her desk in the next room, grinning. "That was perfect!"

"You were listening?"

"Why sure, Miss Lorraine. I have to tape the call so I can transcribe it for his files."

Cynthia came to retrieve the actor's records. "Now then," she said, "you must think about the columns for November."

"I thought Violet did that."

"She called this morning and said she hadn't."

"Damn her!"

"She said you'd say that. I'll get the computer print-outs for November."

At the door, the secretary turned on stocky legs and hesitated. Reading her expression, Lorraine said, "Okay. What?"

"Violet said you should begin the annual predictions, too. They must be completed by December, latest."

When Lorraine bowed her head and held it, Cynthia added, "Violet said to read the past ones, look in her office file for sources. She said you'd do fine."

"What is she trying to do?"

"Make you Violet Day," Cynthia said.

"Miss Day, may we talk?" Detective Leibowitz moved to stand before her.

"As best we can, Mr. Leibowitz."

"About these letters," Leibowitz said. "Can you be certain you've received only three?"

"I'll put you with Mrs. Wheeler. She can—"

"About future letters—" he interrupted.

"You have reason to think there'll be future letters?"

"In case there are. I want to be sure they're handled properly so as not to contaminate any fingerprints."

"Mrs. Wheeler is the person you need to see. Cynthia!"

Herb Leibowitz went to the door, closed it. When he turned, his eyes were two steady black lights of irritation. "Miss Day, you're busy. I came without appointment, I know that. But maybe you don't know what's happening here."

"Are you going to keep our names out of this, Mr. Leibowitz?"

"What's happening is," he said, "some kook is out there killing people. He's taken a fix on you for whatever reason. You're sitting up here thinking about stars while this man is thinking about you. See what I mean?"

"No."

"He sends these letters to you. He's got a sick reason for it. Doesn't that bother you?"

"Should I let it bother me?"

"It would bother me."

"You think this—maniac—is after me?"

"I wouldn't know for positive," Leibowitz said. "But the word 'maniac' is a good term. I don't see any security system here. You got security at your residence?"

"No."

"Would it be prudent to think about that?"

"Mr. Leibowitz, I'm taking over this business for my mother. When she returns, we'll discuss installing a security system."

"When might that be?"

"She'll be back for our annual Crystal Ball, which is Halloween eve and Halloween day."

"Three weeks can be a long time, Miss Day. We got ourselves a serial-type murderer. They don't do what they do for reasons most of us would understand. I'd consider some security precautions."

"I will, Mr. Leibowitz. Thank you."

After he'd departed for the mailroom, Lorraine swiveled her chair to the beautiful eastern view. Palm Beach spread away on the opposite side of Lake Worth. Yachts in the marinas formed thatched patterns on the lake. Traffic wound away south toward Miami. The Atlantic was blue-green and serene.

Behind her, Cynthia gathered the detective's coffee cup and saucer. "You can do this," she said, as if divining Lorraine's thoughts. "You'll be good at it, too. You've spent your whole life getting ready for this."

"But do I want to?"

"It's overwhelming only briefly," Cynthia soothed. "Before long you'll fall into the routine. We'll help you."

The phones were ringing.

"I'm not here," Lorraine announced.

Cynthia punched a button on Lorraine's desk. "Yes? Yes, she is." She extended the receiver. "It's your stockbroker, Mr. Mershon."

It was too much.

Lorraine fretted as the broker spoke of market vagaries.

How could she prepare horoscopes, compose annual predictions, run an office, sell a condominium—

"Nothing precipitous," the broker counselled, "but a slow shift to a more liquid position—"

"How much are we talking about, Mr. Mershon?"

"Slightly more than fifteen million."

"Million."

What would Violet say when she returned to find this business jettisoned?

"Mostly blue chips," the broker continued. "Except for the ten percent the former Miss Day allocates for high-risk ventures."

"*Former* Miss Day? Why do you call her that?"

He seemed surprised. "She assigned everything to you. You are the signatory of record. You *are* Violet Day now."

In the lapse that followed he said, "March twenty-third last. You signed the documents in my presence before a notary."

Dozens of them.

"How long have you handled this account, Mr. Mershon?"

"Forty-two years, Miss Day."

"What's your track record?"

"Our firm has tripled the assets over the past twenty years." She heard a tremor in his voice. "We have consistently produced an after-tax appreciation of twelve percent or better."

"Ever made a mistake?"

The pause was painful. "No one is infallible, Miss Day."

"The worst mistake you ever made?"

"President Eisenhower had an ileitis attack at a time when we had encouraged your mother to buy on margin. She was forced to liquidate assets under duress to cover the margin call. I urged her to stick with the market and it had barely recovered when the president suffered a heart attack. Or maybe he had the heart attack first. In any event, the market plunged again while we were dangerously overextended."

"What did your mistake cost us?"

His swallow was the croak of a toad in her ear. "One million four, Miss Day."

"Did my mother have something to say about that?"

"She said she had confidence in me nevertheless."

"Well," Lorraine said, "so do I, Mr. Mershon. Go ahead and convert to cash. Begin with that ten percent risk fund."

"Thank you, Miss Day."

No sooner had Lorraine hung up than the phone was ringing again. Detective Leibowitz passed her door, returning to the elevators.

"Mr. Leibowitz, come in a moment, please. Close the door."

He did so.

"You know Ken Blackburn," Lorraine began. "What do you think of him? Confidentially."

"In what regard?"

"A person. Policeman."

Leibowitz scratched his neck, his expression quizzical. "One thing I learned about rich people. Never lie. They got ways to get the truth. If it's important, they'll do it. You probably know Mr. Blackburn better than I do."

"I'd appreciate your opinion."

"A good man been a bad route."

"Do you think he could handle my security problems?"

The detective formed an *O* with thumb to forefinger.

"Thank you, Mr. Leibowitz."

As the detective opened the door to leave, Cynthia said, "Line two, Miss Day. It's Ken Blackburn."

Leibowitz grinned. "Mental telepathy," he said. "You believe in that—right?"

Ken's mother watched him finish dressing. He expected her to ask if he'd brushed his teeth. "Will you be back for dinner, Kenny?"

"No, Mama. I'm going out with Lori."

"Lorraine? You could bring her here. I don't mind cooking."

"Another time, maybe."

She flicked a speck from his shoulder, smoothed his shirt.

"Would you like to go with us, Mama?"

"Oh, no," she said weakly, as if bleeding. "Not if it's business."

"I didn't say it was business. Lori, her daughter and I are going to Indian Joe's."

"You'll need money," Marian said.

"I have my credit card, Mama."

"I'll pay you for the lawn work."

"I'm okay." *For about ten more days.*

She looked him over while walking him to the door. "Be careful, Kenny."

It was nearly sundown when Ken arrived. Lori was still upstairs dressing. He strolled out to the swimming pool, where Becky sat, dressed in pink with shoes to match.

"I'm Ken Blackburn, Becky. How goes it?"

She shrugged, peering into the pool. Behind her, lawn sprinklers responded to a timer and filled the air with a misty dew. Ken smelled fertilizer being dispensed with the irrigation.

"Mom says she's known you a long time."

"I lived here when I was your age."

Becky nodded. "Servant quarters."

"You favor your father," Ken noted.

"He says my mom."

"Maybe he sees what he most admires."

She studied him with luminous blue eyes, then looked away again.

"What do you think about your mother becoming Violet Day?" Ken asked.

"Hocus-pocus. Nothing to it."

"Seems that way on the outside," Ken said. "On the inside, there's plenty—columns to write, deadlines to meet. Like being in a new school, afraid you'll goof—everybody waiting to see if your mom is as good as the old Violet Day."

"I can tell you, she isn't. Mom doesn't fall for that star junk."

A breeze caught the fine mist and carried it aloft in a silvery swirl.

"She swore she'd never do this," Becky said. "She told Dad a thousand times she'd never *do* this! They always made fun of Violet. I can't believe Mom will do this."

"But if she does," Ken said, "she's going to need your help."

"I don't know anything about it and I don't want to know. I wish—I wish I could go back a year and stay there."

Ken heard Lori in the house, instructing a maid.

"Tell you what," Ken said, "tonight we'll go someplace awful. I'll take you to a juke joint owned by a Seminole Indian with no ears. He has to wear a headband to keep his hat from falling over his eyes. We'll sit in the same seat where Elvis Presley once sat."

Lori came onto the terrace, high heels clicking on slate tile. She wore gold and diamond earrings, a heavy gold necklace and a stylish lavender silk dress.

"Mom," Becky wailed, "you look like Violet! I can't go with you dressed like that."

"Well, you are going," Lori said evenly. "If I overdressed, I apologize."

They piled into the front seat of Ken's car. As they drove south Lori slipped off the jewelry, dropping it into a small purse.

"Seminole Joe," Lori mused. "I wonder if he'll remember us."

Joe remembered, because Ken had secretly telephoned to warn him. The Indian had a reputation for memory that may have had a basis in fact, but as Joe grew older the legend needed help.

"Lorraine Day," Joe intoned sonorously. "How long has it been? Let me see—twenty-two years, four months and how many days? Ah, yes— six days, five hours and twenty minutes."

"That's unbelievable!" Lorraine cried.

"And this beautiful child," Joe touched Becky's face with a nut brown hand, "I see Tommy Linden in that face."

"You know my daddy?"

"Ken Blackburn," Joe completed his act soberly, "it is good to see you. Why you gone so long?"

They were escorted to a booth beside an opened-screened window that looked down on black waters of a canal. They could hear the whirr of rubber on steel grating as cars crossed a nearby drawbridge. Passing boats sent a gentle wake against barnacle-covered pilings and their seats swayed in sympathetic response as if the entire building might go afloat at any moment.

Joe stood over them, dressed in an open-neck Seminole blouse with rings of beads for a necklace.

"We'd like boiled crab," Ken dictated without asking his companions. "Ice cold beer in frosted mugs and a black horse for my friend, Becky."

"A black horse?" Becky questioned.

"An elixir wrung from the bark of a rare tree known only to the Seminole," Joe said. "Blessed by a high priest with an incantation borrowed from our cousins the Caribs. This we top with the juice of a wild cow, chilled and stirred until it has the consistency of a heavy gel. Upon this delicious elixir we place a milky snow and a ruby-red cherry for flavor."

"Is it good?"

"If it does not please you," Joe said, "we will replace it."

"Oh, I'm sure I'll enjoy it."

When he left, Lorraine squealed like a child. "He said almost the same thing the first time we came here, remember, Ken?"

"I do remember."

"Tommy fell for it," Lorraine laughed. "He went home telling every-body he'd gotten drunk on an Indian elixir."

"Well, what is it really?" Becky asked.

"A blackberry milkshake."

"Aw, gee, Mom—I wish you hadn't told me."

The steaming crabs came in a bucket, with bibs and tongs and tiny implements to pry out the salty white meat. When one bucket was low, another arrived.

Lorraine's laughter was a sound Ken had almost forgotten. It created a nostalgic memory of a time when Tommy Linden sat where his daughter was now beside Lori.

"Remember how Tommy wanted to franchise this place?" Lori reminisced. "We were in the—what—ninth grade? He envisioned Seminole Joes from coast-to-coast. I told him he'd have trouble getting managers to lop off their ears for a job."

"How is your dad?" Ken asked Becky.

"He says fine. He's in Tucson, Arizona, opening an accounting business."

"Speaking of which," Lorraine said, "I began doing Violet's annual predictions this afternoon. She has a list of nine financial consultants she questions for advice on taxes and the market. Talk about slick! Those annual predictions are based on careful analysis of hard data. No wonder she hits so often. Trouble is, I don't know which to believe about my own taxes, much less predictions for next year."

"I should think Tommy would be your best source," Ken said.

"Tommy? He's a nickel and dime accountant. What would he know about world economy."

Ken caught a disapproving glance from Becky.

"Tommy was reading financial magazines and the *Wall Street Journal* when you and I were buying comic books, Lori. From the eighth grade, he could quote the price of commodities. He knew the conversion rate of foreign currencies. He's always been interested in the economy."

Becky listened raptly.

"Yeah," Lori admitted. "Give the little digit his due."

A moment later, "Wonder what he'd charge me?"

"He'll do it because he loves you," Ken said. "When love is the motive, money is an insult."

His eyes met Becky's and she smiled.

"Poor Tommy." Lorraine downed her beer. "There were times when my allowance was greater than his income. But you know, he never touched a dime of it. Hardheaded—"

"Proud," Ken amended.

He watched humor drain away, leaving Lori a little bleary-eyed. "Yeah," she said. "Proud."

Ken pretended not to notice Becky's reassessment as he recalled positive things about her dad.

If the way to a mother's heart is through the daughter—the way to Becky was her father.

So far, so good . . .

CHAPTER
NINE

HE NEEDED another Inez Cumbie . . .

Jaydee moved through the crowded mall unhurriedly. His shirt concealed the pistol stuck in his belt.

He had a dual purpose today. In his pocket was a diamond he'd taken from Miss Virgo in Fort Myers. Originally, a solitaire in a Tiffany setting. He'd pried loose the stone and discarded the mounting. He decided to have it appraised.

The jeweler adjusted his loupe to one eye, holding the gem to bright light.

"Blue," he said. "Good quality. About eighty points."

"How much?" Jaydee asked.

"Retail? Twenty-five hundred maybe."

Twenty-five hundred!

The loupe fell from the jeweler's eye and he met Jaydee's gaze. "Are you planning to sell it?"

"Thinking about it."

The merchant examined the stone again. "Retail is usually double wholesale," he cautioned. "You might get eight or nine hundred."

"Would you pay that?"

He looked up again. "Mind telling me where you got it?"

"My mother."

"She's the one selling it?"

"She died."

"I see."

Across the way a sign advertised the presence of an author autographing books. People stood in line near a table, waiting.

"I'll need to verify this," the jeweler said. "Would that matter to you?"

"No."

The author was gray-haired, small of stature, smiling at her fans.

"Do you have a bill of sale?" the jeweler inquired.

"No."

"I would have been suspicious if you had," he said.

The title of the author's book was printed on a sign in front of the bookstore: THE DYNAMICS OF SELF.

"I could offer six hundred cash," the jeweler stated.

"I don't know," Jaydee demurred. "I'll think about it."

"Possibly seven."

"I'll think about it."

The flash of a camera, somebody taking pictures of the celebrity.

An author should write an excellent letter . . .

"Outside figure would be seven hundred fifty," the jeweler bartered. "Beyond that, I can get it wholesale for the same price."

If he'd offered one hundred Jaydee would have sold immediately. But so much money invited investigation. "I'll think about it." He took the gem, wrapped it in a piece of tissue and returned it to his pocket.

"Why don't you shop around and come back?" the jeweler said. "If somebody offers more I might top it."

"I'll do that."

He ambled through the crowd to the bookstore.

Dr. Gayle Zuckerman . . . psychologist.

A reporter asked questions as the author signed books.

"When did you begin writing, Dr. Zuckerman?"

"After my husband died. My first book, *The Dynamics of Grief* grew out of the intense loneliness I endured. I had a terrible time coping with the loss. We'd always worked together, he and I—"

A waiting customer clucked sympathetically, related her own tale of widowhood. Jaydee picked up a book, turned pages.

The reporter persisted. "Dr. Zuckerman, in your work, you take a personal approach to a clinical subject. One reviewer said you are a classic tragedian cloaked in a psychotherapeutic wrapping."

Jaydee laughed. So did the author. She looked at him.

"What does that mean?" the writer asked the reporter.

Now the reporter laughed. "I'm not sure."

"Perhaps you should ask the reviewer."

Jaydee got into line with the ladies. *She was perfect.*

"Do you have a theory why your books sell so well, Doctor?" the reporter queried.

"We care about ourselves," she replied. "My books tell us how to manage our lives, making our tragedies constructive rather than destructive."

"Absolutely!" a buyer said. "I was going crazy until I read your first book."

More photographs. More questions. Jaydee pretended to read as others surged around the writer. He fell back several times, lingering to listen.

She lived alone. Flagler Drive, she said, a house overlooking Lake Worth. Husband had been a psychiatrist. Only daughter killed in a boating accident along with the only grandchild.

"So I do know about grief," Dr. Zucherman concluded.

The wolf . . . alert but patient. The electric certainty was not there, but this was a carefully reasoned choice. She was his, as surely as he breathed.

"Hello." Her eyes were translucent green, her smile a hint of self-consciousness.

"Would you like me to sign the book?" she asked.

Now he felt it—that rippling electric assurance.

He detected a shift of thought, first bright and gregarious, now searching his face, her smile waning.

"How would you like me to inscribe it?" she took the book from his hand.

Her pen was poised, prepared to write.

"Destiny," he said.

She looked up again, into his head she gazed and now the smile was gone.

"Women are not the only ones who suffer grief," she offered. "Would you like to tell me about it?"

Others were listening, watching. "Sign it, To Destiny," he said.

Destiny—

May you find strength in my book.
(Signed) *Gayle Zuckerman*

Jaydee paid for the book with all that was left of Inez Cumbie's money. He went to a nearby bench to smoke and read. Now and then the author glanced his way, aware of his presence. It seemed to disturb her slightly.
She was perfect.
It should be the best letter yet.

Fog rolled in with the night. Like a blanket the moisture muffled the distant bark of a dog and sounds of water lapping seawalls along Flagler Drive. The moan of foghorns came in mournful notes from afar.

"I thought I'd lost you." Jaydee bound the woman's arm to a chair with adhesive tape.

"What do you want from me?"

"We're going to write a letter." He wrapped tape around her ankle, securing it to a leg of the chair.

"I could write much better with more freedom of movement."

She spoke so matter-of-factly. Jaydee laughed.

When she'd left the bookstore, a manager had escorted the author to her car, which was parked on the distant side of the mall from Jaydee's station wagon. There was no chance to commandeer the Buick she drove; the bookstore man stayed until she'd departed safely.

So he'd lost her. Any other time that would be that. He'd lost others before. But this one—a published writer, perfect for his needs—he refused to let her go.

He remembered snatches of conversation, *Flagler Drive.* He'd searched a telephone book until he found her listing.

"You tied the wrong hand," she advised. "I write with my left."

"No, you don't. I watched you autograph books."

"I presume you didn't like my book," she said.

He stood back, examined his work. Both legs and one arm immobile. "Do you have writing paper?"

"I doubt it."

"A writer without paper," he mused. He wandered into a hallway, then to the den. Beside an electric typewriter, two fresh reams of white paper. He tested several pens, selected two and returned.

"You should write a book about lying," he said.

She followed his movements, her expression more that of curiosity than resentment. "What's your name?" she asked.

"Destiny."

"That isn't your name."

He placed a few papers before her, laying two ball-point pens beside her hand. "Do you know Violet Day?"

"I know the name."

"We're going to write Violet a nice long letter."

"Can't you write?"

"This is *your* letter." He pulled a chair to one corner of the table and sat down. "When were you born?"

"I consider that a personal question."

"It's going to be a personal letter. What month and day?"

"Why do you want to know?"

"It is imperative to the project at hand."

"Imperative," she said. "You seem educated. That's good. It makes it easier to communicate. Tell me, Destiny, are you married?"

"Doctor, let's be about this. I'll dictate the first sentence and the last. The rest of the letter will be yours. Now, write what I tell you."

She looked him squarely in the eye but didn't take the pen. He placed it in her hand.

"Dear Violet Day," he dictated. "Write that."

She took a long breath, exhaled.

"Do as I tell you, Doctor."

"Do *you* know Violet Day, Destiny?"

"Write what I tell you."

"What is the purpose of this letter?"

"We'll get to that."

"What do you hope to accomplish with it?"

Jaydee subdued irritation.

"What does it mean to you?" she questioned.

"Let me tell you what it means to you," he warned. "As long as you keep writing, you will live. When you stop, you die. Understand?"

"No, I can't say that I do. Is Violet Day related to you in some way?"

"Dear Violet Day," he enunciated, ominously.

"You poor boy," she said. "What terrible thing has your mother done to you?"

He sat back.

"Are your parents living, Destiny?"

"Just write the goddamned letter. Stop playing psychologist. You aren't very good at it."

"Then you *didn't* like my book. I feared as much." She dropped the pen and it rolled away. "Let me see if I can guess—your mother is dead, your father absent much of your life—"

She studied his face a moment. "Mother alive. Father absent."

"Dear Violet Day—I am about to die. Write that."

"What difference will this make to Violet Day? She doesn't know me."

He dumped the contents of her purse on a kitchen counter. Driver's license: born April 30, 1920. *Taurus.*

"You seem reasonable enough," Gayle Zuckerman said, calmly. "You have intelligence, education. You comport yourself well. Tell me about your mother, Destiny."

"You may keep this up as long as you wish," he matched her tone. "We'll sit here for hours. Days, if necessary."

"I certainly hope not. I'll have to go to the toilet now and then."

She had more than a hundred dollars in her pocketbook. Jaydee took it.

"Do you need money?" she queried.

"You don't."

"Destiny, I want to help you. But to help, I must understand what's happening here."

Her attempts to outwit him were initially disturbing. But he'd been trained by a pro—Mother could drive a man insane. "Write what I told you," he said.

"I'm sorry. I've forgotten. What was it?"

He sat at the table again, arms extended, hands clasped.

"Oh, yes," she said. "I am about to die, wasn't it? How do you feel about death, Destiny? Do you think it is the end of everything? Do you believe in an afterlife?"

"I see what you're doing. I'm not dumb."

"No, I don't think you are. But I have a right to consider where I'll be after death. Am I going to be plunged into a void, or elevated to a new and better existence? What do you think?"

The low groan of foghorns droned in the night.

"If you believe in life after death," the psychologist continued, "then you must believe your victim would be here, watching you. That seems upsetting to me."

He saw his face reflected in her eyes. Tiny parabolic mirrors returned his scrutiny.

"Do you subscribe to the theories of astrology? I'd like to debate that, if you do."

Jaydee removed today's horoscope from his shirt pocket and spread it on the table.

"Taurus," he said. "Home influences dominate. A child needs extra attention. Expect an answer to an important question."

"I'm home and I'm influenced," she conceded. "Are you the child who needs attention? Maybe you have an answer to my important question—I'd like to hear it."

Trying to confuse him. "Your question, Doctor?"

"What is this going to accomplish?"

He seized her free arm and jerked it down to the chair where he tied it.

"You want to suffer, Doctor?"

"Not really."

"You're going to unless you write that letter!"

"I might agree, if I knew why."

"You *will*," Jaydee seethed.

"I didn't mean to upset you, Destiny. Please sit down."

He put his face close to hers. "I don't want to cause you more pain than necessary, but you will do as I tell you."

"Does the letter relate to you? Your mother?"

He stood up, glaring down at the diminutive figure. *Like Mother.* No changing her thoughts once she set her mind.

He rummaged through cabinets, looked in the refrigerator.

"Where's the bread, Dr. Zuckerman?"

"Would you like me to cook something?"

He found loaves in a bread box on top of the refrigerator.

The telephone rang as he spread butter on a bread slice. It rang again.

"I should answer that," she said.

He smeared mayonnaise on another slice.

"Probably the bookstore calling to be sure I'm home and all right. If I don't answer they'll send someone to look for me.

He constructed his sandwich with slices of avocado, a bed of lettuce, onion and tomato.

The phone quit.

"Do you mind if I have something to eat, also?"

He took a bite.

"There's milk in the cooler, if you want it," she offered.

Jaydee chewed methodically, eyes focused on a point beyond the woman.

He knew how to handle obstinacy. *Ignore her.* It always worked with Mother. Tune her out and go about his business. It worked with anyone. Belligerence melted, animosity evaporated, and soon enough they were struggling to find a way to please him.

Silence. It worked with deceptive students, cruelly contemptuous teachers, conspiring neighbors—and it would work with this psychologist.

She squirmed slightly, trying to hide the movement. "I'll be glad to help you," she said softly. "If I only knew why you want this. Tell me how you feel about the letter. Does Violet Day remind you of someone? Has she harmed you, or someone you know?"

He plucked a crumb of bread from a corner of his mouth, licked it off his finger.

Silence . . .

His weapon against the world.

From a bay window Jaydee looked out at a gray wall of moisture, listened to the doleful lowing of foghorns which came like nautical cows lost at sea.

Almost daylight. His station wagon was parked a quarter of a mile away on a side street. Come dawn, a passing patrol car might take notice.

Gayle Zuckerman dozed, head lolling, only to awaken with a short involuntary cry. She'd drooled on herself. He wiped her mouth and chin with a paper towel.

"May I go to the toilet, Destiny?"

She hunched her shoulders, flexed the fingers of bound hands.

"Are you ready to write?"

"I said I would, and I will," she replied. "As soon as you tell me why. I think Violet Day would want to know why."

"She'll know."

"Then tell me."

He returned to the bay window, let morning air cool his face.

"I must go to the bathroom, Destiny."

The fog was lifting. He could smell the sea.

"How can I write with both hands tied?"

He kept his back to her.

"I don't understand your reticence," she said. "You have only to talk to me about this and I'll help you. I've offered to do so. But it begins with talk."

Voices—Jaydee heard the soft pat of feet on pavement. Joggers on the street talking as they ran.

"I'd like to make a trade, Destiny."

He lit a cigarette, blew smoke through the screened window.

"Let me go to the bathroom. I'll walk around for a few minutes and regain my circulation. Tell me why you want this letter written—and I'll help you."

A moment later, she spoke again. "I don't think you want to hurt me. I see this is important to you. I want to do it properly, but you must cooperate."

He flicked ashes on the windowsill.

"You're a nice young man. I'm surprised you never married. That is what you said, isn't it? You never married? Such a loss for some woman. You're strong, handsome—"

It had been like this all night. She asked a hundred questions, concocted answers to suit herself—and not one word had she transcribed on paper.

Jaydee cooked eggs and pan-fried toast. He sat across from her, eating from the skillet. Her discomfort was acute. She twisted painfully, but when their eyes met she spoke calmly.

"What kind of work do you do, Destiny?"

He swabbed yolk with a wedge of bread. *No coffee.* She didn't drink coffee, she'd said.

"You seem self-sufficient," she noted. "You prepare your food with an experienced hand. Do you live alone?"

By nine o'clock the fog had dissipated. A mailman delivered to a box at the end of the long driveway. From the bay window, Jaydee noticed for the first time a small sign naming the homestead. *Id and Ego.* More joggers trotted past, their feet pattering on damp pavement.

"Destiny, I must warn you," she said. "Let me go to the rest room or I won't be able to control myself."

A few minutes later he heard the trickle of urine. He lit another cigarette. Sea birds skimmed the still waters of Lake Worth. No ships. He wondered where the foghorns had come from.

"See what you've caused?" she accused. For the first time, her voice trembled. "I make no apology for that. I asked repeatedly for a chance to go—"

He spoke with his back to her. "Are you ready to write?"

"Goodness, no! I'll sit here until Hades is an aquatic garden, if necessary. However, if you'd like to talk to me—"

He stubbed out his cigarette, untied her right arm. She stretched it, working the fingers, rotating her shoulder.

Jaydee grabbed her hand, put the pen in it and clamped her fingers. He forced the unresisting hand to write, in block letters: D-E-A-R V-I-O-L-E-T D-A-Y I A-M A-B-O-U-T T-O D-I-E.

When he released her hand, the pen dropped.

"I didn't write that," she said. "You did. Anyone will know I didn't write it."

He towered above her, quivering. He should be at work in less than an hour.

"Very well," she said. "Since you are willing to write it, I'll speak the words and you put them on paper."

The morning passed, the kitchen smelly. Jaydee smoked his last cigarette. *Stubborn. Stupid!*

A woman runner halted forward motion at the foot of the driveway, legs still pumping as she looked this way. Then she resumed jogging.

"I'm out of cigarettes."

"They're bad for your health, Destiny. You should give them up."

Jaydee sat at the corner of the table again very close to her. "You don't know what you're dealing with." He opened his palm, showed her the lines.

"That's the mark of Cain, Dr. Zuckerman. God's curse on Cain handed down to his descendants forevermore."

She examined her own palm. "Mine looks the same."

He took her free hand, turning it. "No, it isn't. Do you lie about everything?"

"Actually, I'm trying to provoke you."

"You're succeeding. My patience is gone, Doctor. I am an evil man and you have vexed me." He crumpled the first sheet and put fresh paper before her. "You will write the letter or suffer. Your choice. Which will it be?"

"As I've said again and again—"

He snatched a dishtowel from a hook, ripped it in halves. He jammed a piece in her mouth, fought away her free hand, tying the gag.

She tried to cough, eyes bulging.

"I prefer not to hurt you," he spoke in her ear. "But I will. No more talk."

She yanked her hand from his grasp, clawing at the gag. Jaydee jerked her arm down, taped it to the chair. She bucked against the restraints, her complexion an ugly blue.

"Yoo-hoo!"

Jaydee froze.

"Yoo-hoo, Gayle? Hello in there."

If he didn't answer—what? Would she go away? Come back with somebody to investigate?

He walked to the front door, the calls more insistent. It was the woman jogger—young, lithe—he knew the strength of fear, debated what to do.

"Gayle? Hello, it's Arlene!"

He unlocked the door, opened it. "Good morning."

She stepped away. "I didn't realize Gayle had company. I'll come back."

"No, it's all right," Jaydee smiled. "We've been discussing her latest book. Have you read it? Hey. Look. Come in. She's in the bathroom."

She looked past him, down the hall.

"You're Arlene, right?"

"Yes."

"She spoke of you. Come in."

She eased past him, still uncertain, then walked quickly toward the kitchen. She saw Gayle Zuckerman and wheeled—Jaydee pointed the gun, malevolently.

"I'm glad you're here, Arlene. We want you to write a letter."

She stepped back, the muzzle of the gun in her face.

"Sit down," Jaydee ordered.

She yanked the gag from Dr. Zucherman's mouth and the psychologist wailed, sucked air, wailed again.

"Sit down, Arlene."

"I won't let you tie me."

"Sit down."

"Are you all right, Gayle?"

The doctor choked, coughing. Arlene reached for the tape that bound her hand and Jaydee shoved her away.

"You sonofabitch," Arlene said evenly.

"Sit down, Arlene."

"Like hell."

Her posture flowed to a stance of defense, fists clenched, feet apart. She was tall, muscled. It was as if she didn't see the gun at all.

"My advice to you," she said, "is run like hell."

He cocked the hammer but she didn't flinch.

"Go and go now," she commanded.

"Arlene—don't fight him—"

"Go, you miserable freak."

He advanced, the gun aimed at her nose, but she didn't yield.

"Arlene—nothing physical—Arlene!"

But she grabbed for the pistol.

Jaydee twisted her arm and threw her face down over the kitchen counter. He pushed the barrel into the base of her skull. She kicked at his shin, jabbed with her elbow.

He pulled the trigger.

The young woman slid off the counter onto the floor.

Jaydee reached Gayle Zucherman with two long steps. "Is that your friend?" he demanded. "Is she your friend?"

Her eyes were glazed.

"Is she your friend? See what you caused? Your friend is dead because of you. You did that."

"Please—"

"Now then, Doctor. One last chance and this is it. Understand me? Write the letter or I'll kill you this minute."

"Destiny—talk to me—"

He cursed, cocked the hammer, put the muzzle to her head. "Write the letter!"

"Let's talk," she pleaded. "Tell me—"

He fired.

CHAPTER
TEN

AFTER KEN took Lori and Becky home, he drove to a public parking sector near The Breakers hotel. There, lulled by the rote of waves, he contemplated the declining hours of his good credit. Dinner and drinks had cost seventy dollars plus pennies, including a tip to Indian Joe. One more debt he couldn't pay—he'd charged it to his credit card. He'd decided he had to do something, to continue this way was irresponsible.

The next morning, dressed in a suit and tie as if for work, he went to the police station on Clematis Street, east of Tamarind Avenue. Herb Leibowitz greeted him with strong Cuban coffee, a fresh cinnamon roll and evidence from the three murders.

Left alone for most of the day, Ken sat in Herb's office and studied grisly photos. The modus operandi was so unique there was virtually no doubt it was the same felon.

Like Inez Cumbie, each victim had been found in her residence bound to a chair, one arm free. The intruder had ransacked the scene where the murders occurred. It was reasonable to assume he'd stolen money. Having complied with his demands, each woman was executed.

The tragedy was sanitized by forensic parlance:
. . . *occipital and parietal trauma* . . .
. . . *powder burns, scorched hair* . . .

The greatest possible damage had been inflicted with a single shot. Shards of skull and pieces of the bullet tore through the pons Varilii, a critical knot of nerve fibers which connected lobes of the midbrain, medulla and cerebellum. The soft metal of the hollow-point bullet flattened and splintered, emerging "anteriorily," taking away most of the face. The enormity of the wound suggested .357 caliber or larger, but ballistics and metallurgical reports failed to confirm it.

Ken swallowed soured saliva, nausea threatening.

He calculated the "angle of entry," taking the height of each victim and the chair to which she was bound. He decided the gunman was about six feet tall, holding the weapon low, but aiming it slightly upward at the base of the skull to create greatest damage.

His hands were cold, muscle fibrillation making him quiver as he sat at Herb's desk undisturbed. *He knew this feeling.*

But there was no way to remain dispassionate. He had to put himself in the place of the killer. Mentally he mimed the attacker's actions, reconstructing the crime in agonizing detail—for it was that way only that he could develop a profile.

A thief. He stole money, articles of underwear and God knew what else. But the theft was an opportunistic act, not a primary one. He'd returned to the scene—to reposition Inez Cumbie's cats, to continue his plunder. Unstained clothing had been found lying over dried blood.

Stealing personal items. *To use in fantasies.*

Ken had discovered Inez Cumbie's body on Monday. This was Thursday. The serological tests were not back from the lab. But the results wouldn't change his opinion—semen or not—these were sexually impelled crimes.

That night, mentally exhausted, he fell into bed by nine and slept. Horrible dreams plagued him. Images from the photographs, data from reports. But this was a part of it, too. The subconscious mind assimilated and collated, producing conclusions in his slumber. So he didn't fight the ghastly visions, but rather, let them flow. Wailing specters screamed his name, the victims pleading as if he might stay their attacker.

"*Kenny!*"

Distantly, vaguely . . .

"Kenny? Telephone!"

He bolted upright, gasping. His mother knocked on his bedroom door, harder. "Kenny—it's Detective Herbowitz."

Leibowitz.

"He says it's urgent, Kenny. Are you awake?"

"Right, Mama." Ken groped for the receiver. "Blackburn," he said.

"You awake?"

"Am now."

"We've got another one," Herb said. "Flagler Drive, south of Thirty-sixth Street."

Few blocks away. Ken rubbed his eyes.

"I'm holding everybody out until you see it," Herb said. "Can you come?"

"Ten minutes as is."

The detective disconnected and Ken sat there, drugged by sleep, phone to his shoulder. *Click.*

Mama, listening on the extension.

Flagler Drive ran north and south along Lake Worth, an old street, one of the first paved in West Palm Beach. Some of the homes dated to the twenties and now stood side by side with more modern dwellings.

Ken had no trouble finding the address. Patrol cars blocked the way, ambulances waited, neighbors gathered. Two vans were set up to record the news.

The house was one of the older ones, built far up a paved drive on a knoll overlooking Lake Worth. The yellow plastic tape of a crime line marked perimeters of the yard.

Herb Leibowitz waited near the house, hands jammed in his pants pockets, chewing a cigar. He started talking without amenity.

"Husband lives four doors down," Herb explained. "Executive type. Comes home about five-thirty last night. Wife, Arlene, works at home. She's a 'potter' he says. Makes bowls out of clay. She goes out to jog every morning, usually stops here to visit Dr. Gayle Zuckerman who is a widowed psychologist and writer. Ever read her books?"

"No," Ken said.

"Mostly woman stuff, I think. How to make cramps work for you, character building—anyway—"

Herb spoke with a low voice, his coal-black eyes traversing the terrain of banyan trees and native growth.

"Anyway," Herb repeated softly, "the wife isn't home. He figures first, no sweat, she left a note. No note. He figures second she told him she'd be out and he's forgot; you know—I do that—the missus tells me she's going to the podiatrist and my mind ain't on carbuncles and corns so I forget."

He squinted toward the waterfront. "I can hear them whisper," he said. "Why do you suppose nobody heard a gunshot up here?"

He yelled at an officer on the street. "Lou! Hey, Lou!"

The man didn't respond. "Acoustics," Herb concluded. "We hear them, they don't hear us."

"Want me to get Lou, Sergeant?"

"Nah. Forget it." Herb munched his cigar. "Anyway, eight or nine o'clock last night the husband begins to fret. He knows his wife comes to see Dr. Zuckerman so he walks up here and knocks—no lights, no answer. He goes home, watches a little TV, about eleven he's gone from fret to pissed. Calls their friends. Calls Dr. Zuckerman. No answer. He comes back, knocks some more. His thinking is now, maybe something happened to Dr. Zuckerman. Maybe Arlene took the old girl to the hospital—but why hasn't Arlene called?"

Herb was moving slowly toward the rear.

"This morning the husband is upset for positive. He comes back and finds Zuckerman's car."

Buick. Locked.

"Husband gets a ladder, goes to peeking in windows. Gets to the kitchen and sees Zuckerman tied to a chair. Breaks in and discovers his wife."

"Who all has been inside, Herb?"

"Husband. Patrolman. Me. When I saw the chair, I called you."

Over the years of Ken's career the smell of blood had become an olfactory anesthesia. One whiff and he numbed, moving through horror as if detached.

"You said sex," Herb stated. "Until now I didn't believe it."

The young woman was on her back, arms flung wide, naked. She'd been eviscerated. A blood-soaked paper towel covered her face.

"Sick-o," Herb wheezed.

"The towel is an attempt to dehumanize the victim," Ken said, as if tutoring. "It's true to type. You see the level of violence has escalated. It confirms what I've been thinking. You'll need a detailed diagram, Herb. Photos—"

"Yeah, yeah."

Ken walked around the room. "Ashes on the windowsill," he droned. "Find out if the women smoked."

"Right."

Ken moved around the carnage into a hallway. The house was a shambles—drawers emptied, books hurled to the floor, pictures ripped off the walls—and in the bedroom amid the vandalism, panties spread on a bed.

When they returned to the kitchen Ken examined a blood-spattered paper on the table.

"Latent impressions—shoot it in oblique light."

"Yeah, Ken," Herb said, irritably.

On the floor, crumpled, another piece of paper. Ken held down one corner with the eraser of a pencil and carefully straightened the note enough to read it.

D-E-A-R V-I-O-L-E-T D-A-Y.

"Herb, have the lab look at this for prints. Use ninhydrin reagent without an acetone base so the ink won't smear."

"Okay."

Ken stood up again, turned full circle. "He made sandwiches. Cooked—egg shells on the counter. He was here a long time. That's true to type, too."

Herb swore gutterally, his face a platinum gray. He gagged, and Ken said, "You can go on out, if you wish. I won't be long."

"I'll wait."

But he gagged again and left.

Ken lifted Dr. Zuckerman's skirt. He looked down her blouse. *Underwear intact.*

He knelt beside the younger woman and examined her hands—he hoped for hair, flesh scratched from her assailant. If it was there, he couldn't see it.

Methodically, he reconstructed the assault: By the blood and bone fragments on the kitchen counter, he deduced her position when shot from behind. The dead do not bleed, they seep. She was dead when he mutilated the body. The woman had intruded; his plans foiled, he'd vented frustration on her.

And for the first time—looking down at the obscenely postured young woman—the sexual aspects were obvious.

Captain Wayne Dilling rocked his desk chair gently. With one arm hung on a file cabinet, Herb mouthed an unlighted cigar.

The captain put on a mystified smile.

"I'm told you're good at this, Blackburn."

"I am," Ken said.

"Maybe you are," Dilling frowned doubtfully. "Me, I'm an anachronism and I know it. I was a rookie about the time you were born. Pounded streets ten years before I sat in a police car, much less an air-conditioned one. In those days every drugstore had a soda fountain. You could smoke in movie theaters. You could buy a newspaper, a Coca-Cola, or make a phone call for a nickel. Hell, I went through a hundred pairs of shoes before I ever saw a marijuana leaf."

Herb chuckled.

"Crime was simple," Dilling said. "A yankee con man or two, a few armed robberies. Mostly burglaries by some migrant worker who'd lost his wad in a crap shoot. Understand what I'm saying?"

"Yes, Captain. I do."

"A cop with a college degree—nobody ever heard of such! Hell, it was twenty years before I saw a homicide I had to solve. Even that was simple. Jealous wife, drunken husband—basic stuff. You remember, Herb?"

"Yep."

"Then the world went Chiquita," Dilling said. "Along came the Cubans, some bad but most good. When a recruit applied to the force he found a new square on the form: language skills. Crime didn't change much, but nomenclature did. *Boleto* instead of numbers, *rameras* instead of prostitutes. You speak Spanish, Blackburn?"

"A little."

"*Un poco,*" Dilling said. "I didn't speak *poquisimo,* but I learned. I had to. *Homicidas nuevos.* New conditions required new knowledge. But I was willing to learn. I still am."

He patted the typewritten profile Ken had prepared. "I don't kick a sack before I know it's empty," Dilling said. "Maybe all I need is some more education here. This profile thing is another innovative technology—is that it?"

"Technology helped."

"I read this so-called profile and parts of it I catch right quick," Dilling said. " 'Smokes Marlboros.' Okay. Ashes on the windowsill, filter butts in the disposal, crumpled pack in a trash can—neither of the women smoked, right, Herb?"

"That's right."

"So, I can buy that," Dilling stated. "The killer smokes Marlboros. Not *positively,* but probably."

The captain turned a page. " 'Revisits the scene.' Dead cats turned over and so forth—I'll accept that. You got good eyes, Blackburn. Detail. You got an eye for that."

"Captain, it's more than deductive reasoning."

"Sure hell must be," Dilling said. " 'Six feet tall.' Not five-eleven, or six-one—six feet tall!"

Ken explained about the height of the chairs, victims, the angle of entry.

"There you go, Herb," Dilling threw up thick hands. "You and me, we're playing Watson to Sherlock Holmes. We can accept that, too, can't we? The killer is six feet tall. At least we can see how Blackburn reached such a farfetched conclusion, right?"

Herb chewed his stub of a stogie, eyes narrowed.

"Let's see," Dilling traced the lines of a page. " 'Above average intelligence—blue collar worker—lives in West Palm Beach but travels infrequently on some assigned route. Lives with his mother.' I admit, I'm stumped, Blackburn. What were your clues?"

"Those assumptions are based on the FBI profile for this kind of criminal, Captain. It is lust murder."

"The FBI knows this—how?"

"They studied thirty-six sexual killers," Ken explained. "Data was collected in various U.S. prisons between 1979 and 1983 by special agents of the FBI. They interviewed the offenders extensively. They consulted the records of prisons, psychiatrists and court transcripts. They also studied the 118 victims of these men—evidence at the scene tells a lot about the lust murderer."

"You believe thirty-six men make a universal?"

"In this case, they do. There were striking similarities in their backgrounds—their childhood experiences, homelife and upbringing. For example, eighty percent of them described their family socio-economic levels as average or better. The mother was at home with the children, the fathers earned stable incomes. Poverty was not a factor."

"That's refreshing."

"But on close investigation," Ken persisted, "there were hidden family problems. Criminal, psychiatric, alcohol, drug and sexual abuse. The parents were so absorbed with their own problems they didn't have time to worry about a troubled boy. Quite often, the parents themselves were involved in some illegal activity. Avoiding the authorities was acceptable family practice. Before the boys reached adolescence, in most cases, the father had abandoned the family."

"Bad environment," Dilling nodded. "We can accept that, too, can't we Herb?"

"This bad environment produced some chilling results," Ken insisted. "The offenders reported childhood and adolescent daydreaming, masturbation sometimes to a compulsive degree, isolation, chronic lying, bed-wetting, rebelliousness, nightmares, destruction of property, fire-setting, cruelty to their playmates and to animals and a poor body image. Poor body image includes self-mutilation."

"Twisted," Dilling relented. "We'll buy that, too."

Skepticism. Damn him.

"The FBI prepared an analysis of twenty-four checklist items on three levels: childhood, adolescence and adulthood. When similarities were statistically significant, the computers made note of it. As a result, if we have certain information about a criminal, we know he is one of two types: nonsocial/organized or asocial/disorganized. And when we know that, we know a great deal about the offender, because he comes from the same mold as other killers like him."

"My curiosity," Dilling mused. "The difference between these two types?"

"The difference is the way each type commits his crime. Ted Bundy was a nonsocial/organized lust murderer. He planned his crime, used restraints, committed sexual acts with live victims, displayed control of the victim by threat and manipulation—he enjoyed their fear. And he used a vehicle in the commission of the crime, luring girls into his automobile."

Dilling listened with practiced stoicism.

"The asocial/disorganized offender," Ken said, "leaves a weapon at the scene, repositions the dead body, performs sexual acts on the dead person, keeps the body and may even move it from one scene to another. He tries to depersonalize the victim. He tends to strike in territory that is familiar."

"Which is our man?" Herb questioned.

"I'm not absolutely sure," Ken confessed. "But it isn't unusual for a lust murderer to be a blend of the two types."

"Therefore it's worth nothing," Dilling concluded.

"No, that's wrong. It takes a year at the FBI school to learn the profiling process, so don't expect me to explain it in an hour. But the value of the profile is obvious. When we know certain things about the murder, we know about the killer. Because of other criminals like him, we now know a great deal about the man we're hunting. In this case, he comes from a low birth order, raised in a home where he was treated with hostility as a child. He is sexually inhibited, sexually ignorant, has sexual aversions. His parents had a history of sexual problems. Don't you see, we know where he's coming from—we know what makes him tick!"

"How does this help us, Blackburn?"

"The profile tells you. He lives in West Palm. He travels infrequently to some specific areas—to Fort Myers and Orlando. We know that by the two women he killed in those places. As he continues, more evidence will help adapt the profile."

"That's interesting as hell, isn't it, Herb?" Dilling pushed the profile to the center of his desk and stood up. "I'd like to hear more about it sometime, Blackburn."

Ken stood, too. He accepted the captain's handshake.

"We appreciate your help, Blackburn. Herb said he called at daybreak and you came right over. We appreciate that."

Being dismissed.

"Captain, each crime will add detail to the profile. A profile can be invaluable to an investigator."

"I know that must be so." Dilling led Ken to the office door. "We'll turn this stuff over to the FBI for analysis. No doubt about it being a serial killer. It'll be interesting to see how close you came with your guesses. Again, thanks."

As he passed, Herb cuffed Ken's shoulder gently.

At the far end of the room, bright lights came on and television cameras focused on Captain Dilling as he issued a formal press release. Concise and understated—by the book.

"Any suspects, Captain?"

"Nothing we can talk about."

"What about a motive?"

"Robbery hasn't been ruled out."

A female voice caught Ken's attention and he paused at the exit. "Captain, is there any connection between the death of Inez Cumbie and these latest homicides?"

"We are waiting for laboratory results and—"

The familiar voice lifted, "Captain, is Ken Blackburn working with you on these cases?"

Now Ken saw her. *Sarah Greenhaw.* She spoke to Dilling but she was looking at Ken.

"He is not working with us," Dilling said.

"Mr. Blackburn is known for his expertise in a particular type of crime." The blonde reporter winked at Ken as she spoke. "I would assume the WPB police would avail themselves of his talents."

"We asked Mr. Blackburn to give us an opinion," Dilling said. "But that's the extent of our association."

"What was his opinion?" Sarah persisted.

"It was inconclusive."

The captain turned away. Cameramen gathered their equipment. Sarah Greenhaw crossed the room with a toothy smile.

"I didn't recognize you," Ken said.

"Nose job. I decided I wanted to do TV news, not print—made the operation a professional expense. Did it before the tax-reform act so it was deductible."

She swept her short hair with a hand up the back of her neck. She had the long lean look of some anorectic models, but Sarah was anything but skinny in just the right places.

"Saw you at the scene this morning." She took his arm, walking along beside him.

"I didn't see you."

"Figured you didn't want to. Maybe don't want to now. Say! What're you doing this evening?"

"I'm broke, Sarah."

"I'll treat. Dinner. You're at your mother's, aren't you? Thirty-seventh Street?"

"Been checking on me, woman?"

"My job. Like a cop. Seven o'clock suit you?" But she pulled away before he answered, running after her camera crew. Halfway there, she turned—chin tucked, pixyish green eyes—and gave a little wave.

It was Ken's first healthy thought about sex since before his trial . . .

CHAPTER ELEVEN

FRIDAY HAD always been Lorraine's favorite day. In high school there were football games, dances and overnight parties. It was football that lured Becky out tonight.

When Lorraine and Tommy lived in Virginia, Friday was anticipated—they went out or invited others in. October was especially beautiful in Virginia, the woodlands painted as if by Andrew Wyeth, the mountains vibrant with autumnal hues.

Alone and lonely . . .

She wondered if Friday would ever have significance again.

Annie and her husband had gone to Pompano Beach to visit relatives. The kitchen was closed, the house empty, the hallways hollow.

Nothing to do and nobody to do it with. Lorraine mixed a pitcher of martinis; at least, that's what it would've been if she'd added vermouth. Now in her bedroom suite she kicked off her shoes and collapsed in an easy chair. She was worn out from working on annual predictions all day. *Never mind.* The gin poured over a handful of Haddon House midget dill tomatoes would help her through the night.

The TV news . . .

"The Palm Beaches were shocked today by the brutal double murder of Dr. Gayle Zuckerman, a nationally known author, and her neighbor—"

Lorraine fished out one of the garlic-laden tiny tomatoes and savored it with a sip of gin.

"Here now, our reporter, Sarah Greenhaw—"

Lorraine had had enough tragedy this week. She reached for the remote control, but the reporter's words stayed the move.

"Five days after the execution-style slaying of retired school teacher, Inez Cumbie . . ."

Gin seared Lorraine's throat as she swallowed awkwardly.

There were pictures of a home on Flagler Drive, of shrouded bodies on ambulance gurneys.

Lorraine saw Herb Leibowitz—and Ken!

"Sarah?" the anchorman questioned, "What do the police have to say about this? Do they have suspects?"

"They say not," the pretty blonde reporter replied. "However, they admit they asked Ken Blackburn for his opinion. Mr. Blackburn, a native of West Palm, was most recently employed by the Dallas, Texas, police department. He is known as a specialist with a particular kind of crime."

"What kind of crime is that, Sarah?"

"Mr. Blackburn says it is 'lust murder.' "

The anchorman swung to face his audience again. "According to sources at the WPB police department there have been at least two other similar murders—one in Orlando, the other in Fort Myers. For that story—"

Lorraine spilled her drink putting it aside. She dialed Ken's home number.

"Marian, this is Lorraine Day. May I speak with Ken?"

"He's about to go out, Lorraine. How are you?"

"I'm fine. It won't take but a minute."

"How is your mother?"

"Violet is all right, Marian."

"She's in Europe I read in the newspapers."

"Yes. She is. Marian, ask Ken if he can spare a minute."

Marian Blackburn made no attempt to muffle her voice. "Kenny? What time are you going out with Sarah Greenhaw? Do you have a moment? Lorraine is on the phone."

A second later, Ken's voice, "Hi, Lori."

"Ken, I saw the news. You were there. Is this the same man?"

"I'm afraid so."

"God," she whispered. "Dear God. Then you think there's a connection with Inez Cumbie?"

"There was a note, Lori, addressed to Violet."

"What did it say?"

"One sentence, block letters. Same message—I am about to die."

The room seemed too large around her. A breeze through opened French doors swirled a curtain.

"Are you all right, Lori?"

"Yes. Yes, of course. Ken, is there any chance you could stop by here?"

He hesitated.

"Anytime will be okay," she said. "As late as you wish."

"I'm seeing someone about seven," he said. "I should be home by ten-thirty or eleven. Would that be too late?"

One of the balcony doors moved in the wind and Lori jerked to stare at it.

"Lori, the bastard is sending notes because he wants to worry Violet Day. He's accomplishing his aim with the letters."

"This is terrible, Ken."

"Yes."

"Ten-thirty, you say?"

"Or eleven."

"I'll see you then."

Lorraine let him hang up first. She went downstairs, moving from room to room, locking doors, securing windows. But getting into the house would be no problem for a determined intruder. She herself had once slipped the latch on the patio doors with nothing more than a nail file. As a youth she'd scaled the trellis to reach the upstairs balconies.

She turned on outside lights along the walkway between the main house and the servants' quarters. Palm fronds swayed, casting shadows that seemed to creep from here to there.

There was no way to keep somebody out if he truly meant to trespass.

Standing in the huge kitchen, the stainless-steel ice maker burped its cargo; the refrigerator hummed.

Not quite seven o'clock. Four hours to wait. *And worry.*

She returned to the upstairs, shutting the balcony doors in every suite, checking windows. Then in her own bedroom again, she fortified herself with gin and finished the jar of midget dill tomatoes. The heavy garlic garnish of the tomatoes created tiny barnacles on her teeth and left her tongue clad in felt.

Suddenly, she wanted to call Tommy. But what could she say—what could *he* do in Tucson?

He would ask about Becky. Is she safe? With whom?

Angrily, as if accused, Lorraine admitted she didn't really know with whom—a football game, at the high school—but she couldn't be more specific than that.

The TV remained on, sound mute, images flashing.

Sarah Greenhaw . . .

It couldn't be the same family Lorraine knew as a child. All those children were endowed with noses that would gratify a Grecian god. Yet, the woman was tall, as all the Greenhaws were, her voice that Lauren Bacall throaty growl that made men want to curl like kittens and purr along.

The telephone rang and Lorraine yelped—she grabbed the receiver.

"Lori, Ken again. I'll break my date and come now."

"No, no!" She heard herself laugh. *Idiot!* "You said eleven and eleven is soon enough."

"You're sure?"

Another carefree chuckle—she did *that?* "I thought we could chat about a possible security system after all. I'll pay a consulting fee with martinis so dry you'll cough cotton."

"If you're sure it's all right to wait—"

"Sure I'm sure. No big deal."

When she hung up, Lorraine slapped herself in the face. "Fool!"

There it was—the sum and summation of her entire life. The essence of her trouble with men! All she'd had to do was quiver a little and he would've come running. Dumb. *Dumb!* She'd never had a good quiver, wouldn't be caught dead with one. So. Now Sarah Greenhaw would get what the distressed damsel didn't while she sat here afraid and alone.

She clapped her hands over her eyes. There was no other word for her, but *stupid!* Ken was out with that fugitive from an aerobics class. Lorraine was sure now it was the same Greenhaw family—some surgeon had possession of her nose.

She detested this feeling. Alone and lonely.

She was frightened.

But even worse—she was jealous.

Sarah didn't ask about Dallas, Ken volunteered the information. She knew anyway, no need for pretense. He even told her about the two girls who conned him on the way home, trying to make the tale humorous, but she didn't smile.

Over her shoulder, beyond the waterfront restaurant windows Ken could see running lights of passing craft. Through balusters of the Middle Bridge, auto headlamps winked a senseless semaphore.

"You know what's bothering me, Ken?" Sarah said. "The way this is changing you. I always thought of you as the epitome of self-confidence. But look at you, sitting here with head hung, unemployed. You shot a bastard who needed shooting. It was a public service! Take your talents elsewhere."

"Not much demand for a dishonored homicide detective, Sarah."

The waiter brought their lobster, refilled the wine glasses.

"Hey, look," Sarah advised, "grab your assets and swing them like a bludgeon. Do what advertising people do—take your negatives and make them positive. You had the guts to do what the public wishes more cops would do—guilty party found, dead and done."

She had an impish way of looking at him. Her eyes were so green they seemed unreal. She was ten years younger than he, born and raised in Palm Beach. They'd hardly known one another in school, meeting really for the first time in Dallas, where she worked with the daily newspaper. He knew of her family, notes compared, things in common, they'd dated on and off for several years.

"I want you to come on my weekly news show, Ken."

"I can't do that."

"That's exactly what you should do! You've got a lot to offer and you're getting nowhere with it—isn't that what you've said?"

"Sarah, I can't."

She put a warm hand over his, leaning nearer. He smelled *vin chablis* and a touch of perfume. "I'm on your side, Ken Blackburn. Come on my show and we'll talk. Two friends back home in the Palm Beaches."

"Talk about what?"

"The creep who's killing people. The way you prepare a profile. We'll talk about you."

"That may be good for a show, Sarah, but it won't help me. If that's your motive."

"It is my motive. Your lobster is getting cold—eat it."

Actually, he'd considered using the media in Dallas. During those terrible days when the press was quoting prosecutors and civil libertarians he'd been castigated with every headline. He'd ached to explain his actions. If only he knew himself—he'd decided to remain silent.

"I'd start out with the whole thing up front," Sarah counseled. "I'd say, 'I killed a man like this in Dallas, Texas.' Then, tell what kind of man he was. Don't be subtle. Don't evade the issue. Tell the viewer what you did."

"That calls for an explanation."

"No," she said. "No! If you tell the viewer the gruesome crimes that man committed, the things you had to investigate—no explanation is required."

Exactly what he'd considered . . .

She sat back, mischievous grin infectious. "Right? I'm right, right? I see it in your face—you know I'm right."

"But what constructive thing will come of it, Sarah?"

"Inez Cumbie and Gayle Zuckerman were killed by a similar criminal. I was told on the q.t. that the young neighbor—what was her name?—Arlene Mertz—she'd been mutilated, foreign objects in her body—"

Patrons at the next table grimaced.

Sarah lowered her voice to a seductive growl. "Am I correct? This is a similar kind of criminal?"

"I think that is so."

She patted his hand. "Now let's eat this crustacean."

But a few minutes later she picked up her thoughts. "Know what I'd do?" she suggested. "I'd start plugging your appearance a week ahead of time. Promo every hour—'the man who knows the killer stalking our citizens.' That kind of thing."

"I do know him."

"I know you know him. And Ken, you can bet your life the killer would be watching, too."

Yes. Reading every word written, listening to the latest developments—he *would* be watching.

"Make that work for you," Sarah challenged. "Look the psycho in the eye and tell him you know him. God, it's terrific, isn't it? What do you say?"

"I'm thinking about it."

She laughed, a xylophone running low keys. "Matter of fact," she said, "this could be a weekly thing. Updates. Delving into the twisted mind of the killer. That ought to scare him."

"No, it wouldn't scare him," Ken said. "The matrix of his criminal act is fantasy. There's no provision in his fantasy for being captured. Some of these asocial/disorganized types attack in broad daylight and crowded areas because they are convinced they cannot be caught."

"There!" Sarah said. "That's the kind of thing I would want to hear. Beat-of-the-heart stuff."

"But, Sarah, what good comes of it? I mean, for *me?* I need to get to work. Herb Leibowitz says I should redirect my career as if I'd retired. He's right."

"Okay. Okay! Try this: Suppose we establish a weekly feature on my show. Crime and criminals. Not just the maniac of the moment, robbers and rapists and—see what I mean? The whole country is paranoid about crime."

"With good cause."

"With *good* cause. Almost anybody knows somebody who's been a victim. The show could encompass the ways and means of protecting ourselves. It could be about the failure of the criminal justice system."

"That's the truth."

"See where I'm going, Ken? It could be endless. Might have syndication possibilities. State if not national. Maybe public broadcasting."

"For which I'd be paid?"

"Subject only to the sponsorship," she said. "If the show catches on, and I believe it will, you could make money."

He tasted the wine to cover his growing excitement.

"This is a natural extension of your knowledge and expertise," Sarah reasoned. "You're handsome, articulate, educated—it'll work, Ken."

"Think so?"

"Betcha baby blues. It's topical, educational and sensational enough to build an audience. The timing is perfect. You're available and there's a man out there preying on our neighbors."

People at adjacent tables were listening. Sarah turned to them. "Am I right? Won't that make a terrific show?"

"You're Sarah Greenhaw, aren't you?"

"Yes. And this is Mr. Ken Blackburn."

"Could I get your autograph for my daughter? She's taking journalism and she's a great admirer, Miss Greenhaw."

Others joined them, adding comment. Sarah played the scene like the glamorous celebrity.

But Ken wasn't part of it. Holding his wine glass, swirling the warm beverage with tiny circling motions of the wrist—he was thinking about the murderer who even now was enjoying news stories about his exploits. The bastard would be buying every newspaper, filled with the thrill the recognition gave him.

Face-to-face—*I know you . . .*

Sarah brought Ken back to the moment. "Then you'll do it?" she queried. "If you tell me I can, I'll begin promoting it with my broadcast tomorrow and throughout the week that follows."

"You think I could make a living at this, Sarah?"

"How much, I can't say. But, Ken—what are you doing, otherwise?"

"Yeah."

"Say yes," she insisted.

"All right. Yes."

She kissed him, then sat back gleefully. "Now, how would you like to end our evening looking at percale and cotton art on a king-size frame?"

"I can't, Sarah. I have an appointment at eleven."

"Um-hm." She waggled a finger at him. "The new Violet Day."

"Woman, stop investigating me!"

She showered him with that enticing laughter she generated so effortlessly. *Chinese wind chimes.*

"Very well," she conceded. "Tonight, I'll put the tab on my Visa card as business, and it won't have been a lie. We're going to be seeing a lot of one another, so I can wait."

"That," Ken said, "is a profit in itself."

Lorraine had drunk too many martinis. Garlic in the midget tomatoes didn't help. After she kissed Ken hello, she discovered he was holding his breath.

"I decided security system might be good 'vestment after all." Lorraine moved away from him. "Monday, talk to Violet."

"All right, Lori."

Her head was swimming, her tongue thick. "We been friends long time, Ken. Childhood."

"Yes."

"Be frank, can't we?"

"Certainly."

"This thing Dallas."

He sat on a chaise longue, clasped his hands and looked at them.

"I have to know," she said.

"I don't know what to say, Lori. I killed a man."

"Thinking 'bout his victims?"

"To be honest," Ken said, "that didn't come to mind at the moment."

"Needed be dead, though."

"Yes. He needed to be dead."

"Temporary—insanity thing—got you off?"

"That was the defense."

"Not insane though."

"Lori, I don't know. I've asked myself a thousand times why I did it. There was no conscious decision involved. Next thing I knew, I shot him."

A door slammed somewhere in the house.

"Talk later," Lori said. "Becky, that you? Come here, please."

Becky entered through their adjoining door and her smile vanished.

"Where been, Beck?"

"Football game, Mom. You knew that."

"Football this late? Where been?"

"After the game, I went out with some friends. First to McDonald's, then to Burger King."

"Now on, hear me? Now on, you go where you say. If you change plan call me. Understand?"

"Okay, Mom."

"Going McDonald's and decide Burger King, call and tell me."

"Mom, are you all right?"

"Li'l business meet. 'Kay, hon—go to bed."

As Becky left, Ken stood up. "I ought to be going, Lori. I'll stop by tomorrow."

"People change, Ken. I got a daughter. Have to think about her."

"Sure you do."

"Hey," she said. "Hey, hey! I'm fond of you."

"And I of you, Lori."

"But people change."

She stumbled and Ken held her arm. He helped her to the bed.

"Okay," she said. "Monday I call Violet. Herb Leibowitz says this job is you."

"Herb said that?"

"Like this." She formed an *okay* with thumb and forefinger.

She wasn't sure what happened next. When she opened her eyes after a long blink, Ken was gone. Becky stood in the doorway.

"Mom? May I talk to you?"

"Come in, Beck."

"Mom, why are you doing this?"

"Violet Day? My job!"

"Doing it for Violet is one thing, Mom. You act like you're trying to be Violet."

"No choice."

Becky pulled at a loose thread in her pajamas. The button fell off.

"You always said you'd never do this, Mom. You don't believe that mumbo jumbo."

"Sweetheart—I gain new respect for Violet these days. Know how she knows about movie stars? Gossip! Divorce and marriage—gossip. She prog—prognost—predicts a coup—been talking to ambassador, senator. I am impressed!"

"Okay, Mom, be impressed. But you can be impressed and do the work without being Violet Day."

"Something bothering you?"

"Yes. I come home. Ken Blackburn is in your bedroom and you're wearing that purple thing with all that jewelry."

"I thought I looked spiffy."

"You look like a Gypsy fortune teller."

"Oh."

"And your breath would kill mosquitoes."

"Li'l tomatoes."

"You've never jumped on me about going out before. Why tonight? In front of company? Mom—what's wrong, really?"

Tears rose in Lorraine's eyes and, despite herself, she sobbed. Becky came to her, asking again, "What's wrong, Mom?"

"Drank too much," Lorraine snorted, tried to laugh but choked.

Becky turned back the covers and Lorraine rolled between the sheets. Her body felt as if she were floating, the room unstable. Becky turned off the lights.

Scared . . .

If she'd said that to Ken, he would have stayed.

Maybe she'd say it tomorrow.

CHAPTER
TWELVE

JAYDEE DECIDED to sell a diamond because now he had two. The second stone had come from Dr. Zuckerman's ring. Jaydee rolled the two gems in the palm of his hand, comparing them. There was no difference he could see. So, why not? He'd lost a day's pay because of Dr. Zuckerman. Almost lost his job as well. *One more time,* Mr. Gus had warned.

Now he was waiting for breakfast while his mother turned the newspaper in search of her horoscope. But the front page distracted her. BRUTAL DOUBLE MURDER.

Jaydee's married sister stood at the kitchen counter slicing bananas over bowls of cornflakes. Her baby crawled across the floor, his sticky fingers webbed with cat fur. In the living room, Lolly's older child watched Saturday-morning cartoons on TV.

"Jesus, Jaydee," his mother interrupted her reading, "will you blow that baby's nose?"

Lolly pushed cats off a chair, delivering cereal to the table. She dunked bananas in milk, listening to her mother's recitation:

"Police say similar murders occurred in two other Florida cities during the past year. They have reason to believe the same killer is responsible."

Again, she halted, "Jaydee, wipe that baby's nose."

Lolly did it using the hem of her skirt.

When Estelle Reaper put aside the newspaper, Lolly said, "Ray thinks he may have steady work if they get that construction project down at Lantana Village."

"Jaydee is going to lose his job before it's over," his mother lamented.

"Better not," Lolly cautioned. "Good money is hard to come by. That's a job you can do, Jaydee. Outside and easy."

"All the time late—he didn't even show up Thursday. Mr. Gus Chambers came by here fit to be tied."

"Jaydee," Lolly chided, "better hang on to your job. Ray hasn't had three days work for a month. I don't know how we make it sometimes."

From the living-room TV came more news about the murders.

"Where were you Thursday?" Estelle demanded.

Lolly yelled at her eldest boy, "Budrow, turn that thing down!"

"He's all right," Estelle said. "Leave him alone."

"Going to be deaf before he's five."

The news story caught their attention and both women leaned to see through the door.

"He cut her open," Jaydee said. "Spilled her guts."

"Goddamn, Jaydee—we're trying to eat here."

But Lolly's expression begged more. "Where'd you hear that?"

"News." *But he hadn't.* There'd been few details.

When the news report passed, cartoons returned, the women resumed eating.

"I met her," Jaydee said.

"Met who—that woman? Hell you say."

"He's lying."

Jaydee went into his bedroom and came back with Dr. Zuckerman's book. He placed it on the table. They stared at the author's photograph.

"That's her," Lolly conceded.

"Where'd you meet her?" Estelle asked.

"Mall."

"What were you doing there? Is that where you were Thursday, spending money we haven't got for a book you wouldn't read anyhow?"

She opened it to the inscription and jabbed it with a finger. "Jaydee, you'd say the sun shined at midnight if a blind man asked you. This says, 'To Destiny.' "

"That's why she gave it to me. He decided not to buy it after she'd signed the book."

"Why would she do that?"

"I helped her carry things to her car."

Jaydee bumped a cat from his chair, sat down again. Lolly had the book now. "God rest her soul," she murmured.

"Told me she was Taurus," Jaydee reported. "See what her horoscope was for Thursday, Mother."

"Doesn't matter what it was. She didn't read the signs right, or she wouldn't be dead."

Lolly spooned food into her baby's fuzzy face. "Doesn't that make you sad, though? Meeting somebody who gets killed?"

"Would if it was you," Jaydee said. "Or Mother. Or Lavern or Aunt Reba." He listed female relatives and acquaintances, each name adding dimension to their imaginations.

"Says here, it was on Flagler Drive." Lolly consulting the newspaper. "You know where Currie Park is? Near there."

"Seems like somebody would've heard something," Estelle said. "She must've screamed and screamed."

There would be people all over town doing this. Reading their newspapers, watching TV. They'd double-check their locks and burn the lights at night. Women would insist their husbands accompany them shopping or to church.

Jaydee had seen this on television crime shows—the way people behave when there's a murder nearby. Especially a murder like this—*brutal*.

He stood up. The diamonds were tiny lumps in his pockets.

"Where you going?"

"The mall."

"The mall? What for? We've got the electric bill to pay. There's no money for foolishness."

"Might look for a job."

"Better keep the job you got," his mother said. "Who else but Mr. Gus would put up with you being late so much?"

When he reached the door, his mother said, "Lock up behind you."

He pulled it closed, backing out. He saw them examine Gayle Zuckerman's book again. Lolly turned the newspaper to read the article another time. She put a hand over her mouth, her eyebrows two mournful tildes, a diacritic response to the article she read.

Jaydee could feel it—people everywhere responding to the tragedy, hungry for facts, protective of their loved ones. He felt like—like the

lone wolf he was, invisible and undetected. As if he were spying on the
world, all of humanity stripped naked as he peeked through a keyhole.

Lolly and his mother were as women would be. Scared—appalled—

That was the word. Appalled.

Indubitably.

The mall was crowded. People milled in wide corridors, waiting for a
jazz band to play. Across from the jewelry store another author was
autographing books. This one was a man.

"You decided to accept my offer?" The jeweler held Jaydee's diamond
under bright light, studying it with a loupe.

Jaydee lit a cigarette, shook flame from the match and dropped it on
the floor.

"Let me weigh this," the jeweler said.

Jaydee didn't want to seem anxious. He blew smoke lazily.

The jeweler placed the stone on a piece of dark velvet and put it
between them on the counter. "Do you know anything about gems? This
one is a brilliant cut fifty-eight-facet stone." He searched Jaydee's eyes as
if he'd lost something. "There are thirty-three facets above the girdle
and twenty-five below. In considering the value, I look at the cut, then
the size, and finally the color. This is a hundred-and-two-point blue.
Deep blue, in fact."

"You want it, or not?"

The jeweler turned the gem with a finger, then wiped it with the
velvet. "Refresh my memory. What was my offer?"

"Nine hundred."

"It was seven-fifty, wasn't it?"

Jaydee flicked ashes, scattered them with one foot. "Seven-fifty,
then."

"Is that acceptable?"

"I'm here."

"Have you taken this to anyone else for appraisal?"

Playing the game, Jaydee said, "I trust you."

"Very well. I'll get a check."

"Cash."

"I have to have a check for my records. I'll write a check, you endorse
it and I'll cash it. It shouldn't take but a few minutes. Would you like to
go have coffee while I do it?"

"Few minutes, you said."

The jeweler reached for the diamond and Jaydee touched the man's wrist. "I might change my mind."

"Sure. It won't take long."

Jaydee pretended to look at items on display. A salesgirl watched him push the diamond on velvet along the counter.

"Here we go," the jeweler said. "Sign it on the back."

Jaydee penned his name.

"Address, please."

He wrote it down.

"Social security. or driver's license number."

"You think I'm dumb?" Jaydee questioned. "It's your check."

"Oh. Yes. Sorry. Force of habit. Let me get your cash."

Irritated, Jaydee watched him count the money twice. When he tendered it Jaydee counted it again. He folded the currency, shoved it in his top pocket and walked out. Down the way, as if to listen to the jazz band, he paused and looked back.

The jeweler was talking to a cop, pointing his way.

"He came in here a few days ago with an eighty-point blue diamond of good quality," the jeweler explained to the two policemen. "I offered seven hundred fifty dollars. He wanted to think about it. Fine. This morning he returns to accept the offer and it's a hundred-and-two-point deep blue diamond of exceptional quality. The difference in the value is thousands of dollars."

The cops caught up to him. "Where'd you get the diamond?" The cop asked.

"My mother."

"She sent you to sell it?"

"No."

"He told me she was dead," the jeweler recounted.

The policeman examined Jaydee's driver's license and the jeweler's endorsed check. "This your address, Mr. Reaper?"

"Yes."

"I want the diamond, of course," the jeweler commented. "But I can't take a chance on stolen merchandise."

"It isn't stolen," Jaydee said.

"You mind if we check this out?" the cop asked.

"Ask my mother."

"She isn't dead, then?"

"No, I took it to sell because they're going to turn off our electricity this week."

"So she could confirm it's her diamond?"

"Yes."

"Why don't we call your mother, then?"

"No phone. Are you arresting me?"

"Not at all. But we'll have to confirm that this is her diamond and she doesn't mind you taking it. You can understand that."

"If you didn't want the diamond you should've said so," Jaydee accused the merchant.

"If your mother says sell, I'll double the amount I paid. I wouldn't cheat you."

"You wouldn't," Jaydee said, "unless you could."

"Let's go to your place, Mr. Reaper." The policeman held Jaydee's arm. "It's not that far away, is it?"

Passersby stared at them.

"I want to talk to a lawyer," Jaydee said. "I might want to sue about this. This is embarrassing."

"No need to be," the policeman soothed. "Take a minute to straighten out the misunderstanding and you've got your money—or your diamond. You did tell the man your mother was dead, didn't you?"

They put him in the rear seat of a patrol car, the two cops up front, a steel screen separating them from Jaydee. He considered dropping the second diamond behind the seat, but they would surely find it, eventually.

When they pulled into his driveway, Jaydee said, "Mind if I talk to her first?"

"Let's talk to her together."

"She may be pissed off."

"We'll see." The cop knocked on the door and Jaydee reached past him to open it. *Locked.* The cop knocked again.

The first thing Estelle said was, "What is it now, Jaydee?"

"Is this man your son?"

"The surest proof that Hitler wasn't all wrong," she said. "What'd he do?"

They told her and Jaydee's mother listened, elbow propped on her stomach, a cigarette between her fingers.

"So?" she said.

"Does he have your permission to sell the diamond?"

"Hell no, but we need the money. Am I going to press charges? He's my boy."

"The jeweler said he tried to sell one diamond earlier this week and returned with a different one today."

"I've got more than one diamond."

"Could you tell us where you got it, Mrs. Reaper?"

"My first husband. A gift."

"Where is he?"

"New Orleans, last I heard. He left us when Jaydee was a kid."

"All right," the patrolman closed his notebook.

"I need a ride back to the mall," Jaydee demanded. "My car is there."

"I'll go with you," his mother said, stonily. Then, with a smile as false as her eyelashes, she asked, "Would you gentlemen care for iced tea while I get my purse?"

"No thank you, ma'am."

A few minutes later, they were riding in the rear of the police car. She rode looking out her window, jaw set.

One of the policemen escorted them to the jewelry store and apologized for "the inconvenience."

"How much did you pay?" Estelle questioned the jeweler.

"Seven hundred fifty."

"You think that's a fair price?"

"No, ma'am, of course not."

"Then pay a fair price or give me back my diamond."

"Would six thousand be acceptable?"

She didn't even blink. "And for the other diamond?"

"Seven thousand for the two," the jeweler said.

"Cash."

"I'll write a check, you endorse it and I'll take you to the bank two doors down. Is that agreeable?"

She looked at Jaydee as if mildly amused. "Trying to rip off your own mother," she said. "Give him the other diamond."

Jaydee did that, face flaming.

At the bank, the teller counted hundred-dollar bills and Estelle put them in her purse.

The first thing she did was buy a new color TV set. Then she purchased clothes and perfume for herself, two pairs of trousers for Jaydee.

"Violet said today would be a blessing in disguise," Estelle chortled.

"I want my share of the money," Jaydee said.

"Your share? You're lucky you aren't eating beans and fatback down at the jail. Where'd you get those diamonds, Jaydee?"

"I found them."

"You lie, and made me lie for you! What else could I do? You're my flesh and blood."

He drove toward home, his mother counting the balance of her good fortune.

"We're going to have a party," she said. "Invite Lolly and Ray and the kids, Lavern and her boyfriend. I'll make guacamole salad and mix up some margaritas. Stop at the store so I can buy Triple Sec and tequila."

He was so furious his skin prickled.

"Maybe I'll go down to the Seminole place and play a few rounds of Indian bingo," Estelle exulted.

"I want part of the money," he said.

But she ignored him. Debating this purchase or that, everything from a new car to used furniture.

His heart pounded with rage—at the jeweler who'd made him look stupid, at the condescending cops who'd brought him home like a child.

Estelle patted his leg. "I don't believe for a minute you found those diamonds, Jaydee. But, okay, our gain is somebody else's loss. Violet Day would agree with that! Our blessing, somebody's curse."

She patted his leg again. "Aw, hell, Jaydee, we needed the money."

She licked a thumb and peeled off five hundred dollars. "Go get your tail bobbed."

His mother bought six cases of beer. Back in the car, she said, "Think I ought to get the phone put in again?"

The engine skipped slightly. *Needed a tune-up.*

As they carried packages into the house, Estelle protected what she had left. "Don't tell Lolly or Lavern about this, Jaydee. They'll be trying to borrow every dime."

That night, with Lolly's toddler asleep on the kitchen floor, Jaydee's mother, Lavern and Lolly and her husband, Ray, drank beer and ate Mexican food. The house reeked of onions and jalapeño.

Morosely, Jaydee slumped in front of the new color television waiting for the news. On the floor, his nephew Budrow foamed around his own thumb, legs extended, watching the TV with expressionless brown eyes. The boy seldom spoke. He tended to flinch if somebody moved abruptly.

"Jaydee!" his mother called. "You're missing the fun in here."

He burped little bubbles of beer, kicked at a cat.

"Budrow?" The child's father paused in the doorway. "You hungry, boy?"

Budrow shoved a purring feline, shook his head.

"Get hungry, you holler," Ray said.

Mr. Gus had come by about the time they delivered the new color TV. He wanted Jaydee to go to Lake Wales, Monday, tend some orchards.

"My car is cutting up."

"You can use a company car. The one with Georgia plates. Somebody from Valdosta will be down for it in a couple of weeks. We might as well drive it."

Usually, Jaydee didn't mind going. But now, with the stories about Dr. Zuckerman, he wanted to be within range of local stations.

News graphics rolled, flickering images of marinas, sunsets, shorelines and condos. *Live eye coverage* . . .

Jaydee punched buttons on the wireless remote until he found the volume. When it blared, Budrow scooted back about half an ass and stopped.

Mostly, it was the same things Jaydee had seen this morning and last night—photographs of Dr. Gayle Zuckerman, her home, the *Id and Ego* sign on the mailbox. There was a photo of Arlene Mertz when she was younger. She certainly didn't look that good now.

The thought made him chuckle.

The new information concerned Dr. Zuckerman's fame and accomplishments. There were quotes from dignitaries, talk of a reward for information leading to an arrest.

As the story continued, Lolly came to sit beside Budrow. Estelle leaned against the doorjamb, rocking a bit, drunker than she wanted anybody to know.

"Jaydee met her," Lolly said to her husband.

"He did?"

"Just a while before she was murdered," Lolly said.

Ray downed his beer, crumpled the can.

Lavern scoffed. "How'd you meet her?" The oldest of the siblings, Lavern had her mother's tendency to grate.

Jaydee didn't have to repeat the story, Lolly told it, even embellished it a little.

"How's that thumb taste, Budrow?" Ray tugged at the boy's arm and the child snatched it away, watching the TV screen.

"Want some sugar on it?" Ray taunted.

But Budrow had catatonia down to a fine art.

"Talk to the police?" Ray asked Jaydee.

"About what?"

"About the dead lady."

"No."

"Jaydee's had enough police for one day," Estelle offered.

"You been in trouble, Jaydee?"

Damn her.

"What, Mama? Did he get in trouble?"

"Not for me to say."

"You already said it," Ray charged.

"Said too much then."

"What happened, Jaydee?"

He raised the volume with the remote control.

"One week from tonight," a blonde reporter said, huskily, "we'll have a man who knows the criminal that killed three area women."

Jaydee heard his own heartbeat.

"Our guest will be Ken Blackburn," the commentator continued. "He will tell us about this killer—the work he does, the way he lives, the fantasies that impel him."

Jaydee lifted his chin slightly, took a slow breath.

"Next week," the woman said, "the man who knows the killer . . ."

"If he knows him," Lolly put in, "why doesn't somebody arrest him?"

"He don't know nothing," Ray countered. "Want another beer, Lolly?"

"Bring me one, too," Estelle said.

"One thing sure . . ." Ray popped the tops of two. "The killer will be watching."

"I tell you somebody who could name him," Estelle said. "Violet Day! She'd look into the future and name his name and where he is."

"Estelle," Ray sneered "you talk like that woman was real. Nobody can see the future."

"She predicts things all the time! Like that hotel fire in Puerto Rico."

"She did *not* say Puerto Rico."

"She said fire. She said hotel. She said people killed and injured."

"She didn't say when and she didn't say where," Ray argued.

"Ray, stop teasing her."

The confrontation changed degrees and Jaydee stepped over Budrow, going to the kitchen. He got a beer and went outside.

Ray was right about one thing.

The killer would be watching . . .

CHAPTER THIRTEEN

LORRAINE had a terrible weekend. Too much gin made her senses painfully acute. The tweet of a bird became cerebral lightning. Her flesh crawled like inchworms in a eucalyptus tree. The sight of food was sickening. But her distress psychologically was worse—she was certain she'd hurt herself in Ken's eyes.

Sunday, having taken a glass of iced water, she was inebriated again, the room swaying as she tried to telephone Violet. The call finally went through late that evening.

Expecting a rebuttal, Lorraine expressed a need for a security system. But Violet didn't question it, shifting the topic to the Crystal Ball.

"We've sent a thousand invitations this year," Violet reminded. "I advised the caterer our theme would be Caribbean, with a touch of voodoo. Have you heard from them?"

"No, Violet."

"Perhaps you should call, Lorraine."

"Violet, about the security system?"

"As you wish, my dear."

"I'm thinking about hiring Marian Blackburn's son. Do you remember Ken?"

"Of course I do. Did he get through his troubles in Dallas?"

Surprised that she knew of them, Lorraine said, "Yes, that's all settled. Would that influence your thinking?"

"No indeed. I knew years ago he'd be back. It's meant to be."

Lorraine heard Violet speak aside to Major Drummond. Her mother returned to say, "Major says that you should take bids on the burglar alarm, Lorraine. But you know that."

The matter decided, she informed Ken, and Monday afternoon he came to the office with the thinnest man Lorraine had ever seen. As the security specialist spoke, Ken seemed to avoid her eyes, her smiles unreturned.

"There are two kinds of systems," the wiry man explained. "Passive and active. A passive system alerts the resident with electric eyes, heat sensors, video cameras and pressure-activated alarms. At that point the police are summoned."

He seemed to watch her from tiny caves beneath the cliff of a neolithic brow, the terrain shadowed by a stubble of beard. "The active system consists of loud bells, sirens, flashing lights. A trespasser knows he's been discovered and authorities are coming. In the extreme, an active system includes high voltage barriers and gas grenades."

"That won't do," Lorraine said.

"Any system works best when it's visible," the security man continued. "High walls, video cameras, armed patrol. When a potential intruder sees that, it's a deterrent in itself. You must think like the invader. If he came to steal, and capture seemed certain, he'd look for easier picking elsewhere."

"But this man isn't coming to steal," Lorraine protested.

"No," Ken conceded, "that isn't our primary concern. It seems to me we need a deterrent that is active, visible and backed with armed personnel."

"Looks that way," the security man agreed.

After the contractor departed, Ken came to sit again. "Have you met my father, Lori?"

"Don't think so. What about him?"

"He's a hard-nosed cop."

"Retired, isn't he?"

"Yes." Ken seemed troubled. "What would you think about my father heading up security? Assuming he'd agree. If he would do it, he's tough, dependable, trustworthy—"

"I don't need a sales pitch, Ken. If you want him, that's fine." Once more she smiled. He didn't.

"I don't know what kind of income he'd need."

"I'm sure it would be realistic."

"I would feel better if he screened applicants, managed the shifts."

"Ken," Lorraine said peevishly, "you see the situation clearly enough. You approached me about a security system and we've decided to do it. The Crystal Ball is less than three weeks away and now I'm convinced there may be some danger to Becky or me. Or the employees."

"Or your guests," Ken added.

The thought hadn't occurred to her. "Then fine," she said. "Do what you must."

"Lori, I hate to talk about money."

"How much do you need?"

For an instant, only an instant, his eyes darted.

"Will you take responsibility for the security apparatus?" Lorraine asked.

"Yes, of course."

"Then, set your salary."

"I'll work up something."

"Good."

"I'll talk to my father."

"Good!"

He stood up, took a step, wheeled and returned to sit again. "You want to know the problem? I don't want a salary. I hear the tone of your voice when we discuss it. I don't want to be your employee. But I do have expenses—"

"All expenses paid. I'll get you a credit card."

"Lori, if I had my way, I'd do this in the name of friendship only."

"Ken, what I need is someone I can trust. How do we put a value on that?"

"Those are my sentiments, too."

"Fair enough. I'll get a credit card for you. Spend what you wish for anything you want. That's how Violet works with Major. It seems reasonable between friends."

There was no pleasure in this transaction, like negotiating a prenuptial contract. "Whatever you are," she attempted, "I like to think you are my friend."

"I feel the same way."

"Good then." Another smile, again forsaken. "Well, fine!" she said. "I look forward to meeting your father."

Ken hated talking to Lori about money. *Rich man's syndrome.* Only commoners found the subject necessary. As he ate dinner, his mother watched him dice meat, monitoring the tempo of Ken's jaw, assessing his enjoyment. He stopped stabbing his food.

"Would you care for more, Kenny?"

"No, Mama. This is great."

"Too salty?"

"No, it's excellent."

Through opened windows came Florida night sounds and cool air fragrant with tropical perfumes.

But he'd gotten what he wanted this afternoon. Now, if he could only get his father's help. His image of the man came with emotional overtones of rejection and adolescent fears. Ken visualized Abel Blackburn incrementally: bulging biceps, thick short forearms and sturdy legs—a piece at a time—furrowed forehead and dark, inquisitive eyes. *Cop's eyes.* He was a genial man to the public, but overly strict at home. He seemed to distrust affection and had never invited it.

"I could make hot chocolate," Marian offered.

"No, thanks Mama. The tea is good. I need to think."

"Can't you think with hot chocolate?"

He quelled impatience. "I'm all right. Why don't you go to bed?"

"I sleep less and less with age."

His thoughts returned to his father. Abel had been a street cop all his career. Others got their promotions, their living standards raised, but not his father. It seemed to Ken that Abel clung to his beat with fearsome authority. It was where he felt like a cop, Abel insisted. On the sidewalks, where temptation is a constant lure, there'd never been a hint of scandal. Nobody ever accused Abel of being unfair.

"This thing with Violet is serious, isn't it?" Marian observed. "It's more than the usual crank mail, isn't it?"

What she hadn't learned from eavesdropping, she'd have guessed by now. "It's serious," Ken conceded.

"Want to talk about it?"

"I can't, Mama."

"Sometimes it helps."

"I can't."

Ken had rehearsed ways of approaching his father. From "Dad, I need you," to "It's a good opportunity."

Then, of course, there was Mama . . .

"Mama, I want to talk to you."

"Sometimes that helps."

"It's about Dad."

"What about him?"

"I'm thinking about offering him a job with Violet Day. They're installing a security system. They'll need manpower, people with experience."

"Your father?"

"If he'll do it."

"He'd be moving here."

"That's what I wanted to talk about."

"It's a free country."

"Mama, could he stay here a few days? Time to look things over. He'll want time to think about the offer."

"Here."

"Yes."

He tried to fathom her expression and could not. She lifted her eyebrows. "First thing, he'll say, Marian could you wash out a few things when you run your clothes? Then, maybe a touch of ironing here and there. Then, maybe add a little starch. Then, be careful of the collars, they have plastic stays in them. Then, oh, how nice I folded everything. Then—"

"Mama, it would be only a few days."

"Then, he drops hints like always—not enough bleach or too much softener and it smells like a woman's blouse."

"Okay, Mama. Forget it."

"I didn't say no."

"Maybe it's not such a good idea."

"First a piece of dry toast while the oven's still hot. Then some butter, not oleomargerine; and guava jelly. Comes a day later and we add two eggs; another day, some bacon. Then he remembers the biscuits I used to bake."

"I said forget it, Mama."

"I didn't say no."

Insects thumped the Florida room screens, seeking light. Ken heard a passing jet murmur as it descended toward the airport.

"First he touches the hand—gratitude, nothing more. Then he squeezes."

"Mama, I'm sorry I mentioned it."

"Then he talks about the catch in his back and do I have a hot water bottle. Spread a bit of Ben-Gay. Now he's so comfortable he falls asleep across the bed, and would it be too much trouble if he napped here a while?"

Ken laughed. "The roast beef was delicious, Mama."

"Iron his pajamas, he'll say. He likes to smell fresh in the bed, he'll say. Doesn't want to offend anyone. He says that. Like we're expecting a crowd."

"I got the point, Mama."

"To make it up, he brings a flower and puts it on the pillow. Like having marital relations is a chore I endure, and he understands. He never understood, Kenny. Never did. He never understood the pressure on a woman married to a policeman. Every morning off to mayhem and every night to bed—I never told you about that."

"No, Mama, and—"

"I never discussed the private things."

"No, Mama. It isn't necessary—"

"Quick. Like it has to be over so he can reach his gun if needed."

"Mama—"

"I say you want to talk about it, Abel? He says, 'Police business.' You say that. 'Police business.' If you are married to a cop and he won't talk police business—there's nothing to say, Kenny."

Ken cleared his throat, standing up. "Supper was excellent, Mama."

"Call your father."

"What?"

"We'll see how it goes. But they sell no-iron shirts now. If he wants a maid, bring somebody."

"You're sure, Mama?"

"Violet needs him. It's little enough to do."

The next morning, Ken used Lorraine's office while she worked in Violet's. Cynthia became his secretary, placing calls to security services, spelling out specifications, soliciting bids on the contract.

Every ten minutes, Marian Blackburn telephoned, interrupting.

"Your father will be here at five o'clock, Kenny."

"Good, Mama."

"Coming to the house. Bathe and shave, he said. From here we go where you want."

"Good, Mama."

"So, where is that going to be, Kenny?"

"I haven't decided. I'll speak to Lori."

"Nothing too fancy," Marian warned. "It makes Abel uncomfortable. He doesn't eat where he has to choke himself with a tie."

"I know. I'll think about it."

"Not Morrison's Cafeteria," she said. "He eats there every week."

"Mama, I have people waiting on another line."

"He likes kosher foods, but they don't agree with him. He'll be burping and flatulent, groaning all night."

"I'll call you back."

He took a call from a contractor. Before it concluded Cynthia was in the doorway. "Your mother."

He jabbed the phone button, switching lines. "Mama—I'm so busy—"

"He likes black beans and rice," said Marian. "Roast pork and applesauce—Cuban style. But he has that every day."

"I'm working on it, Mama."

"I won't know how to dress until I know where we're going."

"I'll call."

Lorraine walked through without speaking. Cynthia on the intercom now, "Herb Leibowitz on the line, Mr. Blackburn."

"Herb—hi."

"We have matching fingerprints that positively link our boy to Inez Cumbie and the Zuckerman kitchen," Herb said. "But the FBI can't come up with a name. That means he's never been in the military service, never been pulled in for a crime."

"Yeah."

"Want to apologize for the short shrift the captain gave you," Herb said.

"No apology necessary."

"Sarah Greenhaw says you're going to be on her show."

"She talked to you?"

"It's on TV—every hour."

"Your mother . . ." Cynthia, over the intercom again.

Ken took her call. "Mama, please, I'm up to my earlobes—"

"A minute," she insisted. "I was thinking. Abel and I could meet you and Lorraine somewhere. How's that?"

"That's great."

"So, where?"

"I don't know. I'll try to decide soon."

"Men get dressed, one the pants, two the shirt, three the shoes," she said. "Women do not dress so easily. I am walking the house in a bathrobe, Kenny."

"Mama, we aren't going out until this evening."

"Clothes to match and not so dated," she said. "Shoes with heels, without heels, accessories like a necklace or earrings. I thought I'd dress the way Abel likes me to—we're trying to impress him, aren't we?"

"Mama, I will call you."

"Just say heels or flats, fancy or plain, we won't be dancing, will we?"

"I'll call you."

He looked up to find Lori listening. "What's going on?" she asked. He told her.

"Café L'Europe," Lorraine said.

"Abel Blackburn is a man of simple tastes."

"What kind of food does he prefer?"

"Morrison's Cafeteria."

"We'll go to Morrison's."

"We need a quiet place to talk."

"Specifically, what kind of food?"

"He likes gefilte fish, bagels, kosher deli; but he also eats Cuban food daily."

Lorraine seemed taken aback. "Does he keep a kosher house?"

"He isn't Jewish, Lori. He's Irish. His mother named him Abel so he could get a job outside Boston. But he grew up in a Jewish neighborhood and the Star of David is imprinted on his taste buds. I see you're busy—don't worry about it."

"Why don't we have dinner at the compound? Call your mother and put her mind at ease."

When Marian answered, Ken laughed shortly before speaking. "We'll be eating at the family compound, Mama."

"I've never been there as a guest." He detected a note of excitement. "If it's no trouble. That would be nice. What time?"

Ken hollered into the adjoining office, asking.

"Six for cocktails," Lori said. "Seven for dinner."

He relayed the information and Marian Blackburn lilted, "Oh, my! Won't this be something? Isn't that nice, Kenny?"

"Bye, Mama."

"Tell Lorraine I said thank you."

He hung up. Lorraine was in the connecting door between suites. They grinned at one another.

Lorraine watched Annie put the finishing touches on the table while Annie's husband, the gardener, ignited Polynesian torches to ward off insects. The patio was spotlessly clean, the swimming pool an unblinking emerald eye. From speakers around the terrace came soft strains of a recorded orchestra, filling the evening with waltzes.

The table was set in silver and crystal, the centerpiece a pyramid of candles shielded by glass flues. Wine chilled in an ice bucket. The portable bar was tended by Annie's husband and he wore white for the occasion.

"It's beautiful, Lori," Ken said. "Perfect!"

In the distance, waves moaned on the shore. Ken paced to and fro, nervously, but Lorraine felt a pleasing sense of security.

"I'm going to be a fifth wheel around here tonight," Becky lamented.

"My father will think you are the most charming of all women," Ken predicted.

"Old men and little boys," Becky said. "How do I look, Mom?"

"You are stunning, Becky. Ask Annie if she needs help."

"Mom, she doesn't. She has two daughters in the kitchen; both will be serving. If I ask, she'll think you're trying to get rid of me. If that's true, say so and I'll go upstairs and watch TV."

"It isn't true."

"Then you two hold hands and pretend I'm not here."

The sound of an automobile in the driveway caused Ken to tense. "Guess that's them," he said.

Marian wore a small white carnation corsage pinned to a flaming red silk dress. Hugging her, Lorraine said, "You look wonderful, Marian."

Ken shook his father's hand formally. "Long time," he remarked. Then, "Dad, this is Lorraine. Her daughter, Becky Linden."

Abel took Becky's hand, seriously. "Your mother doesn't look old enough to have a daughter eighteen."

"Fifteen."

"Fifteen," Abel marveled.

"Well!" Ken clapped his hands softly. "How about drinks, everybody?"

Standing beside his father at the bar, Ken was taller than Abel, better proportioned, Lorraine thought. The elder Blackburn had the physique of an aging professional football player, so thickset his clothes tended to bind.

The men returned and an awkward pause ensued, each taking a sip of martini in the lapse.

"How is your mother?" Marian asked Lorraine.

"She's well. Her lecture series began in London yesterday. I called Sunday for advice, but she has none to offer. Trying to force me into the role of Violet Day. You remember, as a child, I vowed I'd never do this."

"It could not be otherwise, Lorraine."

The men listened without contribution. Finally, they downed their drinks and went to the bar for seconds. Abel chatted with the gardener about liquid fertilizers and the grounds. "How many acres here?"

"Thirteen."

"Tend it by yourself?"

"Several part-time people come when needed."

"Known them long?"

"Long time. Was the martini all right, Mr. Blackburn?"

"What are those little things where the olives ought to be?"

"Midget dill tomatoes. Miss Day is partial to them."

"Skip the tomatoes," Abel said. "I'm a traditionalist."

Marian questioned Becky about school. The men strolled the terrace, voices lowered. Ken pointed at the shoreline, the greenhouse and servants' quarters.

Marian kept Becky talking, but she watched Abel and Ken, her drink ignored. She picked lint from her dress, adjusted the fall of her skirt—like a school girl on a date with an inattentive beau.

Half an hour passed. Conversation was strained, the men withdrawn.

Hoping food would do what drinks had not, Lorraine signaled the kitchen. "We're ready when you are, Annie."

Abel seated Marian with a courtly gesture, his hand lingering on her shoulder.

With dinner, Abel's demeanor altered.

"Matzo balls?"

"We have black beans and rice, if you prefer," Lorraine said.

Abel tucked his chin, looking at Marian. "You always do the perfect thing, Marian."

"I didn't do it, Abel. Lorraine did."

Abel ate with such gusto, Annie clearly worried there'd be enough. He alternated from cheese blintzes to Cuban roast pork with appreciative groans. *Now* he seemed relaxed.

"You'd make a good cop," Abel spoke to Becky, catching her off guard. "Sitting there quietly, but I see your eyes. Always alert, watching. I think you know people, too."

"Is it interesting work?"

"Every day a different way," Abel said. He reached over, touched Marian's hand. "It is difficult for the spouse, though. The worry, the tension, more than anyone should endure."

"So what's the most interesting thing that ever happened to you?" Becky questioned.

"Once," he said, "back when the red light district was legal—"

"Abel," Marian cautioned.

"We got a call from a madam who said she was being robbed. We rushed down there, found the madam tied to a chair. Upstairs, a lady of the evening claimed she'd been raped by the robber before he fled."

"Abel—"

"Well, sir," Abel said, "rape was a capital crime. The lady's price was only five dollars. We had a terrible time trying to decide whether it was a crime punishable by death—or petty larceny."

"Abel!"

Becky threw herself backward, laughing.

"Abel, you tell that child such a story?"

"Marian, I spoke as one police officer to another. Police business."

Becky rejoined with a horrible racist joke that shocked Lorraine. But before she could protest, Abel topped it. The man and girl laughed until tears flowed.

Annie came to the table and leaned down to speak. "Miss Lorraine, there's someone on the grounds. Coming up from the beach."

Ken and his father stood in unison. The moon was half full, the stars an unwinking panoply. "Turn on all the yard lights, Annie," Lorraine directed.

"Is something wrong?" Becky asked.

Ken moved toward the ocean, but his father maneuvered to one side. "Mom, is something wrong?"

"Nothing, darling," Marian interposed. "Somebody lost on the beach. Would you show me the bathroom, Becky?"

"Sure. It's my bedtime, anyway."

The stranger's voice rose in the night. The outside lights came on and flooded the scene. *A drunk*. Lorraine realized she'd been holding her breath.

By now Abel was behind the interloper, Ken reasoning with the man. Finally, the stranger turned unsteadily and walked toward the beach. A moment later, Ken threw an arm around his father's shoulder and both men laughed.

"Somebody visiting a neighbor," Ken reported. "Walking in the dark, he can't find the right villa."

Abel filled his pipe. "How much do you know about what you're doing, Kenny?"

"Not much. That's why I want you here."

Abel tamped tobacco. "What do you know of the resources available? The Palm Beach police, for example."

"Underpaid and understaffed, I'd imagine."

"Not so," Abel said. "Seventy-one man force for an island fourteen miles long and half a mile wide, maximum. Nine thousand permanent residents, becoming 35,000 during peak season. The police department is among the ten best in the nation. In an emergency, they could call on sixty-nine firemen."

"You've done a little study," Ken noted.

"Called a few friends," Abel admitted. "My point is this: You're on an island with three-bridge access. There is excellent police coverage. Seems to me a minimal need is indicated. One guard on the grounds ought to do it."

"I'm not so sure," Ken said. "The letters to Violet Day, reinforced with actual murders—I don't think we should take chances."

"You shouldn't," Abel said. "But when they catch this whacko, these folks will be back to normal. I wouldn't spend hundreds of thousands of dollars for security—"

"Hundreds of thousands?" Lorraine questioned.

"You can make this a fortress," Abel said. "But I don't think it's warranted."

"What do you suggest?"

Abel sucked his pipe, puffing smoke. "Video surveillance. Plenty of lights. An armed guard. Mostly, I'd suggest Kenny do what he does best—catch this man."

"I've lost access to the tools I need," Ken said.

Abel waved the thought away. "Herb Leibowitz is your conduit."

"You know Herb?"

"He called me to ask about you."

"In the meantime," Lorraine worried, "we expect hundreds of guests for the charity ball Halloween weekend. There must be no possibility that anyone could be attacked by this man. I've made the decision to install security, so that's settled. Will you take the job, Abel?"

Marian returned alone and Abel looked at her as he spoke. "I'd like to be here." he said.

Marian lifted a shoulder, dropped it.

"We'll see how it goes," Abel stood. "Through the charity weekend at the least. But Kenny should concentrate on finding this psycho."

"I agree," Ken said.

"Then you'll screen applicants for guards and manage security, Abel?" Lorraine confirmed.

"Certainly." Abel's arm went around Marian's waist. "Incidentally, where are you spending the night, Kenny?"

"I—uh—"

"I asked Ken to stay here," Lorraine said, quickly. "I'd feel safer if he did."

"Is that all right with you, Mama?"

"Kenny, you haven't asked that since you were sixteen."

Becky hollered from an upstairs balcony. " 'Night all!"

" 'Night yourself, copper!" Abel yelled. "Enjoyed the jokes."

"Me, too."

After Marian and Abel drove away, Ken grinned sheepishly. "Have we gotten ourselves into an intrigue, or an imbroglio?"

"I don't know. We'll see what develops."

"Would you like to walk down to the gazebo and listen to the waves?" Lorraine got two glasses and a bottle of wine.

She should have known better. Romance wasn't his motive. As they strolled the moonlit pathway, Ken paused occasionally, taking detours to look behind shrubs.

"Have we lost something?" she asked.

"Nothing to worry about," Ken said. "Just want to be sure that fellow went along home . . ."

CHAPTER
FOURTEEN

DELAYED BY A MEETING with his father at Violet's family compound, Ken arrived at the Stellar Building in midmorning heat and wilting humidity. As he stepped off the elevator Cynthia Peebles called his name.

"Mr. Blackburn, this is Emily Harlow of the *National Enquirer*."

The reporter had the appearance of a child, scarcely five feet tall, with large blue eyes. Such a pretty face—and nothing friendly about it.

"Is there some place we could talk, Mr. Blackburn?"

"You want Violet Day, not me."

"No, you."

"You could use Mr. Drummond's office," Cynthia suggested.

Ken applied a smile. "Would you care for coffee, Emily? Do you mind if I call you Emily?"

She glanced at her watch. "I haven't much time."

Good. Ken escorted her to Major Drummond's domain. The office was smaller than Violet's and starkly modern in decor.

Emily Harlow paused to look at a painting over Major's credenza.

"An original," she said. "Henri Matisse."

"I wouldn't know," Ken still stood.

"It predates Cubism," she observed. "It's called Fauvism, a name

153

given to a short-lived but vigorous phase in the modern art movement. This must be one of the first. It's pure pointillist."

"Won't you sit down?"

She moved to another canvas. "Henri Manguin. Oh! And Charles Camoin. These must be priceless."

Still lingering with one painting, then another, she said, "You're working for Violet Day, Mr. Blackburn?"

"Temporarily. As a consultant."

She stepped back a short pace. "Kees Van Dongen. Someone knows art."

"It isn't me," Ken said, curtly. "Miss Harlow, what do you want with me?"

"Five women were murdered," the reporter said, as she admired the Van Dongen. "Letters to Violet Day. Lust murders you say."

"Have I said that?"

Emily Harlow turned gracefully to the next framed work. "Magnificent. It isn't signed, but I think this could be Raoul Dufy. Have you been hired to catch the killer, Mr. Blackburn?"

"Miss Harlow—"

"Emily," she smiled. "Emily will be fine, since you asked."

"Emily—perhaps you should speak to Miss Day. For that matter, I recommend you talk to the West Palm police."

"I did." She cocked her head, another painting. "Your father is working with Miss Day also, isn't he?"

"Do you mind telling me where you got this information?"

"People call us."

"I'd like to know who."

"All Fauvism," her gesture encompassed the room. "All from the early days of the century. Quite a collection."

"Miss Harlow, I have a busy schedule."

"I know you do." She faced him now. "I only wanted to confirm a few facts for my story."

"Do you believe a sensational article will be beneficial to this case?" Ken questioned, pointedly.

"We do print sensational things," she said, "but we verify all information. You have to admit this is a story that will have great appeal. Letters from murdered women, a psychopath stalking one of the so-called seers of our time. One wonders why Violet Day doesn't use her professed powers to conjure the man's name and face."

"I think you will be doing a disservice to the unfortunate women who have been victims, Miss Harlow. May I make a proposal?"

She waited—iced blue eyes.

"Suppose we work together. As the case develops I'll keep you informed. But you hold this story at least until after the Crystal Ball."

"Your purpose?"

"To avoid complications that will arise if we're flooded with copycat letters, and to avoid the possibility of a worse copycat, another killer trying to share the attention. I would agree to give you an exclusive, at the proper time."

"No."

"So this article is written already."

"I could edit a bit, but the story is set. I only wanted to check my facts. I enjoyed the art. My minor in college was impressionism, my thesis was on the Fauvism period."

She paused at the door. "Incidentally, the term 'Fauvism' came from a Paris critic's description of a small bronze shown amidst the first collective expression of this style. He called it 'a Donatello among the wild beasts.' *Chez les fauves*."

"Emily, an insensitive article aimed at Violet Day is really a low blow. She has no control over the murderer. Are you going to do that to her?"

"I'm not going to protect her. However, the thrust of my story isn't Violet Day. It's you."

"Thanks. I really need that."

"You sound so wounded," she said. "Are you appearing on Sarah Greenhaw's TV show this Saturday?"

"Will you please hold the story until after the Crystal Ball?"

"Are you going on Sarah Greenhaw's show, or not?"

"I am, but it isn't an attempt to capitalize on—"

"*Chez les fauves*, Mr. Blackburn. Violet Day is among the wild beasts. That's a news story to her millions of readers."

Ken followed her to the elevator. She stepped in and turned to face him, unyielding and cold.

Chez les fauves.

The more Ken thought about it the angrier he became. But then, logically, there was no way to keep this quiet. The evidence was circulating in ever widening circles—ambulance attendants, forensic scientists, the FBI—cops talked to cops, anybody could have called the *Enquirer*.

The TV show made him fair game. He'd worried about that. Worried about Lori's reaction, too. Thus far they hadn't discussed it.

He waited until that night to tell Lori about the *Enquirer.*

"Well, that's it," she said. "They'll make Violet look like a charlatan. As for divining the identity of the murderer, Violet has never pretended to predict anything but tendencies. That sounds hollow even to me. Lord, how did I get into this? Becky is going to endure the ridicule of her friends just as I did in school. There's nothing I can do but defend us. Damn it."

"The reporter said I'll be the thrust of her story, Lori."

"Even then, we can imagine what that thrust will be."

Rogue cop . . . serial killer . . . prophetess . . .

Worse: *Killer cop hired by prophetess . . .*

Even worse: *Crazed killer cop . . .*

"Monday," Lori anguished, "the national media has been invited to a press party to publicize the Crystal Ball. What can I say to them?"

"Do you want me to distance myself from you?" Ken asked.

"Of course not. Tell Abel to work on that security system."

Later, Ken left the family compound and stopped by home, looking for his father.

"Abel isn't here," Marian said. "He's at Violet's office."

"Doing what?"

"You know your father. 'Police business.' "

It was after ten o'clock when Ken entered the office foyer. He heard laughter from Major Drummond's office. The door was partially closed but he could see his father, feet on Major's desk, chair reared back, holding a glass of purloined liquor from Major's stock. Teasing Donna Wheeler—and *she*, responding like a winsome girl, "Aw, get out of here, Abel!"

"No, I mean it," Ken heard Abel say. "I would've guessed you to be about my age. Whatever your diet, stick with it."

Ken pushed open the door and Abel looked up. "Hello there, lad. Come have some Scotch."

Mrs. Wheeler patted her hair. "Do you need anything else, Abel?"

"No, angel—thanks."

She left without speaking to Ken, closing the door behind her.

"Dad, what are you doing here?"

"Just what you asked. Going over personnel, past and present. A hell of a thing, this computer. Did you know it's linked to other computers all over the world? Donna was showing me how to reach New York, London, Tokyo—"

"Dad, what *are* you doing here?"

"I told you. Personnel files. Stuff that'd surprise you. Surprised me, anyway. Hey! I didn't know you were a straight-A student. Four Ivy League scholarships—why didn't you take one?"

"Florida State University has the best department of criminology in the nation. There's a file on me?"

"Honor roll student." Abel sucked a cluck from the side of his mouth. "Then went into police work. Why did you do that?"

"I expect it was because of you, Dad."

Abel smiled. "How about that?" He finished the last of the Scotch and tossed the empty bottle into a wastebasket with a horrendous clatter.

"Dad, the *National Enquirer* is doing a story on Violet Day and the murders. Evidently I'm featured. Lori says we can imagine the way they'll treat us."

" 'The Ghost of Elvis Presley Fathered My Baby,' " Abel said. " 'Alien Sperm Discovered in Swimming Pool.' "

Ken sat down, tiredly.

Abel patted the screen of the computer. "This piece of machinery is phenomenal," he said. "There's a file on anyone ever employed by Violet Day. A hundred twenty-something. Births, deaths, awards, diplomas, marriages, children—you want to know something about somebody, Donna Wheeler can call it up."

"Have you found a disgruntled employee?"

"Not a one. When they come to work here, they've been checked from birth to date of employment. Then the files are kept current. Every living employee can be located because they receive gifts at Christmas, flowers when ill, extra money if the need is perceived. Donna says they're intensely loyal, and I believe it. Look at her! Still working because she wants to."

Ken massaged his eyes, wearily.

"I can count the zits on your backside with this computer," Abel said. "If you ever got a traffic citation, it's in here. Every newspaper item about you is here. Tells who you dated and where you lived. Incidentally, why didn't you marry that woman at Florida State? Was it because she was divorced?"

"No."

"Because she had a teenage daughter?"

"No, Dad. Joanne Fleming was from a different world. She'd been married to an attorney, she was a professor, she socialized with politicians—our backgrounds didn't mesh. I ran for sheriff and if I'd won, things might've been different. But I didn't win."

"Interesting the similarities between her and Lorraine," Abel mused. "Divorced, with child, different worlds—"

The comment rankled Ken. He was seeing his father in a strange light; a bit tipsy, flirting with Donna Wheeler to inveigle cooperation.

"Major Drummond set up this computer network," Abel said. "He's responsible for bringing this organization into the mainstream of modern communications. They run a financial empire, were you aware of that?"

"More or less. Dad, let me drive you home."

"This little screen," Abel tapped the CRT again, "can deliver information on nearly anything you can imagine."

"We could stop for coffee," Ken offered.

"Violet is quite a woman. *Women*, actually. Ask this machine about her and it'll run for hours. Lorraine, her mother, her grandmother, her great grandmother! You know why they settled in Palm Beach?"

"Henry Flagler invited her to a lawn party."

"His first wife did. To read the palms of their guests. When coming down the east coast to Palm Beach, Lorraine's grandmother took it as an omen that Flagler's railroad passed through Jupiter, Mars, Venus, and Juno, Florida. They've called it the Celestial Railway ever since."

"How about it, Dad? Go for coffee?"

"Hey, boy!" Abel roared. "Are you listening?"

The unexpected intrusion of the father he'd always known hurled Ken back to resentful childhood.

"I'm not babbling to hear the sound of my own voice," Abel growled. "I'm making a point, if you're listening. Donna Wheeler knows how to make this computer yodel and do the two-step. I asked her if she could get into the National Crime Information Center and she said she could, if she knew the entry code."

"Your point?"

"Why can't you use this thing to track the killer?"

"Because we do not have access codes to the NCIC, or the FBI, or local police files. Because it would take thousands of hours to sift through data if we did have the access codes. Because a computer can only find what's recorded and what we need won't be."

"Give me for instance."

"By the profile," Ken said, "the killer was probably in trouble at an early age. I need a list of juveniles who came to the attention of the law in the past twenty years. Then I'd look for kids ordered into psychiatric clinics—then, kids who were charged with sexual molestation; then, children who were charged with cruelty to their peers, or cruelty to animals—bestiality, for example. Then, I'd hunt for youthful arsonists, attempted suicides—"

"Juvenile records are destroyed after a prescribed time," Abel stated.

"I know that. That's why a computer won't help. What I need is no longer available."

Going down in the elevator, Abel filled his pipe, pensively. "Modern technology, and it still comes down to hoof beats and hard rides."

"Same as always. Let me drive you home."

"No," Abel said. "I'm sober."

"They're tough on drinking drivers here."

"That's reasonable, if you're sober."

Abel lit his pipe, talking as he puffed it. "You're saying it takes years to find a felon like this."

"Usually."

"Do you have plans you can share?"

"I know him," Ken said, evenly. "I know his soft spots, the pieces of his ego most tender, the deepest darkest secrets he thinks nobody knows. But I know him. He's going to see it. Then it'll be him and me."

Unsmiling, Abel puffed his pipe, staring at Ken. Then, with a quick nod, he got into his car and drove away.

Sarah Greenhaw perched on a high stool behind Ken, speaking to his reflection in the brightly lighted mirror. Sweat gathered in his palms. Ken hid his hands under a barber's bib spread over his body to protect his clothing from spilled cosmetics.

"This *Enquirer* story changes things," Sarah said. "We can't ignore it, Ken."

COP STALKS VD KILLER . . .

"No, no," Sarah instructed the makeup artist. "Take the arch out of his eyebrows. You have a handsome face there, but let's keep it virile and masculine."

"Yes, Miss Greenhaw."

Sarah's vision shifted slightly, meeting Ken's eyes. She smiled. "I want authority, not sexy."

More instructions to the makeup man. "Male—think male!"

"I'm thinking, Miss Greenhaw."

Sarah held a clipboard, a copy of the *National Enquirer*.

"I had planned this half-hour to be you and me and the killer," she said to Ken. "But now, we must address the connection with Violet Day."

"I'd rather not," Ken said.

"Hell, you have no choice!" she cried. "Letters to Violet Day—you were *raised* by Violet Day!"

"That's not true. I lived on the compound. My mother—"

"Precisely," Sarah interrupted. "The truth is what we need to get to. Your lifelong association with Violet Day. Your connection there now. Your background—the Dallas thing. Have you thought about that?"

Little else. Ken closed his eyes as the makeup man powdered his face.

"Look," Sarah reasoned, "all you have to do is follow my lead. We have clips to run; I'll recap the cases, the police conjecture on the sequential events preceding the murders. We have shots of the malls, of the victim's homes, Steadicam shots approaching the scene of the murder as it might have been seen through the killer's eyes. Don't bother yourself with any of that. I'll ask a question now and then. Keep your answers brief and to the point. Incidentally, the Florida Net is picking this up for state wide distribution."

Ken felt his chest constrict. He wiped his hands on the bib surreptitiously.

"Don't be nervous," Sarah said. "You're going to do fine."

"If I make a mistake, we can back up, right?"

"No," she said. "This is taped, but it's final on the first take. Ken, you'll be great."

She leaned toward the mirror, examining the finished product. "I still don't like the eyebrows. Give me some shag on the brows."

"Yes, Miss Greenhaw."

Then, too quickly, it was time. The set was that of a den or home library. Books on shelves, comfortable chairs, a maze of lights and cameras, cables and technicians—they fitted Ken with a lavaliere microphone, placed a clip to his collar and snaked the wire down the inside of his jacket.

"I don't want soft lighting," Sarah directed the director. "When it goes to Ken, give me mood and strength."

"You got it, Miss Greenhaw."

Ken tried to remember the points he'd memorized, the way he'd say them.

"Keep your voice down in the chest," Sarah advised, as the studio lights shifted to them.

"Good evening," her voice was down—somewhere right below the cleavage. Ken had a nightmarish image of himself speaking contralto to her bass. "The news of the week in the Palm Beaches . . . " Sarah intoned.

Ken pressed his palms against his trousers, unsure where to look. Follow the red light, Sarah had prompted. She stared into the camera, her image on a studio monitor seemed to gaze back at him—delicious green eyes, steady and hypnotic.

"But our major story . . . "

Ken saw old snapshots of Inez Cumbie, her life flitting by in still shots—smiling with her husband, Eugene, accepting an award, giving a speech—retiring—and *dead*. The body pushed into an ambulance.

"Less than a week later . . . "

This time, the writer, Dr. Gayle Zuckerman . . . more a public figure—there were scenes where she was one among several celebrities . . . autographing books . . . interviews on national talk shows . . . and *dead*.

"Her neighbor and friend . . . "

Arlene Mertz. Laughing . . . husband . . . *dead*.

Ken heard his name as if in a roaring wind tunnel.

"Degree in criminology, expert in forensic science, a specialist in profiling lust murders . . . "

Like mechanical carnivores sniffing the air, the cameras rose and postured, settled and wheeled, circling, red lights winking—profile, full face, then closer, closer . . .

It had a dreamlike quality. A surreal timelessness. He heard his own voice—it was not contralto. Deep, resonant, softly spoken.

"I killed a man like this in Dallas," he said.

"Tell us about that, Ken."

And he did. Unemotionally, without apology, properly pensive.

"What kind of man was this criminal?"

Terrible. Heartless. Sadistic—but behind those words were thoughts that had begun to creep into Ken's consciousness. They came in the night, sometimes. They popped into his brain over breakfast, or while driving, even during conversations which had nothing to do with crime—a human, breathing, alive . . . and *dead.*

"The *National Enquirer* says Violet Day raised you . . . "

Lived there . . . home . . .

"Now, into your lives, fate has cast another killer—a killer much like the one you shot in Dallas. This one forces his victims to write Violet Day—horoscopes are attached to the letters—they begin, 'Dear Violet Day: I am about to die.' "

It was like . . . like a whiff of blood—he was numbed. Stepping through the carnage. The professional policeman.

A commercial.

Great, Ken. Great!

"Ready on two!" Disembodied hand flashing fingers, *four, three, two*—

"What makes such a monster, Ken?"

Very professional. Controlled. A dissertation on the murder matrix, the forces of parental neglect, the crushing warp of emotional isolation, the constant abuse to self-esteem, the miserable role models of failing adults, disdain for authority figures, the desperate childish attempt to find order in a disordered lifestyle, the development of fantasy in which *he* had control over *them.*

"The murder matrix could fit many of us," Sarah Greenhaw said. "That should cause parents to pause and consider their affect on children."

Ken had a sudden memory of Abel, shouting, "Hey, boy! Are you listening?"

Another memory. Sitting alone, frightened by a bad dream, calling for his mother, and Marian wasn't there—the lights were off. He'd gone in his pajamas to the main house, climbed the trellis to peek in Lori's window—there she was, *Marian, holding Lori's hand . . .*

"How can you state that this killer is a blue-collar worker—that he lives in West Palm Beach?"

He explained the FBI research, how profiles are based on other murderers and their histories, the telltale evidence that marks them and betrays their similarities.

More commercials . . . constant reassurance from Sarah. Ken's chest ached from tension, he couldn't blot away the sweat seeping from his palms. He saw his image on the studio monitor and couldn't evaluate it—weak or strong?

"Ken, we have a few minutes remaining. If you could speak directly to this killer, what would you say?"

Now. His moment. The instant he'd waited for! Ken stared into the camera, armed with the knowledge it had taken a lifetime to accumulate—he held the audience with a prolonged silence, peering— peering into the killer's eyes.

"I know you," Ken said.

The camera closed, slowly, ever so slowly.

"I know the bad dreams you had as a child. The way you awoke, screaming, and there was nobody who heard or cared. I know the way you sat in a noisy room with a dozen people—all alone. They didn't care about you, and you knew it.

"I know the games you played with yourself. The way you hurt yourself and felt almost no pain. You were a little proud of that. You cut yourself, burned yourself, even practiced hanging yourself—nothing could hurt you. I know about that."

Abel: spare the rod, spoil the child.

Abel: good grades. Did you cheat?

Abel: absent and not missed, overpowering when present.

Everything Ken intended to say evaporated on his tongue. The penetrating psychological insights hung in his mind—they'd hurt, yes, God, they'd hurt if he said them aloud.

Dumb . . .

But, not dumb.

Who was there to applaud the achievements? Who ever encouraged a faltering step forward.

"Ken?" Sarah spoke softly.

Tears streamed down his cheeks and he swallowed hard.

"I know you," Ken said to the eye of the camera, to the eye of the killer, to the depths of the man's soul.

"I know you, because—but for the grace of God, there go I . . . "

CHAPTER
FIFTEEN

IN THE AFTERGLOW of fading day, Jaydee pulled into a roadside diner. From Lake Okeechobee came a musky odor of rotting hyacinths, over-riding the faint scent of chemicals which still clung to his clothes.

"Hey, Mister!" Two girls hitchhiking. "You from Georgia?"

He was driving the unmarked ORGRO car with Georgia tags.

"How about a ride?"

Normally he'd have spun a lie, secretly sneering at them, but he wasn't in the mood.

He'd driven down from Lake Wales in search of a place where he could get the West Palm Beach television signal. In an expensive motel room, sipping canned cola, he'd settled down to watch the show. It was not about him alone.

Ken Blackburn . . . cop.

Or, he had been; until he shot a man in Dallas. So-called expert.

In the sanctum of the room, sitting with shod feet on the bed, Jaydee watched news film done really well—going toward Inez Cumbie's house, then up the driveway of Dr. Zuckerman's. There were pictures of Inez Cumbie, Dr. Zuckerman, that other woman. Glimpses into their

165

lives; knowledge that held special intimacy for Jaydee—like knowing a famous person under discussion, or *being* a famous person, incognito.

Completely unexpected, they spoke of the *National Enquirer*—and Violet Day.

Well, about time!

He'd sat forward, eagerly. The woman commentator read aloud: "Dear Violet Day . . .

Finally it was revealed: Blackburn knew Violet Day. He grew up in her home. Employed by her now—this pseudoexpert with so much intelligence.

It couldn't have been more electrifying.

The letters had been received and read, passed among them no doubt, kindling fear and a need for this former cop.

But then they played a trick.

Ken Blackburn looked at Jaydee as if the TV screen no longer existed, the space between them vanished. It was shockingly direct and personal.

I know you . . .

Jaydee drew back into his chair. It was a trick, he *knew* it was a trick, but that didn't keep the shivers off his spine.

The bad dreams . . . nobody cared . . .

The walls thinned and disappeared around him, or so it felt to Jaydee. The mirrors were windows with strangers just beyond. He could almost hear the whisper of his name.

He'd paid for the night, but he left the motel immediately. He thought he saw people staring. A passing patrol car slowed as if to take second notice.

His first inclination was to flee—go home to West Palm. But it *was* a trick! He'd stopped at a convenience store and bought the *Enquirer,* then come to this diner.

"Eating, or not?" a waitress interrupted his thoughts.

"Menu," Jaydee said.

"On the wall. We're out of pork chops."

He ordered a hamburger steak smothered with onions. Outside in the amber vestige of evening light, the younger of the two hitchhiking girls slapped her legs, fighting mosquitoes. The girls busied themselves examining their parcels—a battered cardboard suitcase and a bundle.

Jaydee turned pages of the tabloid.

COP STALKS VD KILLER.

It was an awful headline. At first he thought it was medical! They should've used Violet Day's name.

But he decided the editors had done it on purpose. The facing page carried another headline: HORRORSCOPIC! It was about the daughter of Violet Day, heir to the throne of "America's most popular stargazer."

So. The former cop had known her a long time. "Attended the same exclusive school," the writer reported.

The show *was* a trick. Designed to make Jaydee feel exposed and vulnerable. All that talk about childhood—trying to outsmart Jaydee—pretending to be so intellectual. *Faking.* Like Violet Day—faking perceptions he did not possess.

So!

What had changed here? They knew no more than before. But he knew *infinitely* more—that Violet Day had been ignoring him; that Ken Blackburn was an extension of her, working *with* her.

When he thought back on it, there were a lot of lies in that show. He'd never tried to hang himself. That was stupid.

As for hurting himself, it was a test. It took courage to cut the flesh. He'd drawn blood plenty of times, but it wasn't *hurting* him.

"Mind if we sit down?" the girl did so even as she asked. "You're the fellow from Georgia, right?"

The younger girl was speckled with welts and spatters of insects smacked.

"Listen, my name is Diane. This is Sissie. Tell you what," Diane bartered. "Buy us a square meal, give us a ride to the next town and we'll show you something you never saw before."

Jaydee raked his gum with his tongue, assessing them.

"Best few bucks you ever invested," Diane promised. She used the window as a mirror, but watching the cop.

"Make it worth your while," Sissie said.

The waitress stood over the table. "You eating, or what?"

The girls looked at Jaydee expectantly.

"Sure," he said. "Why not?"

Diane sat beside Jaydee in the front seat, Sissie in the rear. "I'm really sorry, Diane."

Lost a diamond.

They'd almost reached West Palm Beach and it was after midnight. "Ten-thousand-dollar ring!" Diane had wailed.

A few minutes later and it would've been too late. Jaydee was going to an abandoned warehouse he knew.

"What's your name?" Diane broke the silence.

"Destiny."

"Destiny? Your mother must've read a lot of paperback novels."

They rode with the windows down, unhurried. Jaydee had to think this through. It wasn't likely the diamond was still there, not in a place like that. Less likely it was worth ten thousand dollars.

"You know any place we could sell it?" Diane spoke again.

"Maybe."

The wolf among lambs . . .

The constant chorus of Everglades amphibians rose and fell above the rush of wind through their windows. Diane lit a cigarette, extended it to Jaydee and he took it. She lit another for herself.

"What kind of work do you do?" But she didn't really care, was gazing out her window even before he replied.

"Entomology," he said. *A word Mr. Gus used.*

They reached Canal Point and Jaydee swung south along Lake Okeechobee.

"I guess bugs are good for something," she said. "But I don't like most of them."

Surprised that she knew "entomology," Jaydee let it drop.

The diner was empty except for a man behind the counter. Jaydee pulled in, turned off the motor.

"Leave our stuff here, Sissie. Destiny will look after it."

"Lock the door if you get out," Sissie said.

When they were inside, he glanced back at the bundle, the cheap suitcase. Lock the doors?

"He has the diamond," Diane came to report. "But he wants five hundred dollars reward."

Jaydee started to open the door and she bumped it shut again. "You don't want to get in this," she cautioned. "The cops come, find out Sissie is a minor—they'll want to know where we got a ten-thousand-dollar diamond."

His pistol was under the front seat. Go in there and shove it in the man's face!

"Be best if we give him some money," Diane reasoned. "We'll pay you back out of our share when we sell it tomorrow."

He had four hundred dollars remaining. He gave her one bill. "Better let me take it all," she said. "I'll bargain, but if it takes the whole amount you'll get it back in the morning. What's a few hundred, Destiny? Tomorrow we'll have lots of money."

He gave her the cash, and as she walked away he retrieved his gun from under the seat, shoved it in his belt, tugged his shirt out to cover it.

Five minutes later, he knew he'd been had . . .

He'd never been so furious. Trying to second-guess them, he drove first north, then east. Back to Pahokee—enraged—he went as far south as Belle Glade, on around to Clewiston.

For hours he drove aimlessly, the barrel of his weapon a talon in his abdomen; he cursed aloud, intuitively taking side streets, burning rubber as he regained the main highway.

He stopped at an all-night service station. As the boy pumped fuel, Jaydee asked, "Seen two girls—one about twenty-three or four; the other fifteen or sixteen?"

"What they driving?"

"Don't know."

"Not tonight."

Jaydee got out to pay and the attendant tried to charge him tax on the amount the pump said.

"Tax included in gas sales," Jaydee said.

"Not here."

"Yes, here."

"I got to charge tax."

Jaydee drew his gun and backed him into a corner.

"You think I'm dumb? You trying to cheat me?"

"No, no, hey—I'm sorry. I'm sorry. Forget it."

Jaydee cocked the hammer, shoved the muzzle into the cringing boy's face.

"You call the cops," Jaydee said. "You do that. I'll come back and get you. You believe me?"

"Yes, sir. I'm sorry."

Jaydee snatched his change, stood menacingly over the attendant. "Just call the cops," he warned.

Driving away, he watched in his rearview mirror. But the man didn't run out to catch Jaydee's tag number. It saved his life.

Enough. He'd had all he was going to take. Violet Day controlling his life with her horoscopes, Mother taking money that was his—*his!* Now, those girls . . .

He knew this territory well, traveled it several times a year. Slicing through the Glades, the highways spread away to Fort Myers west, the town of Okeechobee north, Miami south. He tried to guess which way they'd go.

He finally decided they wouldn't have gone anywhere. To a motel in Pahokee, that would be smart. They'd thought he was from Georgia headed for West Palm Beach.

He returned to the diner, found the back alley exit they'd taken. He surmised where they had parked, then patrolled the blocks around there; all streets returned to the main. To the motels.

Which motel?

Not the one where he'd been, surely. Too expensive. Too many papers to fill out with name, address, driver's license number and auto license . . .

He analyzed the things they had said to him—setting him up, psychologically. In retrospect, it became abundantly clear: They wanted him to think they were running from the law. They enlisted his assistance— dangled the diamond for bait, appealing to his greed—it had to be stolen, where else would they get such a prize? He decided it didn't exist. Or, if it did, it was a bauble.

They would have contingency plans—suppose he'd insisted on confronting the manager at the diner? By then, Sissie must've been gone, through the bathroom window, out into the alley to get the car. Or—on foot—to a nearby motel.

Would he call the police?

Enraged, duped, and feeling stupid—would any man call the police immediately? He'd have to admit carnal motives, a minor involved, his willingness to share in the sale of a gem that *must* be stolen. *Stupid*, the cops would think.

Jaydee narrowed the possibilities to a small mom-and-pop motel. The parking lot was filled, half a dozen pickup trucks and two cars.

They worked nights. They'd sleep late.

He parked where he could see, but not be seen. Then he proved to himself what he already knew—the suitcase and bundle were weighted, filled with rags.

Okay. He slumped in the seat, squinting at the sunrise, watching the graveled drive of the motel.

He had patience—it was Sunday.

What better thing had he to do?

It was noon and he'd almost decided he must be wrong. Then Diane appeared, packing bright blue Samsonite luggage in the trunk of a late model Ford Mustang. With binoculars he carried for use in the orchards, Jaydee focused on the vehicle. *Palm Beach County* tag.

A maid moved from room to room dragging a cart behind her as she collected linens, replaced supplies.

The sun warmed. Sweat accumulated under his clothing. Waiting, watching . . .

Sissie. In shorts and candy-striped blouse, silk scarf around her hair. Diane settled in on the driver's side, donned sunglasses.

Jaydee started his motor, let it idle. He too put on dark glasses, lowered the sun visors. As they rode slowly past his position, Sissie was checking her map, Diane alert for oncoming traffic. They hadn't noticed him. Jaydee fell in behind, separated by two other automobiles.

They didn't go far—a restaurant on the outskirts of Belle Glade. Parking behind the place, they backed the Mustang to a fence, hiding the tag. He gave them time to get inside and comfortable, order their food. Then, Jaydee got the longest screwdriver in the company tool kit. He went directly to their Ford and punctured the radiator. He knelt; the green drip of liquid told him—they wouldn't go far . . .

From the back of the building, a large fan blew hot air out of the kitchen into an alley connecting one street to another. A thin, hungry dog stood on his hind legs sniffing trash barrels.

In his car again, burning with vengeance and a sense of satisfaction, Jaydee waited . . .

It wasn't long.

When they reached the Ford, Diane stretched languorously, extending her arms overhead. Through his binoculars, Jaydee saw Sissie dab ointment on insect bites. They consulted the map. He could almost read their lips.

"Home," Sissie seemed to say.

Diane slapped the map onto the dashboard and sat in the open door as Sissie ministered to her wounds.

The doors slammed. Motor started. They left by the alley. Jaydee waited for them to turn. He stayed with the main street, catching glimpses of them at crossings. When they emerged, Diane headed east.

There were two breaks in a straight shot from here to West Palm. Six Mile Bend came first. At that dogleg in the highway a lane fell away to the southeast ending at Brown's Farm near the Loxahatchee Wildlife Refuge.

With a ruptured radiator it was as far as they'd get. Jaydee let them pull ahead almost out of sight.

Years ago, dark canals had bordered this highway. That was back when the Everglades teemed with reptiles. It was common to see alligators sunning on the banks.

But today, the muck fields were no longer a rich humus almost black to the eye. Constant draining had exposed millions of years of decay and, according to Mr. Gus, the soil actually rusted, like iron.

They passed the Agricultural Experiment Station, a few black and white Holsteins sharing meager pasture with hump-backed Brahman cattle.

The sky overhead was incredibly blue, but on the horizon rising vapors formed thunderheads which would fall later as rain. The wind in Jaydee's face was warm, the pistol in his lap.

The spoor . . .

There was no connecting road.

The overheated car balked. Jaydee stopped, half a mile back. He pulled off onto the soft shoulder.

As he focused the binoculars, Diane lifted the hood. Steam rose to join the clouds. She walked to the center of the highway, turned full circle. Sissie's door opened, but she didn't get out.

He imagined their shock when he confronted them. He concocted a conversation that would follow—fumbled lies, the clumsy alibis.

What to do with them? No, that wasn't the question—*when* to do it, that was the question.

"Well, hello again," he would say.

Distantly, wavering in undulations of heat from the asphalt, a car approached from the east. Diane ran to the far side of the road, her thumb extended. The car raced past and she gave a vulgar sign with the same hand.

"I'd like to have my money," he'd say.

If they hesitated he'd end it right there.

He removed his sunglasses, wiped his sweaty brow with a sleeve.

When he reached them they would know he was omniscient, like the wind, he was everywhere.

Another car, shimmering like a mirage coming from the east. Diane waved her arms, jumped up and down.

Jaydee cursed softly. It was stopping.

Diane leaned down to talk to the driver. She pointed at her vehicle, looked west. Then, happily, she gestured for Sissie.

Damn.

But Sissie didn't come. Diane went to her car, obviously arguing, urging.

No sign of Sissie.

Finally, Diane grabbed her purse, hurried back to the waiting driver and got in.

Jaydee opened the trunk of his car and raised the lid, covering the Georgia tag with his legs, bent as if to retrieve a spare tire.

"You need help, too?" The driver slowed. Jaydee waved him away.

With his back to the departing car, he shut the trunk and watched the diminishing reflection in his rear window.

It couldn't have been more perfect.

Isolated. Their motor ruined. And now Sissie alone.

Like a doe exhausted, Sissie shifted from one leg to the other, trembling. "Easy," she said. "Easy, Destiny."

His stance lupine, he aimed the gun at her face.

"Okay, Destiny. You're really angry. I don't blame you, I really don't. Listen, okay?"

The muzzle was sighted between her eyes. She stared at it. "Destiny—please—let's talk."

He could smell her. Perspiration and unguents and cheap perfumed motel soap.

"You want your money," Sissie affirmed.

"I want my money."

"Sure you do. But Diane has it."

He drew back the hammer and it clicked into position.

"Wait-wait-wait," she cried. "There's money in the trunk. I'll get it."

She fumbled with the keys, dropped them, rounded the car. He swung the gun at arm's length to follow her.

"Double your money, okay, Destiny? Please don't point that thing at me."

But he held; rock-steady and deadly, he held—he saw himself in the car windows, face shaded by dark glasses and two days of beard.

Her upper lip hung on her teeth. She made croaking sounds, swallowing. When she lifted the lid of the trunk, Jaydee said, "Step back."

"Let me get your money."

He motioned her away with the gun.

Clothes hanging in a travel bag . . . expensive luggage—*a pistol.* He turned the snub-nosed weapon in his hand. "Were you going to shoot me, Sissie?"

"No sir. I swear it."

"But Diane would."

"Honest to god, I don't think she would. She never shot it in her life."

"What good is it if you don't shoot?"

"Scare somebody off. Two girls alone. Scare them off, sure."

Behind the spare tire he found a zippered bank bag. Inside, sorted by denominations, *hundreds of dollars* . . .

"Stole all this, did you?"

She shrugged, helplessly.

In a purse, identification: Diane Feldman's driver's license—a social security card—and this girl, according to other documents, was Patricia (Sissie) Feldman, age fifteen, Diane's sister.

"You take your money and go, okay, Destiny?"

He zipped the bank bag shut, tucked it under one arm. "All right, Sissie Feldman, you're under arrest."

"Arrest!"

"Anything you say may be used against you," Jaydee recited, lines from cops-and-robbers shows. He made her lean against the automobile, feeling her body—firm, rounded buttocks—

"You're a cop?"

"Get in the car," he said. He stuck his gun in his belt, going around to the driver's side.

"I told Diane not to mess with you," Sissie wailed. "I told her!"

"Put your head down and keep it there," Jaydee commanded.

"Why?"

He grabbed her arm, shoved her. "Because I said so."

He pulled away—there were no other cars—no houses—

It couldn't have been more perfect . . .

CHAPTER SIXTEEN

SUNDAY MORNING. Lorraine sat on the east terrace waiting for breakfast, the thick Sunday edition of the Miami *Herald* on the table. They were in the news and she felt selfish for worrying more about that than the victims themselves.

Inez Cumbie's letter had given Lorraine a feel for the woman. It was written like a poem which captivates first by cadence, then gathers new meaning with each successive reading. And out of those poetic passages came a voice Lorraine imagined to be modulated and pleasant.

Husbands enviably have a special grace regarding all yesterdays; eventually yesterdays emerge sweet and blissful, loving, utterly euphoric, with all grief only nebulous—only lovely dreams.

Then, on television, photographs of the woman added a mental picture of a gentle, kindly, caring woman with periwinkle-blue eyes, a smile flirting at the corners of sensitive lips.

There wasn't an accusing word in the dead woman's letter. But she died because of Violet Day. Inez Cumbie, Dr. Gayle Zuckerman, Arlene Mertz—the women in other cities—*because of Violet Day.*

So then, for strangers she'd never met, Lorraine grieved. It crept upon her in idle moments, jarred her from sleep, a web of sadness clinging to her consciousness.

But now the purity of her grief was altered. Now she was forced to think of herself and the potential for suffering to come.

Ken's TV appearance and the newspaper stories had had an immediate impact. The telephones rang constantly. Reporters pried, friends inquired, business associates worried. Saturday, Becky discovered the story.

"Mom! We're in the *National Enquirer!*"

"I know, Becky."

"It says Mr. Blackburn killed a man."

"I read it."

"It says a killer is after us, Mom. Is that true?"

Before Lorraine could answer, Becky threw down the newspaper. "So that's why Mr. Blackburn is here. Sniffing around the bushes like a guard dog—we hired a hit man, right?"

"Becky, please. No contrived disputes."

"Why didn't you tell me, Mom?"

Those had been Violet's very words when she telephoned earlier this morning. "Well, yes, Lorraine, you talked about a burglar alarm but you didn't say anything about a murderer!"

Before she'd finished her first cup of coffee, Tommy was on the line, damning with innuendo, heaving his famous sighs of preordained defeat.

"I realize you must be busy, Lori." *Neglecting your duties as a mother.* "With all you have on your mind, you may not have considered your alternatives." *Self-centered, thoughtless.* "It's Becky I'm thinking about now."

As if she weren't.

"I want Becky to come to Arizona, Lori."

"Becky might like a say in this, Tommy."

"Lori, she's a child. Children might insist on staying in a war zone. But that isn't a mature judgment."

The conversation ended in shortened sentences and mounting rancor. The intimation was, Tommy would see a lawyer, if necessary. *His* interest was *his* daughter.

Becky brought Lorraine back to the moment, coming onto the terrace, plopping in a chair. "I guess you saw Mr. Blackburn on TV," she said.

"Yes." With new eyes, she'd seen him.

"Pretty sexy," Becky noted.

Sexy to Sarah Greenhaw, too. Her voice husky and crooning, Aegean eyes darting like tiny green lights signaling *Go* as they caressed Ken's lips, chin and hair.

The telephone rang and Becky grabbed it. "Spookville. Little Specter speaking."

If Violet heard that . . .

"Mom, it's the Witherbees. They want me to come play tennis."

When Lorraine hesitated, Becky said, "They have a guard at the gate and he packs a pistol."

"You may go, Becky. But if your plans change, call me; *before* you change your plans, call me."

After accepting the invitation, Becky hung up and confronted Lorraine. "You're giving me mixed signals, Mom. Last night it was don't worry. This morning you want me to punch a time card. Which is it? Worry, or don't worry?"

"Be prudently cautious, but not obsessively so."

"How about Ken Blackburn? Is he prudent or obsessive?"

"I don't know what you mean, Becky."

"Is he a bodyguard, or guarding your body? Is he a guest or employee? Is he convenience, or necessity?"

Lorraine sighed so heavily it pulled Becky to her.

"Mom, you've got to level with me, okay? I can't go around second guessing what's happening. Don't you remember how it is to be a kid? Things are important that you've forgotten were important, maybe. Like sex and money—no big deal if you've got it, pretty critical if you don't. I'm under your thumb, Mom. You can sling me around with indecision, pack me off to a convent, restrict me to my room. I'm really helpless, don't you see that?"

"I do see it, Becky."

"So you got to promise to level with me. Okay?"

"Okay, Becky."

The girl kissed her, stood back. "You and me, Mom. If you want to talk, say the word. About this killer. About Dad. About Mr. Blackburn—especially about Mr. Blackburn. You know—girl talk."

Lorraine ate breakfast on the terrace. Ken was in the guest cottage. He'd come home late last night. Sleeping late today.

The story in the *Enquirer* would have been distressing, but coupled with Sarah Greenhaw's show, it left Lorraine feeling vulnerable. The newspaper gave the impression Ken had always been a rogue cop. Another shorter item described Violet Day, Lorraine and Becky. The mention of Becky was the most unforgivable part of that.

But the TV show was more directly aimed at Violet Day. Ken worked here, he'd admitted. Grew up here. His mother was part of the household staff, he'd said, making it sound so impersonal.

If Lorraine's reaction was indicative, Ken had won the admiration and sympathy of his audience. He'd stated his case without apology, but with regret and sensitivity. He was photogenic, had charisma, a quality theater people call "presence." When he spoke, his tone was masculine, commanding.

When he looked into the camera, speaking to the wanted man, tears rose in Ken's eyes, his face taut, *but for the grace of God . . .*

When he tried to draw comparisons between himself and the brute he sought, it was an absurd attempt—and yet, last night when she reconsidered it—this morning still thinking about it—

Ken's performance had changed the way she perceived him. He could have said they were a "second family." But he didn't. He might have mentioned things they'd shared; were there none?

What had he felt as a child living on these grounds? This was a home that was not truly home for him, she realized. Yes, he could roam the compound, even swim in the pool if he asked permission. He was *accepted,* with certain limitations perhaps, but accepted nonetheless.

"Mom?"

How long had Becky been standing there?

"You've been staring at Mr. Blackburn's cottage for an hour, Mom. Why don't you take him some coffee?"

"I thought you were going to play tennis."

"See the racket? See the shorts? I came to check out. Mom, is there anything I can do?"

"No, darling."

Alone again, Lorraine watched Ken's door. If he glanced out his window, he could see her. If so, why didn't he come up? Unless he felt uninvited. Could it have been that way when Ken was a child? Uninvited meant *isolated.*

When he spoke on television of bad dreams and unheard cries, it rang with sincerity. *Nobody cared . . .*

She wished she could deny that. But until Ken's recent return, how many times had she called or written him? Had she ever been to his mother's home in nearby West Palm?

Marian had raised her and yet there had never been correspondence between them. After Lorraine married Tommy, she'd lost track of them. Of course, Ken was the child of an employee and—

That's how he saw himself. *Son of the nanny.* He must've sensed a distance to keep, the shallow depth of their concern.

Defensively, Lorraine reminded herself she'd been conditioned to this lifestyle. Servants were as essential as electricity and indoor plumbing. Except when absent, about as appreciated. *Like sex and money*, Becky had said.

Ken had described his father as a strict disciplinarian. *Hard-nosed cop, tough, dependable*—nothing warm about that.

Meantime, his mother had been with Lorraine.

She reassessed their dinner party a few nights ago. Ken had been ill at ease, trying to smooth the way between his estranged parents. His repayment was probably the emotional currency of a lifetime. *Incidentally, Kenny, where are you spending the night?*

At the time, it seemed romantic. Abel with his arm around Marian, Marian in her red silk dress with white corsage.

But what about Ken?

In a single breath, the dominating father stole away Ken's mother and expelled his son from their home. Unintentionally cruel, but cruel nevertheless.

And Ken? He reacted as he always had, absorbing the rebuff, accustomed to being maneuvered to suit the needs of others.

"Miss Day?" Annie, ready to clear away the breakfast remnants. "May I get you anything before we go to church?"

"I'd like to take Mr. Blackburn coffee and cinnamon rolls, Annie. Tell me where they are and I'll get them."

"No, ma'am. I'll get it."

"Have you time, before church?"

"Yes, ma'am. Plenty time!"

Loyalty came with a sidecar: *obedience.*

Lorraine had married Tommy with such strong expectations—demands, really. She expected him to move where she wished, buy the house she preferred, take trips at her whim and where she desired. Even her pregnancy was dictated by Violet—to ensure that Becky would be born under signs most favorable.

Approaching the finality of divorce, in a sudden moment of desperation, Lorraine had said, "I love you, Tommy!"

"I know, Lori. But you don't need me. I've decided that love is really a degree of the need two people have for one another. You don't need me at all. If I try hard, maybe I won't need you."

Annie brought a breakfast tray: linen napkins, china cups, hot cinnamon rolls.

"If there's nothing else, Miss Day, I'll be leaving now."

Tomorrow in the Violet Day offices there would be a publicity party designed to promote the charitable Crystal Ball. Reporters would be searching for a story that had nothing to do with charity.

Everything had changed. Yesterday was eons past.

Lorraine carried the tray toward Ken's cottage.

She no longer deluded herself that it was a friend she went to see—it was a stranger she wished to know. Maybe she'd tell Ken about Tommy's theory—mutual need was the definition of love.

Then, she'd tell him how much she needed him . . .

Ken knew by the set of Abel's jaw how angry his father was.

"There's some coffee left if you want it, Dad."

Lori had brought it, woke him with tender strokes, murmuring his name. A dream, Ken had thought. She spoke of mutual need and of long respect.

"This is where you and your mother lived?"

It was Abel's nature to stall before a confrontation. Whether to heighten the interrogation or to gather courage, Ken was never sure.

"Yes."

Abel pulled open sliding glass doors and stepped out onto the patio overlooking the ocean. A Bahama squall was building, the surf rising. "A man would spend a fortune for such a view," Abel said.

"Dad, what's wrong?"

The thud of collapsing waves muffled seagulls' screaming in the wind.

"What does a man learn in one of those college criminology classes?" Abel asked.

"Sociology. Statistics. Forensic science."

"Criminal psychology?"

"That, too."

"So a man would learn from a book how a bad guy thinks. He'd learn about the value system of such a criminal. He'd learn about peer pressures and childhood heroes who were role models for such scum."

"What is it, Dad?"

"But even if he didn't learn from a book," Abel said, "a cop learns such things on the street."

It was a reprise from childhood. Not yet certain how he'd erred, Ken could only wait. He sank into a deck chair and poured the last of the coffee.

"The *National Enquirer* did what you'd expect," Abel said. "You can't control them. But that TV show."

TV show.

"So you wanted a spit shine on your armor, a chance to bite back," Abel said. "TV is a good way to do it. Safe way to attack without interruption. Tell your side of things. I can understand."

He looked at Ken steadily. "Am I right?"

"Something like that."

Abel's pipe made tiny gurgles as he sucked it. "College education," he said, as if it were humorous. "Bad Guys 101. But you know, Kenny, a classroom will never teach what a man can learn walking the beat."

"Dad, why don't you get it out so I can follow you?"

"I think you follow me, Kenny. Deep down inside, you must have some notion of what you've done."

"Spell it out," Ken said.

"You looked that sick bastard in the eye—I know you—but for the grace of God, you said. What did you mean, exactly? You wanted him to know he had a kindred spirit?"

"Actually, I hadn't intended to say that. I—"

"What did you suppose he was going to do?"

"My intention was to shift his focus to me. I intend to catch him."

"I'm sure you will. Somebody will. Meantime, he goes to a telephone book and looks up 'Blackburn.' He doesn't know to look up Violet Day, 'Guest Cottage.' What does he find? *M. Blackburn;* with your mother's address on 37th Street."

"I want him to direct his anger at me, Dad."

"He will. I didn't learn it from a book. Gut feeling. Getting to you may become very important. Obsessive-compulsive, a shrink might say."

Ken forced himself to sip coffee, control his expression.

"You got a telephone call this morning," Abel said. "If I'd answered, I'd have known what it was, but your mother got there first."

Ken's last breath went as if into a vacuum.

"Male," Abel reported. "Slight Southern drawl. Low voice. Didn't seem to be disguising it. Asked for you. Marian said you weren't home. Like I say, if it'd been me I'd have known to deny I knew you. Your mother doesn't understand police work. After all these years, she still thinks we're little boys playing games. She asked if he'd like to speak to me instead. He sent you a message."

"When did the call come in?"

"Thirty minutes ago."

"Caucasian?"

"That's my guess. Flaunted his vocabulary. Imperative . . . indubitably . . . words like that."

"Did you call Herb Leibowitz?"

"No, I didn't. I figured you and I better go see what it's about. You expected this, didn't you?"

"No, I didn't."

"Books don't teach street smarts," Abel said, coldly. "See, Kenny, I'm surprised it happened so quickly, but I'm not surprised it happened. Of course, if I'd known what you were going to say on television, I'd have had a tape recorder set up. As it is, we lost that chance."

"The message?"

"He said he left something for you—a warehouse."

Ken stood up to go and Abel looked him over. "I'd change clothes. That floral shirt is too busy to look good on TV. You want to make your best impression, don't you?"

As Ken changed, Abel lit his pipe again. "I told your mother she should go to my place in Miami. She says no, this is home. She has a pistol, she says. Never fired it. Didn't know it was unloaded and can't remember if she ever bought ammunition. Surprised to learn it has a safety. But she has the pistol, mildew on the grip and a spider's nest in the barrel."

Abel swore softly in Spanish.

"I'm ready, Dad."

Abel looked him over again, making a mockery of it. "That's better," he said. "You TV stars have to think about image."

Torrential rain pelted the metal roof, reverberating through the empty warehouse in a roar. They had to shout to be heard. It was like working in a drum.

Ken knelt beside a horribly disfigured female torso. *Mid-teens*. He flexed a finger, testing rigor mortis.

"How long you guess?" Herb Leibowitz yelled.

"Couple of hours!"

Her clothing was draped on a nearby wooden flat, the kind used to transport goods in a storage area. If she had worn panties, they were gone.

"Could've been a copycat," Herb hollered.

Could've been . . . *but it wasn't*.

"Not much similarity," Herb suggested.

The victim was younger. No note to Violet Day, no evidence a letter had been attempted. The victim was not tied to a chair. She had not been shot.

Ken stood up, turned in a slow circle. Water poured from the eaves. Reporters huddled near a personnel door, inside, out of the elements. Walking the warehouse, Ken pointed to tire tracks in silken dust. Herb nodded.

Good tread. That too broke the profile. The assailant should be driving an old car in poor condition. The man Ken had profiled would have attacked his victim on familiar grounds—

"Copycat," Herb shouted. "Got to be!"

It was the classic asocial/disorganized scene. The body had been mutilated after death. She'd been postured to shock the viewer, an attempt to horrify.

Inscribed on the inside of her thigh in black block letters: FOR KEN.

Madmen could be flexible. The profile was not infallible. Sometimes the modus operandi changed . . .

As suddenly as it began, the rain ceased. Their ears rang with the memory of it. They tended to shout unnecessarily.

"Herb?" a forensic examiner motioned them over. "The shorts and blouse have a dressmaker's label. It says, 'Especially Designed for Diane Feldman.' "

"Tag it and bag it."

"That's the name in the blouse," the examiner said. "In the shorts it reads, 'Sissie Feldman.' "

Jolted, Ken turned to stare at the corpse.

The face was discolored, distorted, death by strangulation.

He knelt, seeking any trait he remembered . . .

There was a scar in the left eyebrow. He visualized her lifting that eyebrow with exaggerated suggestivity, "Know what we mean?" Sissie had inquired.

Then, the fingers—the fingernails chewed to the quick.

Ken squeezed the lobe of her ear—she'd worn earrings that, on consideration, seemed expensive for a girl in her straits.

"Herb, I think I know this girl."

Suddenly, the scene was no longer impersonal residue from a vicious assault. This was the same minor—the same child—*Jesus!*

Ken started to stand, but staggered. Herb grabbed his arm.

"Jesus, Herb—"

"It can't be the same man," Herb said. "He saw you on TV. That's the connection."

As if that would make Ken feel better. As if that explained anything!

He swallowed repeatedly, fighting the urge to vomit. He saw Sarah Greenhaw and a film crew; police officers looked away. A technician covered Sissie and her two bare feet protruded.

Everybody so professional. *Insensitive.*

Herb had a hand on Ken's shoulder. "Put your head between your knees," he suggested.

Ken experienced waves of cold and heat simultaneously. *God. Damn the bastard, God!*

"That's a shock," Herb sympathized. "Finding you know somebody this way. A real shock."

The thought of Sissie, young and lovely, in the hands of someone so cruel and sadistic—Ken glanced back at the blanket, the thrust of her knees made twin tents over the torso.

The killer enjoyed that.

Creating this obscenity—

He enjoyed it . . .

CHAPTER
SEVENTEEN

"IT'S A SMALL WORLD isn't it, Herb?" Captain Wayne Dilling flicked cigarette ashes at a wastebasket. "Our resident specialist is not only in the thick of it, he now knows the victim. What are the chances of that? One in a million?"

Ken met his gaze.

"Goes on TV," Dilling said, "tells us he *knows* this man. My wife says, why aren't you using this brilliant detective?"

"I'm available," Ken said.

"Hell, you're unavoidable! Question is, what are you doing and why?"

"I told you. I've been hired by the Violet Day organization to establish protection for them. Their best protection is apprehension of the criminal."

"These two girls—Diane and Patricia Feldman," Dilling consulted Herb's report. "Also-known-as Sissie Feldman—they pulled a scam, took you in."

"That's right."

"It *is* a small world," Dilling mused, coldly.

"Captain, my association with the department doesn't have to be official. But I can help you."

"Blackburn, if your act were clean, I'd be the first to welcome you with open arms. But I have this nightmare. You're out there playing the vigilante—maybe shooting this sonofabitch—the ACLU and every other activist group in North America would be on us like wet cement. We don't need that; we aren't going to have it, either."

"Captain," Herb said, "I told you what the FBI reported. This Dr. Joanne Fleming—"

"Joanne?" Ken questioned. "What?"

"She says," Captain Dilling said, "if we have you, we have the best. However, she's coming down later this week. The FBI recommended her."

"She's good," Ken stated.

"She insists you are as good as it gets," Dilling said. "Then come to find out you two nearly married. Like I say—small world."

A long pause ensued. "Herb wants to bring you in," Dilling rocked in his chair. "Says we ought to be using any help we can get. Suppose we do that, Blackburn. Unofficially, because it can *not* be official. Is that understood?"

"Yes sir."

"Now you've got this psycho sending notes on the body of his victim—"

"Captain," Herb interceded, "we think Diane Feldman is dead. The two girls worked together. But if she isn't, Ken believes she could describe the killer."

"You need Blackburn for that?"

"I want him to go over the transcripts, every interview. We've talked to hundreds of people, at the shopping malls, the neighbors and friends of the victims. Maybe I'm missing something."

"Assuming you were involved, Blackburn, what would you do?"

"With the power to alter things?"

"For the sake of discussion."

"First, I'd create a task force. I'd have them study several articles by John E. Douglas and Robert K. Ressler of the National Center for the Analysis of Violent Crime."

"The subject is lust murder," Herb offered.

"The purpose being," Ken said, "to make these investigators familiar with the type personality we're after. They should know the kind of man he is—how he's likely to behave and interact with people."

"You have faith in this profile thing," Dilling said.

"Absolutely! Ressler, Douglas, Ann Burgess and several others with the FBI Behavioral Science Unit have created an invaluable tool for the cop on the street—but it's useless unless understood."

"Granted that," Dilling said. "Then what?"

"Part of the pattern of the asocial/disorganized felon involves the area of attack. Our man kills here in West Palm—he lives here! But he also killed in Fort Myers and Orlando. What would take him to those areas often enough to feel familiar with the territory? His work, maybe."

"A traveling salesman," Herb suggested.

"Visiting relatives," Dilling said.

"In any event," Ken continued, "this must be home. This is where he is, most of the time. I'd have someone call on businesses that have service routes to Fort Myers and Orlando. We need a computer, too."

Dilling listened, but was noncommittal.

"Send a man to the juvenile courts," Ken said. "Talk to the old-timers. Somebody might recall kids who got in trouble years ago."

"That'd be thousands, Blackburn."

"That's true! But when the task force understands the mind of the criminal, they'll know the answers to listen for. This man, as a child, did certain things a case worker would not forget. Cruelty to animals and playmates, setting fires; I've been through all that with you before."

"Anything else?" Dilling queried.

"Somebody knows his history," Ken said. "When I go on TV next Saturday, I'll lay it out piece by piece; his psychological background, warning signals in adolescence, the kinds of family and social stresses around him. Maybe somebody will recognize his profile and call us."

"Anything else?"

"Yes. I need a permit to carry firearms."

"Unequivocally no, Blackburn."

"Captain, I've been hired to help guard the Violet Day compound and offices. I need the weapon to keep my job. You have no legal basis for refusing a permit."

Dilling mashed the butt of his cigarette into an overloaded ashtray. "Blackburn, you've taken a highly visible stance in this. You've presented yourself to the public as an expert. So far every frightened senior citizen is pulling for you. They're scared and going to be more so. You agree?"

"Yes, I do."

"But if you get a license to carry a weapon, continue to present yourself as the Lone Ranger, and somehow, even if accidentally, you kill this felon—do you know what will happen?"

"I think so."

"Those same grateful citizens will hear another side of the tale," Dilling warned. "There will be charges of ineptitude on our part for allowing an unstable citizen to carry a gun—you follow me?"

"Yes."

"They'll see you serve time or go bankrupt fighting in court, Blackburn."

"I realize that."

"Okay." Captain Dilling sat back in his chair. "Get him a permit, Herb. Share any information you deem expedient."

"Thank you, Captain," Ken grinned, despite himself.

"If you disappoint us," Dilling said, "we're going to hurt in a lot of places."

"I won't disappoint you."

Dilling nodded. He didn't seem so sure.

The Violet Day staff had assembled in Donna Wheeler's office, a glass-enclosed cubicle overlooking the mail room and computer center. In suites above, the press had gathered, awaiting Lorraine.

"Ken," Lorraine said, "you know my mother."

"I thought you weren't due back until the end of the month."

"I cancelled the tour!" Violet exclaimed.. "What else could I do? Horrid stories in the newspapers—comedians making us the butt of jokes! If we become a laughing stock, Lorraine, it will hurt us for years to come."

"What kind of jokes?" Ken asked.

"We all know Violet Day," Major Drummond intoned. "There's bad news and good news. The bad news is Violet was struck by a train. The good news is—she knew it was coming."

"If that's the worst," Ken said, "we're all right."

"Oh, it gets much worse," Major stated. "Variations of the same theme, but bloody and insensitive."

"How many are up there?" Lorraine questioned Cynthia Peebles.

"Sixty-two guests at last count."

"Lori," Ken said, "we need to talk."

"Ken, I'm thirty minutes late now. Damn the press!"

On Donna Wheeler's desk lay the front page of a London tabloid: *The seer who predicts world events seems helpless to guess the motive of a diabolical killer* . . .

"We can't keep them waiting," Violet fretted. "Whatever the outcome, we must go up, Lorraine."

"Hold on," Ken said, firmly. "You can't do this without a plan—it *will* be a disaster. Let's think a minute."

"I think I'm ill," Lori said.

"Violet," Ken softened his tone, "it was a mistake for you to cancel your tour, rushing back. It accents a bad situation and that's exactly what shouldn't happen. This man will be overjoyed to discover he has caused you to alter your life. It's what he's been wanting."

"Be that as it may," Violet said. "I intend to stay."

"All right. We'll treat your presence as if it were planned. You can introduce Lorraine as the new Violet Day."

"Yes," Violet agreed. "That's good."

"Having done so," Ken advised, "step back and don't say another word. If they ask you questions, no matter what they ask, defer to Lorraine."

He took Lorraine's shoulders, "Be positive, Lori. Control this. There are ground rules for confronting a hostile group of reporters."

"Believe me, I'm listening."

"Don't give negative impressions. If several people speak at once, select the question you want to answer. What's the purpose of this Crystal Ball?"

"Charity. But they won't ask about charity."

"Pretend they did. As if one of the voices had posed the question—answer it with the information you want divulged."

"Yes," Violet said. "That's good."

"Formulate your replies in such a way they can't be refuted," Ken counselled. "For example, they'll probably ask if you think your guests will be in jeopardy. What do you say?"

"I—he—there's no reason to think this man would hurt my guests."

"That's not credible," Ken said. "You should say, 'We are taking all necessary precautions, we've hired all the necessary security people.' "

"They'll ask what precautions," Major said.

"To which you say," Ken tutored, "it's not wise to reveal the security measures but—and be emphatic—*believe me*, my guests will be secure."

"The celebrities may be." Major played adversary. "What of the general public the next day?"

"Again, I say," Ken took Lorraine's role, "it is unwise to reveal the measures we've taken. But you may be assured, even if this man were in the crowd—there would be nothing he could do."

"Good show," Major applauded.

"You're beautiful, Lori," Ken encouraged. Her dress was soft and feminine, Royal blue under fiery red hair.

"If you hit a snag," Ken led her toward the elevator, "direct their attention to me while you recover. Anything relating to logistics, your guest list—tell them you don't want to answer for obvious reasons of security. You're going to do fine, Lori."

In the elevator, Ken continued. "You won't yield to terrorist tactics. Think of the agencies who depend on this for funding . . . mention other charitable functions in Palm Beach that might falter. You are the vanguard. You are fulfilling a public need. So this isn't strictly public relations—it has value to the community."

"That's good," Major spoke behind Ken. "Good, Lorraine."

Forget publicity for charities served. When the elevator doors opened, sixty-two reporters from fashion, society, gossip and news departments turned like a predatory school. Lorraine moved through them, preceding Violet. Each guest wore an identification tag. "How's the food?" Her gaiety was mock, talking too loud.

"Miss Day," somebody shouted, "are you going to cancel the Crystal Ball?"

Ken mounted the platform at one end of the room. "Ladies and gentlemen, for anyone who might not know, may I introduce the lovely Violet Day!"

"I want to welcome each of you—"

"Louder!"

Violet cleared her throat, lifted herself regally. The old pro on a familiar stage. "Welcome! Our theme this year is Caribbean, with a touch of voodoo just for fun. But as most of you already know, it will not be my party. As of now, I am no longer Violet Day. My daughter is. And here she is, my friends—the new Violet Day!"

For a few moments, Ken dared to believe the drinks and hors d'oeuvres had mellowed the audience.

"The first night is for our honored guests, the celebrities who donate items for auction," Lorraine said.

Violet followed Lorraine's words, inadvertently mouthing the speech as if by ventriloquism.

"The next day is for the public," Lorraine said. "Last year, we raised nearly half a million dollars which benefited such benevolent groups as—"

"Miss Day?" a reporter interrupted. "Have you seen the *National Enquirer?*"

Well, damn. Lorraine paused. "Yes, I saw it."

"Maybe we could hold questions until Miss Day completes her opening remarks," Ken said, loudly.

"No," Lorraine took a breath. "Let's get this out of the way. Folks, I am very distressed about what has happened."

"Is the story true?"

"As far as I know, the story is true."

Notebooks riffled. Tape recorders activated. Microphones thrust at Lorraine as TV lights glared.

"We did not know the people involved in these tragedies," Lorraine said. "They came to our attention only when we received letters directed to Violet Day. At that point, I contacted Ken Blackburn, a longtime friend, a former police detective. He agreed to investigate and found the body of Inez Cumbie, the retired West Palm school teacher. Since then, Mr. Blackburn has remained to help us cope with a senseless and dreadful chain of events."

She didn't wait for questions. Beginning with their first notice of the letters, Lorraine brought the reporters to date, revealing everything that had transpired.

When she finished, a brief lull followed.

"What affect has this had on you, Miss Day?"

"I am grieved, of course. We all are. But we can't allow a madman to halt a worthwhile project. Too many organizations depend on the Crystal Ball for their annual budget. Should other charitable balls be cancelled, too? Palm Beach is known for generosity."

"The *Enquirer* posed a provocative question," somebody said. "If Violet Day can predict natural disasters, why didn't she predict this?"

"Because," Lorraine replied, "when we make a prediction, it is founded in data we've researched. Deteriorating roadbeds of a railway line suggest an accident may be imminent."

Violet blanched.

"If we learn of inadequate sprinkler systems in a particular hotel," Lorraine said, "or we hear they are plagued with labor problems and an overworked staff, we know it invites tragedy. We assess earthquake faults for tremors. Our craft is science—research first, celestial tendencies a strong second.

"You're saying the stargazing is hokum?"

Violet's chin quivered. Major held her elbow.

"I'm saying no such thing," Lorraine countered. "I'm saying we *know* what we know because we are well-founded in data. But to deny the pull of the stars is to ignore the tides and the eclipse of the moon or sun. Celestial influences have been recognized for centuries—and my great-grandmother was one of the pioneers who turned from purely heavenly to more earthly considerations."

"Will your guests be safe?"

"We have taken security precautions. Believe me, they will be safe."

"What kind of precautions?"

"It would be foolish to reveal them," Lorraine smiled. "But *believe* me, everyone will be secure. If this terrible man were standing in the crowd, he could do nothing."

It was like being on a battlefield amidst the whine of shrapnel. There was no interest in any good that would come from the Crystal Ball. No recognition of monetary goals and what their sums could accomplish. The reporters ignored those comments, returning to the macabre, almost hopefully.

"Have you consulted the stars for a reason why anyone would kill people, forcing them to write you?"

"As I said," Lorraine attempted, "we first begin with a fact, then we turn to the heavenly charts. We know nothing of the person doing these things. We have no idea why. The police assure us his crimes are sexually motivated. What more can I say?"

Moments later, it was over.

"The shortest press party ever," Donna Wheeler observed.

"Don't worry about it," Cynthia consoled. "You did the best you could under impossible circumstances."

Visibly shaken, Violet kissed Lorraine lightly, patted her shoulder in quick strikes. "We'll meet at home," she said.

Lorraine pulled a magnum of champagne from a tub of ice, selected two glasses.

"All right, people," Mrs. Wheeler clapped her hands, "let's clean up and get out of here."

Lorraine led Ken to her office. He shut the door, popped the cork. They drank morosely.

"My mother is very upset," Lorraine said. "I've destroyed the mystique in horoscopes."

"Maybe you strengthened it," Ken suggested. "It gives me more confidence knowing there's logic involved."

Lorraine reached toward him and Ken took her hand.

"If you think this afternoon was rough," Lorraine spoke to herself, "wait until tonight . . . "

It was after dark when Ken and Lorraine arrived at the family compound. A cooling breeze swept in from the ocean, drawn by ascending thermal currents on land. Mockingbirds sang evensong. Still sitting in the car, Lorraine sighed.

"As a child," she said, "I knew the seriousness of a transgression by the setting Violet selected for a reprimand. On the terrace, it's hardly worth mentioning. If it's her suite upstairs, I'm in for a motherly rebuke. But if she's downstairs in the den—"

Ken squeezed her hand. "I was proud of you this afternoon. You did well; you'll handle this, too."

Lorraine sighed again. "Okay. Darn it. Let's go."

"Lori, I'll see you in the morning."

"You leave me and you're dead meat."

"This is a family matter, Lori."

"Dead meat!"

Ken paused, reached to kiss her.

"Mom!" *Sotto voce* in the gloom. "Be careful!"

"Becky? What is it?"

"Dad is here!"

"Becky—where are you?"

The girl stepped from shadows inside the four-car garage. "I thought I'd better warn you. Dad's inside."

"Warn me about *what?*"

"Mom, I'm not naïve. Here you sit with your motor hot—"

"Becky, don't be ridiculous."

"Okay! Don't say I didn't try. Hi, Ken."

"Hi, Becky."

As the girl strode toward the main house, Lorraine groaned. "What is Tommy doing here?"

She answered her own question. "Break out the repeaters; circle the wagons."

The den. Violet rose from behind a massive antique oak desk. She wore a lavender exercise suit, matching running shoes, and a diamond ring that refracted light from the Tiffany lamp.

"Why didn't you call me back about Becky?" Tommy demanded.

"I'm sorry, Tommy. Things have been so hectic."

"Did you speak to Becky about going to Arizona?"

"Not yet. Tommy, you remember Ken."

Ken started to speak, but the man turned away.

"Lorraine," Violet began, "I want the birth dates of the victims of this atrocious criminal. I intend to run a chart on this sordid affair."

"Violet," Lorraine labored, "it wouldn't be smart for us to interfere. The police will do their jobs."

"Interfere? I intend to help them."

"With horoscopes and planetary influences? Don't you see how that looks? If the newspapers hear of it, their derision will only get worse."

"Tommy, darling," Violet's tone altered, "would you mind brewing tea? You know the kitchen, don't you?" Then, "One thing is obvious, Lorraine. Something has shaken your faith. There were certain statements you made this afternoon—about the data collection, the way we work—"

"Violet, I'm sorry, I really am. But this is no time for hocus-pocus, as Becky calls it. We're dealing with a real-life, honest-to-god tragedy. I cannot stand there and play the mystic with reporters."

"Mystic?" Violet said.

"Yes, mystic! As if there were magic formulas and alchemists percolating in a laboratory! This is a time for rock-solid sincerity. No nonsense."

"Nonsense," Violet repeated the word, looking at Major. His expression was inscrutable. "Have I anyone to blame but myself, Major?"

"No one," he said.

"Obviously I have failed somewhere."

"Violet," Lorraine implored, "you haven't failed. I admit I didn't appreciate the mechanics of astromancy before, but now I do. I'm impressed!"

Violet bit her lip, paced a step away and back again. Her blue eyes darted about the room, coming to rest on Tommy as he reentered.

"The tea?" she asked.

"I told Annie. She's working on it."

Returning to Lorraine, Violet's expression flowed to disappointment. "I'm not going to waste time defending myself and my work."

"Violet," Lorraine insisted, "it isn't required!"

"A skeptic is best won from the inside out," Violet stated. "Never you mind that mankind's struggle to foretell the future is as old as society itself—certainly older than any system of science."

Lorraine attempted to speak and Violet shushed her.

"Thirty-two thousand years before Christ, Cro-Magnon man read the sky and marked the seasons by notches in a bone," Violet said. "In that time, the benefit was mundane. Primitive man could use celestial readings to follow migrations of animals, plot the growth of plants. What the heavens told him was invaluable."

"Violet, I know that."

"Yes, you know," Violet responded. "But you don't *feel*, Lorraine. 'Let there be lights in the firmament of the heavens—let them be for signs and for seasons.' Genesis 1:14."

"Violet—"

"Lorraine, I wish to speak. May I?"

Lorraine sat down, glanced at Ken.

"Never you mind," Violet continued, "that astrologers have read portents of the heavens with great accuracy for centuries. Nigidius, Ptolemy, Nostradamus—and more recently, Evangeline Adams, who predicted in 1931 that the United States would be at war in 1942. Edgar Cayce—"

"Violet," Lorraine said, shortly, "a history of prophecy won't convince anybody of anything."

"Quite true, Lorraine. I'm sure we could list a comparable group of reknowned disbelievers. But for what it's worth, thousands of people live desperate lives, wounded by disease and poverty. It is not possible to do an individual horoscope for each of them—so our newspaper feature is the next best thing, general though it may be. Millions of readers turn to their horoscopes for the slightest hint of encouragement."

"Yes, yes," Lorraine said. "I realize the value."

"It is not given to me to understand how astrology works," Violet said. "But my life is proof of it. Your life, too. Read the words you write, Lorraine! Tommy is Virgo: not especially tall or robust, unless Sagittarius or Jupiter are important influences. Strong and capable of hard work, nevertheless. Always busily involved in assessing his surroundings and relationships . . . deeply sensitive, he presents a cool exterior that is difficult to penetrate . . . there are two types, the neat and the careless—Tommy is neat—he demands perfect order and harmony. Lorraine, I didn't write that to fit Tommy. Tommy fits what is written. I knew before you married him—can you deny that's the description of Virgo?"

"No."

"And a description of Tommy is Virgo. I could go around this room, sign by sign—and it is invariably so."

"I know, Violet. It's astounding."

"Yes," she said. "It is. For reasons I do not comprehend, it is astounding and true. So, I will not spend my time defending myself and the work we do. Better that I employ my talents in a productive way. Kenny?"

"Yes, Violet?"

"I want these birth dates," Violet said. "Can you get that for me?"

"I think so."

"If only we knew the birthday of the murderer himself," she said. "But, we don't. Another thing, Kenneth—I will need the letters from the victims, the originals, if possible."

"It isn't possible, Violet. The originals are in Washington at the FBI labs. Besides, they're evidence and the police won't release them."

"Copies must do, then."

"We have copies," Ken said.

"Good, good," Violet massaged her hands and smiled at Major Drummond. "We will banish the skeptics, Major."

"If anyone can, Violet, you can.

"And so we shall," she vowed.

CHAPTER EIGHTEEN

JAYDEE'S MOTHER was on the telephone, sitting at the kitchen table with his oldest sister, Lavern. The room was hot and fetid, doors and windows locked. The newly installed phone came with an extra-long coiled line that could be stretched to any part of the kitchen. Jaydee stepped over it, looking in the refrigerator for beer.

"Have you a pedigree on that one?" Estelle queried someone afar, clamping the receiver to her shoulder with head cocked.

"Who's she talking to?" Jaydee asked Lavern.

"Cat breeder. California."

"What's this?" Jaydee pointed at an array of cat-fancier magazines spread on the table.

"Mama's going to breed cats."

"Cats? We have cats!" They prowled the counters, rubbed his legs, mewing for food.

"Seal point," Estelle repeated what she was told. "Write that down, Lavern. Three hundred dollars plus air freight to West Palm."

Lavern tossed her short, bronze hair, writing on a legal-size pad. There were more pages filled with similar notes.

"Lavender point Siamese," Estelle repeated a long distance quote. "Four hundred, with papers, excellent pedigree."

"Cats," Jaydee said. "Who cares?"

"People pay good money for purebred cats, Jaydee. You'd be surprised."

His mother still wore her bathrobe. Jaydee dodged stalagmites of manure, moving to the counter to make a mayonnaise sandwich.

"Blue point," his mother related, "four champions in the line—a thousand dollars."

A thousand dollars for a cat? Jaydee went into the living room, hurled felines off the couch and turned the pillows. The cartilage in his ears hurt. He'd spent forty dollars for a *Sony Walkman* radio so he could continue listening to the news even while working.

"Jaydee," his mother called, "I want these cats fed."

He turned on the television and raised the volume.

"We're up to our ankles in cat shit, Jaydee."

"I'm eating!"

He'd been pleased with news reports earlier in the day. *Grisly, gruesome, sadistic.* They gave more details, but they didn't reveal Sissie's name, yet.

For the first time, CNN carried the stories. Mr. Gus said CNN was heard all over the world.

". . . press conference at the Violet Day offices in West Palm Beach . . . "

Jaydee sat up, expectantly.

There she was. Violet Day herself. But a moment later, the new Violet Day stepped into the scene.

"Jaydee, did you hear me?"

"I heard you!" he screamed. "Goddamn it."

His mother's rejoinder was surprisingly mild. "But I didn't hear you answer me, Jaydee. I never know if I'm getting through your hard head."

He raised the volume again. They could hear it next door.

" . . . received letters written to Violet Day. At that point I contacted Ken Blackburn . . . "

A shot of the detective, standing near the old Violet Day. A cat sniffed at Jaydee's sandwich and he backhanded it across the floor.

"Jaydee, will you please turn that down?" Lavern stood in the door. "We're trying to talk long distance. Jaydee, do you hear me?"

"Will you shut up?"

"Turn it down, Jaydee."

He'd missed some of the dialogue. Lavern reached the TV and decreased the volume.

"You ought to pay attention, Lavern," Jaydee said. "Somebody killing women. Could be you."

They were listening, now.

" . . . can't allow a madman to halt a worthwhile project . . . "

Estelle clucked her tongue. The telephone was ringing. "Get that, Lavern honey."

" . . . our craft is science—research first, celestial tendencies a strong second . . . "

Jaydee's mother came to sit beside him. She recoiled. "Jaydee, you need a bath if you go out tonight."

"Mother, will you shut up?"

" . . . we've taken security precautions . . . "

"Poor Violet," she said. "Dreadful."

Lavern called from the kitchen. "Mama, it's a breeder in Chicago calling collect. Should I accept it?"

"Yes, Lavern." But Estelle didn't hurry, watching the news as she sidled toward the kitchen door.

" . . . police assure us, his crimes are sexually motivated . . . "

Then it ended. Jaydee stood up, abruptly. "You made me miss some of it. Damn you!"

"Well, Jaydee, ex-cuse me. Ex-cuse me for breathing."

"Goddamned cats." Jaydee kicked at one. "Next time the news comes on, keep your mouth shut."

"Well, Jaydee, ex-cuse me. Excuse me for—"

He crossed the living room, through the kitchen to the door. Locked. He yanked it, fumbled, snatched it open.

"You think this lock will keep him out? You think he can't get in? Wait until he sticks a knife up you—"

"Jaydee, where are you going?"

"—spills your guts, with your heart still beating—"

"Mama," Lavern said, "this man is long distance. Jaydee, if you're going to talk filthy just get out of here."

"Know what he does to them?" Jaydee taunted. "Have you heard what he does?"

"No, and I don't want to hear," Lavern snapped.

"They scream and cry and beg—"

"How would you know?"

"It'd be me stopping him," Jaydee said. "Him and me—you'd be screaming, trying to hide."

He yanked the door shut behind him. The glass chattered in the frame. Looking back through the curtain he saw the women still as statues for a moment. Then his mother took the phone.

What had Violet said? The new Violet—what did she say? Something about security precautions.

" . . . *believe* me, everyone will be secure . . . "

He'd caught only part of the next sentence.

He could do nothing.

That's what she said.

Could do nothing . . .

Could do nothing . . .

Two Violet Days now; that detective, Blackburn. Hundreds of guests.

They raised good money at the Crystal Ball, he knew that. The Palm Beach newspaper covered it every year.

Rich people and famous—selling clothes they wore in a movie, or something from their homes. From the rooftop of a nearby condo, he'd watched through binoculars—people bidding good money for junk.

He'd forgotten his beer. Out of cigarettes.

Jaydee drove to Palm Beach, taking the Middle Bridge. He swung north along Ocean Boulevard.

Then, with a shock, he realized he was following the new Violet Day and her detective friend.

They turned in—disappeared down a driveway.

Jaydee stopped, peering out the windows in fading light. He didn't see anything new. No guards at the gates.

He considered going in there, right now.

" . . . security precautions . . . "

No. Not now.

He wasn't stupid.

But he could get in. He could fix them, if he wished.

He shifted into gear, moving away.

He could get them all, if he wanted to.

Not sure how. But he could.

That'd show them.

Twice Jaydee had been out the Belle Glade highway to check on Diane and Sissie's Ford Mustang. He had the keys and Diane's driver's license with the Juno Beach address.

She wasn't there. Wasn't going to be, either. The doors of the rambling Spanish-style house were sealed with warnings not to trespass. *For Information: Internal Revenue Service.*

The second time he went back to the Ford, the trunk had been jimmied, the luggage gone. So he'd missed Diane. Not that he cared. He'd made a profit, that was sure. The zippered bag held nearly two thousand dollars cash.

Now, driving through downtown West Palm, ten o'clock at night, his nerves crawled.

Department-store windows reflected the coming season. Halloween pumpkins set in pastoral scenes, witches on broomsticks, ghosts and goblins—well-dressed mannequins followed his passage with glassy stares.

He stopped at a small Cuban bar to buy cigarettes. It was a place Mr. Gus liked to frequent, with dark booths and a mature clientele. Mr. Gus didn't like noisy, boisterous youths, but he didn't like the senior citizens any better.

"Cut the federal deficit," he'd say, "stamp out the old folks."

Social security saved, he meant.

Jaydee took a booth in a far corner, ordered draft beer.

Grandmother.

The thought seeped into his consciousness unbidden. He never thought of her deliberately. It depressed him.

Well, *she* didn't. But he couldn't think of Grandmother without thinking of Granddaddy.

The only happy time in his life was then. Granddaddy took him fishing, taught him to string a lure; they lived in a "stick" house on the canal, the building held aloft of the marshy terrain by tall cypress pilings.

Anytime his mother was absent she sent Jaydee and his sisters to stay with Granddaddy.

His beer arrived and Jaydee said, "I asked for a pitcher."

"Coming."

He bumped ashes off his cigarette, glancing around at other patrons, but only dimly aware.

The last time he'd cried was when Granddaddy died.

"It's the best thing, Jaydee," his grandmother had reasoned. "Granddaddy lived too long."

Maybe he wouldn't have died if they'd taken him to a hospital. But that cost good money.

He'd detested his grandmother for letting it happen. He hated his mother for concurring.

"Hell, Jaydee, everybody's got to die sooner or later and Granddaddy is no exception!" That's what his mother said.

Lavern didn't even weep. Lolly had, but not Lavern. Lolly cut flowers in the park to put on Granddaddy's grave and for a while she would go over to the cemetery and talk to the air, as if Granddaddy could hear her.

Years later, when Jaydee told Mr. Gus about it in a rare moment of confidence, Mr. Gus said, "Cut the deficit, Jaydee—people need to die when it's time."

He didn't like Mr. Gus after that.

There'd been a thousand dollars insurance. It had to be divided among the heirs. Jaydee's share was a few pennies over a hundred dollars, but he never got it. Grandmother had to pay for the funeral, she said. The cheapest one cost more than she had.

When she died, nobody wept. Nobody cut flowers or talked to the air. There wasn't anything they had to say. Except "Just as well"—Mother said that—"everybody has to die, and Grandmother is no exception."

Besides, she'd lived too long . . .

Jaydee swilled the beer, smoked cigarettes; his flesh was a hive of bees in motion.

Another thing Mr. Gus didn't like in his long list of things was rich people. Sopping up the cash flow, he said. Getting the best for less.

To prove his point, he suggested Jaydee drive by a plush grocery store where the wealthy shopped, and compare prices to markets where poor people bought. "Rich people's prices are lower," he'd claimed.

It was true.

Jaydee didn't care for him, but Mr. Gus didn't lie.

The only thing Mr. Gus liked less than an old person or a rich person was an old rich person.

"Me," he said, "when they force me out to pasture, I'm going to kill myself. Do it as a kindness to the world. None of this sapping the economy for me."

"More beer?" the proprietor inquired.

"Got beer."

"Something to eat?"

"No."

"See the sign? Booths reserved for two or more."

"I see two empty booths," Jaydee said.

"Because there aren't two or more."

Jaydee thought about that a moment. Then, moving to stand, he deliberately knocked over his pitcher spilling beer across the table and floor. With a theatrical recovery he hit his glass and it shattered.

"Ex-cuse me," he said. "Ex-cuse me for breathing . . . "

Mr. Gus rubbed a thumb over his coated tongue to moisten it and turned a sheet on the clipboard. "Witherbee place is on Ocean Boulevard. Near Violet Day."

Jaydee was filling the truck with ethyl.

"Take a spray can," Mr. Gus directed. "Mrs. Witherbee wants her ferns sprayed."

"With what?"

"Water."

Rich and dumb. Paying to water plants.

"Careful with that gas, Jaydee. Half a cup of fumes can explode like dynamite. Cap the tank when you finish."

Mr. Gus hop-stepped to change stance, easing his bad leg. He went down a list of duties, the route to take.

Jaydee had already washed the truck. Mr. Gus didn't allow a dirty truck in Palm Beach. "It advertises a sloppy operation," he said.

Last night, he dreamed he'd captured Violet Day, the old one, and somehow he held the younger. He'd made them read their horoscopes before he hurt them. Then, as he finished, the detective arrived— horrified and disarmed. In his dream, the man had gone insane with grief.

Jaydee realized he'd hollered in his sleep. His mother woke him, calling his name.

"Bad dream, hon?"

Just as he was dozing again, she said, "Me, too."

She'd stroked his back, patted his bottom.

"Jaydee, I smell gas," Mr. Gus said.

"Spilled a little."

"A little is all it takes. Run water over that spill and wipe it dry before you go."

Mr. Gus put a pressure spray can in the cab. "Forty pumps max," he said. "Don't be lazy about it. More than that and it puts too much pressure on the gasket."

There'd been practically nothing on the news this morning. *Investigation continuing*, the announcer said. No mention of Sissie's name.

Jaydee bought several newspapers, scanned them. The Tallahassee *Democrat* and the Orlando *Sentinel* noted the murders, but with less detail than local papers.

He might have thought people weren't noticing, but Mr. Gus carped about his wife—

"Can't take a pee without company," he'd said. "Be glad when they catch the sonofabitch."

Yet, pedestrians continued their peregrinations—a new word he'd learned on CNN this morning. It meant travel from one place to another.

"Guess I'll be peregrinating," Jaydee said to Mr. Gus.

"Did you cap the fuel tank?"

"Yes."

"Shut off the fuel pump?"

"Yes."

It was sunny, with fluffy clouds riding a high breeze. Jaydee planned his route to pass the Violet Day mansion several times, as if he'd looked for the Witherbees and couldn't find it. In Palm Beach, it didn't pay to loiter. The cops checked your driver's license, made sure your permit was current and the decal properly posted on the windshield. They hovered, the cops did, and doted if anybody complained.

There was activity on the Violet Day grounds. Men surveyed the perimeters, brick masons were adding to the gatehouse. Precautions in progress.

Jaydee detoured to a condo he serviced weekly, taking the elevator to the roof. There, in broiling midday sunshine, he focused his binoculars and studied the Violet Day compound.

He saw nobody but the gardener.

Finally, last on his list, the Witherbees—to water the ferns.

"Jaydee, you say?" the old woman questioned.

"With ORGRO."

"Service entrance to the side."

"I came by the side. The guard let me in."

"You want—what?"

"Water the ferns."

"The ferns!" She stepped away, letting him enter. The portico was cool, arched doorways, high ceilings.

"I want them misted," she said.

"Yes, ma'am."

"That thing make a mist?" she indicated the stainless steel tank strapped to his shoulder.

Jaydee demonstrated, with the first fern. The spray was so fine it fell like dew.

"That's what I want," she said. "Ferns you don't water. Ferns you mist."

"Yes, ma'am."

There were dozens of ferns—on the patio, around the oblong swimming pool. Jaydee had to refill the cannister repeatedly, pumping precisely forty times to create proper pressure.

As he worked, the lawn sprinklers activated—the spray there was equally as fine.

The mist rose in gossamer swirls, creating miniature rainbows over the perfectly tended lawn. Their system was a good one—not as good as Violet Day's, but more than adequate for the area. Around fenced tennis courts, the moisture fell precisely where it should.

"You misted the ferns on the gallery?" Mrs. Witherbee was following him, checking up.

"Not yet."

But she knew that.

"Don't forget the galleries."

In a few moments, the smell of moist soil and foliage was a heady mix, the backyard several degrees cooler as vapors spewed.

And then it hit him.

A way to do it.

"Not too much," Mrs. Witherbee called from below. "It's starting to drip from the bottom. Mist it, mist it."

Jaydee got so excited he nearly fell from the ladder.

"Misty, misty," the woman cried.

He twisted to look over the yard behind him. Like fog, almost—

And it quit.

Birds broke into voice. The lawn gleamed as if bejeweled. The plants seemed greener, more lush.

"That's fine, young man. Thank you."

He was trembling with this concept, this *brilliant* idea.

But it had to be tested. He wasn't stupid. Things could go wrong, so he had to be sure.

Jaydee loaded his equipment into the truck and drove off the grounds. Across the street, slightly south of the Witherbee's men at Violet Day's were setting markers—planning a fence, maybe. Taking precautions.

Where could he go? Some desolate area where he could work without fear of intruders.

He was impatient with traffic, rocking his body behind the steering wheel.

He remembered the Belle Glade road, the dogleg at Six Mile Bend, the deserted lane to Brown's Farm near the Loxahatchee Wildlife Refuge.

It was so late Mr. Gus had gone home. Jaydee locked the truck and dropped the keys through a mail slot into the office.

He took the portable sprayer with him. At a country service station he bought one gallon of gasoline.

Thirty minutes later, he passed over the Six Mile Bridge. Diane and Sissie's car was gone.

He turned south, the lane dusty and unpaved. The smell of muck-lands and fallow fields dried his nostrils like talcum powder.

The sun hung low, the highway hidden by a stand of bamboo. Cattle egrets foraged for a final tidbit before dark.

Jaydee pumped the sprayer forty times. When he squeezed the nozzle, the smell of gasoline overpowered all other aromas.

Good.

He locked the nozzle open, laid it on the ground. Fumes accumulated, spreading.

Jaydee lit a cigarette—tossed the match.

Instantly, and with surprising volume, the earth erupted in a fireball, licking at his face, driving him backward.

Jaydee scrambled away, shivering—
Yes!
It worked. Beyond his most fervent hope—it worked!
Two Violet Days . . . the detective . . . hundreds of guests . . .
It couldn't be more perfect!

CHAPTER
NINETEEN

"THE STATE LAB and FBI sent back the victims' letters," Herb Leibowitz reported to Ken. Annie delivered a carafe of coffee and they sat on the terrace watching workmen go about their labors.

"The Inez Cumbie letter is the one that'll nail the killer," Herb said. "They found his prints on her letter, in her kitchen and at Gayle Zuckerman's house. He makes no attempt to cover himself."

"Because he's convinced he can't be caught."

Herb drank coffee, watching laborers. "This security system. Curiosity—what's it going to cost?"

"About three hundred thousand."

"No way but grade-A, when you got money," Herb said. "Even a rich man's java tastes better."

A few minutes earlier, Ken's father reported that he'd selected six men for guards from dozens of applicants.

Herb spoke, gazing away at the ocean. "This lady professor from FSU is coming in tomorrow morning. You have a problem with that?"

"No problem; should there be?"

"So you can meet with her?" Herb asked.

"No problem."

"Captain Dilling wants you two for positive about this profile. Reconcile any differences. Then, he wants Dr. Fleming to meet our task force and lay it out. That agreeable?"

"Fine."

"Unless maybe you have something to say?"

"Can't beat Joanne."

Herb tasted his coffee again. "We got a computer. Slow, but it'll do."

Except for Christmas cards Ken hadn't contacted Joanne in several years. He dreaded meeting her now.

"Two men from the Palm Beach County Sheriff's department," Herb listed his task force. "Five from City, two from Palm Beach City, one from the Florida Bureau—"

When he thought of Joanne, Ken ached—not for what was but—

Would he have changed anything?

"Eleven, including me," Herb concluded. "Experienced homicide—hound dogs, all of them."

Ken nodded, half listening.

"We've interviewed hundreds of possible witnesses," Herb said. "I got transcripts, if you want to see them."

"Any leads?"

"Nothing."

Workers scaled extension ladders, installing remote-control video cameras, adjusting the arc of their revolutions. Tommy Linden arrived in Violet's Mercedes and Herb took note.

"Mind a personal question?" Herb asked.

"What?"

"The ex, right?" Herb nodded his head sidewise toward Tommy. "He complicating things for you?"

"No. Why is that personal?"

Herb looked at him without expression. "Maybe it wasn't."

"Tommy and I were two sides of a triangle when we were kids. We're old friends."

As if to refute it, Tommy walked past without greeting. Herb stroked the tip of his nose, deliberately preoccupied.

"Anything else, Herb?"

"Guess not. Are you doing another TV thing Saturday?"

"Yes, why do you ask?"

"This lady professor wanted to know. Said she saw you on cable news."

"Did she say anything else?"

"Nothing important."

"Like what?"

"Said you'd gained an ounce or two. Little gray at the temples. Kind of thing a lady would say."

If she were a former lover . . .

Reading his expression, Herb said, "It breaks up my day, you know— watching you operate."

Herb turned to leave and stopped, snapping his fingers. "You wanted copies of the letters to Violet Day. I forgot."

"I'll get them tomorrow."

"Eight o'clock too early?" Herb questioned. "To meet Dr. Fleming?"

"That'll be all right, Herb."

"She's staying at the Brazilian Court here in Palm Beach. She suggested there. If that's convenient."

"Brazilian Court it is."

Herb shook his head, bemused. "No way but grade-A," he said.

As the detective departed, Abel approached. "Any more coffee?"

"Help yourself, Dad."

Abel sat down, legs spraddled. "Won't be an inch of grounds we can't see when they finish this job. It's a good system."

"Expensive—it better be good."

A moment later, Abel said, "Did you know these folks own a Lear–35 jet? The pilot says it carries 6000 pounds of fuel; at 6.7 pounds per gallon, that's 895 gallons. Buck-fifty a gallon. Plus the salary of the pilot and copilot. Insurance, maintenance, hangar rental—sometimes weeks go by and it sits there. Other times, the pilot said, they call him in the middle of the night to fly all over the world. He once flew to Boston to bring back lobster for a dinner. I wouldn't worry about the cost of a security system."

"Nobody wants to waste money, Dad."

"This whole island is fantasy land," Abel said. "The Palm Beach *Daily News* is known as 'The Shiny Sheet.' Good name for it. I read an article about that paper. It said 19 percent of their subscribers serve as

company chairmen or presidents; 34 percent serve on boards of directors; 54 percent claim a net worth of more than a million dollars! I
wouldn't worry about the cost of anything."

"Okay, Dad."

"Fantasy land. They named their junior college after the movie actor,
Burt Reynolds."

"Good for Burt."

"An estate recently sold for eighteen million dollars," Abel said. "If
you want to see hoity-toity, drop by Worth Avenue at the Esplanade.
Bonwit Teller, Saks Fifth Avenue—these people spend three hundred
thousand the way you and I spend a grand."

"Okay, Dad."

"You!" Abel said. "You're at a place men dream of."

"What do you mean?"

"Heir apparent to Major Drummond."

"Dad—"

"Let me tell you! Drummond drives expensive cars, has priceless art
works and he flies that Lear–35 anytime he wants to."

"Dad, stop poking around in Violet's personal affairs."

"Drummond is a powerful man, Kenny. But he's walking away cold
turkey, turning it over to Lorraine. She needs her own Major Drummond. The salary stinks, but the perquisites are good."

Abel stood up to talk to a contractor.

Poor Lori . . .

The thought might have made Abel laugh, but it saddened Ken. The
other morning when she brought coffee to his cottage, she'd spoken
almost desperately. She *needed* him, she'd said.

Ken watched Abel, resenting his father's disdain.

"Annie," Ken called. "Could you bring me a phone?"

Abel turned and winked.

Ken dialed Lori's office. Cynthia put his call through.

"How would you like to have a quiet, romantic dinner for two?" Ken
asked.

Lori giggled mischievously. "Sounds delicious."

"No talk about anything that doesn't make us smile," Ken
said.

"That does sound good."

"Pick you up at the office after work."

"Five-thirty. Ken? Thank you."

When he hung up, Abel was grinning.

Ken resented that.

Lorraine was waiting when Ken arrived at the office. His attire caught her by surprise. He wore shorts, tennis sneakers and no socks. His shirt was strictly tourist, with palm trees and coconuts.

"You remember The Hangout?" he began.

"Yes?"

"And those grilled-cheese sandwiches with salty potato chips and dill pickles on the side?"

A shiver of anticipation surprised Lorraine. She hadn't felt that tremor since the last time she'd gone to The Hangout, during high school.

But more than youth had passed.

Ken parked under a streetlight where loitering youths made Lorraine worry whether the car would be safe. They walked half a block and paused.

"This is the place isn't it?" Ken questioned.

It was. But it wasn't. The name had changed. Lorraine recalled the resonance of recorded music, the pulse of laughter and familiar shouts—that much remained, but of a different tenor.

Inside, her eyes becoming accustomed to the dark, she knew Ken was having second thoughts.

Along the soda-fountain-turned-bar, long-haired men with coal-black eyes assessed her. They wore blouses opened to the navel, heavy gold chains and earrings.

Oh, great. The place was now a Cuban bistro for singles. "La Bamba" reverberated from the jukebox. The smell of sawdust and beer were pungent.

Seeing their predicament, a bearded heavyset man stepped from behind the bar. "Need a table?"

"Something romantic," Ken attempted.

The bartender led them to a rear booth and waited for their order, despite a sign that read "No Table Service."

"Remember those grilled-cheese sandwiches they used to make here?" Ken asked the bartender. "Big salty potato chips and dill pickles that made your saliva squirt."

"Don't serve food here."

"How about draft beer?" Ken asked, lamely.

"Dark or light?"

"Light."

Ken squinted, peering into shadowed recesses. "Was it always this noisy?"

"I think it was."

Men were staring at her. Lorraine shifted her position, knees toward the wall. She covered her diamond ring with her other hand.

"Ken, would you like to go someplace else?"

"Might as well. No cheese sandwiches."

They paid for beer they hadn't tasted, returned to the car.

This time, Lorraine drove, Ken riding with his hands folded in his lap. When she turned south on Lake Worth Avenue, he asked, "Where're we going?"

"The Bahamas Club."

"I'm not dressed for it."

"We'll sit where we can't be seen."

A doorman parked the car. The maître d' followed Lorraine's instructions, placing them well away from everyone else.

"Our specialty for the evening is—"

"I'll tell you what we want," Lorraine interrupted. "Four grilled-cheese sandwiches."

"Yeah!" Ken brightened.

"Lots of salty potato chips—"

"And dill pickles."

"Not kosher," Lorraine advised, "dill. The kind that makes saliva squirt."

Soberly, the waiter took her order. "To drink?"

"Chocolate milk shakes."

"I'm sorry, madam—"

"Beer, then. Domestic."

Ken moved his chair with stiff-legged hops to sit beside her. He took her hand, looked into her eyes.

"I'd like to kiss you," he said.

"I wish you would."

His lips were pleasantly soft, the tip of his tongue touched hers. He started to withdraw, then kissed again.

When he sat back, he said, "I've always wanted to do that."

"I'm glad we waited," she smiled. "It's always better when you wait . . ."

* * *

Lorraine grinned at her reflection in the dressing table mirror, humming as she brushed out her hair. Dinner had been the world's most expensive grilled-cheese sandwiches and they'd eaten three each!

When they arrived home a guard stopped them at the entrance. Laughing in the dark as she and Ken walked arm-in-arm, Lorraine caught a glimpse of Violet on a balcony, saw the curtain move in Tommy's bedroom.

After Ken left, Becky came to sit on Lorraine's bed. "I don't want to go to Arizona with Daddy. He says I must. Must I?"

"He's worried about you, Becky."

"He treats me like a child."

"You are a child."

"What could happen to me here? We'll be living in a prison—that horrible wall and guards with guns."

Lorraine scrutinized her own face in the mirror. She didn't feel nearly forty. Did she look it? "Becky, do I look—healthy?"

"Sure."

"Do you think of me as old?"

"Mom, you're going to bed alone. You look fine."

Lorraine swept her hair with a brush, trying a new style.

"Actually, we could crash in the airplane, or get hit by a car," Becky said. "I'm safer here."

"Becky, it's your decision."

"Is it really?"

"I admit, I don't see your objection. It could be a nice visit with your father."

"Then, I'll go to Arizona for Thanksgiving or Christmas."

"You could go then, too."

"Mom, don't you see what Daddy's doing?"

"He's trying to protect you, Becky."

"He's using psychological warfare! He's suggesting you have failed as a mother, putting me in danger, somehow. Because you failed, he had to come to my rescue. We shouldn't fall for it."

"Becky, I don't think that's fair."

Tommy was down the hall in a guest suite, waiting for a decision. Kicked about by Violet and ignored by Major, he'd been insulted with innuendo—and hurt, knowing Ken and Lorraine had a—"thing," Tommy bitterly called it.

"All these years," Tommy had declared at breakfast, "he's been waiting for his opportunity and here it is."

"Tommy, that is idiotic."

"Even when we were dating he was always along."

"He's your friend, Tommy."

"Obviously," Tommy had sneered. "Lurking, lusting. Tell me, Lori, did you two have an affair while we were married?"

"Tommy, I regret so many things about you and me, but infidelity is not one of them. I regret the way I treated you, the things I said—"

And suddenly they were crying, holding one another.

"Mom? Are you all right?"

She was lost in thought, remembering this morning.

"I love you, Lorraine," Tommy had cried. "I'll never stop loving you."

"Then why did we divorce?"

His answer was pure truth. "We'd begun to destroy ourselves. I'm not sure why. I wish it weren't so."

"Mom, are you all right?" Becky repeated.

"Yes, Becky. Tell your father what you've decided."

"Should I go?"

"For the right reasons, yes. If you want to share a part of yourself in these fleeting moments, go. If you would like to have memories of your father at this point in your life, yes, go."

"I don't want to, Mom. I wish I did, but I don't."

"Tell him that, Becky."

"He's so pitiful!"

"Do *not* tell him that."

"Could you tell him?" Becky pleaded.

"No. You must do it."

"He could stay here, couldn't he?"

"Tell him that, too."

"But he won't." Becky stood up, slapped her nightgown to flatten it. "I feel so guilty and I hate feeling guilty."

Lorraine pulled the girl to her lap.

"You want me to go, don't you, Mom?"

"Becky—"

"It must be difficult kicking off an affair with a teenager peeking out of the shrubbery."

"Becky, that's silly talk."

"Can't kiss without cutting your eyes."

Lorraine laughed.

"Mom, are you going to be okay?"

"Of course I am."

"Kids at school say the killer is really after us."

"They don't know that."

"They say he cuts women open and—awful things."

"Becky, they're going to catch this man. There are a lot of people looking for him. It's only a matter of time."

"And I'm one more thing to worry about."

"Yes, that's true."

"I know." Becky stood up, tugged her garment to loosen it.

"Whatever you do," Lorraine said, "I'll agree."

"I know, Mom. You're good about that."

Becky kissed her and practically ran to leave the room.

Beyond open French doors, a symphony of crickets played alto to a bass section of frogs. The smell of the sea was pleasant to perceive.

Lorraine went to the balcony without thinking, then ducked back when a guard looked up.

Instantly, she was indignant over this loss of privacy. Now she not only had to beware the public, but the people who protected her from the populace.

She saw lights go off in Ken's cottage and wished she were there, curled around his body.

She heard Becky's voice from Tommy's balcony, the father's even-tempered reply.

She yearned for the simplicity of workaday living, lives devoted to survival with the weekly anticipation of a paycheck.

No, she didn't.

Lying to herself.

She had everything—and nothing.

The guard coughed in the dark, a reminder he was still there, hopefully alert.

He coughed again, harder, longer.

"Do you have a cold?" Lorraine called, impulsively.

"No, ma'am. Swallowed a bug, I think. Ought not to walk with my mouth open."

Now *that* was simplicity.

CHAPTER
TWENTY

WHEN LORRAINE came down for breakfast, Ken was on the terrace talking to a woman in her mid-forties, attractive, well-dressed.

"I still think of Marcie as sixteen," he was saying. "What ever happened to her boyfriend, Charlie?"

"He's bumming around Europe trying to find himself," the woman said. "He and Marcie correspond occasionally."

The woman noticed Lorraine before Ken did and indicated as much with a flourish of a hand.

"Lori!" Ken rose. "I'd like you to meet Dr. Joanne Fleming from Florida State University."

Joanne Fleming extended a hand with an explanation: "Ken and I are very dear friends from long ago."

"Joanne is here to help profile the murderer," Ken said. "She's staying in Palm Beach at the Brazilian."

"How nice."

"I made arrangements to meet Ken there this morning," Joanne explained, "but discovered the restaurant isn't open this early. I didn't know how to reach him, so I gambled and came over. I hope you don't mind."

"No, of course not. Please sit down, Ken." He did so, on the very edge of a chair.

"I'll ask Annie to serve breakfast," Lorraine offered.

"No, no, no," Ken protested.

But Joanne smiled:

Ken hunched his shoulders. "Coffee, maybe."

After an awkward pause, Ken grinned through a grimace. "It was a nice surprise finding Joanne here. We haven't seen one another in—"

"A long time," Joanne said.

Nothing so cold as an old flame extinguished. But Lorraine thought she saw Ken raking the coals. "You look terrific, Jo."

"I've gained weight. Marcie gave me an oven mitt with a lamb appliqué that says, 'Ewes not fat; ewes fluffy.' "

"Ewes certainly not fat," Ken laughed nervously.

Joanne turned to include Lorraine. "We're after a concensus on a profile of the criminal. Independently, at the request of the West Palm police, I prepared one which was compared to Ken's."

Ken's attitude altered, "Are we in disagreement?"

"Not necessarily. But I'd like to know how you reached some of your conclusions."

Becky's appearance halted conversation. Introductions completed, Becky said with single-minded determination, "I'm going, Mom. I went in last night to say no, and I'm going! Daddy raised his eyebrows, up in the middle, down on the ear side. I couldn't refuse. The words fell out of my mouth and I stared at them like I'd thrown up. I can't believe it."

"It may be a wise decision, Becky."

"Becky reminds me of Marcie," Joanne said to Ken. Then, to Becky, "Marcie is my daughter. She was about your age when I knew Ken, years ago."

Becky hesitated, respectfully, and faced Lorraine again.

"If you tell me to stay, I will. I really want to stay. I'll never catch up my lessons at school."

"Taking a trip?" Joanne inquired.

"I have to go to Arizona until they catch the man who's trying to kill us."

Pleasantries vanished. "You've made the right decision," Joanne said.

"But Mom wishes I'd stay, don't you, Mom?"

"Naturally, Becky—"

Reassured, Becky said, "It won't be long, though. Then we can be together again."

"Jo," Ken asked, softly, "where are we in disagreement?"

"We'll discuss it later, Ken."

"Minor, or major?" Ken persisted.

"Maybe we really should leave now," Joanne addressed Lorraine. "I'm only here for the day and we do have things to discuss."

"I'll see you this evening, Lori." Ken bent low. She thought he was going to kiss her, but he didn't.

Amenities completed, Ken walked toward his car with Joanne holding his arm. She halted by a bed of flowers, as if to admire the blossoms.

"Don't worry, Mom," Becky said. "On her best day she never looked as good as you, and she knows it."

Lorraine tried to laugh, but choked on it.

"Every time you looked away," Becky reported, "she sneaked a peek at your legs and behind. You've got great legs and Ken likes your behind."

"Becky—you say the most outlandish things."

Becky munched toast, eyes narrowed, watching the charade of posturing adversary Joanne Fleming stooping to smell a bloom.

"Nah," Becky said. "You got to love first, before love begins with her. That's the type she is, Mom."

"Becky, really—"

But she was enjoying it and Becky knew it.

"Bucket of bolts," Becky said. "Shake, rattle and roll."

Lorraine pulled the girl close enough to kiss.

"Besides," Becky concluded, "he doesn't love her; he loves you."

"Oh?"

"He sneaks peeks too. Not just the legs and behind, either. He looks at *you*."

"Thanks for the information," Lorraine joked. "When I have him in my power, you let me know."

"Oh," Becky said, "you've got him now. Probably had him when you were kids. But he's like Daddy. He's afraid to let it show."

Seeing the seriousness of Becky's expression, Lorraine stopped smiling.

"One big difference between Daddy and Ken, though—"

Becky saw her father about to join them.

"You won't be Ken's boss," Becky lowered her voice. "He won't let you push him around."

"Morning!" Tommy said, cheerfully. "Did Becky tell you her decision?"

"Yes, Tommy. I think it's a wise move."

"Good!" He kissed Lorraine's forehead lightly. "Then we'll probably fly out of here after the weekend, if you have no objection."

Becky was watching Ken open the car door for Joanne.

"Who's the woman?" Tommy asked.

"Her name is Joanne Fleming," Becky provided. "She's a psychologist or criminologist or something."

Tommy looked from Becky to Lorraine.

"An old friend of Ken's," Lorraine added.

"Old and very *dear* friend," Becky added.

"Hm," Tommy shook out a napkin, dropped it in his lap. "She didn't look that old to me."

Becky laughed. "Daddy—you're so cute!"

A waiter adjusted venetian blinds to block the glare of sunlight across Ken's table. "Bloody Mary, Jo?"

"That's fine."

On their way to the wharf-side restaurant, they'd talked more as strangers than intimates, recalling people they once knew. Jo's daughter, Marcie, was an attorney now working with abused children in Tallahassee. Jo's former husband had remarried, "beginning a new family." Ken wasn't interested, and Jo didn't want to talk about it, but these were the topics they held in common.

Now, with drinks before them, Ken squinted his eyes, watching pleasure craft ply Lake Worth; the water seemed jet black under a cloudless sky.

"Where do we differ on the profile, Jo?"

Ken swiggled his drink with a stalk of celery. *God she was beautiful.* Those round brown eyes were unwavering.

"Maybe we don't differ," she suggested. "You have him down as asocial/disorganized and so do I. He exhibits nonsocial characteristics but he's primarily asocial."

The waiter came for their order. Joanne requested West Indies salad, chilled shrimp and remoulade dressing.

"I didn't want to discuss this in the presence of Lorraine Day and her daughter," Joanne said. "Because the major problem I have is with you, not the profile."

"As long as we agree on the profile itself—"

"The profile is not all there is to this," she said. "I saw you on cable news. You seemed on the verge of revealing the profile technique. You won't do that, will you?"

"As a matter of fact, I intend to."

"Which will ensure a change in the man's modus operandi."

"At this point, we have him pegged."

"Until he's imprisoned he is not pegged."

"Hey," Ken said, "I didn't come to fight."

"You are letting your emotional involvement endanger lives, Ken."

To disguise irritation, he sipped his Bloody Mary and studied a passing yawl.

"You were in Tallahassee when a newspaper quoted my profile." She referred to the serial killer who got away. "The murderer saw it, resented it and came after Marcie and me. You know how this man will respond."

"It turns his focus on me, Jo."

"Ken, I understand why you've done what you have. I even sympathize with you. You wanted a public defense of yourself."

"You've been talking to Captain Dilling."

"Yes, I have. But any psychologist would see your motive."

"Jo, I don't want to argue."

"Somebody needs to say this to you, Ken." She leaned nearer, "Somebody who cares for you."

"Okay, Jo. I did it to redeem myself. But it will also focus the killer on me. He's already called my mother's home."

"Which endangers her."

"It's a contact!"

"All right. Let's think about the future victims. You've incited this man, accelerated his violence."

"Typically asocial," he said.

"Except now his impulse is not altogether sexual—the act is sexual, the impulse isn't. The last victim was a statement to you. It was also a warning. Lorraine Day is wise to send her daughter out of state."

Face flushed, she paused as food arrived.

"Asocial believes the world is against him," Joanne resumed, softly. "He sees himself as an 'evil seed' beyond the norms of society. He can't bond to anyone, emotionally."

"I know that, Jo."

"I know you know it, Ken. That is what makes a public relations attempt unforgivable. You must not spell out profile techniques publicly. It serves no purpose."

"All right."

"I'm going to say things you know as well as I," Joanne continued. "You need to remember that the only pure emotion a lust murderer feels is frustrated rage. Everyone is against him. These murders are a way to punish the world."

Ken nodded.

"We know what his upbringing was, the assaults to his ego—so, yes, you know the nerve endings. But heaping your abuse upon abuse he's already endured is not productive."

"Okay. Damn it. Okay."

She touched his hand. "Remember he's probably above average intelligence. He may fixate on you, murdering as a way to punish you— making you responsible for the crime. That's the way he feels about it, anyway. The world is responsible, not him."

"Your point is made, Jo."

A long lapse finally became uncomfortable and Ken realized they were staring at one another.

"Do you love Lorraine, Ken?"

"Why do you ask?"

"She loves you." A flash of bitterness soured a smile. "You are a good criminologist, Ken. You are a fair psychologist. But when it comes to women, you always were a bit obtuse."

She checked her watch. "I have to meet Herb Leibowitz at one o'clock."

"I'll give you a ride."

"No. I'll get a cab. Let's part company here. May I buy your meal?"

"I can handle it."

"Ken, if there's ever anything I can do—"

"Thanks, Jo."

"Try writing now and then, you lug. Marcie and I are fond of you."

"I'd say I would, but you know better."

She kissed him on the cheek and held him down with her hand on his shoulder. "Stay wary of this man, Ken. He has the instincts of a predator. You should not underestimate him. If he can hurt you or anyone you care about, he'll do it."

Watching her walk away, for an instant Ken visualized those hips beneath him, her hands caressing his back.

"Anything else, sir?" the waiter inquired.

"No," he said. "I've had enough."

Up on the terrace, Lorraine, Violet, Major Drummond and Tommy Linden were having evening cocktails. Ken could hear the music of family conversation. Beyond them, unnoticed and efficient, Abel spoke to one of the guards.

The small living room of Ken's cottage seemed claustrophobic. He opened the sliding glass doors, pacing anxiously. Herb Leibowitz had promised to come by after Joanne met with the task force. That was hours ago.

Ken sat in a deck chair, put his feet on the railing and jiggled away nervous energy with pumping legs. The sun had set, creating a deep purplish glow that brought everything into brilliant display. Vermillion waves curled to collapse on the pink sandy shore. Seagulls were jagged dabs of a painter's brush against a canvas of rose-red clouds.

He forced himself to think those descriptive thoughts, trying to dispel haunting suspicions.

After leaving Joanne this morning, he'd come back here to reexamine everything. Defensively, he'd concentrated on the profile, as if to be correct in that made him correct overall. He'd begun with the fifteen-page FBI crime analysis reports, the first step to the profile procedure. He'd studied his own observations, the critical classifications of nonsocial and asocial.

Things he needed to hear . . . from somebody who cared . . .

He'd tried to convince himself that Joanne was jealous of Lori, still resentful over a love affair that ended—professional pique, surely! She'd been more intent on attacking him than the profile itself.

Yet a mature man must question himself as well as his detractor.

He knew psychology, it was his stock in trade. He also knew intellect alone cannot penetrate the darkly foreboding secrets the mind hides from itself. If intellectual rationalizing could get past the self-protecting walls the mind erected, there would be no need for psychiatrists. He was well aware that Joanne probably saw him better than he saw himself.

He had a sudden, unexpected vision of Dr. Gayle Zuckerman's home, the small sign which named it Id & Ego.

The id was the part of the psyche hidden in the unconscious. It was the primitive well where instinctive energy begins. From the id came those animal impulses which seek satisfaction in the pleasure principle. But before the beast of impulse could be unleashed, it was modified by the ego and superego. Thus was born civilized man, who tempered the rage of desire with thoughts of what others may think of his actions.

Facing that smirking murderer in Dallas, hatred and rage rose from Ken's id without a second of reflection, and he killed the man.

Why? A thousand times—why?

It destroyed his career, warped his life, altered his personality. In that alley, at that instant, the primordial demand for vengeance was so overwhelming that his ego and superego failed him. He'd fired until the hammer fell on spent shells. And why?

Vengeance. For the assault on mankind; for the victims who could not avenge themselves! *Punishment.* For crimes so bestial nothing but death could be just. But not for vengeance and punishment alone, he knew that. The courts would dally, lifting the murderer to the status of celebrity. Under the pretense of justice, lawyers and judges would create endless appeals as they selfishly clung to the maker of headlines.

To convince himself that he'd dispassionately dissected his motive, Ken had thrown out *vengeance* and *punishment,* substituting the word *pity.*

The lust murderer was a deformed personality. He was emotionally disfigured by forces beyond his control, a freak who couldn't help himself.

So, killing him was a charitable act. The eradication of a suffering animal. Had he lived, he would have been subjected to the pokes and probes of his keepers, like a specimen under a microscope. They would peel his personality, seeking the defective id, studying the damaged ego and superego which had failed to filter heinous impulses.

But no, it wasn't pity. Ken could find no iota of pity within himself. What he felt, when he analyzed it, was sickening, disgusted, unadulterated revulsion.

His senses struck dumb by a flash of passion, he'd killed a man who needed to be killed. *Temporary insanity*. The attorneys so declared and a court had decreed.

He stood up, paced in the dark, only to sit again and stare at the night.

On Sarah Greenhaw's show, from a place in him he didn't know, *But for the grace of God . . .*

Isolation, loneliness, the tendency to fantasy—*if somebody ever hurt my mama, I'd stick pins in him and burn him and . . .*

The difference was, the lust murderer began to think, *If anybody hurt me . . .*

In the course of learning about them, Ken had disassembled the personality of lust murderers. With each new insight, he'd thought, *but for the grace of God . . .*

Like a medical student who sees deadly symptoms in himself, Ken began to think he was a law officer and not a criminal, more from luck than design.

He'd been a bed wetter. He'd never considered himself physically attractive. He'd suffered nightmares, headaches, loss of appetite. He'd been a lonely child, isolated in this cottage, fantasizing about being "up there" on the terrace, a part of the family.

What his childhood had engendered, Vietnam accentuated. He'd volunteered, an act which now seemed suicidal; he'd debated a tattoo, a form of self mutilation; he'd destroyed property without qualms; suffered rebellious, murderous inclinations . . .

His chest hurt, his breathing labored. God, who was he to pass judgment on anybody?

"Kenny?" His father at the front door. "Kenny, are you there?"

He tried to compose himself.

"Mind if I come in?"

His throat was dry.

Behind him, Abel turned on a light in the living room. "What're you doing in the dark, boy?"

Ken extended a hand to hold him off.

"Kenny?"

His hand quivered and Abel stared at it.

He loathed himself for weakness. Abel expected strength, admired nothing less. *The way a boy should be.*

"Dad, I killed that man—"

He couldn't say it. *Because I saw myself in him.* He couldn't say it!
"Where were you?" Ken cried. "I needed you, Dad!"
Suddenly, Abel seized him in a hug that smothered.
"Dad—I killed him because—"
"I know, Son," Abel soothed. "I know—"

CHAPTER
TWENTY-ONE

VIOLET CLOSED the drapes in her office, activating the computerized planetarium projected onto the ceiling. Lorraine placed a copy of Inez Cumbie's letter on Violet's desk. "May I bring you anything else, Violet?"

"No, darling. Close the doors as you leave."

With her chair tilted back toward the planetaria, Violet would meditate for hours. Concentrating on the constellation Taurus, Pleiades specifically, she would inhale deeply, exhale rhythmically. The computer would shower her with artificial meteorites.

Anyone can do it, Violet would say, *but shouldn't.*

Lorraine shut the connecting door between their offices. Donna Wheeler shuffled mail she'd selected for Violet Day's attention. Cynthia was poised with her stenographer's pad, awaiting Lorraine's dictated responses to letters.

"From Des Moines, Iowa," Mrs. Wheeler began. " 'Last year you promised I'd gain love. I gained forty pounds, but no man. Suggestions?' Signed, Corpulent Capricorn."

"Dear Corpulent Capricorn," Lorraine replied. "Try men, not meals. Venus ascending, gain still a promise."

Mrs. Wheeler numbered the inquiry and went to the next. Lorraine closed her eyes. *Five days until the Crystal Ball . . .*

"Are you all right, Miss Lorraine?" Cynthia asked.

"Yes. Next letter, Mrs. Wheeler."

"Next one," Mrs. Wheeler announced. " 'I was born eight weeks premature, a woman in a man's body. Am I what I am, or what I should have been?' Signed, Virgo."

"Dear Virgo: Be Virgo, but think Scorpio, if that pleases you. Obviously, you have the ability to perform that feat."

"That's too flip," Mrs. Wheeler said.

"And sexist," Cynthia agreed.

"The letter isn't a joke," Mrs. Wheeler chided. "The question is critical to the writer and it should be treated as such."

Irritably, Lorraine rocked her chair, tried again. "Dear Virgo: You are what you are, be what you will."

The secretary and Mrs. Wheeler looked at one another.

"Skip that letter," Lorraine ordered.

Mrs. Wheeler put it aside, choosing another from a pile of thirty.

Ken had said, Friday, that he'd decided not to do another television appearance. In Lorraine's presence, he'd telephoned Sarah Greenhaw to withdraw. *Because,* Ken had said, *he was inciting the murderer.*

"This is from Libra, New York City," Mrs. Wheeler commenced. " 'Parents black, I'm white. Angry! Can I change?' "

"It's all right with me, if it's all right with your mother," Lorraine said.

Neither woman smiled.

Lorraine sighed. "Let's do this tomorrow. I'm not in the mood."

"That happened to your mother sometimes," Cynthia said. "Don't worry about it, Miss Lorraine."

"You're going to have to treat this more soberly, Lorraine," Mrs. Wheeler admonished. "Your readers are serious, you must be also."

Alone, Lorraine retreated into the adjoining rest room and washed her face with cold water. She lifted her head, chin dripping and saw her reflection in the mirror.

Curly strands of red hair eluded control; her complexion was a pale mask blotched by Florida freckles. What could Ken see in her? Yet, before the Crystal Ball press party, he'd said she was beautiful.

"Lori?"

"In the bathroom, Ken."

"Cynthia thought you weren't feeling well."

"I'm all right." She flicked off the bathroom light and returned to her office. "Violet is in there plotting charts and conjuring tendencies concerning us all," she said. "She has the copies of letters from victims."

"If that pleases her," Ken said, "why not?"

Lorraine stood at her desk, looking down at the correspondence Mrs. Wheeler had read.

"What do you say to a gay man who thinks he was born under the wrong sign?" she asked.

"The proof of the pudding is in the eating."

"Mrs. Wheeler says not to be funny."

"If a letter is difficult to answer, why bother?"

"Maybe I won't."

"What do the stars say?" Ken teased.

"The stars don't dictate such things. People can *be* anything, signs notwithstanding."

"Tell him that."

She pushed the letters away. "Becky left for Arizona this morning."

"I drove them to the airport, Lori."

"Oh, that's right. Did Tommy ever soften up?"

"No."

The telephone rang and Lorraine tensed. "New York realtor, Miss Lorraine."

Ken thumbed through the correspondence as Lorraine listened to yet another sales pitch regarding the New York condominium.

"Miss Day, they are now offering twelve hundred dollars a square foot. Please—*please,* let me accept."

"We'll take that." She hung up.

"This one's good," Ken said. " 'The pill didn't work. Can failed birth control affect an unexpected child?' "

Another phone call. Through the new two-way mirrored wall Lorraine saw Cynthia shunt the caller to someone else.

"What's wrong, Lori?"

"Nothing, Ken."

He put down the letters, waiting.

"Nothing! I'm out of sorts. This whole situation is twisting my life into knots—Becky had to leave town, Violet is in the Boogey Room doing incantations—"

She expected him to smile, but he didn't.

"We've had a couple of hundred cancellations for the Crystal Ball. They give varied reasons, but we know why they aren't coming."

"The fewer guests, the easier security," Ken noted.

"There won't be fewer guests. We've had over three hundred calls from people who normally wouldn't come at all! But these are so-called free spirits, the ones with orange hair and Mohawk styles. They generally take off their clothes and jump in the pool before the evening ends. They seldom bring items that auction well."

"Tell them not to come."

"It wouldn't do any good. Rich, spoiled rotten—Major calls them the Drug and Thug Troops."

Ken saw Herb Leibowitz step off the elevator and went out to meet him. Lorraine gazed through the mirror—a disinterested voyeur.

"About Diane and Patricia Feldman," Herb reported to Ken. "The father is Charles K. Feldman."

He turned to Cynthia. "Okay to smoke?"

"We'd rather you wouldn't."

Herb grunted, mauled the cigar. "Family home in Juno Beach."

"It should be staked out."

"Did that. Don't hold your breath. Feldman was convicted of mail fraud and other charges. He's in minimum security at Eglin, Fort Walton Beach. The feds seized his property—first for tax evasion, but that fell through. Then, claiming it was purchased with illegal income. Haven't proved that either. It's still in court."

"Have you talked to Feldman, Herb?"

"Started to." Herb adjusted his tie in the new mirror, unaware he could be seen from the other side. "Apparently Diane's alive. The warden says she's been trying to call her father. He can call out a couple times a month, but she can't call in. She wouldn't leave a number. Said she'd be there for visiting privileges."

"When?"

Herb looked at his watch. "About three hours. I thought I'd ask the Fort Walton police to pick her up."

"No," Ken reasoned. "It would be better if we did it. You still have to tell the father about Sissie, is that right?"

"No way I can get there in three hours, Blackburn."

Ken reentered Lorraine's office without knocking. "Could I use the jet right away?"

"Certainly. Where do you want to go?"

That easy . . .

"Herb and I have to be in Fort Walton Beach in a couple of hours. You remember Sissie Feldman, the last victim?"

"Yes?"

"Her sister Diane will be in Fort Walton trying to visit their father. He's in prison there. Diane might be able to describe the killer."

Lorraine was on the phone immediately. She had Cynthia call the airport, then Fort Walton to secure a rental car.

"You know how it is with white collar criminals," Herb expounded. "You chase a guy, put him away and become friendly in the process."

"What about it?"

"An agent at the FBI office knew the name right away. Wish I'd called there first. We ran them down through those designer clothes. Anyway, the FBI guy says Diane was a student at Rollins College when her father went to trial. Very bitter, she was. The second girl's a minor—that'd be Sissie. She was committed to foster care until she gained her legal majority, or until her father goes free, whichever comes first."

"The plane will be ready by the time you get to the airport," Lorraine advised.

"Anyway," Herb continued, "all the property was impounded, including several automobiles. But a Ford Mustang is missing."

"You put out an a.p.b?"

Herb looked stung. "Of course."

He spit dryly as if to dislodge tobacco, then picked up his thoughts. "In addition to a car, they took items of unknown value, including several diamonds."

"Good, Herb. Good."

"FBI has been hunting the girls. One of those low-priority things. They're on the NCIC, so they'll stumble sooner or later, that was the FBI thinking."

"If you're going," Lorraine said, "go!"

Ken started for the door, wheeled and kissed her. "Be careful," Lorraine said.

Riding down in the elevator, Herb revealed what he knew in a low monotone. He held his cigar in anticipation of open air and the chance to light it.

"Feldman was a known gambler, attracted a certain segment of society—con men, mostly. He did pretty good in the stock market, but when he took a tumble he stretched the rules to recover. Nothing really major, but the Securities and Exchange Commission cited him several times. The FBI had been trying to nail him for some shady deals in the Midwest and couldn't. They used the securities thing as a hook to put him away."

Herb drove them to the airport, radioed his office to say he was going to Fort Walton, would be back later today.

"The mother skipped out when the girls were babies," Herb related. "FBI says she couldn't be located. They tried, to help Sissie stay in a home environment. Meantime, Diane grabs her sister, a car, the jewels, and they vanish. That's been nearly nine months. They're on the computer for taking the car; no accusation of running a scam."

"Leibowitz?" Captain Dilling's voice on the radio was unmistakable.

Herb turned into the airport, going to the private hangar section. "Yes, Captain?"

A sleek silvery jet stood on the tarmac, a uniformed pilot waiting.

"You're going to Fort Walton and back today?" Captain Dilling questioned.

"Yes I am."

"How're you going to do that?"

"That's a what?" Herb questioned Ken.

"Lear–35."

"Lear–35 jet, Captain. Ken Blackburn is with me. About the Feldman girl—I told you."

The Captain acknowledged the information, signed off.

Herb came to a stop, chuckling.

"Breaks up my day," he said.

When Violet emerged from her office, she was ashen. She came to Lorraine and hugged her, clothing slightly damp as if from a feverish sweat.

"Major and I are going home."

"Are you ill?" Lorraine questioned.

"No, darling."

At the door, as an afterthought, "Where is Kenny, Lorraine?"

"He took the jet to Fort Walton Beach. The detective Herb Leibowitz is with him."

With a tense smile, Violet leaned on Major's arm. "Let's go home, please."

After they left, Lorraine went into her mother's office. The letters were spread across a credenza. On Violet's desk were wheel graphs depicting the twelve astrological signs. She had designed a horoscope for each victim, using different color pencils to draw the overlapping results on a single chart.

Fiery triplicity, a note said . . .

On other papers, Violet had calculated the eight motions of Earth through space, with mathematical computations to reach her deductions. *Axial rotation, orbital rotation, precessional motion . . .*

The wastebasket was overflowing with mathematical formulas, printouts—Lorraine smoothed one, studied it.

Inez Cumbie . . .

What Violet attempted, Lorraine realized, was a common horoscope not for one person or two, but linking every individual involved—as if Ken and Major and Becky and everyone else were pieces of a whole person.

Repeatedly, she found the notation: *Fiery triplicity . . .*

It referred to Aries, Sagittarius and Leo, the fire signs. A triangle on the graph connected them.

Fire could be good—it cooked, warmed, cleared fields, mesmerized the viewer.

But it could also burn the body it had comforted, destroy the home it made pleasant, roaring until all was consumed.

Fire was the indiscriminate element. It was what one made of it. Controlled, it was invaluable. Uncontrolled, it could be tragic.

In occult physics, the balance of negative and positive forces was the basis for any horoscope.

There were endless scribbles placing the Sun, Moon and rising signs . . . and the results were weak. Page after page of ill omens predicting—
What?

Under Violet's chair, trash had spilled. But in the center of her broad, modern executive desk she had a single piece of paper. *One line.* "Form is mortal; essence, immortal."

A shiver rose along Lorraine's spine, goosebumps flowering on her arms.

Hey—*she* didn't fall for this!

Hocus-pocus, Becky called it. But like the pernicious tentacles of superstition, a nameless fear grew from a seed of dread and Lorraine spread more papers, reading them through.

Fiery triplicity . . .

Negative . . .

Beneath that, the worst aspects of the triangle: "Ruthless and self-imposing; zealot, fanatic; destroys the efforts of others and diminishes life forces—imposes own authority—"

If such a horoscope had been prepared for a client, it would never be released. It was a portent of hazardous times.

But surely there must be good here, something positive!

"Miss Lorraine." Cynthia was at the door. "If it's all right, I'm going home."

"Yes, Cynthia, go ahead."

Lorraine reminded herself, she did not believe in this!

She'd been imbued with mumbo jumbo all her life, letting Violet manipulate their existence by the guideposts of stars.

Astrology was upon her as prejudice on the children of racists. Absorbed like the Haitian fear of voodoo doctors with perilous skills.

The telephone was ringing, but she ignored it.

When she left, Lorraine locked the office, rode the elevator alone in a nearly empty building. The parking garage seemed cavernous, her footsteps echoing as she strode toward her car. Go home. Hot bath. She wouldn't even indulge Violet with questions—that would give credence to dire prophecy.

She drove toward the Middle Bridge. Her brain replayed a phrase like the mental litany of a song captured and wished forgotten.

Fiery triplicity . . . fiery triplicity . . . fiery . . .

Ken hung up the telephone and turned to Herb. "No answer." He was trying to call Lori. Their plans had changed.

A mistake, the warden had said. Visiting hours were tomorrow, not today.

"So we down a few brews, eat a steak and rinse out our underwear," said Herb, putting the best face on it. "Can you loan me some money?"

"Anything a credit card will buy."

Meantime, a multimillion dollar jet and crew waited at the Fort Walton airport.

"Don't sweat it," Herb insisted. "You got that Day woman right here," he pointed at the palm of his own hand. "The pilot and co-pilot have to be somewhere. Might as well be here."

Ken drove the rental car back to the airfield and notified the crew they were delayed through tomorrow. He dialed the family compound.

"Miss Lorraine has retired, Mr. Blackburn."

"At this hour, Annie?"

"Came home, had a bath and went to bed."

"All right, Annie. Give Miss Lorraine a message. I'm in Fort Walton and will return tomorrow evening."

"No way but grade-A," Herb said, cheerfully.

The detective shared none of Ken's worry about taking advantage of Lorraine's generosity with the airplane. Driving into town, Herb sighed as if contented.

"I like the way you operate, Blackburn . . . "

CHAPTER
TWENTY-TWO

ESTELLE REAPER'S party began on Friday and was still in progress Monday nearly midnight. *Spending all the money*—Jaydee's share as well. Bossing him around like a moron child. "Get the man a drink, Jaydee!" *The man*. A stranger. The house was full of them, devouring food, drinking booze. His mother had finally opened the doors and windows, but a sweet smell of pot hung in the air.

"This is a very famous cat," Estelle took an animal out of a pearl-white plastic cage and placed it on the kitchen table.

"Cost a thousand dollars," Lavern boasted.

Several people oohed and aahed. Even a cesspool had its eddies. Jaydee took a beer from the refrigerator and the last of little pimento cheese sandwiches with no crusts.

"A very famous Siamese," his mother reported.

Jaydee had become acutely aware of fame these past few days. One newspaper article compared the "Violet Day" killer to Ted Bundy, a man who had killed dozens of women. The story mentioned Charles Whitman, who armed himself with ammunition, ropes, a radio and food, climbed a tower in Austin, Texas, and proceeded to kill fourteen people, wounding thirty others. A man named Richard Speck had slain eight nurses in Chicago. James Huberty went into a fast-food restaurant with a machine gun. Sylvia Seegrist opened fire with a rifle in a shopping mall, killing three, wounding seven.

"But, the article said, "a spree murderer was not the same as a serial killer." *Jaydee was a serial killer.* It said that.

The writer defined a serial killer as someone involved in three or more separate homicides, "with a cooling off period between attacks."

Yep. That was him.

Example: Christopher Wilder, an Australian-born race car driver who abducted women from shopping malls. He posed as a fashion photographer, promising to help them become models if they let him take photos. Wilder's classification changed from "serial" to "spree" because he stopped "cooling off" between slayings.

It pleased Jaydee to be different from the others. He was not like Leonard Lake and Charles Ng, who murdered as they made video tapes to sell. He wasn't like Ted Bundy, preying on young women of a certain physical description, for purely sexual gratification.

Nor was he a Herbert Mullin, of Santa Cruz, California, who killed fourteen people of varying types—a priest, a young girl and an elderly man included. Mullin's victims unluckily crossed his path, his murders based on psychotic impulses, as well as his fantasies.

Now that he had a plan, Jaydee envisioned himself the most famous of them all. People would write about *him* in years to come.

The longer he considered his idea, the more perfect it seemed. Gasoline in the sprinkler system, the clock set to start with the Crystal Ball in progress—

"Telephone company calls me up," Estelle played to her freeloading audience, "eight hundred dollars long distance, they said. Hell, there was no way I could owe that much, I said. Besides, I hadn't received a bill!"

The phone had been cut off.

Jaydee eased past bleary-eyed revelers, went into the living room. The TV was on, but nobody was watching it. Two more cat cages were stacked in a corner, the animals cowering inside.

"Jaydee, bring your sister a beer," Lolly said from the couch. But he ignored her, stepped over Budrow asleep on the floor with his thumb in his mouth.

"Ray," Lolly redirected her plea, "bring your wife a beer, will you?"

The weekend had been perfect for Jaydee, despite his mother's party. Newspapers featured articles about the new Violet Day and the charity function due to begin Friday. There were pictures of galas past, famous people who had attended then, others expected this week.

"Will the Violet Day Killer discourage your attending?" a columnist had polled celebrities. Not at all! To express solidarity, people were coming who hadn't intended to.

Jaydee was so pleased not even Mr. Gus could upset him.

"Where's my spray can, Jaydee? It isn't in the truck. It isn't in the storage room or office."

Of course it wasn't. It was a melted mess in a scorched field near Loxahatchee Wildlife Refuge.

"Stolen," Jaydee had suggested.

It was interesting watching Mr. Gus change colors. Veins protruded from his neck and forehead, eyes widened; he stamped his good leg, moaning about the bad one. He threatened to take it out of Jaydee's wages. Later, he lapsed into a lecture about responsibilities and re-liabilities and other *bill*-illities. Talking like a father, he'd said. Dutch uncle. Finally, he put a forgiving arm around Jaydee's shoulder. But then he got wound up again and changed colors once more. He couldn't file for insurance because the deductible exceeded the value. Besides, Jay-dee hadn't called the police to report a theft. The spray can was a loss. Period.

They only worked half a day today. Jaydee serviced his station wagon: points, oil change, filters; he rotated the tires and balanced them.

He drove to a marina in Fort Lauderdale, a place he'd called long distance just before they cut off the phone. He wanted a particular kind of binoculars.

It was one of those naval stores where employees wore white trousers and canvas deck-shoes. The manager had a captain's hat with gold braid on it.

"You can't buy better binoculars than Swift," the salesman said. "11x80."

"Heavy," Jaydee commented.

"Seventy-eight ounces. Observation binoculars. You'll need a tripod, which we carry in stock. At four hundred seventy dollars, they're a good investment."

Jaydee focused on a long row of yachts outside.

"Very good visibility in low light," the clerk persisted. "You said you needed that."

"I do."

"Superb optics, coated lenses. At a thousand feet you have a viewing width of two hundred thirty-six feet. Easier to find your subject and stay with it. See what I mean?"

"These are the strongest you have?"

"Stronger magnification, you mean? No, we have 20x80. But your width of vision at a thousand feet is only one hundred eighty-three feet. In dim light you'll have difficulty finding an object, especially if it's moving."

Jaydee bought the 11x80, with carrying case and a tripod. He also purchased a lightweight folding stool.

Nearly six hundred dollars all told.

Before coming home tonight, he'd gone to a condo where he made deliveries regularly. On the oceanside, south of Violet Day's compound, from the roof he had a view of Palm Beach North. He positioned his tripod and sat on the stool, searching the scene far below. The clerk was right, it was difficult to find something in the dark. But he did, finally. The tripod was essential. When he tried to handhold the binoculars the image jumped and danced.

There . . .

With the tripod set to pan, he swiveled the glasses, sweeping the grounds. He saw a guard at the gate, vehicles in the driveway. The greenhouse reflected lights from Hawaiian-type torches being installed around the yard. Open flames licked the air. *Good.* That would ignite the fumes nicely.

The binoculars were superb. He could distinguish faces even at that distance—almost three-quarters of a mile and twelve floors down. He could see what he needed to see.

"Jaydee, hon!" his mother called from the kitchen. "Bring me that lavender point Siamese from the living room."

He shut his bedroom door. Somebody in the bathroom was retching. Jaydee lit a cigarette, dwelling on his plan.

Friday afternoon he would make his usual delivery to the Violet Day compound. For several years he'd done so, a few hours before the Crystal Ball began. There was no reason to think this year would be different.

Carefully, in the most minute detail, he imagined every step he'd take—the way he'd get to work before Mr. Gus, the time it would take to pump five hundred gallons of gasoline into the tank where chemicals and fertilizers were normally transported.

Everything was vivid and real—the way he'd back to the pump house, the voices of unsuspecting people around him, the fall of hammers in last-minute construction, the musicians setting up sound systems.

He would screw the hose to the stainless steel reservoirs—not an ounce would escape. And if it did! The truck was large and old, such vehicles always smelled of gasoline.

The gardener would ask the same dumb questions, as if Jaydee were stupid. "What mix you got here?"

Then, as always, the gardener would complain about the ripping up of his yard, the damage to plants, the toil required to mend it. He would walk away . . . "Lock up when you finish," he'd say.

Second by second, Jaydee fashioned the events as they would unfold. The insides of his thighs tingled, arousing him.

He'd be right there on the condo roof, convective currents sweeping up from the swimming pool and warm patio below. Through the new binoculars, he'd watch the rich and famous dancing, drinking, unaware of their impending doom. Only he would know.

He'd decided to set the sprinkler system timer for eight o'clock. In years past at eight, Violet Day appeared at the stage microphone. Even from the condo roof, if the wind was right, he could hear voices, the faint patter of applause.

The bright eye of the party lights would be a momentary jewel in the night.

And then—

He gripped his crotch with the vision.

First, they'd screech a little—*surprised*—no harm done, though. It would take a few moments for the underground water pipes to empty as the gasoline pushed through from the reservoirs.

They'd laugh, joke about the misty spray—some would actually jump over and around the nozzles, playfully. Somebody would smell gas—

Jaydee drew on his cigarette, sucked it deeply, teeth bared.

They'd run this way, then that. They'd scream. Musicians would spill off the stage, employees would scatter.

They could go east to the ocean, or west to the street—but new fences blocked adjacent properties.

As from the pressurized spray can, only hundreds of times more powerful, five hundred volatile gallons would spew in the night, settling on clothing as a deadly dew, beading hair and eyebrows, choking nostrils for only a second—maybe two—until it reached the torches . . .

"Jaydee," his mother rapped the door. "Jaydee, you hear me?"

He drew smoke from his cigarette, sucked it down.

"Jaydee, open the door. I've told you about locking this door."

"What is it?" he yelled.

"Where's Granddaddy's pistol?"

"I don't know."

"I looked everywhere for it."

"What do you want with it?"

"I want to show it to somebody."

"I don't know," he said.

"It was in your closet!"

"No, it wasn't." It was under the seat of his station wagon. That's where it'd stay, too.

"That gun might be an antique, Jaydee. Look for it."

He inhaled smoke in the dark, the plan beginning to replay in his mind.

The flush of a commode awoke Jaydee. For several minutes he listened to repeated coughs, nasal snorts, a man trying to clear his sinuses.

"What do you like for breakfast?" Estelle's voice came through the uninsulated wall. "Can you stay that long?"

"Long as you'll let me, babe."

Another one.

Jaydee stretched, scratched himself, yawning. Mr. Gus said there'd be no work today. No work, no pay; but Jaydee didn't care.

Tuesday: four more days . . .

The man in the next room was talking about shotguns.

"Ten-gauge if you can get it," he was saying. "You shoot somebody with ten-gauge deer load and it'll blow him half in two."

"I need some kind of protection," Jaydee's mother replied.

"Ten-gauge," he reaffirmed.

The tone of voices changed. "You like the Seiko?" Estelle questioned.

"Helluva fine watch. What'd it cost?"

"It's not nice to ask that! It's a gift."

A moment later, she banged on Jaydee's door. "Jaydee, you awake?"

"Yes."

"I want this house cleaned up today."

He listened for retreating footsteps. "Jaydee, you hear me? This place is a mess."

Suddenly, she squealed and the man laughed.

Under the covers against Jaydee's nude body, silken panties formed a nest. He tucked one between his legs, staring at the wall.

In his sleep, he'd decided to drive by Violet Day's compound. By midmorning he wanted to be on top of the condo, using the observation binoculars to assess the situation.

He rubbed himself with the underwear, pulled it out to see which one it was—Miss Virgo, from Fort Myers. He selected another. Sissie's.

"Why are we going in here?" she'd asked.

"Do as you're told."

"There's nobody here. What is this?"

He had sharp mental images, like color snapshots in quick sequence.

"Aw, naw," she'd said, sensing some of what was to come. "Naw, now—I won't let you do it."

She had no choice.

Jaydee stroked his abdomen and thighs with the panties, remembering . . .

She tried to dash away but he knocked her down. She came up stumbling, crying—it was interesting the way she never screamed, not once.

She shoved at his chest, trying to run again.

He grabbed her from behind, his arm around her neck, lifting her feet from the floor. She kicked, she gasped, clawing up at his face, then his arm, then the air.

Mentally, he savored the rest of it—the way she flopped when he turned her onto her back, every piece of clothing removed.

"Jaydee! You got to work today?"

"No—goddamn it!—leave me alone."

"Who is that?" the man asked Estelle.

"I'm related to him by marriage," Jaydee's mother answered. "He's my son."

"He know I'm here?"

"Doesn't matter."

She hammered the door again. "Jaydee, I want you to meet Harold."

"Go away."

"We're going down to play Seminole Bingo and try to win back some of my money. Jaydee, you hear me?"

"Go away!"

"Let him sleep," Harold urged. "His day off. A man likes to sleep late."

"Sleep his life away if I let him."

More goosing, more giggles from Estelle.

Jaydee pulled Sissie's underwear to his chin, his morning beard snagging the fine fabric. He rubbed it over his eyes and mouth—remembering—

His mother and her new man were back in the bedroom. *Squeals* . . .

Jaydee pictured his first exploration, Sissie's inert form spread on the warehouse floor.

The detective, Blackburn, was wrong about lust. He didn't have sex with her or any of them.

"You're an animal," he heard his mother say.

"Just a little bunny."

The distraction caused Jaydee's images to waver and he turned in bed, covering his head with a pillow.

Remembering . . .

It had begun to sprinkle . . . a metallic ping of raindrops hitting the metal roof of the warehouse . . . clouds swept over the sun and shade engulfed them. He could hear the contractions of his car's motor cooling nearby, inside the building.

It was good until then.

He had imagined Sissie was Violet Day, spread before him on the concrete, palms up, fingers curled. But thoughts of Ken Blackburn intruded.

His reverie was disrupted by the sounds of passion in the next room, the rhythmic creaks of bedsprings, the thumping of his mother's headboard against a wall.

Animal . . .

Jaydee sat up, shaking.

Ruined it.

Ken Blackburn and Violet Day. Playing experts to stupid people like Jaydee's mother.

He dressed, angrily, listening to the rising tide of sexual expressions, his mother's headboard knocking the wall with increasing tempo.

Jaydee gathered the underwear and put it in his secret place through a hole in the Sheetrock paneling. He felt for the mementoes he'd been collecting since childhood, the things that helped him relive the moment.

One good thing, though—his mother was debating a shotgun; she wasn't depending on Violet Day now—scared, that's what she was.

He tied his bootlaces, raked his hair with a brush.

As he unlocked the door and stepped into the hallway, his mother called, "Jaydee, don't forget what I told you."

"Let him go," the man murmured.

Jaydee made his way through a throng of cats, kicking this way and that. Out the back door, into his station wagon. It was barely daybreak, morning shadows fell across the streets in pale gray patterns.

First to Violet Day's—trucks lined the street outside, others down the driveway. Workmen delivered lumber. The guard watched them pass without question.

That's how it would be—no questions. Usual delivery.

Jaydee circled back, going south to the condo. The elderly woman who managed the place was washing sidewalks with a water hose. She was nearly blind and mostly deaf, so Jaydee went, as usual, straight to the elevator without challenge.

He set up the tripod, attached the heavy binoculars, placed his folding stool.

In the light of bright morning sun, he could see everything—even the gardener was recognizable.

Men were erecting a stage. Others were digging a hole in the east part of the lawn. It looked like a large grave!

Jaydee panned his binoculars slowly. Near the pump house they were setting up a row of canopies, long tables, vats for cooling drinks.

He studied the terrace—nobody there, yet. No sign of Ken Blackburn, or either of the Violet Days.

The swimming pool deflected light from the rising sun. These binoculars were wonderful. He could see the front door of several cottages down near the ocean, each unit with a small patio—but unoccupied, evidently.

Jaydee lit a cigarette, resting his eyes a moment.

He would get to work before Mr. Gus . . .

Fill the tank with gasoline . . .

The truck would lurch and groan as he backed to the pump house for his usual delivery . . .

"What mix you got here?"

Jaydee held his crotch, elaborating on the vision. He saw it as if in slow motion . . . smelled the odors of imagined foods, heard the voices of unsuspecting people . . .

He massaged himself, accomplishing now what he'd failed to achieve at home in bed with the panties.

It couldn't have been more perfect . . .

CHAPTER
TWENTY-THREE

"LORRAINE?" Violet's voice was a gentle echo from childhood . . . *time for school* . . .

Lorraine groaned, pulled the covers over her head, curling away.

"Hot coffee," Violet enticed, "Annie's best biscuits, orange blossom honey—"

"Violet, I don't want to get up."

"We'll dine on the balcony," Violet crooned. "Listen to the mockingbirds sing, watch the sun rise. Come along, now."

Splashing her face in cold water, Lorraine thought, *four more days.* She slipped into a robe and joined her mother. Predawn fog lingered over the lawn below. The Atlantic was still as a pond. A mockingbird trilled.

"We haven't done this in a long time." Violet poured coffee. "There is no dawn so beautiful as Palm Beach. Miguel loved the break of day."

Lorraine's father. Violet hadn't spoken of him in years.

"Alas, Miguel," she said. "I never forgave him for dying."

Killed. Racing at Le Mans. Lorraine had no memory of him.

"Thank God for Major," Violet said. "I knew the instant I saw him,

he would be with me for the rest of my life. I knew it about Kenny, too—
even when he was a child. Have you heard from him?"

"No. He's still in Fort Walton Beach."

"What do you think of him?" Violet inquired.

"I think he's a good friend."

"You love him."

"Is that a question or a statement?" Lorraine smiled.

"I know what I think; what do you think?"

"I guess I've always been fond of Ken."

"You love him."

"I suppose I do, Violet. Does it worry you?"

"Does it worry you?"

"Violet, I'm not awake enough to play this game adroitly. Why don't
we take a linear approach—what's on your mind?"

"You and Kenny."

"Perhaps you should be asking *his* intentions."

"He'll make no move without invitation," Violet concluded, soberly.
"That's up to you."

The mockingbird had run through his repertoire. morning stars were
fading from view.

"You don't remember your grandmother," Violet veered to another
subject.

"No."

"She would wake me every morning, bring me out here for breakfast
from a tea cart like this. At first glance, it was a warm and thoughtful
gesture. In fact, it was her way of extending my education. While we
waited for the sun, listened to the birds, she'd recite tales of faraway
places and ancient times. Do you remember Pharsalus? she'd ask. No,
I'd say, I don't remember—what is Pharsalus?"

Violet assumed the manner of her own mother, " 'Pharsalus is the
place in Greece where Caesar defeated Pompey, 48 B.C.' "

Animating her dual roles, Violet the child questioned, " 'Was I
there?' "

" 'Indeed! You were the oracle to Julius Caesar, a meteorologist and a
prophet.' "

Workmen were arriving on the grounds below, awaiting the hour
when construction was permitted by local ordinance.

"In that life," Violet recounted, "Major was Titus Labienus, commander of Caesar's cavalry. Major was handsome, courageous. I was madly in love with him, my mother said. But alas, Miguel was not there. He was never meant to be my partner in this lifetime, your grandmother told me. But you were—my mother spoke to me as a child about my child yet unborn. You were the servant girl to Titus Labienus. I suspected you were his mistress, but never mind. It was a long time ago."

"Thank you for understanding," Lorraine teased.

"Yes!" Violet laughed. "It is funny, isn't it? Of course, when I was a child the stories seemed exceedingly real."

"Why are you telling me this?"

"It's the kind of thing my mother did to me, Lorraine. By the time I married, I couldn't distinguish fact from fiction. Were the scenes I recalled from this life, my mother's lips? Or from a former life in 48 B.C.?"

"You did that to me," Lorraine said, softly.

"Not like she did to me," Violet insisted. "After I learned to read, I was required to study Black Arts, occult texts, endless calculations concerning astrology. And always, always, my mother insisted it was I who participated in the origin of the subjects, hundreds of years ago."

"Why are you saying this to me?" Lorraine asked.

"Because I don't know what's true anymore, Lorraine. I sincerely believe that what is meant to be, will be. But your grandmother had an uncanny ability to predict things that—all my life—have come true."

"You were an impressionable child!"

"She foretold my marriage to your father, his death, your birth, Major Drummond's lifelong affect on me. She predicted Major would take her fortune and multiply it a hundred times with technologies as yet uninvented—"

"Violet, I saw the printouts in your office."

"Fiery triplicity. Mother told me it would be so."

Lorraine shivered, shook it off. "Fate may be inevitable, Violet. But do we invite our fates?"

"We do."

"If you believe something dreadful is about to transpire, let's change our plans! Cancel the Crystal Ball."

"If your grandmother could predict events of my life in 1927," Violet said, "I doubt I could alter the course, even if I tried."

"Then, tell me what you think you see?"

Violet put aside her coffee cup and turned to Lorraine. "I see you very happy, living with Kenny for the rest of your lives."

"Is that what this is about? Lord! Violet, I thought you were worrying about the man who's been killing people."

"But I see this happiness only if you make the move, Lorraine. Kenny cannot. He will not—if you love him, say it. If you want him, let him know."

"Were you talking about the Crystal Ball?"

"Oh, that." She stood up.

"Tell me," Lorraine insisted.

"Don't worry. Nothing you could do would alter it for better or worse." Violet smiled, not altogether happily. "I'll send Annie for the tea cart."

Below, men dug a barbecue pit on the eastern end of the lawn.

Four more days . . .

Ken and Herb sat in their rental car under the shade of an oak, watching the building where Diane Feldman must go to visit her father.

"Hard time this ain't." Herb looked across neatly trimmed lawns and whitewashed, stone-lined walkways.

Eglin Air Force Base contained one of the federal minimum-security facilities known to critics as "country club" prisons. Here in balmy semitropical clime, eating decent meals and sleeping on comfortable beds, white-collar criminals suffered a restriction of freedom but little else. They wore no stripes or chains.

"Whatever happened to public degradation, corporal punishment, execution and banishment?" Herb lamented. "There was a time when the sentence was commensurate with the crime!"

Ken remembered a class in criminology at Florida State University. "The treatment of criminals," the professor had said, "rests on the four R's: retribution, restraint, rehabilitation and reintegration."

"You go in there"—Herb pointed at the penal section with his cigar—"you meet psychiatrists, psychologists, social workers, sociologists—and finally, the warden. They talk about vocational and educational 'opportunities.' I tell you, Ken, it's worth breaking the public trust just to get your teeth fixed. Dental bills being what they are—"

"Heads up, Herb." Ken noted a young woman walking toward them. She wore tan slacks and a red blouse.

Herb adjusted a side mirror. "Is that her?"

"Not sure yet."

With the sixth sense of a fugitive, she halted.

"Wait until she goes inside," Herb said, as if Ken had asked. "Too hot to chase her down."

She selected a bench, sat down and lit a cigarette. Casually, she surveyed the scene.

"Bet a buck it's her," Ken advised.

Her hair was different, but she could have bleached it since Ken last saw her. She used the little finger of the hand that held her cigarette to wipe corners of her mouth. Carefully, ever so carefully, she studied the area.

"What do you think?" Herb questioned.

"Let's go see."

Ken backed out and turned in her direction. They had done nothing untoward, but she saw them coming and stood up.

Herb put his cigar in the ashtray and opened the door before Ken stopped. The girl moved as if to flee.

"Diane," Ken called, "we need to see you about Sissie."

She hesitated. Herb blocked escape.

"What about Sissie?" she asked.

Now Ken was out of the car. She recognized him and swore softly. Herb seized her arm. "We have bad news," he said.

Ken sat on the bench and patted the place beside him. "Sit down, Diane."

"What about Sis?"

"She's been murdered," Ken said.

"Oh God. Oh, God—you're lying, aren't you?"

"I wish I were."

She dropped her cigarette and began to cry. Ken pulled her to him. "I'm sorry, Diane."

"Have you told my papa?"

"Yes."

"Our money was gone. The pistol, too. I thought Sissie took it. But she'd left her clothes. Took my driver's license, but she doesn't drive. Why would she do that? I kept asking myself. Why would she do that? I had the car towed in by a mechanic Papa knew. He said the radiator was punctured. Couldn't have been a rock, he said. Somebody punched a hole in it."

Herb pulled a handkerchief from his pocket, looked at it and decided not to offer. He went to the car, got a packet of tissues and broke them open.

"Did you tell my father about me?"

"No."

She blew her nose. "I've forgotten your name."

"Ken Blackburn. This is Detective Herb Leibowitz. We're from West Palm."

"Poor Sissie. I should have stayed with her. I tried to get her to go back to town with me."

"Need to ask some hard questions," Herb said.

"I don't know anything."

"Maybe you do," Ken suggested. "Maybe it was somebody you hit— he saw Sissie and recognized her."

They went inside to a conference room. Through wire-mesh grating, they could see inmates clipping shrubs, raking leaves.

"The last mark was in Pahokee," Diane related. "Met him in a diner—you know how we worked."

"Yes."

"Sissie didn't like the looks of him, but I insisted. Mosquitoes were eating her up. I used to say we could make a living renting Sissie to lawn parties—one mosquito with a hundred people and it always went for Sissie."

She swallowed hard, dabbed her eyes. "She was about to start her period—cramps—so I said let's take him."

"What kind of car?" Herb took notes.

"I don't know. Cheap. White. No radio, no chrome trim. Working stiff car. Vinyl seats. He was traveling. That's what we always looked for—clothes in the rear seat, Georgia tag. He drove toward West Palm. Usually, if the mark goes one way, we head the other. But we were trying to get home to find out about Papa's house. Do you know about Papa?"

"We know."

She wiped her nose.

"What did he look like?" Ken questioned.

"Early thirties. Shaggy hair, darker than blond. Rough hands. I said he was a working stiff."

"Any idea what kind of work?"

"He said entomology. But I think he lied."

"Ento . . . " Herb looked to Ken. "Spell that."

"Bugs," Diane said. "Insects."

"Why do you think he lied?"

"If some married guy wants to make it, he'll lie about everything. Jailbait wiggling a finger. He's going to lie. He asked if I knew what 'entomology' was. I did, so he shut up."

Herb moistened the tip of his pencil on his tongue. "Color eyes, how tall, wearing what?"

She told him what she seemed to remember. Then, "He said his name was Destiny."

"Destiny."

"That's what he said."

They allowed the girl to visit her father. Herb telephoned West Palm with the name and description.

"We're going to bring her in and try for a composite," Herb said into the receiver. "Meantime, search telephone and city directories for the name Destiny. Could be first or last. Vehicle registration, driver's license. Hey, and listen, he was driving a car with Georgia plates. Get Georgia in on this."

"He's not from Georgia, Herb."

"Ken says he's not from Georgia," Herb relayed. "Check it out anyway, but do it last."

In the next room, the tearful father and daughter embraced. Ken read Diane's lips, "Love you, Papa . . . "

"Think of anything else?" Herb questioned Ken.

"Public and parochial school records; call businesses connected with entomology."

"Entomology," Herb spoke into the phone. "Bugs! You know, bees, termites, ants, roaches, spiders—"

"Not spiders, Herb."

"Scratch the spider," Herb said.

Thirty minutes later they were four miles high, flying south in the Lear jet. Down below, the fleece of cirrus clouds looked like finger waves on a graying head.

"You aren't arresting me?" Diane questioned.

"No."

"I'm sorry about your money," she said. "If I can get a job, I'll pay you back."

Riding in the plush seat of a high-flying jet, sipping Scotch and water—the money didn't seem important.

Right now, Ken was thinking of Lori and the Crystal Ball.

Destiny . . . a real name, or an omen?

Ken closed his eyes, head back on the seat. He wished he could go home. *Home.* It was more than a place. It included people who truly cared for him.

Make the first move, Violet had said. So all right. Lorraine waited in Ken's cottage feeling more foolish than predatory. She wore her sexiest lace underwear, a sheer dress and a hint of perfume. She'd put fresh flowers on the bedside tables. The lamps were a soft glow. She'd selected music by Mantovani . . .

It was as appealing as a trap could be.

The telephone rang.

"Hi, Mom."

"Becky!"

"Am I interrupting anything?"

"Why did you call here instead of the main house?"

"I could say 'Is he there?' and you could say, 'Is who here?' and I could say 'You know who,' and you could say, 'Oh, no—or yes.' Is he?"

"No, he isn't. How's Tucson?"

"Dry."

"Are you and your father getting along?"

"He isn't trying to buy my love, I'll say that. We've eaten at McDonald's and Burger King every day."

"I'm afraid Tommy's approach to food is as fuel, Becky. Once he swallows, his stomach doesn't know steak from hamburger."

Becky laughed. "Is that original?"

"No, it's from a play, *Rain.*"

"So!" Becky said. "What's happening?"

"Getting ready for the party Friday night."

"You know what? I didn't realize how exciting you are until now."

Or, how boring Tommy is.

"Something is always happening around you and Violet. Here—you know. Dad thinks watching *Sesame Street* makes breakfast an event. An old movie on TV is really zingy if we pop corn in the microwave. I mean, Mom—ho-*hum!*"

"Look for his strengths, Becky."

"I do. I really do. I see he's reliable, faithful, gentle and smart. But that sounds like a Labrador retriever."

A long, adolescent pause. "Are you really alone, Mom?"

"Yes."

"There's been a lot of television news about the man who's after us."

"Don't worry, Becky. Ken says they've found a girl who may be able to help produce a drawing of the man. They also learned his name— Destiny. It won't be long before they catch him."

Becky lowered her voice. "I hear Dad. I only wanted to say I was thinking of you—and appreciate you. Kiss Violet for me."

As Lorraine hung up, Ken walked in. She wheeled, like a child caught in a forbidden act.

For an instant he seemed startled. "Hi there." He took in the setting with a glance. "What's up?"

"I put charcoal in the grill," she said. "Two steaks marinated for tenderness, Chablis—"

He lifted his head, a nod incomplete.

Suddenly this didn't seem so wise. Questions arose in Lorraine's mind that should've been considered before. Suppose he rejected her? Or worse, did not reject her but wanted to?

"This is too important to me to mess it up," she said. "I'm not very good at it. I never have been. You can just say no and I'll forget it."

Now the nod completed, chin down.

"Violet told me you'd never make the first move."

"You don't have to do this, Lori."

"I hadn't thought of it as an obligation."

He smiled, awkwardly it seemed. "I won't hold you in emotional bondage, Lori."

"I came to make a confession and a plea," she said. "See, the truth is, I've decided I love you, Ken. I say 'decided'—which means admitted to myself. You've never encouraged me, you know. Except when I stole the money in school."

He nodded, soberly.

"Why did you protect me?" she asked.

"I didn't want you hurt."

"How did you know I took the money?"

"I saw you. I was always spying on you."

"Oh."

"You said confession and a plea?"

"If I'm making a fool of myself, forgive me."

"What do you want me to do, Lori?"

"What I've always wanted, I guess. I'd like you to love me. If not that—maybe pretend to."

He pulled her into his arms and held her a very long time. Then, he kissed her. It was not like the kiss in the restaurant, playful, teasing—this kiss was enduring.

"Ken, I love you."

"You don't have to say that."

"But it's so."

"Then," he smiled, "dreams do come true . . . "

Palm fronds rustled beyond the guest cottage windows, the smell of sea air pungent as it swept through the room. She'd never imagined that sex could be so wonderful. Lorraine traced Ken's chest and torso with the tips of her fingers. Hairy and muscular—Tommy's smooth chest had worried him more than a balding head.

"What are you thinking, Lori?"

"What a beautiful body you have."

He kissed the tip of her nose.

"I worried about doing this," she said. "I need you too much to drive you away."

"Lori, I spent my youth wishing for you."

She snuggled nearer. "I don't know where the years go," she said. "One minute I'm a school girl. The next minute I have a daughter the age I was a moment ago. Somewhere along the way, I lost control. I never should have married Tommy."

"He's a good man."

"How can I be this age?" she asked, softly. "How can I have allowed the best years to slip away? Everything I really wanted—like you—I was afraid to go for it."

He sat up on the bed and twisted to look down on her. "Lori, if you see things differently tomorrow—or at any time—it's okay. I worry about people taking advantage of you. I don't want to do that."

"Do it, do it."

He looked into her eyes so deeply and sadly Lorraine felt compelled to pull him down on her chest.

Please love me.

"I do," he said, as if she'd spoken. "I love you . . ."

CHAPTER
TWENTY-FOUR

GOING TO WORK, Jaydee pondered the state of his life. Last night on television they displayed a drawing of him. Caught by surprise, he'd waited for his mother's reaction.

"I hope they catch him real quick," she said.

Only Lolly seemed to give it a second thought. "That man looks familiar, doesn't he?"

"Everybody looks like somebody," Estelle had concluded.

This morning, the same drawing was in the newspapers and, somehow, it seemed more like Jaydee than it had on TV. He felt more exposed now. Every stranger was a threat, any lingering glance became a dangerous inspection. But, never mind, tomorrow was the day.

He turned off the highway, driving through waist-deep fog toward the fenced grounds of ORGRO. He parked his station wagon and locked it. In the distance, on the highway, automobiles were tiny ships afloat on a sea of vapors.

When he entered the office, Mr. Gus grinned toothlessly. His teeth were in a goblet on his desk. Jaydee smelled liquor.

"Got us a big order from the sugar mill at Okeelanta, south of Belle Glade," Mr. Gus said. "They're doing aerial spraying and they'll need several tankloads of pesticides. That's where you'll be tomorrow."

"Tomorrow? I deliver to Palm Beach tomorrow."

263

"Go to Palm Beach today."

"I can't do that," Jaydee said, firmly. "They expect me tomorrow. That's my regular day."

"What do they know, one day from the next? You'll be a day early, so what?"

Mr. Gus turned order sheets on a clipboard, reciting as he went. "Palm Nursery, fifteen hundred gallons of nitrogen; Seminole Landscape, a thousand gallons. Then the mixes—"

Jaydee rocked from heel to toe. Mr. Gus was messing up his plan. He hadn't filled the tanker with gasoline and even if he had, to deliver this early would be a mistake. The gardener might notice the sprinkler clock had been reset. No, tomorrow was the time, just before the Crystal Ball, as he always did.

"Damned gardeners think they're botanists," Mr. Gus grumped. "This one to Violet Day—ten-five-fourteen, he wants. Eight-eight-eight won't do; it has to be ten-five-fourteen mix. We'll send him ten-ten-ten, what the hell does he know?"

Jaydee knew how to set the timer for eight o'clock. But he wasn't sure he could make the timer skip eight o'clock tonight and tomorrow morning, waiting until eight o'clock during the Crystal Ball.

In a small dressing room adjoining the office, lockers lined the wall, mute testimony to more prosperous days before cheaper granulated fertilizers began to take the market. Jaydee selected a clean pair of light blue coveralls and a baseball style cap with the ORGRO logo on the front.

"Why can't I go to Okeelanta today, Mr. Gus?"

"Because the crop-hoppers won't be there with the planes until tomorrow."

"I might get most of Palm Beach done today," Jaydee tried to work it out, "except maybe one or two deliveries. I could squeeze them in between loads to Okeelanta, tomorrow."

"No, Jaydee, damn it. Do all the Palm Beach deliveries today. If you miss them today, forget it until next week—so *don't* miss them."

His face burning, Jaydee walked past his boss, on the way out.

"Hold on, Jaydee, don't go off half-cocked."

He didn't like Mr. Gus anyway. Sitting there pretending to be so casual about it. Messing up the plan.

"Do you know where you're going?"

Like Jaydee was stupid.

"Palm Beach, you said."

"Palm Beach *where?*" Mr. Gus waved the order sheets. "Do you know the mix?"

Mr. Gus stood over him as always, monitoring the gauges, counting every drop.

"I read some place that an unmarried man doesn't live as long as a married one," Mr. Gus rattled. "I find that hard to believe—living with my wife and her being what she is. Damned back hurts, she says. Like my leg doesn't. Watch your meter, Jaydee."

Mr. Gus tapped a gauge with his finger. "Close enough, Jaydee. Stop it there."

Jaydee pulled down a hose from another tank to complete the mixture.

"The police banging on my door, nine o'clock at night. Does she say, Gus is sleeping? Hell no, wakes me up!"

Jaydee's heart leaped. "Police?"

"Third time this week," Mr. Gus said. "I told them they want to see me, here's where I am nine of the best hours in a day. Be here, or don't wake me. But my wife sees a badge and she comes shaking the bed."

"Three times?" Jaydee forced himself to study the meter.

"Three times this week. Slow the flow there, Jaydee."

"What did they want?"

"Asking if we go to Orlando and Fort Myers."

"What did you say?"

"I said we have offices in Orlando, Jacksonville and Valdosta, Georgia. We cover the Southeast. Are you watching the flow?"

Jaydee stopped short of the mark, approached it with tiny quick squeezes of the nozzle trigger. "Why'd they want to know about that, I wonder?"

Mr. Gus was checking the gauge.

"They say what they're after, Mr. Gus?"

"You, maybe."

"Me?"

Mr. Gus chuckled. "Joking, Jaydee. They asked if we had an employee named Destiny."

Destiny . . .

Jaydee followed back to the office. "What did you say?"

"What do you think I said? You're the only employee."

"You said that."

Mr. Gus turned to stare. "You in some kind of trouble, Jaydee?"

"What kind of trouble?"

"How would I know? You're the one asking about the police."

"I don't like cops."

"Yeah. Until the first time you need one. You got a full day, get going."

Jaydee returned to his station wagon, pulled his pistol from under the seat. He unzipped his coveralls, stuck the weapon in his belt and zipped up again.

Destiny . . .

He drove east out of view, circled back and rejoined the Belle Glade highway. He needed time to think, a safe place to do it.

Loxahatchee Wildlife Refuge. That's where he'd go. He shifted gears, gaining speed.

How could they know the name Destiny?

He recounted every move, every letter mailed, every victim—*of course!*

They'd found Sissie. That led to Diane. He'd told Diane his name was Destiny.

Your mother must read a lot of novels, she'd said.

Sure, that was it. She knew what he looked like. Her description helped construct that dumb drawing. To him it looked like him, but obviously he couldn't judge the likeness. If his own mother didn't recognize him, how would anyone else?

His frustration narrowed to Mr. Gus. Messing up the plan. The perfect plan!

One thing sure: Jaydee wasn't going to Palm Beach today. Since nobody expected him a day early, there should be no complaints when he didn't appear.

Second thing sure: He would make his delivery to Violet Day tomorrow afternoon—2:30 promptly.

He left the paved highway, driving south toward the refuge. The truck labored over softer soil.

He'd dump his load where he'd burned the spray can.

Then, he'd wait until late, after Mr. Gus went home. He'd get back to the office with the truck while nobody was there. He wouldn't gamble about tomorrow morning—he'd fill the tank with gasoline tonight.

Jaydee turned off the motor and lit a cigarette. Cattle egrets stalked insects on the narrow lane ahead. Already the temperature was climbing. It would be hot sitting here all day. But he had it to do and do it he would.

Third thing sure: This would have to be the last time.

But—he smiled—he was going to get them all.

Once more was enough.

Ken drove toward the West Palm police station with Diane beside him, weeping. They'd been to the morgue, a traumatic necessity delayed until today.

"It didn't look like Sissie," Diane sobbed. "But it was."

Midmorning traffic held them to a walking speed. Ken rolled down the windows, despite the air conditioning.

"More like my baby than my sister," Diane cried. "I raised her from a baby."

Over the years, he'd encountered hundreds of horrified, despondent survivors. Some required theological assistance, others wished to be left alone. Then there were those who, in the throes of loss, would commit suicide within the hour, if not protected from themselves.

Diane needed to talk . . .

"I hate this town," she seethed. "I grew up here and I despise it. Everything and everybody is so artificial."

"A place is what you make it, Diane."

"I know." She blew her nose loudly. "You're right. It would've been the same anywhere. Papa says he's a businessman, but 'promoter' is a better word. Sissie and I grew up listening to him and his con man friends. Filled with high good humor and fast talk to put a mark at ease. Driving expensive cars, draping their women in diamonds and furs—"

She honked her nose again. "They talk about millions won and lost. Wheeler-dealers. 'The Cadillac Kids.' Alligator luggage and ruby tie tacks—"

She wiped her eyes and stared out the window a moment. Trapped in traffic, they weren't moving.

"They came looking for sanctuary and a stake," she said. "Papa was always available. They were his friends, he'd say. But when he got arrested I called everybody in his address book. Not a one came to help. Busy, they said, or broke; more likely running from the law."

Working her way through it trying to allocate blame for Sissie, Diane sobbed. "I didn't know what to do. No house, no money. I couldn't make tuition at Rollins. Sissie was terrified, going to a state-run foster home. I bitch about the con men, but we did it, too."

She lit a cigarette, turned off the air conditioner and rolled down her window. "Papa sent Sissie and me to a dude ranch in Montana one summer. They chased cattle into chutes, forcing them through vats of a stinky white chemical. To kill ticks, the cowboys said. I was thinking about that this morning before you came to pick me up."

"What about it?"

"Destiny smelled like that. Cattle dip. Not strong, but like he'd been handling it. Maybe he wasn't lying about entomology."

She'd spent all day Wednesday looking at endless pages of photos— known sex offenders, felons at large. They were returning to look at more this morning.

As Ken passed the police pound, Diane said, "They've got my Mustang. There it is. Sissie knew Destiny wasn't a good mark. I knew it, too. Scuffed boots, worn jeans. But, hell, we'd been stuck in Pahokee for two nights. He was the best shot we had. Something the police artist didn't show—"

"What?"

"Destiny had sleep-eyed ways, but his eyes were different. I tried to tell the artist, but he said we were after configuration."

Ken pulled into the parking lot.

"I thought Destiny saw through us," Diane said. "I was giving him our line and his eyes were that one degree between cold and freezing. Like he had me figured but was playing along. Something missing in his eyes—that's what the drawing didn't show."

"Can you describe it?"

"It isn't what's there, it's what isn't. Character, maybe. The kind of thing that comes from living long, but *living* . . . He had creases around his eyes from the sun. But no lines from smiling or from pain."

Ken now knew for certain—this was the man.

"He was like somebody who never felt an emotion enough to have it register."

"That's because he doesn't feel things as we do."

Ken escorted her into a room where mug shots waited.

The moment they were alone, Herb reported to Ken. "There is no

Destiny. From Miami and two counties north—no Destiny. It's a lie or a nickname."

"They checked variations?"

Herb traced a list, "Destin, Destry, Doostin, Dustin—about forty variations. We went through driver's licenses, auto registration, union memberships—every computer list we could find. Nothing."

"School records—looking for a dropout?"

"Nothing." After a moment, "Thanks for taking Diane to the morgue. I'm no good at it. Never know what to say."

Another moment. "Right where we were," Herb complained. "We've had two suspects and both had alibis. I hope that composite lights up the switchboard."

Ken telephoned Lori at the Stellar Building. "Missed you this morning," he said. He'd left her asleep in the cottage.

"Missed you. Sure was nice."

"Sure was."

"More of the same tonight?"

"Most definitely."

When he hung up, he saw that Herb had been listening. The detective winked, knowingly, and touched the palm of his hand.

Ken shut the office door and leaned against it. "Herb, there's something I have to get off my chest. These asides about Lori are insulting to me in general and to Lori in particular."

Herb met his gaze with impassive black eyes. "You're right. I apologize."

As Ken turned to leave, Herb cleared his throat. "About what I said—"

"Forget it."

"It's one of those moronic things an immature person says. You're right, it was insulting."

"No big deal. Let's forget it."

"Truth is," Herb persisted, "Lorraine Day is a beautiful woman. She's got class. Her mother's a bit dippy—no offense."

"No offense taken."

"She says I was a cohort in Caesar's army."

Ken laughed.

"Thing is," Herb said, "I said what I said to feel you out. When you didn't bite on me I figured I was right and it hurt my opinion of you. I worried that a nice lady with so much class was being used by a man she needed at the moment. Understand?"

"I do now."

"I feel better," Herb said. "You two fine people deserve the best."

"Thanks."

"Know what a cohort is?"

"An associate, companion."

"Used to be a military unit," Herb provided. "One of ten divisions in a Roman legion. I guess I was one of those."

Walking down the hall Ken passed the room where Diane was looking at mug sheets.

Right where they were . . .

And the Crystal Ball was tomorrow . . .

Bedeviled with gnats by day and mosquitoes that night, Jaydee had rolled up the windows and smoked cigarettes as a repellant. In the heat of his truck, perspiration soaked his clothing only to evaporate, leaving a salty residue that chaffed the flesh. He itched incessantly.

Shortly after three o'clock in the morning, he drove back to ORGRO, earlier than planned. And a good thing, too. He hadn't reckoned the time it took to pump five hundred gallons of gasoline.

Designed to fill the fuel tank of a truck, the antiquated pump delivered a mere 100 gallons in thirty minutes. His hands cramped from squeezing the nozzle. Finally, he tied it open and climbed down.

He used Mr. Gus's electric razor, selected clean coveralls. No point inviting suspicion, looking unkempt.

When he returned to the truck the pump made a coughing noise; the reservoir was dry.

He barely had time to move the truck before Mr. Gus drove up.

"You're early," Mr. Gus said.

"Ready to go."

"You are, are you." Mr. Gus looked around. "What time did you get in last night?"

"Must've been right after you left."

Mr. Gus limped around the truck. "How'd you get home?"

"Drove my wagon."

Mr. Gus sucked his lips in. "What're you up to, Jaydee?"

"What do you mean?"

"You're lying."

"About what?"

"Look at your station wagon. The windshield is covered with dew. It's been there all night."

"Okay. I walked. I had car trouble, Mr. Gus. Didn't want to worry you."

"Ready to go to Okeelanta?"

"That's right."

"What'd you put in the tank?"

"What you told me."

"What would that be?"

"Malathion."

"I didn't tell you anything," Mr. Gus said. "Malathion isn't what they ordered."

He rapped the tank. "It isn't full, Jaydee. Want to tell me what you're doing?"

Jaydee walked past him into the office. He went to the locker room, unzipped his coveralls and took out the pistol.

In the next room Mr. Gus thumped over to his desk.

"Mr. Gus?"

"What is it?"

Jaydee waited in the locker room, pistol in hand.

"What is it, Jaydee?"

The creak of the swivel chair and steps across the floor placed the old man. He came through the door as if expecting a surprise.

Jaydee leveled the gun.

"Jaydee?"

He pulled the trigger and Mr. Gus threw up both hands, staggering. "Jaydee! Wait, wait!" Mr. Gus fell, quivering. Jaydee put the muzzle to his head and fired again.

Smoke hung in the air, spent powder sweet to the nostrils.

He pulled the body into the dressing room, closed the door, turned off the lights and locked the office. He tossed a clipboard onto the front seat of his truck. Gasoline sloshed as he backed around chemical and fertilizer tanks.

There were few visitors at the distributorship. With a two-man operation, no one would be surprised to find them both gone.

After tonight, maybe he'd go someplace else. California or Oregon.

He'd thought about it before.

But he hadn't the perfect plan. If he thought about it long enough, sure—he'd go to California.

He stopped at a restaurant catering to the blue-collar trade. He bought several packs of cigarettes from a vending machine and selected a booth. Nearby, a man was reading the morning news—the drawing of Jaydee on page one.

It didn't matter.

Nobody would recognize him.

His mother hadn't. Lolly didn't.

Jaydee ordered six eggs over medium, two rashers of bacon, a double order of biscuits.

"My, aren't we hungry this morning?" the waitress teased.

He ran through the list of things to remember.

After the delivery . . .

Like Charles Whitman in the Texas tower . . . food, canned drinks . . .

He didn't dare go home for anything. In case the police were watching. In case Lolly had decided she knew the man in the drawing.

She didn't though.

He knew it, as surely as the morning sunrise—he knew he was invisible from this minute on. He could stroll through the herd undetected.

"There you go, husky," the waitress chided. "Eat it all, or you don't get dessert."

Like he was dumb.

"Coffee," he said.

Yeah. Today was the day. Two-thirty this afternoon.

All he had to do was occupy himself until then.

Meanwhile, the plan began to replay in his mind.

It was perfect . . .

CHAPTER TWENTY-FIVE

JAYDEE DECIDED it would be wise to wait out the morning back down at Loxahatchee. There, watching waterfowl and listening to the hum of gnats, he'd suffered the interminable tick of time. The dial of his watch had fogged with condensation. His flesh had gone rosy within the oven of the cab.

Finally, a few minutes early, he decided to go.

The truck rumbled, the windshield permanently etched by dust and sand. Heat radiated through the uncarpeted floorboard and gas fumes were thick despite opened windows. He had put his pistol beneath the seat and it chattered on metal as he followed the commercial truck route around West Palm. He crossed the north bridge to Palm Beach and turned on Ocean Boulevard. It was slow going along this usually serene residential street. Spanish bayonet grew near bricked walls, pampas grass formed ornamental screens. The terra-cotta tile roofs of mansions could be glimpsed among coconut palms and bougainvillea. The perfume of sweet acacia overcame fumes of petrol momentarily, and he found it repugnant.

A uniformed guard stood in the street directing traffic. Jaydee turned at the familiar entry. Another sentry stopped him.

"You got one hour, Bud." He gave Jaydee a pink card. ALL VEHI-
CLES MUST VACATE PROPERTY PROMPTLY 3:00 P.M. NO EX-
CEPTIONS!

Blocked by delivery vans, Jaydee lit a cigarette. Men unloaded ice and
cases of food and liquor. Tents stretched over long tables. The cacoph-
ony of reggae music was a din upon a din, men shouting orders, work
crews checking this or that.

Jaydee adjusted his sunglasses, leaned out, "Can you let me by?"

The truck preceding him pulled away and Jaydee crept past the
kitchen and side terrace. To his left, papaya and banana trees surrounded
the greenhouses. He saw the fruit of citrus within the glass building.

"Come on, come!" somebody shouted, and Jaydee shifted to double-
low for traction.

"Where you going with that thing?" a security guard hollered.

"Pump house."

"Jeeze, get on with it!"

For a moment, he had full view of the festivities to be: dancers in
costume, black men playing oil drum instruments, huge speakers that
blasted the ears with every note. Cooks in long white aprons and
mushroom hats tended pits, the smell of barbecue tantalizing.

There, on a terrace beside the swimming pool, he saw Violet Day the
younger, and Violet Day the elder. Also . . . Ken Blackburn.

Jaydee leaned forward against the steering wheel, enjoying the moment.

"Hey, pal, you asleep?"

The face in the truck window was florid. "I'm yelling move it, move
it, and you sit here like a rock. Now move this damned thing."

"I need to get to the pump house. My way is blocked."

The officer went ahead, berated the next driver and Jaydee inched
forward.

At last.

He backed the tanker toward the pump house and put the vehicle into
neutral, set the handbrake. He walked past caterers and bearers, people
rushing to meet the curfew before they must leave the grounds.

He was pulling a hose from a reel at the rear of his truck, dragging it
across the drive to the pump house door.

"What are you doing?"

The man wore no uniform, but he was armed and unmistakably a

cop—thick torso and bulging biceps. A tag on his breast pocket identi-
fied him. ABEL BLACKBURN—SECURITY.

"Delivering fertilizer."

"Fertilizer?"

The gardener appeared. "It's our usual order," he said. "The day after
the party I have to put the lawn together again."

The gardener turned to Jaydee. "Ten-five-fourteen mix?"

"Yes."

Deflected, the policeman moved away, hurrying people, reminding
them of the time.

"Lock the pump house before you leave," the gardener instructed.

"I'll do that."

Jaydee pulled his hose inside and paused.

The system was a beauty to any man in the business of landscaping.
Two five-hundred-gallon tanks. Four six-inch pumps, each of which
delivered eighty gallons per minute. The Smith injector was one of the
best to be had.

Jaydee removed a cap from the holding tank, screwed the hose to it
with a collar nut. He glanced out—nobody watching. He flushed sludge
from the bottom of the tank. Then, returning to the truck, he activated
the delivery pump, shoving volatile petroleum where fertilizer should
have been.

It took twenty minutes.

Jaydee used the time to shut off the cocks for the greenhouse, side
lawns and front yard. He concentrated the flow into 296 misters spread
over the region of the party.

"Got anything for me to sign?" The gardener leaned through the
doorway.

"No. Mr. Gus said don't bother."

"Be sure to lock up."

"I will."

Then, the critical moment. Jaydee pulled the door closed, knelt
beside the holding tank and opened the automatic control box. It was a
clock showing twenty-four hours to the day in thirty-day cycles. It could
be set with tiny metal pegs on a rotating wheel. At that moment it was
off. Jaydee turned it on.

Eight o'clock. He positioned the peg that would start the system. He
shut the box.

Usually, the sprinkler system drew concentrate from the holding tank at a ratio of 1 gallon fertilizer to 100 gallons of water. Jaydee altered it. *One hundred percent concentrate.*

When the pumps activated, the lines would first be flushed of water—a mild inconvenience to the guests. But moments later, gasoline would rise in misty cones from nearly three hundred sprinklers.

Anyone smoking might ignite it. An electrical arc could set it off. But if not, the open flames of the lanterns would certainly do it. He now knew the grave-like hole in the yard was a barbecue pit. He anticipated the conflagration would begin there.

In an instant, the compound would become a ball of fire.

And the world would know—

Jaydee rewound the hose. Officers were blowing their whistles, "Three o' clock—everybody out!"

Two Dade County panel trucks had arrived. Men in flak jackets led German shepherd dogs. Others carried metal detectors. *Bomb squads.*

The animals could sense a few grains of explosive. But gasoline was not something they had been trained to notice.

Jaydee moved unhurriedly.

He saw the two Violet Days and their men go into the guard building at the head of the drive.

With a song in their throats and champagne toasts, surrounded by fame and fortune—it would be ended. Out of the earth would come fluid under pressure, a fine flammable mist, at the rate of one gallon per minute per misting head.

It was only a matter of time . . .

Under a no-smoking sign in the security room Abel was puffing his pipe, reporting to Ken, Lorraine, Violet and Major.

"Nine video monitors," Abel said, indicating the screens, "show every foot of the grounds. Remote control"—he touched a button and one of the cameras swept an area, then zoomed to a close-up of men stoking the barbecue pit. "Sitting here, a guard can see a fly in a salad bowl." He demonstrated another camera making a visual pass over canopies, tables laden with food and ending at the pump house where a workman coiled his hose, preparing to depart.

"High resolution, state-of-the-art," Abel said, proudly.

"Very nice, Abel," Violet seemed appreciative.

"We've hired every off-duty deputy and police officer available," Abel said.

"How many is that?" Major questioned.

"Eighty-two."

"Eighty-two! Giving a million to charity might have been less expensive, Violet."

"Our responsibilities don't end here," Abel admonished. "Most of your invited guests are staying at The Breakers, with an overflow at the Hilton and Brazilian Court. We have to take precautions there, too."

"Abel knows what he's doing, Major," Violet said.

"At what cost?"

"We've arranged for buses to transport guests from the hotels," Abel related. "For those few who will insist on driving, we'll have valet parking."

"Abel," Violet cautioned, "I do hope you won't inconvenience our guests with metal detectors and vulgar searches."

"No, ma'am. If they're invited guests, on the list, they won't be inconvenienced. If they're media and have proper press credentials, they're fine."

"Advise your men accordingly," Major mandated.

On the monitors Ken saw automobiles, trucks and vans pulling away slowly.

"We haven't tried to keep up with anybody at this point," Abel seemed to read Ken's thoughts. "They come and go. But from now on, if they don't have clearance they're out of here. Bomb squads are covering every inch of terrain. By party time, this place will be secure."

In a rack on the wall, thirty hand-held shortwave radios were ready for distribution. Following Ken's eye, Abel grinned. "Best you can buy. Five-mile range and it'll receive or transmit in a steel girder building."

Violet yelped and raised a hand as if to stay conversation.

"What is it, Violet?" Major asked.

"Inez Cumbie!"

Violet's eyes were wild as she looked from Major to Lorraine, then she grabbed Ken's arm. "Something was there. Reading her letter, *she* was there—I said so, didn't I, Major?"

She wheeled, blue eyes skipping. "That is how it is in our business, Lorraine—insights for those who dare to see."

Violet shook Ken's arm. "I've been talking to a dead woman, Kenny.

No, no—she's been talking, I wasn't listening. Come with me. Major, call Herb Leibowitz!"

A grandfather clock ticked sonorously, then tolled four. Lorraine stood at Violet's side, Violet turning pages of Inez Cumbie's letter.

"You can do this, Lorraine," Violet murmured. "Let your mind go free."

"Do what, Violet?"

"Listen to Inez Cumbie—"

Herb chanced a glance at Ken and smiled, painfully.

"Let this be a lesson, Lorraine," Violet said. "It is always this way in our business. The signs are there for those of us blessed with sight."

Major Drummond was behind them looking over their shoulders.

"I don't see anything, Violet," Lorraine said. "I've read these letters dozens of times, just as you have."

"Darling," Violet pressured, "she tells you about her husband, Eugene. She tells you they loved word games—crossword puzzles—look at it. She's speaking to us, Lorraine."

"Dear God," Lorraine cried. "Anagrams! He's about thirty-three years old! He has shaggy brown hair!"

"What?" Ken started to rise and Major motioned him down again.

"How much is a kilo, Major?" Violet asked.

"Two-point-two pounds, Violet."

"The man weighs ten times that times eight," Lorraine said. "One hundred seventy-six pounds!"

"Yes," Violet said. "What else?"

"He says he has the sign of Satan in the palm of his hand—the shape of an hourglass."

"Do you believe this?" Herb spoke to Ken.

"He's over six feet tall," Lorraine added. "Strong jaw. Large ears. Big hands."

"Sleepy eyes," Violet added.

Ken could sit still no longer. He stalked across the room and stood beside Major.

"Gray eyes—a blue wagon—that would be an old station wagon! With a faded sign on the side that reads O-R-dash-dash-O."

Major was writing it down.

Lorraine looked up at Ken. "His name is J.D."
"If this is real," Herb said, "I'm a cohort. Mind showing me how you get this?"
"Anagrams," Lorraine marveled. "See, Ken, read this."

Always gallant, Eugene's altruistic bent overwhelmed/ underwhelmed the 33 worst in the history studies; he also graded generously, yet he and I realized better reports orally, were normal.

Lorraine scanned the page, picking up another passage:

We eventually instructed grades higher than kindergarten in long, overheated—the Indian-Mexican émigrés suffered the environs naturally—they invariably mastered elements so equitably, I grew haughty, too.

"Here's another one," Violet said.

Husbands enviably have a special grace regarding all yesterdays; eventually yesterdays emerge sweet and blissful, loving, utterly euphoric, with all grief only nebulous—only lovely dreams.

"Bless her heart," Lorraine said. "Bless her brave heart." She put her finger on another paragraph:

So, in deference, Eugene carried all responsibilities for any delays, especially delinquent students in general, not ordinarily responsive, doting, asinine, stricken homeroom delinquents always staying here overtime.

Ken read as Lorraine traced sentences.
"The first letter of each word in selected paragraphs. Like this one—"
" 'Never again make early judgments, darling,' he said."
Ken picked up the letters, jotting them on Major's pad. *N-a-m-e-J-D—he said.*
Violet smiled sadly. "Talking to a dead woman."

The guests were arriving. Violet and Lorraine had gone out to receive them. Across the hall in Violet's den, Major worked with ladies from Palm Beach civic clubs who had come to help organize the charitable aspects of the function. Items had to be labeled for auction tomorrow, descriptive teasers added to raise the bids.

"So what do we have now?" Ken pondered aloud. "Name J.D. Could be initials, the 'D' for 'Destiny' after all."

Herb was on the telephone trying to reassemble the task force downtown.

"Ask your computer operator to feed the initials J.D. into the machine, Herb."

"Ladies!" Major's voice rose from the den. This is the scarf Meryl Streep wore in the movie *The French Lieutenant's Woman.* But that's not enough to sell it. We want to mention John Fowles who wrote the book and the critical acclaim Miss Streep won for her portrayal of both Sarah and Anna. What else? We want to say this is more than a piece of silk—it is an intimate item, Miss Streep's personal memento, and she grieves to part with it . . ."

"The initials J.D. raise nothing, Ken," Herb spoke aside from the telephone. "Is there something we could add to it?"

"Working stiff," Ken recounted Diane's words. "Smelled like cattle dip." He added notes from Inez Cumbie's anagrams, "Old blue station wagon. Have the computer run auto registration again—for owners with last initial D, first initial J."

"It's too late, Ken. The Florida offices are closed and the state computers are down."

"Damn it. Okay. The faded sign on the station wagon read, O-R-dash-dash-O. Feed that into our computer."

"Asking what?" Herb demanded.

"Business names. Ask for businesses beginning with O-R."

Herb relayed the information, chewed his cigar, gazing out French doors at the party in progress.

"Computer jock wants to know in what context."

"Any business we've contacted. Chemicals, nurseries—"

A moment later, Herb grunted, "Spell it." Then, "ORGRO, Ken. O-R-dash-dash-O—ORGRO."

"The fertilizer people?"

Herb switched ears, asked for more information.

Major kept things moving in the den, circulating among his volunteers, commenting on their work. "Good description," he said. "That's what sells—"

"One of our boys has talked to ORGRO," Herb reported to Ken, "asking about Destiny; they're west of town, out the Belle Glade-Pahokee road."

ORGRO—it fit. Ken felt an electric thrill.

"Yeah?" Herb spoke into the phone. "Spell that."

He hung up, removed his cigar and looked at it, suppressing a smile. "ORGRO is run by a man named Gus Chambers. He has one employee. Unmarried, Caucasian male, about thirty-six years old, lives with his mother. Delivers pesticides and fertilizers. Makes occasional trips out of town."

"Send somebody out to ORGRO again."

"Even as we speak," Herb stated.

"Got a name for the employee?" Ken asked.

"Reaper," Herb grinned. "Jaydee Reaper . . ."

Lorraine was poised beside Violet to welcome their guests. Between greetings, Ken spoke to her quietly. "His name is Jaydee Reaper, Lori."

"So glad you came," Violet kept saying.

"Wouldn't have missed this for the world, darling!"

There was a nervousness, a war-zone tension. It became obvious when a speaker blew out in a sudden explosive pop. An instant of stunned silence was followed by artificial laughter, then voices rising again, slowly.

"Herb brought Diane Feldman to the security office," Ken continued. "She's watching the monitors. If she sees Jaydee—Destiny—she thinks she'll recognize him."

Chefs turned ribs over glowing embers. Decorated tables held a mountain of delicacies—fresh crab, boiled shrimp and lobster. The focal point was a twenty-foot-long ice sculpture of dolphins cavorting in a frigid surf.

"Are they going to arrest him here, Ken?"

"If they find him they will."

Flaming Polynesian lanterns lined walkways and marked the limits of festivities. An arrangement of small brightly colored tents provided guests amusement with costumed fortunetellers, or a voodoo doctor offering occult advice to those who wanted it. Other tents were equipped with computers which produced an astrograph upon request.

"I'll be gone awhile, Lori," Ken explained. "We think we've located this Reaper fellow's home address."

"I wish you could stay, Ken."

She shivered under his arm. "Believe me, Lori, he isn't here. In this crowd he'd stand out like a bruised lip."

The reggae band beat an infectious rhythm as dancers performed onstage. In the loggia, adjacent to the pool and terrace, a large orchestra attired in white tie and tails prepared for more sedate dancing later.

Out on the Atlantic, small craft bobbed in the last of the sunshine.

"Now tell me, Violet," a gravelly voiced actress accused, "you invented this story about the madman, didn't you? I'll be so disappointed if nothing really happens."

"Damn fool," Lorraine murmured.

Cases of liquor were stacked behind the bars, tenders serving drinks ranging from exotic to mundane. Familiar faces of entertainers from Hollywood to Broadway mixed with industry moguls. Their raiment was eclectic—shimmering gowns and tuxedos, designer jeans and running shoes—the overdressed and the elegantly understated; bejeweled and casual.

Palm Beach galas were never late-night affairs. Most guests attended too many parties to indulge beyond a decent hour. Guests tonight, tomorrow host and hostess. Everything was planned to a social formula: drinks, dining, the birthday song for Violet, then dancing. It would all be ended before eleven.

It was gaudy and it was regal. Rebellious rock stars reveled in costume and wild hairdos, or shirts open to the waist, men *and* women. Old money scions were a picture of assurance and reserve. True to style, the performers constantly performed, for their mentors, producers and directors.

"This is my daughter," Violet said repeatedly. "She is the new Violet Day."

"You have hip boots to fill, my dear—"

"Yes, I know."

Ken waited impatiently, conspicuously wearing his pistol and shortwave radio.

"We cannot yield to the wretched types who would destroy our last bastion of civilized debauchery," a famous author proclaimed.

Internationally recognized names dropped like rain as the famous and nearly famous evoked images of stars and superstars conspicuously absent.

"I heard Bruce Springsteen would be here," somebody lamented. "Is that true?"

"He's in Europe."

"Damn. Pity."

An aging actress had joined dancers onstage, giving an enthusiastic if somewhat arthritic show for the crowd. She wasn't getting much encouragement.

"Have you tried the West Indies salad?" Lori heard a woman ask. "Bit vinegarish."

"It's supposed to have vinegar, my dear."

"Yes, but domestic?"

"Hello!" Violet greeted another guest. "Have you met my daughter? She's the new Violet Day."

The last glow of sundown passed in shades of titian, nightfall inviting a gentle breeze from the sea. The wink of boat lights were fallen stars riding gentle waves.

From the entertainment world came many youthful millionaires. At one of the bars, a young man brazenly shaved cocaine into snortable rows. The smell of marijuana rose in the night. Distressed, Lorraine asked Ken to intervene.

"No," Violet ordered. "Leave the guests alone."

"Like hell. Throw the bums out, Ken."

But he didn't. He asked them to be discreet.

"The day of the refined celebrity is past," Lorraine said, peevishly. "They don't worry about major studios or bad public relations. The only thing these people have in common is wealth."

"This will pass," her mother said. "We have about an hour before the birthday song and then you may leave. Meantime, smile, Lorraine!"

"Ken?" the voice from his shortwave was Abel. "Herb Leibowitz at the front gate."

"I'm going, Lori. Be back shortly."

She squeezed his hand, tried to brighten her smile. "When you return I'll be ready for a hideaway for two."

"Maybe they'll have fireworks," a New York dancer said. "We need something after the buildup."

Despite Violet's best efforts, the crowd remained subdued, standing in clusters, drinks in hand.

Lorraine linked her arm in Ken's and walked with him. "This served a purpose years ago. It raised money for charity, brought national attention to Violet Day. But this is the last, so help me!"

A man in bright yellow suspenders strolled past. He wore a brilliant red shirt, melon-colored trousers that fell only to his calves exposing fancy silk stockings. His shoes were old-fashioned, two-tone brown and white wingtips.

The man jostled a guest, then apologized profusely and wiped away spilled drink. He helped the offended patron adjust his jacket.

Ken spoke into his radio, "I think we have a dip."

"Peacock?" Abel's voice answered. "Yellow suspenders."

"That's the one."

"He works for us."

"What?"

"Checks anybody who looks like he's packing a piece," Abel said.

"A pickpocket?"

"One of the best."

Ken hooked the radio to his belt. "What are we doing here, Lori? This is crazy."

"Yes," she kissed him warmly. "Crazy. Please be careful, Ken, and hurry back."

CHAPTER
TWENTY-SIX

HERB TURNED SOUTH on the Dixie Highway. Police officers had preceded them, moving into positions surrounding the address of Jaydee Reaper.

Ken rode with Herb in the detective's car. The pieces had begun to come together. The radio crackled. "Herb?" a voice said. "There's nobody at ORGRO. But there are a couple of cars. One is an old station wagon with what's left of the word 'ORGRO' on the sides."

"Get a warrant. Stake it out and stay out of sight."

"Herb"—the same voice—"we telephoned the manager's wife. She says her husband hasn't been home yet, but that's not unusual. He goes to a bar now and then to ease a bad leg. Want us to try and find him?"

"Send somebody else," Herb directed. "Keep an eye on that station wagon."

Herb recognized some of his men and pulled to the curb. It was a neighborhood of never-fashionable, mostly concrete-block houses with identical front stoops, driveways and a separate garage in the rear. Children in costumes were going door to door, trick-or-treating. Herb rolled down his window to speak with an officer.

"Fourth house on the right, next block," the policeman said.

285

"There's somebody there. I walked past and looked in. An older woman, a young woman and a couple of children."

"Any men?"

"None I could see."

"Everybody in place?"

"Waiting for you."

"I don't want gunfire with these children in the neighborhood," Herb said. "Fire only if fired upon. Pass the word on that."

"Yes, sir."

"Okay," Herb commanded. "Ken and I will take the front."

He pulled away from the curb, advancing slowly, mindful of young-sters running in the darkened street. Herb parked his unmarked vehicle squarely outside the front yard. He and Ken walked to the porch.

"Mrs. Reaper?" Herb spoke through a screened door. "Is Jaydee home?"

"Jaydee? No. What do you want?"

She turned on the porch light and Ken felt vulnerable. Herb displayed his badge. "May we come in, Mrs. Reaper?"

"What is it this time?"

Ken saw officers coming over a fence at the rear, others moving toward the garage. Next door, a woman screamed at her children. Inside, the TV blared.

"We'd like to come in, Mrs. Reaper."

She sighed, the exasperated expulsion of a woman put upon, unlatch-ing the screen door. Herb entered first.

"Is Jaydee in trouble?" the younger woman asked.

"Who are you?" Herb questioned.

"My name is Lolly. This is my mama and Jaydee is my brother—is he in trouble?"

"We'd like to speak to him."

Other men were coming through behind them.

"What is this?" Mrs. Reaper cried. "You can't barge in here like this!"

The television was too loud. The room smelled of kitty litter. Cats in cages sat in a corner.

"You're letting out my cats!" Mrs. Reaper pushed Ken aside and snatched the screen door closed.

"May we have permission to look through your house, Mrs. Reaper?"

"I'm not so sure," she balked. "You got a warrant or whatever?"

"We'll get one if we must."

"I'm not so sure—what do you think, Lolly?"

"I want to know what's going on," Lolly said, nervously. She jiggled a baby, her other child watching the TV.

"Where could we find your son, Mrs. Reaper?"

"How the hell would I know? At work, most likely. Call Mr. Gus, he can tell you."

"What time does Jaydee get home?"

"When he pleases. He didn't come home last night. Out of town, probably. Call Mr. Gus Chambers."

Some of the men carried shotguns and wore helmets. Bulletproof vests and dark blue uniforms signified the seriousness of the situation.

"Tell me what this is about," Mrs. Reaper said, firmly, "or get out of my house."

On a table lay a book. *Dr. Gayle Zuckerman.* Ken picked it up.

"Lolly, go next door and call Ray. Tell him to get a lawyer and come over here this instant."

"What lawyer, Mama?"

"Do what I tell you! Go call Ray."

"No ma'am." Herb blocked passage. "Before you go anywhere, I want to know how to find Jaydee."

Ken had opened the book, reading the author's greeting: *To Destiny.*

"We have rights," Mrs. Reaper stiffened. "We don't have to talk about anything and I don't think we should, Lolly."

"Please," Lolly pleaded, "tell us what's happened. What is this about?"

"This," Ken extended the book. "It's about this—"

"That!" Mrs. Reaper forced a laugh. "Aw, hell, if Jaydee stole a book, I'll pay for it."

Herb read the inscription.

"You know how boys are." Mrs. Reaper seemed tortured. "Jaydee said that lady gave him the book. We knew better, didn't we, Lolly?"

Lolly was wide-eyed, the baby bouncing.

"Said he helped that lady carry things to her car—hell, I'll pay for it. How much is it?"

Behind her, an officer opened a bedroom door, his shotgun ready to fire—then to the next door—

"I've told Jaydee about lying," Mrs. Reaper said. "You do the best you can, you keep a God-fearing Christian house. You do the best you can—"

"Mama," Lolly said, "this ain't about a book."

"Then, what, Lolly? What is it about?"

Herb spoke to a fellow officer, "Get a warrant and make it snappy."

"Whoa!" Mrs. Reaper laughed, theatrically. "There's no need for that. The neighbors will be watching. Embarrassing. But I've been embarrassed before by Jaydee. Okay. What do you want?"

"Look around the house," Herb said, grimly.

"Okay. Look. Go ahead."

Herb spoke to the same officer, "Get the warrant."

Men stepped over and around yowling cats. Into the kitchen, down a hallway.

Herb lit his cigar. "Mind if I smoke?"

"Lolly, turn down that TV, honey. Would any of you gentlemen like a beer or a glass of iced tea?"

"Jaydee's in real trouble, isn't he?" Lolly asked Ken. "I saw you on TV."

"I'm afraid so."

"Something really bad," she said.

"I'm sorry."

"Hurt—hurt—hurt somebody."

"Or," Mrs. Reaper said, "I could make a pot of coffee. We still have coffee, don't we, Lolly?"

Lolly was weeping. The baby began to cry. On the floor, sucking his thumb, the little boy scooted forward on his buttocks and turned up the volume again.

"Mrs. Reaper," Herb tried anew, "it is important that we find Jaydee. We need to do it now, it can't wait. Where would he be likely to go? A friend, maybe?"

"He has no friends."

"Male or female?"

"Not to know about."

"Is there a particular place—a bar, or restaurant?"

"Not to know," she said.

"You say he didn't come home last night? Is that something he does often?"

"If he goes out of town. Sometimes he sprays groves out of town. Mr. Gus could tell you."

"Do you have a telephone, Mrs. Reaper?"

"Out of order."

Herb spoke aside to another policeman. "Get in touch with Mick out at ORGRO. See if the manager has been located."

Mrs. Reaper was on the couch now, her robe tucked modestly. She stroked a cat.

"Mr. Gus can tell you," she said. "He would know . . ."

Herb left men hidden in the area, the two women confined to the house. Now, driving out the Belle Glade highway, Ken sighed wearily. "The murder matrix," he said. "It fits the profile, Herb."

"Murder matrix."

"You want to see Jaydee Reaper as a child, look at that little boy glued to the TV. The house is crawling with cops, his mother crying, his grandmother shouting—and he didn't stop sucking his thumb, his eyes never left the television."

"Yeah."

"Isolated, alone in a crowded room."

"Yeah, I saw it."

"Everything that child feels is blunted. He exists in a world apart. Did you see the way he held his testicles, oblivious to anything but the TV?"

"Be hunting for him in a few years, I guess."

"The grandmother—'You know how boys are.' Beating the authorities is a part of that child's cognitive mapping—us-against-them mentality. In his fantasies he is struggling to control an uncontrollable environment. He'll find violence exciting—setting up an opiod response."

"What's that?"

"Adrenaline—he'll get hooked on it. Like men who court death driving fast cars or climbing high mountains—opiod means like an opiate, a drug. He'll get gratification from the high of it, then the violence will begin to escalate."

"Depressing," Herb said. "That's the place, isn't it—off to your right—is that ORGRO?"

They turned onto oyster-shell bedding, tires crunching. A policeman stepped from the shadows.

"Mrs. Chambers is on her way, Herb. I sent somebody after her."

"Okay, Mick."

"Damned mosquitoes will carry you off out here."

"Get in while we wait."

"I'll take the mosquitoes over that cigar."

Around the bulbs of bare security lights, insects whirred.

Finally, another car drove up. A short, plump woman got out. "I'm Doris Chambers," she said. "I don't know where Gus could be."

"Do you have keys, ma'am?"

"I brought a set, but I don't know which is which."

She gave them to Mick and he tried several on a ring until the gate lock parted.

"That's Gus's car," she said. "Jaydee's station wagon."

"What could they be driving, Mrs. Chambers?"

She looked around the fenced area. "The small tank truck, apparently."

"You say you can tell where Jaydee is by a log?" Mick questioned.

"The order sheets. They're on a pegboard inside."

Mick unlocked the office door and she turned on fluorescent lights that hummed overhead.

"Here we go," she picked up a clipboard on a desk.

Mick was in the next room. "Herb. Better come look at this."

Ken glanced in the doorway, then grabbed for Mrs. Chambers as she passed him.

"What is—oh, my God! Is that Gus? Oh, my God!"

Ken shielded her with his body.

"Is that Gus?" she screamed.

The body lay on the floor, one arm lifted in rigor. For the first time, Ken saw blood beneath their feet. He maneuvered the woman outside. "No, no! Was that Gus?"

"Call forensics," Herb ordered, mechanically. "Get the medical examiner."

Mick was on the telephone.

Ken helped Mrs. Chambers to Mick's police car, knelt beside the open door in agonized silence as she wailed and rocked.

"Ken?"

"Yeah, Herb."

"The order sheet says Okeelanta. South of Belle Glade."

"Mrs. Chambers, may I call someone for you?" Ken asked.

Herb, on the radio, issued bulletins to state police and the sheriff's satellite office in Belle Glade.

"We kept no money here," the woman cried. "Why would anyone shoot him?"

"Mrs. Chambers, I'm very sorry."

"Gus never hurt anybody."

Ken got into the car beside her. "Mrs. Chambers, do you have family?"

Other officers arrived and somebody took Ken's place.

"Shot his boss," Herb said. "Why would he do that? Didn't steal his wallet. Does this fit that profile?"

"Not sexual. No."

"Had to know somebody would find the man. Had to know we'd be on him soon after."

"Chambers must've known something," Ken said. "Stood in Jaydee's way somehow."

The men were looking at one another, neither aware of the lingering stare.

Ken turned back to the woman. "Mrs. Chambers, we have to know— can you describe the truck Jaydee is driving?"

"Tank truck. To haul pesticides and liquid fertilizers. It's not a new truck. Oh, God, oh, God—"

"Maybe we're wrong," Herb reasoned. "It wasn't Reaper at all. This just doesn't fit."

"Herb!" Mick called from the office door.

"Yo?"

"He didn't go to Okeelanta."

Herb swore in Yiddish.

They ran to the cruiser and Herb asked the dispatcher to patch him through to Mick by radio. "Mick, call Palm Beach police. Looking for an ORGRO tank truck. Call the sheriff and state patrol, every unit they can spare. Give them Jaydee Reaper's description and mark it hot."

Herb turned toward town, tires hurling shells behind them as he gunned the motor.

"Where would he go, Ken?"

"I don't know, Herb."

"Hey, hey," Herb said, sharply. "This is your thing!"

"I don't know!" Ken tried to clear his mind. "He'd want to hurt Violet. Hurt me. He can't get in there, Herb. Dad has the place locked up."

"Someplace else then. Where?"

"It would be—damn it, I don't know—it would be a place familiar to him."

Herb lifted the microphone. "Mick—get a list of every place ORGRO services in Palm Beach."

"I'll try, Herb."

"There's nothing he can do," Ken insisted to himself. "He isn't suicidal. Homicidal, but not suicidal. Whatever he does, he'd want to get away."

"Then, what?"

They crossed the middle bridge on Royal Poinciana and halted. "Which way?"

"I wish I knew, Herb."

Police cars were coming, lights flashing. Herb got on the radio, "Mick! Tell everybody to kill the flashers, and no sirens."

"Right, Herb."

Then, completely unexpected, Herb reached over and held Ken's neck. Very calmly, almost brotherly, he said, "This is what you know best. This is what you do. Remember what Violet said, reading the letter? The signs are there for those with sight—you have the sight. This is your moment. Think like the bastard thinks. Where would he go?"

"Someplace to—to watch, maybe."

"To watch."

"The party."

"Like a high roof."

"Maybe."

Diminutive figures in the garb of ghosts darted from house to house. Out of the dark came Day-Glo skeletons swinging plastic jack-o'-lanterns filled with candy. Herb moved the car at walking speed, alert for a heedless child.

Ken remembered his own Halloweens past. The beach condominiums were always good territory. Tourists seldom expected callers, and caught unawares, they gave money instead of sweets.

Witches in peaked hats crossed the roadway recklessly, their masks leering in the headlights. Chaperones hurried to keep pace with their ghouls.

Herb circled methodically, down one block, up another, through parking garages.

"Herb?" Mick on the radio. "You wanted a list of places served by ORGRO in Palm Beach. I found it on a rotary directory here in the ORGRO office. I'll name places with a Palm Beach address, starting with the last letter of the alphabet."

Mick's voice became a slow litany. Nurseries, hotels, condominiums. One of the familiar names turned Herb toward a high rise nearby.

"Herb—look there."

Tank truck.

. . . estates, golf courses, greenhouses . . .

Herb pulled past the truck, looking in the window. He stopped and they both got out.

". . . private residences next, Herb . . ."

Herb on one side, Ken on the other, guns drawn, they snatched open the truck doors and gazed across an empty seat.

". . . Witherbee, Thomas, Samson . . ." Mick's voice was a singsong.

"*Oy vey,*" Herb murmured. "I'll find the landlord. You stay with the truck."

". . . Nelson, Monroe, Lancaster . . ."

Ken leaned back to look up. *Twelve floors.*

". . . Farland, Edwards, Day—Hey, Herb—Day! Violet Day."

"Mick, this is Blackburn." He gave the address. "I think we've found him. We need backup."

"Roger."

Ken ran to Herb. The detective was bathed yellow by the glow of a lightbulb over the manager's office.

"You're who?" an elderly woman challenged.

"Police!"

"Nobody by that name here."

"Herb, Violet Day is one of his deliveries. That's probably how he got started on this fixation—I'm going up."

"Wait for a backup, Ken."

But Ken was running. He reached the elevator and it wasn't available. He stepped back, looking up. The shaft and a freestanding stairwell rose parallel to the main building, but were set apart for fire exit. Every apartment faced an opened walkway overlooking the grounds below. He heard children screeching, "Trick or treat!"

Taking the stairs two at a time, at each level he looked for the elevator. On the fifth floor he found it.

"Let go of the door, son."

"My mommie is coming."

"Let it go."

"Sir," a mother called, "we're going up."

"No, ma'am—police. Take the children below."

Ken pressed a button and the lift rose one floor. The children had punched every button. He drew his pistol, made certain it was fully loaded. At each level the elevator halted, the doors opened. More little tricksters.

"Lady, take your children below. Police emergency."

He heard Herb, gasping, feet pounding the steel and concrete stairs.

On the eleventh floor Ken abandoned the lift. As he emerged on the top flight, a tenant in slippers and a bathrobe was dumping garbage down a chute. "Which way to the roof?"

"End of the corridor. Is that a gun?"

"Yes, ma'am. Police. Go inside and stay there."

Behind him, empty, the elevator arrived, yawned, and closed to descend.

"Abel," Ken spoke into his shortwave radio, "this is Ken."

"Yes, Kenny."

"We think we've found Jaydee Reaper. It's a condo roof about three-quarters of a mile from you. Clear the yard, Dad."

"Clear the yard? Kenny, there are four hundred people out there."

"Clear the yard! Do it now."

He approached a metal fire door and with his back to the wall, pulled it open. The lightbulb had been broken, the passage absolutely black.

Herb lunged into view, holding his chest, gasping. "Wait," he rasped. "Wait."

A step at a time, his own ribs aching from exertion, Ken felt his way up the ascending well. Pieces of the broken bulb crunched underfoot.

Herb hurled aside the lower door and blocked it, his panting so audible Ken said, "Herb, shut up!"

He eased the upper door ajar. A warm breeze swept past him and took the portal out of his hand.

In the distance, strung like luminous diamonds, north Palm Beach lights curved away in a beautiful arc. With his naked eye, Ken could see the glitter that was the Violet Day compound.

And there, sitting on a stool at the edge of the roof—Jaydee Reaper, his back to Ken, peering through a huge pair of binoculars.

Ken heard Herb wheezing behind him.

"Jaydee," Ken said. "Don't move."

In the same instant, Jaydee moved, so quickly that Ken was not prepared. *As if the man expected him* Jaydee threw himself aside, rolling away in the dark.

"Police!" Herb yelled. "Hold it!"

Ken saw the flash, heard the reverberation—a missile whizzed by his ear and he dropped to one knee.

"Police, Jaydee!" Herb hollered. "Ken, you're blocking me!"

Then, there he was—rising from the dark of the roof, a silhouette against a glow of lights beyond. Ken held the man in his sights.

Another flash and Herb flung himself away.

"Goddamn it!" Herb screamed. "Shoot him!"

He had to. Ken told himself that. *He had to shoot.*

Thinking he'd wounded Ken, Jaydee advanced, his pistol held with both hands, pointing.

Ken fired . . .

CHAPTER
TWENTY-SEVEN

TENSION AND THE VOLUME of the reggae band had given Lorraine a headache. The evening breeze died and the party threatened to do the same. Circulating through the crowd with her mother, Lorraine tried to lift the mood with a joviality she didn't feel.

Barbecue ribs simmered on a grill, hickory smoke rising. Here and there, liquor laughs in the bubbles of conversation.

A uniformed guard touched Lorraine's elbow. "Abel Blackburn wants you and Miss Day in the security room."

"Is something wrong?"

"He says to clear the grounds."

"Oh, dear." Violet walked rapidly, Lorraine hurried alongside.

Major was already there. "If they've caught the man," Major reasoned, "what could be the problem?"

"I don't know," Abel replied. "Kenny said clear the yard and do it now."

"Then we shall," Violet agreed.

Abel reached for his radio to give the order and Violet stopped him. "If officers start herding people, it might cause undue alarm. I'll go onstage and ask them to leave."

"No," Abel said. "I don't think you should be out there."

"What *is* it?" Major demanded.

"Mr. Drummond, I do not know." He pushed Diane Feldman to the door, "Go on out, sugar."

"Can you reach Ken on that radio? Ask him!"

"Kenny," Abel called, "come in."

"If Kenny says clear the grounds," Violet commanded, "let us do it without delay."

"Kenny—can you hear me?"

"What time is it, Major?" Violet asked.

"A few minutes until eight."

"They're expecting me onstage at eight for the birthday song. I'll go now and explain that we have a problem."

"Kenny? Come in."

"Dad—" Ken was breathless. "Where is Lori? Violet?"

"They're here, Kenny. Listening."

"Ask them what ORGRO means to them."

"I know what it means," Abel said. "Fertilizer. They made a delivery today."

"Dad, it's got to be something in the pump house. Get those people out of there."

Immediately, Violet ran toward the stage.

Abel reached past a guard, redirected a video camera to the pump house door. "It's locked."

"I'll find the gardener," Major stated.

"Dad?"

"Ken, goddamn it, we're doing it, son."

"Don't fool around! Get those people out of there."

"Okay," Abel said to himself. "Okay." He used his shortwave radio. "Attention security personnel. We have an emergency. Move these people to the street, away from the pump house. Do it calmly, but do it now."

On the monitors, Lorraine saw Major here, there, looking for the gardener.

"Ladies and gentlemen!" Violet's voice rose from the speaker system.

Applause began, people turning to face the hostess.

"Ladies and gentlemen, I am so sorry," Violet said, "but I must ask you to go to the street immediately. Please do not delay—go to the street at once."

"Dad?" Ken's voice. "Dad?"

Abel was outside in the driveway. Lorraine lifted the microphone, asking the sentry, "How do I use this?"

"Push the button to talk, let go to listen."

"Ken, this is Lori."

"Lori—stay there, darling."

"Ken, what is it?"

"We got Jaydee Reaper. He was watching the compound from a roof south of you. He killed his boss, Lori. I don't know why—interrupted something—it may be nothing, but let's not gamble. Tell Dad to hurry."

"They're working on it, Ken. Are you all right?"

"Yes. Lori, I'm looking through binoculars—can't they move any faster?"

Lorraine yelled at Abel. "Faster, Abel!"

"Let's go, let's go," Abel urged. Some nearly ran, others strolled deliberately. There were those drunk, or high or unconcerned. "Come along, people! Let's go!"

"Officer, what seems to be the trouble?"

"Lady, we can't talk now. Go to the street."

Onstage, Violet impelled and soothed simultaneously. Major was at the pump house door trying to batter it open with his shoulder. Where was the gardener! Behind Violet, musicians put away their instruments.

"Jaydee won't talk, Lori," Ken spoke on the radio. "Something is wrong there. Reaper asked Herb for the time."

"The time? But what—"

Eight o'clock! The birthday song. Lorraine ran to the door of the building. "Violet—run! Run!"

Her voice did what nothing else could—somebody screamed and, instantly, people shoved and fled. A security guard helped a woman to her feet.

"Violet!" Lorraine screamed. "Get out of there!"

"Do not run," Violet spoke to the crowd. "Do not panic. You boys at the food tables, help people to the street . . ."

Major slammed against the pump house door and fell back. He looked around, picked up a stick and tried to lever the hasp.

"Violet!" Lorraine started for the stage and Abel seized her. "No. Stay here."

"Eight o'clock, Abel—it must be something at eight o'clock!"

Major's stick broke and he cast about for another.

"Lori, are you there?" Ken's voice. "Lori, darling—hello, Lori!"
"Ken, it must be aimed at the birthday song. Eight o'clock. Ask the
man if that's it."
"He won't talk. Lori—don't go out there."
"It's a minute, maybe less!"
"Lori, stay away from the pump house."
On the monitor, Major attacked the door with all his strength. Violet's
dress caught a breeze and lifted like a diaphanous curtain. "Move along,
please," she was saying. "Please go to the street . . ."
"Abel," Lorraine said, "my mother."
"I'll get her."
Lorraine turned to the guard in the security room. "What time is it?"
"About thirty seconds to eight, if my watch is right."
"Lori, are you there?"
"Ken—yes—Ken—"
"Stay there."
"Yes, Ken."
"Hey!" somebody shouted.
"Ken," Lorraine said into the radio, "the sprinklers came on."
The crowd moved like wheat in the wind, first one way, then another.
Abel stopped, yelled at Violet, then wheeled to escape.
Major at the pump house door looked across the lawn.
"Run!" Violet yelled. "Run!"
"Ken," Lorraine quavered, "I smell gas—"
With a *whoosh,* flames raced over the scene, a massive fireball
churned. The oxygen momentarily consumed, a roiling mushroom
lifted slowly—but then, a second fire erupted, licking the yard, into
tents and under canopies, torching trees.
A last, indelible image of Major—running through volatile spray,
trying to reach Violet. She extending both arms to him—and the inferno
engulfed them . . .
Jaydee cackled, "All *right!"*
Ken blinked, blinked, trying to regain his vision. The close-up view
had shocked his eyes, producing temporary blindness.
"Eight *o'clock!"* Jaydee chortled.
Ken dived for the man and Herb jumped to stop him. Ken shoved Herb
with such force it sent the detective sprawling. He seized Jaydee by his
belt and collar, hauling the handcuffed figure toward the edge of the roof.

"Ken!" Herb hollered. "No, Ken!"

Jaydee screamed obscenities, hooked a vent with one foot. Ken snatched him free, dragging him toward the precipice.

"Ken, no!" Herb screamed. "No!"

With his hands bound, shoulder wounded, Jaydee was helpless—he snapped at Ken's leg, teeth clicking.

At the edge, for an instant, Ken let him look down twelve floors to the lighted pool and terrace below. Then he hurled Jaydee into space and grabbed him by the ankles.

With a screech, Jaydee went out the length of his body, stiff with terror, and fell to bump the side of the building. There, upside down, his fingers splayed behind his back, he screamed.

"Ken," Herb crawled toward him. "Don't do it. He isn't worth it."

A police officer called up from the stairwell, "Herb? You up there?"

"Get an ambulance!" Herb yelled. "Stay there." Then, softly, "Don't do it, Ken. For Lorraine. Don't let go."

"Stay back, Herb."

"Herb!" Another cop.

"Get away!" Herb shouted.

Herb was so close Ken could smell the cigar on his breath. "If you drop him," he said, "I'll swear he jumped. But don't do it."

Jaydee was blubbering.

"Ken, this is not the way," Herb reasoned.

Ken made a quick move as if to release Jaydee and the man squawled.

"What have you been telling me?" Herb insisted. "He couldn't help himself. You said that. The little boy sucking his thumb? You want to go after him before he gets started? Reaper is the head on a pimple, Ken. There's more to the infection than him. Ken—don't drop him."

"Stay back, Herb."

Someone else reached the roof and Herb cursed the man vehemently. "Go below! Keep everybody off this roof."

"Yeah. Sure, Herb."

Jaydee wailed. Urine seeped through his trousers. Ken saw fire trucks racing north, claxtons blaring.

"How about his mama?" Herb questioned. "His father? Where will you stop?"

"Ken?" Lori's voice on the radio.

Herb scampered to the instrument, "Come in, Lorraine."

"Is Ken there?"

"He's listening."

"Ken—do you hear me? Are you all right?"

Ken's legs cramped, his arms painfully stretched; Jaydee's boots were slipping through his grasp.

"Ken, can you come home now? Please come home."

Herb reached past Ken and took a handful of Jaydee's pants. "So, what say, Ken? If we drop him, we'll say he jumped. But it isn't the way."

Ken nodded. They hauled Jaydee onto the roof, face down. He croaked, coughing, vomited.

"You okay?" Herb questioned Ken.

"Okay."

Herb went to the stairwell, shouting. "How long do we have to wait for a backup?"

Officers poured onto the roof.

Ken took the shortwave. "Lori, can you hear me?"

"Yes, darling."

"How bad?"

"Bad, Ken." He heard her sob. "Violet and Major . . ."

Sirens warbled. Somebody read Jaydee his rights. The compound was a black hole, surrounded by flashing lights. Smoke rose to a cool air mass and flattened like an anvil, halving the face of a full moon.

"Ken, are you coming? I need you."

"Okay," he said. "I'm on my way . . ."

CHAPTER
TWENTY-EIGHT

IN THE LIVES of most men, time is calculated by dial and calendar. By the setting of the sun and rising moon, primitive cultures marked the past. But, Ken thought, time had to be reckoned in more ways than the chronology of human indicators.

Eight weeks. An eon ago.

He had come downstairs for breakfast, but halted in the wide, open hallway. Outside, the December sun was brilliant as it can only be in the clear skies of Florida by winter. A cool breeze swept past him, up the stairs to open windows.

He would never again enjoy a moment without thinking, fleetingly, of Jaydee Reaper. Imprisoned for life, Jaydee forfeited a succulent steak cooked to order, the sip of an especially good drink, the satisfaction of making love to someone who loved him. Maybe that was the true punishment for such criminals. Those joys were denied forever.

A stranger might never guess the tragedy that had occurred here. New sod covered some of the scars of scorched earth. The pump house and guest cottages had been rebuilt. Where heat had blistered and soot had stained, men scrubbed and painted the evidence away. The emotional scars would never vanish, however.

Lori sat on the terrace, gazing across the pool and lawn toward the ocean. She was unaware of Ken, lost in thought. She spent a lot of time lost in thought these days.

Nothing was as before. He, Lori, Becky—a family now. How could he ever have imagined that this position would be unsatisfactory? If he was major domo to the new Violet Day, it felt as comfortable as a well-worn glove.

"Everything is as it should be," Lori had commented one night. "Despite all that has happened."

As if, in fact, eight weeks ago was an eon past . . .

"Morning, Ken!" Becky came downstairs with the bouncy gait of youth. "Seventy-six degrees," she said. "It doesn't feel like Christmas Eve, does it?"

And yet it did.

Peace on Earth . . .

"Well?" Becky paused at the door, "Are you coming out for breakfast?"

Their arrival stirred Lori and she accepted kisses from them both.

Becky collapsed in a deck chair, took a deep breath, smiling. "Snow and fir and crackling logs," she said. "*That* is Christmas."

They were flying to Switzerland this afternoon, but Becky didn't know it yet. The trip was part of her gift. They'd be staying at a chalet in Lucerne.

"Telephone, Mr. Blackburn," Annie delivered an extension to the patio table.

Tommy Linden's voice was upbeat. "Hi, Ken! Merry Christmas!"

"Hey, Tommy. You want to speak to Becky?"

"Not yet," he said. "How's Lori?" .

"I think all right."

"Becky, too?"

"You know the resilience of youth."

"Thank God," Tommy said, soberly. "Listen, Ken, as executor of Violet's estate, I have to fly to nine countries and two dozen cities. I'll be in Europe next week. I don't want to impose, so feel free to deny me."

"What is it?"

"I wondered if I could stop by Lucerne. You and I could discuss some details while Lori and Becky ski."

"That would be fine."

"Been reading Lori's columns. They're better and better. More mature."

She was a believer now and the columns reflected it. If she lacked the second sight of her mother and grandmother, Lori more than compensated with common sense and a flair for writing.

"Incidentally," Tommy said, "I finished the legal work for Diane Feldman, as you asked. We settled with the government so the family home will be hers."

"Good, Tommy."

"She talks like she wants to go back to college. Thinking about accounting, she says. Asking me about Arizona. Who knows, right? It may be in the stars."

A lingering scent of burnt wood surprised Ken and he shot a glance at Lori. She smelled it too.

"Okay!" Tommy said. "Let me speak with Becky."

Becky retreated with the phone to a far chair, babbling about remedial studies to catch up with her classmates.

"To me," Lori said, "Christmas is tinkling chimes, poinsettias and Annie's turkey."

Annie came onto the terrace, her expression so acutely distressed that Lori asked, "What is it, Annie?"

"A letter, Miss Lorraine. From overseas."

Becky hung up and joined them, staring at the envelope. The ink was deep purple, the cursive script painfully familiar. From—*Violet Day*.

Lori handed it to Ken. "I can't," she said.

Regular mail. Posted nine weeks ago. He slit the envelope, removed lavender stationery. A lock of hair fell into his lap and instantly, he had an image of Violet.

Ken read aloud:

My Darlings:

I shall entrust this to the slowest bellman in the slowest hotel known to civilized man—knowing it will take many weeks to arrive by land and sea.

Tomorrow, Major and I will fly home to see about a terrible story we're reading in the newspapers. But that is not the point of this letter.

By now, whatever happened, has happened. I have little doubt you will read this sadly. That is the point of my letter.

*First of all, you know that Major and I love you with a passion
tested by time and travail. Our lives have been intertwined for
centuries and, I know, we will intertwine for millennia to come.*

*I shall not dwell on what is soon to transpire. At this juncture, it
is past and you know it yourselves. But I did want to explain why I
did not tell you 'up front' as Becky likes to say.*

*It would have served no purpose but to worry you needlessly. My
mother foretold it before any of you were born. It was in the stars
and I accepted that.*

*Becky will ask me to prove the value of my craft, as indeed
Lorraine asked me and I once challenged my mother, who did the
same to her mother. A stranger will change your lives; an old friend
will come to help. But more proof is always demanded. Let this
letter be that proof. I write it before the events which are predestined.*

*As you read this, I am with you. I kiss your cheek as a breath of
wind, I stroke your hair and behold you lovingly.*

*Please do not be sad, my children. Major and I are going ahead
to prepare for you.*

So then, this is only good-bye, until next time.

A gust of wind came off the ocean, fronds of palms rustled and
sighed. Ken put the letter back into the envelope.

"It's one of Violet's tricks, isn't it, Mom?" Becky scoffed, tearfully.

"If it is," Lori said, "it's a good one."

Indeed it may have been. But in Violet's den, they'd found similar
letters posted over the years, sealed and never opened—designed to be
"proof" to the new Violet Day. As Ken and Lori read them through,
comparing them to their diaries, Violet triumphed again and again.

"All right," Lori said, huskily. "We're going to Switzerland, Becky.
We'll ski until we turn blue or break a leg."

Becky laughed, then fell silent.

The wind stirred, palms whispered.

It was time for Christmas. The past was past.

Everything else was in the stars . . .

KEEP TRACK OF YOUR READING
AT THE LIBRARY

This page is provided for patrons who wish to have a record of the books they read at the library.

You may mark this page with a number (like a birthdate) or a simple symbol (like a star) or even your initials to keep your own personal reading record!